Hardly a Challenge

Max Thornton

Published in Australia by Silverbird Publishing Pty Ltd.

First published in Australia 2024
This edition published 2025

Copyright © Max Thornton 2024

Cover design, typesetting: WorkingType (www.workingtype.com.au)

ISBN: 978-1-922958-86-0

The author has chosen Max Thornton as his penname for the
story of his journey through life, and it bears no resemblance
to any person who may have the same name.

With the exception of those who have given permission,
the names of people and places have been purposely
changed or deleted.

Contents

Preface

The stars of the southern cross represent our geographical position in the southern hemisphere, the Commonwealth star symbolises our federation of states and territories and the crosses stand for the principles on which our nation is based; namely, parliamentary democracy, rule of the law and freedom of speech. The Australian flag should be treated with respect and dignity.

In Australian schools, the flag was raised every day at morning assembly by the children and lowered again after school.

Children were taught at school and by their parents the importance of the national flag and its principles, which would hold them in good stead as they walked their way through life. Children were raised by the flag and its principles. It was the expression of Australian identity and pride.

This is the story of one man who grew up during these times and ventured down his own road of life. It's a story of love, sadness, determination and, hopefully, encouragement for those in need of some inspiration. Believe you can and you're halfway there.

Prologue

A kid's paradise

Max Thornton was born in a regional town in Australia in the early 1940s. He and his twin sister, Dorris, were the proud children of their parents, Fred and Alice.

When the twins were seven months old, Alice was changing their nappies on the double bed. When she turned to put Dorris in the cot, Max fell off the bed and broke both his little legs. After some time in hospital in traction, he spent the next five years in callipers. As time went on, the men at the factory where his father worked made a special trike for Max because he couldn't bend his legs to pedal an ordinary one. It was a three-wheeled trike with pegs on either side of the front wheel to steer with his feet which enabled him to keep his legs straight. The handlebars were also straight, to push and pull to move the trike forward. Little Max could now get along without having to bend his legs.

The war was ending, but Fred had not participated due to meningitis – or so they were told. Just say, like many families in those days, they were struggling financially; perhaps not struggling, but certainly had no money left for creature comforts. The family never owned a car, so their travels were by public transport, but this cost money, so on most occasions, their travel was by foot.

Fred worked as a lagger, insulating pipes in ships' hulls and ceilings in factories with what we now know as a death substance called asbestos; this finally claimed him some forty years later. Alice worked in a local factory and often picked up other work she could get to help with the family's finances. Most of Fred's work kept him away from home, travelling to and staying in Melbourne and Tasmania. When he went to Tasmania, Alice would go with him and Max and Dorris would go to their half-sister's farm in Balliang.

Skeletons in the cupboard! Someone once said, if you can't hide the family skeletons, you might as well make them dance. Max and Dorris suspected that, before they were born and Alice married Fred, she was seeing a married man. Whether she knew that at the time, who knows – a child was born, and her married lover pissed off. They were always told he had died (Fred was probably told the same), which they learnt later in their adult lives wasn't true.

In those days, that sort of behaviour wasn't tolerated, and her parents banished her from the family. When Max and Dorris were young, they were told their grandparents on Alice's side were dead, which wasn't true, and Fred's parents were in England. So, they never had any grandparents to go and visit.

Their half-sister's name was June and her husband, their brother-in-law and Steven's father, was Ross Peters, the greatest man Max ever knew, who was born there. Max owes him most of his early learning and mentorship. Their farm was half an hour from Bacchus Marsh on the back road to Geelong. Ross told Max they could manage on five hundred acres, 'but it's getting harder'.

They spent most of their early days at the Balliang East school, a small one-room classroom where each row of desks was for a different class. The sixth grade row only had two desks, and after Grade Six, you went by bus to Bacchus Marsh High School.

Max was only a kid, but he was interested and loved being on the farm, which was actually between Balliang and Anakie. Max always thought it sounded like somewhere Ginger Meggs and his mates would hang out. It was a great place to grow up. There was a large dam for the cattle which was fed by a deep creek, and in the winter, the creek overflowed down a washway and refilled the dam. The creek was known to the kids as Rainbow Creek. The creek was the southern boundary of the property and ran for ten kilometres through several farms. The creek was fed by the main town reservoir, so was never dry. Along the banks were large willow trees that provided shade for the rainbow trout to lay their eggs when they swam upstream from the reservoir to spawn and provided shade for Max and Steven when they fished for the trout. (Max would eventually have three nephews: Ralph was only three and Murray was yet to be born, so Ralph seldom had much to do with the activities of Max and Steven.)

When they weren't helping on the farm, which was nearly all the time, they would fish for the trout or catch the yabbies in the shallow holes of the creek or fish there at night with a lantern for eels. Along the banks of the creek were a few peppercorn trees that were home to big fat green caterpillars. If they couldn't find worms, they could use the caterpillars to catch the trout. When they came out of their cocoons, they were butterflies of all the colours of the rainbow, brilliant and vivid colours that could never be copied.

Max said to Steven, 'God, I love this place!'

There was an abundance of gum trees to fire their shanghais (what they called a slingshot) at or just climb and build a tree hut. Slugs for the slug gun were expensive, so if they had used all our pocket money, they would be left with their shanghai; the stones were free.

And then, as if to spoil the fun, Max said to Steven, 'Bugger, we are being called to go get the cows for milking.'

Max knew how many cows were milked because he and Steven, his nephew, got them in while chancing their luck with the bloody bull. Max liked it better when he was on the horse – the bull couldn't outrun the horse. And he couldn't tell you how sore their fingers got as little kids helping sew up bags of wheat in the paddock, which probably weren't all that many as far as a count for the day was concerned.

There was a large, long chook shed, from which the eggs were sent to the Victorian Egg Board. Milk containers were picked up with the fresh milk on a platform from the roadside outside the farm and sheep were raised for the market and their wool, and cattle for beef to the butcher. All the farms in the area were versatile with different products; if one went down, they didn't lose their income. Even as a kid, Max understood how sensible that was.

They rode their bikes to school in the summer and their horses in the winter when the roads were flooded. Max said all the kids would meet at the gravel road intersection where the windmill stood in the corner of the paddock and ride to school together. There was a paddock with stalls and feed for the horses while we were in school. Max being Max, he had a special friend. Her name was Leone and after school, they would sit with their horses or their bikes in the paddock and eat the plum puddings (also known as onion grass) that grew in the paddocks. Max said one day when he got home, Ross said, 'I saw you with "Lehowneee" in the paddock after school.' Mind you, Max said there was never any hanky-panky. At Max's age, he didn't know there were other things you could do with 'it' other than wee.

Max came to realise how hard life was for his other family on the land. Max said, 'I once watched my brother-in-law, Ross, getting the water to the chook sheds. There was a square steel tank on cast iron wheels that he towed behind an old Ford truck to back down to the edge of the dam. A pitchfork stuck into a bucket was used to manually bucket the water into the manhole in the top of tank. When it was full, it was towed back to the chook shed.'

Max said he owed a lot of his early hands-on learning to that farm. This is where Max first learnt to drive – even if he did drive the truck into the gatepost with his nephew Steven in it when they shouldn't have been in the truck in the first place.

Max said he remembers going to Ross's father's farm, which was the neighbouring farm. His name was George, although Max and Steven called him Mr Peters. In an old wooden shed, he had a big black 1946 Oldsmobile Ace series 66 sedan that was their family car, but the best part of the farm was the long open sheds that held the old farm machinery. It was, Max reckoned, a kid's paradise for climbing, pushing, pulling levers, pretend driving and sitting on all sorts of tractor seats and climbing on the hay bales. 'A nice time of my childhood life,' Max said.

The rabbits on the farms in the area were in plague proportions and shooting them became too costly. Ross had an old car similar to a Model T Ford with the canvas roof cut off and running boards to stand on. Max was sometimes allowed to go with the men at night who would stand on the running board with a net attached to a broom handle, jump over, net a rabbit and snap its neck. It was not unusual to get fifty or so rabbits in one night, so of course, at least one meal every week was rabbit stew, baked rabbit or rabbit pie. Myxomatosis was released in Australia in 1950 and became a successful biological program for eradicating the rabbits that threatened Australian farmers. Max said he could tell if a rabbit had myxomatosis by looking to see if there was a discharge from the eyes and/or the nose.

Max couldn't understand how the sheep worried about the foxes only to be eaten by the farmer who was supposed to be looking after them.

*

Travel took its toll on Fred and Alice. They finally moved from their quiet country dwelling to the big smoke in Melbourne where Max and Dorris continued their schooling.

Alice's brother, Jasa, and his wife, Mary, had been the caretakers of a large two-storey school. Good references, written of course by Uncle Jasa, had enabled Max's parents to secure the position and become the new caretakers of the school. To Fred and Alice's delight, the caretaker's house came with the job and after Uncle Jasa and Auntie Mary moved out, Max and the family moved in.

The house was a white single-fronted weatherboard, small

but well maintained. The front lawn had been laid with thick buffalo grass, as with most houses in the street. Along the inside of a white wire mesh fence and gate were rows of pink and white rhododendrons giving the place a homely and peaceful feeling. Running down the right-hand side between the house and the fence next door was a bitumen path extending to the rear, with a tall green trellis gate. Just off the back veranda was a bungalow, which Max was quick to claim as his own, where he could fire his slug gun darts into the back of the wooden door, listen to the radio on his self-made crystal set or sneak out in the night to climb on the school's two-storey roof with a mate, Joey, to catch pigeons while they slept.

The outdoor toilet had a pan that could be removed from the back of the toilet. The night cart man would remove it, put it on his shoulders and carry it to his truck, known locally as the 'shit cart'; hence, the term 'flat as a shit carter's hat'. Max said he was standing outside the local Coles store one morning when the shit cart came round the corner and a row of pans came spiralling off the truck with the contents spilling down the footpath and into the entrance of Coles. Max said it was a really shitty mess and absolutely stank. The people were stuck inside Coles – no way were they coming out through the shit!

At home, there was a wooden shed three steps off the ground where Fred's tools and Max and Dorris's bikes were kept – if Max had been bothered to put his in there. Max's bike was always an issue.

His father would say, 'Christ, Max, you need a bloody steamroller, not a bike. Stop riding it up and down the gutters. I'm sick and tired of fixing it. How could you possibly snap the front bloody forks?'

Behind a small lilly pilly type of hedge was another small open shed that led through old high wooden gates to a blue stone laneway. This is where Uncle Jasa would have kept his two-seater baby Austin with the dicky seat where Max and Dorris had many a ride on their previous visits to this house.

There was a bird cage in the back yard where Max's father kept two rosellas. These parrots would taunt the dog by sticking their heads out through the wire cage, whistle and call, 'Toby, Toby'. Eventually, the dog hid under the cage and when the parrot stuck its head out, the dog bit it off. Max's father went off his tits and said, 'If that dog does anything else, he'll be going to the wood merchant's yard.'

When they were little, Dorris would be invited to other little girls' parties, and for some unknown reason, their mothers thought, as Max was the twin boy, he should also be invited. 'I dreaded having to go,' Max said, 'The girls made you feel like an idiot; you could tell by the way they were saying, "What's he doing here?"'

Yeh, well, Max thought, *in fifteen years, I'll bet it will be different. When I turn up at the party, they'll be saying, 'Who's this spunky looking kid? Come on in, baby!'* At one of the parties, the girls said he had to be the big bad wolf in the game. This little bugger of a girl chased him down the side way and while he was trying to get out of the gate, she buried the garden hoe in the back of his head!

'What a little shit she was,' said Max. 'I had to go on the tram with my mother, who had to be called from work, to take me to the Royal Children's Hospital with a towel on my head to have my head stitched up.'

To reduce expenses when income was tough, Alice would attend the school at the end of every year to buy the second-hand schoolbooks that were handed down from students the year before. Max was captain of the school football team; however, he never made it to the school cricket team. Most times at school assembly, he got a mention by the school principal after kicking one or two goals at the school's previous footy match. This was a winner for him with the girls and they allowed him to sometimes have a sneak look at the bottom of their petticoats behind the school incinerator. He was a talented sportsman, a bugger of a kid and probably spent more time at the principal's office than any other kid at the school. When the report card came in from school each year, Fred would say, 'I see nothing has changed, Max', as he read the comment: 'Max is a disruptive influence in class.'

Chapter 1

Learning and living

The alarm went off at 4:30 am in his bungalow at the back of the house. Max ignored it several times before his black-and-white fox terrier, Toby, who faithfully accompanied him on his morning paper round, was licking his face and pulling on his pyjama coat.

'You've got to be joking, Toby. It's pouring rain outside,' Max said.

He headed outside with Toby who commenced biting the tyres of his bike. Max hated these early mornings, especially this morning, but he needed the pocket money, so he and Toby headed for the local paper shop. It was still dark, but the lights were on inside and several other boys were already there, rolling and wrapping the papers to put in the hessian bags that hung over the bikes' cross bars. Toby curled himself up just inside the entrance and waited for Max. The shop was warm and inviting, and as Max rolled up his papers, he could see behind the counter rows and rows of cigarettes – Turf, Capstan, Philip Morris, menthol cigarettes, Marlboro and many others – and as he placed the papers in his hessian bag, his mind was on how he could buy a packet of fags and keep it on the sly in his and Joey's lane hideaway. Well, that would have to be for another day.

The first house on Max's paper round was number 35, Primrose St. Argh! Yes, Mr Selly's house, the school principal.

'Well,' Max said, 'this is for the strap I got two days ago.'

He threw the paper short of the veranda so it landed on the lawn in the rain.

'Good shot,' Max said to himself. 'Old Selly will, of course, dirk me to the paper shop but if Roy, who opens the shop early for the paper boys, doesn't tell him who delivers his papers, I should be safe. If I get called to the principal's office tomorrow, I'll know why, won't I?'

The rest of the paper round was uneventful, with all papers landing under cover without any broken windows or placed inside covered letterbox paper tubes. By the time Max and Toby arrived home, they were both as wet as a shag.

Max and his twin sister were luckier than most kids. Where time management was required, they only had to walk across the road to school from the caretaker's house. Yet Max was always finding things to do at the last minute, like a quick repair job on his take-everywhere shanghai, or 'ging' as some kids called it. *I guess the only downside of Dad being the caretaker*, he thought, *is if I'm not careful, I could keep running into him as he performs his duties, like emptying bins and general maintenance, and then sometime during the evening at home, I'll be waiting for it ...*

'I saw you doing this and that, and what were you and Joey doing up behind the incinerator with those girls?'

Max had found that a simple excuse in the least words as possible was the best reply – he had lots of practice– so he said, 'Just talking, Dad.'

'What? Don't give me that! You must think I'm some sort of halfwit,' his father said.

'Now, come on, Fred,' his mother said, 'the boy has told you that he wasn't up to no good.'

Good old Mum to the rescue!

Max did, however, get tired of comments from teachers, like 'It's hard to fathom how one twin can be so thoughtful and no problem when the other one – well, there's no explanation' and 'You might be good in the sports arena, Max, but you've a lot to learn in a class environment'. Max's answer, using the short answer theory, was 'She's a girl'.

Max also sold papers on his allocated corner, with traffic lights and a pub on his side of the corner, his stack of papers on the footpath and some under his arm. When the lights turned red, he would walk down the line of cars selling papers to the drivers, yelling *Herald, Herald*, and on Saturday nights, yelling *Herald and Sporting Globe*. He had a lot of customers in cars that always bought a paper on their way home. The trick to selling one was to be in the line of cars when the lights were red. Max always had a cunning move up his sleeve. Selling a paper to a driver when the lights were just about to change green, he would fumble in his money bag till the lights went green. The cars behind would blow their horns and the driver would say, 'Keep the change, son.' Then there were the stingy bastards who would say, 'Catch you tomorrow, son, on my way through.' He also had his regulars in the pub. Sometimes, they would buy him a lemon squash in a small glass called a pony.

Max said, 'Riding my bike home on Saturday night after selling papers, I can still smell the vinegar and see the steam coming from the hole in the newspaper parcel with the potato cakes inside it.'

It was mostly accepted that paper boys could ride the tram a couple of stops to sell their papers and then ride the tram back to their corner. On one particular tram ride, the peroxided blonde tart, dressed as a conductor in a shitty brown uniform and a brown ticket and money bag, chewing gum like a camel chews its cud, said out of the corner of her mouth full of chewie, 'Get off the tram'.

'Bloody bully,' Max said, 'the tram's going.'

'I don't give a shit,' she said, 'Get off or I'll push you off.'

Shit! Max thought as he looked out the tram door. There were no doors on trams then, just the open doorway. With no cars coming, he jumped, papers went everywhere and although he was knocked around with gravel rashes and bleeding, he had survived. Max's father and the newsagent reported the incident, but wouldn't you know it, heard nothing back. Well, that didn't surprise Max. He thought she was probably screwing the boss, and by the look of her, anyone else who was interested. *Well, I guess,* he thought, with life in general, *sometimes you're the dog and other times the tree.* Little did Max know but soon his turn to be the dog was coming.

Joey's father had driven him and Max to the Exhibition Buildings in Melbourne to the car show and they caught the tram back home after the show. The tram was absolutely packed with people were hanging off the running board.

Somewhere in among the crowded tram, a female voice screamed out, 'Get off the fucking running board, the tram's not moving until you all get off.'

As she got off the tram to abuse those on the running board,

'Oh, joy,' Max said to Joey, 'that's her! That's her, mate, the floozy who threw me off the bloody tram.'

Max thought, *I can't let the opportunity escape. What can I do?* With that, he reached up and pulled the cord twice – ding, ding – and the tram took off, leaving the floozy behind on the tram stop. The driver must have seen her in his mirrors or heard her blood-curdling screaming and he stopped the tram fifty yards down the road. Everyone on the tram was pissing themselves laughing. *Lots of dogs on the tram*, Max thought, *and they're all pissing on the same tree.*

All the local kids went to the Saturday afternoon pictures at the Padua Theatre. On the way there, Joey and Max passed a shop that sold leather goods and stacked up high against the window were many suitcases. It was a large window, so when you leaned on it, you could get some movement. Max and Joey would keep doing this until the suitcases started to rock and eventually all fall over. This Saturday was no different.

Joey said, 'Look, Max, this bloke has stacked the cases up against the window again. You'd think he'd learn and stack them a little bit away from the window.'

'Buggered if I know,' said Max,' but let's see how many times we can do it before he learns. Come, help me push.'

Down went the cases. The next thing they knew, they were both grabbed by the scruff of the neck by two policemen who had been sitting in a car waiting for whoever was doing this every Saturday afternoon. The police station was next door to the picture theatre. Max and Joey were lectured and locked in a cell for an hour. They missed most of the pictures before they were let out. It frightened the life out of them.

They would have to find something else to do. Joey said, 'I reckon we get a box of matches and some beer bottle caps. We can peel the cork off from the inside the cap, put the match heads in and put the cork back in the cap, then put it on the tram line.'

'You reckon that will work?' said Max.

'You just watch this, Maxi boy,' said Joey, as he put the cap on the line.

They sat on the tram stop seat and waited.

'Here comes the tram now,' said Max, 'so get ready to run.'

When the tram ran over the bottle cap, there was a loud bang. The conductor leaned out the open doorway to see what the noise was. Max and Joey gave him the finger and ran like hell. The kids were coming out of the pictures now and one of them told Max if he lay on the tram line, he would give him sixpence. The girls were saying, 'Go on, Max, do it, Max, do it, Max', so of course Max did it and ate his sixpence worth of potato cakes on the way home.

When his sister, Dorris, got home, she went straight to their parents' room and blabbed, 'Max's been lying on the tram line. I saw him lying on the tram line.'

The next sound Max heard was, *'Max, get in here!'*

The fact that Dorris was Max's twin sister didn't change his opinion that she was a little shit who would go out of her way to involve Max if it meant there was any chance he could be blamed if anything went wrong. The outdoor toilet at one house they lived in had three concrete steps going into the toilet. Somehow, Dorris fell down the steps and split her head open. She said that Max had pushed her and took great delight in smiling and pointing at Max, hoping he'd get a belting. She would deny any of this, of course.

'You know, when I think back,' Max thought years later, 'she was a little bugger. If we were both given a bag of lollies or an ice cream, she wouldn't touch hers until I had eaten all of mine, then she'd start licking the ice cream in front of my face or show me a lolly and then put it in her mouth. The only reason she's still alive today,' Max said, 'is because she stopped doing those nasty little sister acts as she got older, and we are now as close as twins could and should be. She has no idea how to drive a car properly, but what would big brother know?'

'You don't know everything, Max,' she told him many times. 'You're only an hour older than me, Max,' she would say, 'and I'm getting tired of you telling me what to do.'

'Well, that was a waste, wasn't it?' Max said, 'because you haven't been listening, Dorris. But I love you anyway.'

And having said all that, if anything actually happened to Max or he was hurt, she was always there, fussing around and mothering him and caring to make sure he was all right. She could be such a little bugger and then such a change. Max thought, *How could you ever understand female thinking?*

Chapter 2

Max and Joey

oey was a skinny kid and Max's good mate. They were the same age, twelve years old. Joey was slightly taller with wispy hair, a square jaw and blue eyes that seemed to wink when at a certain angle to the sun. He had the look of confidence and knowledge of someone much older than he was. He was a kid you could trust under any circumstances. Max had always reckoned he wouldn't dob you in, even if someone was pulling the hairs out of his crutch with tweezers. His fingers on one hand were sort of bent, and his mum had told him he would have to have them fixed one day. It always looked like his pants were going to fall down, and sometimes he was called Slim or Picket.

It was Saturday afternoon. Max and Slim were heading for the local creek, as they often did on a Saturday if they weren't going to the footy, but not before they filled their pockets with just the right sized stones, or as they called them, yonnies. This often took some time to find. It was very important to get just the right size for your shanghai; that was the considered opinion of every kid who owned one. The ride to the creek was always spectacular with the original handlebars of the bike removed and replaced with a straight piece of pipe, a cigarette packet clipped to the rear spokes to make it sound like a motorbike, a side mirror and, of course, a wire aerial attached to the back wheel nut with the must-have foxtail on top. They had a well-versed route to the creek down all the laneways – some with smooth concrete while others were bluestone – stopping only to remove a particular bluestone block and retrieve their well-hidden packet of ten Turf cigarettes and box of matches. Sometimes, there were other kids at the creek with shanghais, and the battle would begin until some kid stuck his head up at the wrong time, got hit and went home bawling. A truce was usually called, and everyone went their own way, which was always good because they weren't getting any of Max and Joey's cigarettes.

'What's that down there in the creek, Max?' said Slim.

'Don't know,' replied Max. 'Looks like an old shirt in the creek full of sand, air and water'.

They poked it with a stick and a yellowy face and head came up out of the water with eyes bulging out of their sockets.

'Bloody hell!' said Slim.

'Shit!' said Max.

'You stay here, Max,' said Slim, 'and I'll ride to the police station and tell them.'

'Bullshit! I'm not staying here with the body,' said Max, 'You stay here. Don't be such a bloody sook. You don't have to stand here and stare at it.'

Max took off on his bike. On the way to the police station, Max was thinking, *'You beauty! I'll have to show the police where it is and I'll get a ride in the police car, lights flashing and sirens blaring. Can't wait!*

Max rushed into the police station, all out of breath and there sitting at a desk was a chubby middle-aged copper.

'What's up, son?'

Max said, 'Well, you're not going to believe this ...'

'I've heard a lot of stuff in my time, boy. I doubt whether you're going to surprise me,' said the copper.

'Well, bugger me if you're not surprised, sir. Joey and I found a dead body in the creek,'

'How do you know it's dead?' the copper said.

Max replied, 'You've got to be kidding me! His face is a real sickly yellow, his eyeballs are bulging out of his head five times further than yours and when we poked his legs with a stick, his whole body came up out of the water stiff as my mum's ironing board.'

The copper made a couple of phone calls and said, 'Right, let's go. Show me.'

Talk about a letdown. It would have been more exciting to stay with the body, thought Max, as they climbed aboard a little Austin A40. By the time they got to the creek, three proper police cars were already there. *I could have got back quicker on my bike*, thought Max, and there was Slim, the centre of attention, giving statements to the police waving at me and giving me the finger, big smile on his face. But Max did get a ride in a real police car to go back and get his bike so he gave Joey the finger and made sure Joey saw him smiling at him.

Some months later at about 8 pm, there was a knock on the Thorntons' front door.

'Fred,' said Alice, 'there's someone at the door. I hope it's not someone checking if we have paid our radio and television licence.'

But it wasn't; it was the police. Fred answered the door to find a young copper holding his black police bicycle.

He said, 'Does a young boy named Max Thornton live here?'

'Yes, he does,' said Fred, 'What's the boy done now?'

'The boy's done nothing illegal, Mr Thornton. In fact, he's a bit of a hero. He and his mate, Joey, found the missing man from the nursing home in the creek and I'm here to see that he gets his share of the one-pound reward, which is ten shillings. I have already given his mate, Joey, his ten shillings.'

Max was called to the front door, his mum close behind.

'Here you are, son, and well done,' said the young policeman.'

Alice said, 'You see what a good boy we have, Fred. He's a hero.'

Max just smiled and thought, *I'm keeping all this as ammunition for the next time I'm in the shit.*

The caretaker's job required both Max's parents' input when cleaning the classrooms, of which there were twelve downstairs and four upstairs. They had fireplaces, so in the winter, apart from cleaning the classrooms, the fireplaces had to be cleaned out and reset for the next day, and the wood had to be split and carried to the classrooms. This had to happen every day during the winter months; what a task! This sort of thing fell by the wayside later in life, though the wood was still purchased and they still had to split and carry the wood. Dorris and Max helped where they could after school.

The ever-alert Max, while carrying wood to his classroom and looking for any advantages, looked for any copies of upcoming exam papers. He never found any but still managed a C grade pass to secondary school with the comments: 'Max is a disruptive influence in class', and 'We know he is brighter than he shows us. He obviously has other ambitions on his mind, and we wish him well in his future endeavours.'

*

Max and Joey would soon be going to secondary school and their billycart racing days would come to an end.

'Let's give the carts one more run down Kamikaze Hill. Five bob to the winner,' Max said, offering up the challenge to Joey.

'You'll lose your money, you dill. You haven't won a challenge yet. Okay, you're on.'

Kamikaze Hill, as all the kids called it, was the steepest hill in the area. It was a mile long with one vicious bend halfway down. It was so steep that cars needed first gear to get up it. Both Joey's and Max's carts were the fastest carts in the area, riding on four, top-of-the-range ball bearings: larger ones at the rear, smaller ones at the front given to them by Joey's father, Mick, who was a toolmaker at the Holden plant at Fisherman's Bend. Whenever they needed a new box, an undercover raid on the box factory took place on a Sunday night. Over the fence, select a box of their liking from the ones stacked in the yard, over the fence with the boxes and away they'd go.

The word got around about the challenge of the two fastest carts in the area. Some of the kids were at the start, others at the finish, but the smart ones were waiting at the sharp bend halfway down where the carts would be going full bore with no brakes. There was a strange-looking kid with a pigeon chest who had obviously pinched his sister's scarf to wave the start. Away they went, with kids yelling, 'Go, Slim', 'Go, Max'.

Slim didn't get a good start; he still had one leg hanging out of the box. Max was three cart lengths in front, grinning like he'd just eaten his sister's last lolly as the bend came up fast. Max made the mistake to take one last look to see where Slim was. The kids were right – the bend was the place to watch. Up over the gutter the cart bounced, ejecting Max out over someone's fence into their garden. He had blood running down his right arm coming from a deep six-inch-long tear in his hand made by the bent six-inch nail that kept the front ball bearing on the axle. All this happened in front of Slim. He slowed his cart by scraping the wheels on the gutter and ran back to see if Max was all right.

After using his and Max's hankies, he said, 'You owe me five bob.'

'Bullshit,' Max said, 'You never finished the race.'

'What! I came back to help you. Fair go, mate.'

'All right,' Max said, 'I'll give you two shillings and sixpence; how's that?'

'I love you, mate, but sometimes you really are bloody lousy.'

But Slim did go with Max to hospital to get his hand stitched. It wasn't long before Max was going to the hospital with Joey.

Max said, 'Yeah, well, if you could ride a bike properly, squashing my fingers between the white posts at the park when you were dinking me, it wouldn't have happened. How could I forget? I've still got the scars!'

Chapter 3

Growing up

It was 1954 and Queen Elizabeth II was touring Australia. All the school kids were to perform a flag-waving ceremony and maypole dance on the Melbourne Cricket Ground while the Queen drove around in an open vehicle. Max was dressed in a white shirt with white shorts and a red cummerbund.

'I'm part of the of kids making ER, "Elizabeth Reigns", signs. What are you doing, Dorris?' asked Max.

Dorris replied, 'I'm doing the maypole dance, and guess who is in my group?'

'Buggered if I know,' replied Max.

'Margery Atkinson, that's who,' said Dorris.

Max said, 'Who cares?'

Dorris had great delight in saying, 'Yeah, well, I know you fancy her a bit, Max. Do you want me to tell her you like her?'

Max, using his short answer style said 'No!'

The school had started to organise the big dance routine and parade to be held at the Coburg Town Hall. This was where all the kids at the school were on show. The day came where they paired boys and girls by height and age, boys on one side of the auditorium and girls on the other side.

Then Max saw her – Margery Atkinson, a young girl in the spring of her life, the time when a young girl's fancy turns to love. She was luckily his height and age, so his chances looked good, and he knew she had a bit of a crush on him. She was such a lovely girl. She was wearing a yellow summer dress with a small pink bow on each of the short sleeves, white bobby socks and yellow sandals with a butterfly catch. She had long flowing blonde hair, small breasts and eyes as blue as the ocean that when you looked into them that silently said, 'I love you, Max'. That's what Max reckoned anyway.

'Okay,' said Miss Whitaker, the dance teacher. Her name was Lois, but they called her Miss Whitaker. 'You first, young Max Thornton, come out here.'

Here we go, thought Max. Margery Atkinson was standing right in the front row of girls. *Can't miss*, he thought. A chill ran down his spine. Miss Whitaker went straight past Margery and picked another girl. *Shit, no. Not the fat one! It's the end of the world*, thought Max.

'This is Karen, Karen, this is Max. You two will be partners for the rehearsals and you two will be leading the whole school onto the dance floor on the night.'

'Hello, Max', she said.

Max looked her over. She had a round, chubby face the size of a dinner plate and she looked like she could have been hiding balloons. *Why couldn't they pick partners by equal weight?* thought Max. Her eyes, unlike Margery's, said, '*You put your hands where they shouldn't be and I'll kick your arse.*

And so came the big night with Max and his bulldozer partner. She did, however, look a picture in her rather large ball gown, he had to admit as they waited at the front door. 'Move in now', the order came, and the music started. So, Max and Karen led the whole school into the town hall. He couldn't get over how big the dance floor was. It was polished to a high shine with sawdust sprinkled over it. They danced their way in. She was good on her feet, he had to admit. She was also strong and, as such, had made herself the dominant partner. He doubted his feet were even on the ground as she swung him around, going through the routine they had all learnt.

Then it happened. In the middle of the dance floor, she slipped onto her arse and dragged Max down with her. *Shit, shit, shit,* thought Max, *I'm never going to live this down. Four hundred people watching, including my parents. All I need now is for my sister to have seen it. She will spread the news as fast as she can.*

Wouldn't you just know it? Slim and the love of Max's life, Margery, danced past. Slim had that smartarse look on his face and gave him the finger. Max, however, the debonair and suave kid that he was, casually bent down, kissed Karen on the cheek and helped her up. She returned the kiss on his cheek and said, 'You are my knight, Max. Thank you.' The gallery of parents and relatives stood and applauded. The dance teacher, Miss Whitaker, smiled, winked and nodded at Max. He imagined his mother saying, 'See that, Fred? What a gallant thing for the boy to do, how lovely. I'm so proud of him.'

At least he hoped that what she was saying. More ammo to be used at the right time.

*

The summer Olympics were held in Melbourne in April 1956. Max was in the 3rd Brunswick Scout Group, and they were helping out at Festival Hall for the boxing. Max's job was to carry buckets of water to the ring. He obtained lots of autographs and a hit on the head with someone's mouthguard.

Not only were the Olympics here but television had arrived as well, albeit black and white. Since taking the caretaker's job, Fred and Alice's finances had improved enough to buy a three-in-one Philips television, record player and radio.

They also bought a second-hand piano for Dorris and Max to take music lessons, much to Max's horror. Music lessons and piano practice would be a drag and as interesting as a tour through the crematorium, although his sister Dorris took to it with gusto and loved it. The piano teacher looked like a bent-over ninety-year-old spinster, although as Max grew older, he realised she was probably only fifty. Max hated it. If you didn't have your fingers and hands arched enough, down would come this thin, long cane across the knuckles. After some time of purgatory, Max managed to snivel his way out of the piano lessons.

*

Essendon had just beaten Carlton at Windy Hill, 9-13-67 to 5-9-39. Slim and Max had gone to the game. Slim had slopped his pie and sauce down the front of his Essendon jumper and lost his bus money to go home.

'See, you're lucky I only gave you two shillings and sixpence instead of five bob for the cart race, so I have enough money for your bus fare and mine,' Max said, 'You're like a bloody baby – can't get along without me.'

John Coleman, the Essendon full forward, had gone into the Sacred Heart hospital for a knee operation. The hospital was only a short bike ride from Max's place, so he grabbed his football, which was almost buggered from being kicked on the bitumen and gravel, and headed off to the hospital. When he got there, he asked to see Mr Coleman.

'Sorry, son, no visitors allowed,' he was told.

What bullshit! Max thought, *He's only had a knee operation, hasn't had a leg amputation, for Christ's sake, so I'm going up anyway.* Max snuck up the stairs and was creeping along the passage, looking in the rooms from the door to find him, when a lady who said she was the matron said, 'Hey, what are you up to? How did you get up here?'

'I'm looking for Mr Coleman's room.'

The matron said that no visitors were permitted to see him on his request and said, 'Out you go, young fellow.'

'I made out like I was walking to the stairs until she had gone, and then I snuck back,' Max said. 'I looked in the last room and there he was, sitting up in bed. Just as he saw me, so did the matron.'

'I told you, no visitors, young man. Now, out!'

Mr Coleman said, 'It's okay, Faye. (That must have been the matron's name.) Let him in for a few minutes.'

Max went into his room. Coleman was a really nice bloke, and of course, Max had on his Essendon footy jumper. He asked him a few questions about footy and when Max was last at Windy Hill. Max gave him an earbashing about kicking goals, and Coleman signed his footy.

'You'll need a new one of these soon, son. The bladder is poking through the lacing.'

He wrote down Max's name and where he lived and then Max thanked him and left. Two weeks later, an almost new football arrived for Max; it was probably one of Essendon's training footballs. The note said, 'I hope you kick many goals, Max' and it was signed 'John Coleman'. Max had a grin on his face for a long time and couldn't wait to skite about the football, especially with Joey, who was going to hear about this for as long as Max could draw it out. He told Joey that John Coleman said no one else was allowed to kick it but Max. As time went by, everyone kicked it and it would soon look like the old one.

*

The Scouts were planning a trip to Tasmania for two weeks and Max was saving his paper round money to help pay for the cost. The scout master was a fantastic bloke; he was like a second dad to everyone.

'We all gave him our pocket money,' Max said, 'and he had it all written in a book. When he gave you money, he would adjust your amount.'

Max brought his mum souvenir teaspoons from all over Tasmania. She just smiled and said, 'Thank you, Max'. He now knows how she felt about bloody teaspoons.

They flew to Tasmania in a Douglas DC-3 Dakota from Essendon airport, the first time on a plane for all the kids. Some of them were sick. They travelled all over Tasmania in a picnic/furniture van and slept on the floor in various scout halls. The vehicle that transported them to sail home on the *Taroona* was a side loader bus of medium size with five doors on each side and a bench seat that went right across to each side door. Max said it was a fantastic holiday, thanks to a dedicated man.

Max had been practising in the back yard on a plank over

a log like a springboard for the Scouts' Victorian swimming carnival. On the night, Max came second in the three-metre diving. He was quietly pleased with himself until his father told him he was the first person to come last. Yes, Max thought, I wasn't the best, but it was my best and I can't do any better than that, so my father can get stuffed.

The day came for the family discussion as to which secondary schools Max and Dorris would attend. Most of the discussion was centred around where their further education would lead them and how much it would cost if they went as far as university, money that the family just did not have. They needn't have worried where Max was concerned. He viewed going to university like going to the dentist for a root canal. It just wasn't going to happen. He viewed himself more of an 'up the guts with tons of smoke' and a hands-on man. In the end, it was decided that Dorris would go to high school and Max to a tech school where he could opt out after Form 3 (Year 9) and start an apprenticeship.

While waiting for tech school to start, Max saw an ad in *The Sun* calling for applications for a suitable young person to be trained as a cartoonist. The position would be a cub cartoonist, with full employment for the successful applicant. Max could draw and paint almost anything, so he applied. His father wasn't pleased; he wanted Max to do an apprenticeship. *The Sun* sent Max four drawings: a cartoon, a seascape, a two-storey building and a maze of line and dots. These drawings had to be copied to the exact scale with a pencil. Max completed the task and sent them back, and it wasn't long before he received a letter asking him to come in for an interview. His father went off his brain.

'There's no bloody future in drawing, and bugger-all wages.

Take the advice I'm giving you and do a proper, structured apprenticeship.'

His father was speaking out of his clacker. He wasn't from that side of the street; he just wanted Max to do what he wanted Max to do. Max is still angry at himself for not standing up to his father, but 'in your defence, Max, you were only a twelve-year-old boy, so don't beat yourself up about it,' commented his mate, Slim, later in life.

Dorris came home from high school one day and said to Max, 'There's a boy at school that said he wanted to plant his carrot in Mavis's garden. I know she hasn't got a vegetable garden.'

Max could hardly contain himself and said, 'One day, Dorris, I will remind you of this conversation.'

Max started his education at the tech school. His subjects were maths, English, plan drawing, art, clay modelling, engineering, sheet metalworking, woodworking, welding and chemistry. His father once asked him which part of school he liked best. He used his short answer technique and said, 'Going home time.'

Max had now managed to come to terms with his lot in life. He was the vice-captain of the footy team and what you might call an average student, which suited him just nicely, thank you. Joey was not a footballer but just as talented a cricketer as Max was a footballer. Slim often had to be asked several times how many runs he had made; the answer, when squeezed out of him, was always high double or triple figures. Slim was not blasé about his talent, unlike Max, who could not wait to tell you what he had done and how many of the opposition he had thumped.

Slim was going to be a motor mechanic; it was his dream.

Max had always thought it was good choice for him. Being skinny, he could slide under the front of a car and come out the back. They hooked up with three other kids at tech, not bad kids, just rough and tumble. Like Slim and Max, they were all going on to apprenticeships at the end of Form 3. They named themselves the Fury of Five.

On one occasion, Max said goodbye to his mum as he left for school, only to find out his bike was gone. He ran back inside, yelling to his mum, 'My bike's gone. Someone has stolen my bike!'

'Are you sure? Have you looked everywhere?'

'Yes, and it's not there.'

'Well, you'd better go to the police station on your way to school and I will give you a note for being late.'

'Someone has stolen my bike which was in the back yard at home,' Max told the police. 'They must have snuck in overnight and pinched it.'

'All right, son. Don't get excited. Give me the description and we will let you know if and when we find it.'

Max left and headed for school. He caught the bus home after school, sitting and thinking about who would steal his bike. As he looked out the window, the bus was going past the second-hand comic shop, and there was his bike, leaning up against the window.

'Shit, now I remember. I went to the comic shop last night and walked home with Alan. I must have forgotten that I rode my bike there,' Max said to his mum.

'Well, Max, you will have to go back to the police station and explain what happened.'

'Well, that's going to make me look like a dickhead, isn't it?' he replied.

'So be it. You're such a scatterbrain, Max.'

After completing his mandatory three years at tech, Max was ready to start an apprenticeship. Since he wasn't going to do cartography at the *Sun*, he wanted to be a motor mechanic. But no, his father pushed him in the sheet metal direction. Once again, he failed to stand up for himself and took his father's advice, which, once again, looking down the retrospectoscope, proved to be wrong. His father took over the role of finding a place to start the apprenticeship. Remember, Max was only fifteen and, in his father's defence, he guessed that back then fifteen-year-olds didn't go by themselves for apprenticeship job interviews. Max was to start work in a factory that made hot water units: gas, electric and briquette. They also made guttering and air-conditioning ducting. At this stage, Max would not be commencing his apprenticeship for another three months.

Everyone had to earn their keep in the household in those days. If you didn't have a job, no one gave you money, so you had to bloody well earn it. So, Max got a job for three months as a telegram boy in the city at the Melbourne General Post Office. Well, that was an eye opener. He even had a telegram boy uniform. Max loved it, travelling up and down in lifts in and out of the big stores like Coles, Myers, LP Alexander and Allen's music store. He would stand for ages watching the little man tap, tap, tapping on the window at the LP Alexander tailor shop. As he plied in and out of office buildings and courtrooms, he always hoped that one of the telegrams would be to let someone know they had won Tattersall's and they would give him a huge tip. Never happened, though.

If you had to deliver a telegram to the suburbs, you would be given a metal disk with a number, and out the back of the post office, a little man sat in a cage full of red Postmaster General bicycles. You gave him the number and he gave you a bike.

Max said, 'Can I have the one with Sturmey-Archer gears?'

'What?' the bloke said, 'Whoever do you think you are? This is not Toorak. They are all fix-wheeled. Bloody prima donna! Get on the bike and go.'

Max was sorry to see his term end at the GPO, but he knew there was no future in delivering telegrams.

Chapter 4

A job and a car

Well, here we go, Max thought, standing in the upstairs office in his new ill-fitting bib and brace, dark blue overalls, a folding three-foot yellow ruler in the side ruler sleeve, pen and pencil in the top allocated spot, ready to go. *How cool this is going to be*, he thought, *I'm going to make hot water systems.*

Down the stairs he went into a large factory where he was met by the foreman, almost a replica of Slim, much taller but just as skinny. He had a thin pockmarked face, obviously from his younger days with a bad case of pimples. He was about thirty years old and had what Max called a crooked grin. He was quietly spoken with no smartarse comments about the new apprentice. Max was pleased to think this foreman would be the one to oversee his training; however, he would soon learn there were others in the factory who were not as considerate.

The tradition in those days, and no doubt it's roughly the same today, was that the new apprentice got all the shit jobs like sweeping the floor, cleaning all the oily metal fibres from the machines and, the worst job of all, where someone in the factory had their hole punched in the wrong place. Well, Max thought, *I bet the second-year apprentice here thinks it's great.* After about three weeks, Max got his task of soldering spouting corners together. The angles were already cut out by a machine – so much for learning how to do it at trade school. For the first week, the solder was lumpy and looked like a pigeon had sat there and shat on it. Max wondered what the plumber who would be using it would say. He'd think some poor bugger was soldering with their feet.

As time went by, and with more tuition from the foreman, Max's soldering looked like it was done by a machine. But the shitty jobs didn't go away, like cleaning the toilets and sweeping the floor. Max was told he was sweeping the floor the wrong way. How could there be a right and wrong way to sweep the bloody floor? He'd have to speak to his mother about that. 'Don't keep taking the mountain to Muhammed, take Muhammed to the mountain,' they told him, whatever that meant. Max thought, *I'll have to speak Mum about this as well.*

The foreman's name was Bruce and he travelled to work by train, like Max did. Sometimes he would bring his car to work, a 1945 Ford Pilot. Black, of course – Henry Ford said you can have any colour you like as long as it's black. He said black dried quicker than any other colour on the assembly line. Max had to travel from their caretaker's house by train to Flinders Street and then by another train on the Frankston line. His worker's weekly ticket cost nineteen shilling and sixpence out of his weekly apprenticeship wage of four pounds nineteen and six shillings, of which he paid his mother one pound for board.

Back at the factory, Max had moved up in the world to the spot-welding machine where he spot-welded small box-like frames to go onto electric hot water units. These frames separated the elements and thermostats in the outer housing of the unit; a boring job, but he was getting there. Soon after, he was cutting galvanised sheets in the hydraulic guillotine and rolling them through the power rollers for the outer cases of the hot water units.

'At last,' Max said, 'here's a new apprentice. Now the shitty jobs are his.'

Fair dinkum, this kid, Morris, was so uncoordinated you wouldn't trust him to help you put your hat on. Max showed Morris how to use the rollers. The galvanised sheets were four feet wide and eight feet long. You needed to kick the length of the sheets under the rollers, then feed the front of the sheet in so it rolled up on itself. It was a hot day and Morris had his bib and brace overalls undone with the straps hanging down. As the sheet rolled in, so did the straps of his overalls, slowly pulling in the rest of his overalls in as well, along with his dick! By the time Max got there, the damage had been done. Luckily, the machine couldn't take all of the bunched-up overalls, so he only lost the first half of his dick.

Max was tasked to take Morris four doors down to the local clinic. They slowly walked down, with Morris walking like he had shat in his pants. There were a lot of people in the waiting area and the girl behind the reception desk said, 'How can I help you?'

Never letting moments like this go by, Max said in a loud voice, 'This man has rolled his dick into the mechanical rollers.'

Women in the room cried out, 'My God'. The men grabbed hold of their crotch and said, 'Shit!'

Morris was married as it turned out, and Max guessed any

extramarital activities would be out of the question for some time to come.

The factory had a Hungarian welder who kept mostly to himself, a nice bloke and a prankster at times. He wore a blue beret with a small stalk on top. Max was in the room where they kept all the fittings required to make the units when Morris came in.

Max said, 'What's up, Morris?'

'The welder wants me to get him a hat full of nail holes.'

Max said, 'Well, go and get his hat.'

The welder's hat was on the steel dressing-down bar and the welder must have been off somewhere, maybe in the toilet. Morris came back with the hat.

Max, with a smirk on his face, said, 'Right now, go over to the lead block, use the hole punch and put as many holes in the hat as you can. The welder will be absolutely beside himself.'

Morris took the hat back, whichwas the welder's pride and joy, and the whole factory watched as the Hungarian welder went right off his tits. He looked up at Max and pointed to him. He knew who had egged Morris on.

He came to Max later on and said, 'It's my bloody fault. I didn't think he'd be stupid enough to do it.'

Morris wasn't finished yet – far from it. He was cutting four-foot galvanised sheets in the hydraulic guillotine into two-foot strips, and because he failed to use the guard, cut the tops off eight fingers. When we all ran over, sure enough there in the tray on the offside were eight finger tops cut just below the nails. That was the final straw for management. We had a little farewell party at the factory with drinks and tied sixpence in the corner of hanky for his tram fare. As they watched Morris get on the tram, they all waved him goodbye. Max hoped he would find his place in life somewhere along the way.

There were two owners; the one who oversaw the work in the factory thankfully didn't come down into the factory very often. He was a bad-tempered prick and a bully who took great delight in mimicking the workers who had afflictions. No one knew how to take him; he had a split personality like Jekyll and Hyde. Although Max wasn't happy doing what he was doing, this man played a big factor in his leaving the factory after he finished his apprenticeship.

When Max started his apprenticeship, he joined the local football team as it was very close to where he now worked and trained every Tuesday and Thursday night. It had been very convenient once his family had moved into the area. The Glenhuntly Football Club was in the Federal Football League, two leagues down from the Victorian Football League, the VFL. During his playing days, Max won two best and fairest awards along with two broken noses, a hamstring, dislocated shoulder and a broken scaphoid. Max said they were good days and he wouldn't have traded them for anything else. Eventually, due to too much time off work because of injuries, he had to stop playing.

*

The caretaker's job had worn Fred and Alice down so Alice's sister, Amy, offered them a house they could buy with no deposit and no interest on easy payments. The family soon moved to their new house in Malvern – well, not new, but this was their own.

Alice was one of four sisters and Amy seemed to be the one with the money. She also owned a fantastic two-storey house with attics, basements, big polished carpeted staircases and what Max called a dungeon. The staircase had banisters on which Max and his cousin Keith slid down whenever Max was visiting. The house had been made into a six-bed aftercare hospital where Max's Aunty Amy was the matron, with two nurses and a visiting doctor. The family lived upstairs.

Max's cousin, Keith, was a quiet unassuming kid who was never going to die from the over-pumping of adrenaline. He and Max were as different as chalk and cheese. Unlike Max, Keith was the studious type and was said to be the boy in the family to make something of himself. He had the backing of his parents with money, but unfortunately his ambitions weren't all that high; that's what Max thought, anyway. Sadly, Keith eventually died of a brain tumour.

Max was once asked if he could explain what his auntie's house was like. He said he probably couldn't explain its true worth, as in a mental picture, but there was something compelling about English-style manor architecture. It was grandiose and classic, yet cozy and charming, with a long gravel driveway and vines covering the walls at the front of the house and narrow, curved windows grouped together with coloured flowers in planter boxes on their ledges. It had slate roof shingles and a very large chimney in the front of the house and the rear. He remembered as a small kid going into the house for the first time. There were things he'd never seen before – cords hanging down from the ceiling with white knobs to pull the lights on and off, coloured wallpaper stuck to the walls everywhere, huge ceiling fans that looked like they could lift up a plane, stamped metal patterns across the ceiling and thick, bright-coloured carpets that felt like you were walking on grass in bare feet. Max couldn't get over the size of the polished stairs with their thick carpet and large polished handrails. At the top of the stairs was another handrail that you could look over to see downstairs. As a kid, he had spent many a time running up and down them and sliding down the banisters until he heard his auntie's voice: 'Max, stop running up and down the stairs. You will wake the patients.'

*

Due to different trades and living in different suburbs, Max and Joey didn't see as much of each other now, but once they both had cars, things changed. Joey had just got himself a 1954 Vauxhall Velox Vagabond, a snazzy looking convertible; you couldn't wipe the smile of his face. Everything comes to those who wait, so they say. Joey was getting nineteen pounds. Max thought, *See, so much for my old man's bullshit with apprenticeships. What did he know? He never did one.* Now that he was earning seventeen pounds and sixpence, he might be able to afford the payments for his own car.

One Saturday morning when Max was sorting out his finances, he asked his parents if he could pay ten bob less in board so he could buy a car on hire purchase. His father was all for it and Max knew why: he would have to take Fred all over the place fishing. He said to himself, 'Let's get the ten bob sorted out and get the car. There'll be plenty of time to come up with evasive action where Fred is concerned.' To Alice, he said, 'Just think about it, Mum, I can take you shopping so you won't have to push your shopping jeep home full of stuff.'

Fred and Alice looked at each other. His mother winked at Max and said, 'Okay, son, go and find a car.'

He knew his father wouldn't want to go. What a blessing! What Fred knew about cars you could write on the back of a postage stamp and still have room for the Lord's Prayer if you wrote really small.

'Thanks, Mum, for the reduction in the boarding contribution.'

The doorbell rang.

'Who's there?' called Max.

'It's me, dickhead, Joey. Open the bloody door. Oh ... hello, Mr and Mrs Thornton.'

'Hello, Joey,' they replied.

Max's parents liked Joey. He was a good honest kid, although, like Max, they were hardly kids anymore.

Joey looked at Max's mum and grinning, said, 'Did he manage to get ten bob knocked of his board?'

'You're a bastard,' Max replied. The answer, using Max's answering technique, was 'Yes'.

When your mother asks you if you want a piece of advice, it's only a formality; you know you're going to get it whether you answer yes or no.

Alice said, 'You make sure you two remain friends through thick and thin.'

Max's smartarse reply was, 'What does that mean?'

She said to Joey, 'Go find a car and take this idiot with you.'

Most car yards were small. Kevin Dennis Car Sales on the corner of Punt Road and Swan Street in Richmond, however, had cars lined up outside, flags flying, and unscrupulous salesmen everywhere coaxing the poor sucker off the street. They were nothing but vultures; you could walk in off the street with no money and without a deposit of any kind, and drive off in the car of your choice, only to find out very quickly you couldn't afford the payments and subsequently the car would be repossessed. The salesmen didn't care; they went on selling cars and collecting their commission. Max and Joey stuck to the regular small yards.

They now visited their third one, Honest Harry's Used Cars in Sydney Road, Brunswick. They were eyeing off a green 1956 FJ Holden ute when, in a flash, Honest Harry materialised out of nowhere.

'Hello, boys. I see you've got an eye for detail. Nice looking unit. It's in perfect condition,' he said.

'Lift the bonnet and fire her up,' Joey said.

Max and Joey then stuck their heads under the bonnet to look and listen.

'I don't know what I'm looking for,' Max said.

'No, but I do, Max,' Joey said.

Harry, if that was his real name, stood there smiling like he had already sold the car to a couple of young blokes who knew bugger all about cars. Well, he was in for a shock, wasn't he? Joey marched up to him.

'You must think we were born yesterday, mate. Listen to the tappets and gudgeons banging like my outdoor toilet door in the wind, and the big end bearings don't sound that hot, either. I wouldn't mind betting the sumps full of thick truck oil.'

The look on Harry's face instantly changed. Max could read his mind: he was obviously thinking the skinny one's a bloody mechanic.

Harry, not to be outdone for a sale, said, 'Come into the office, boys. I'm sure I can do a better deal than the price advertised.'

Max said, 'Well, I won't be buying this, will I?'

'Hang about,' Joey said, 'If we can torment him down to a realistic price, we'll take the car to my dad's workshop, and you can help me rebuild the motor and anything else that needs to be done.'

And so Max became the owner of the green 1956 FJ Holden, blowing clouds of blue smoke down Sydney Road, Brunswick. In time to come, utes and panel vans became very popular, particularly when the Sandman Sin Bin hit the market – an upmarket panel van with waves and other things painted down the sides, windows and curtains with mirrors, a mattress and glass and cup holders all factory fitted. When parents saw one of these go by, they could only hope their daughter wasn't inside. As promised, Max's car went to Mick, Joey's dad's workshop, and from Friday night to Sunday night, Max and Joey rebuilt the engine. Joey did all the important stuff that was needed: feeler gauges and timing lights, piston rings, gudgeons, shell bearings and big end bearings were replaced. All that was left to do were the shock absorbers. The pong box (exhaust) and muffler would have to wait for another day. It wasn't a new car – who could afford that? Not Max nor Joey – but the FJ was now purring like a kitten and, anyway, 'Joey,' Max's mum said, 'the older you get, the better you get – unless you're a banana'.

Max's Aunty Dolly, another one of his mother's sisters, had a holiday house at Anglesea where Dorris and Max would sometimes go to stay. Uncle Harry was a grumpy old bugger.

Max heard him say, 'I don't mind that girl staying, but that bloody boy ...! I keep telling him not to run up the rocks on the driveway and now he's gashed his knee open.'

Well, some years later, now that Max had a ute, Harry

wanted him to move his office furniture from his architect's office in the city to a new one in St Kilda. So, for the sake of peace with his mother, Max agreed. It took him all day Sunday carrying chairs and desks up and down stairs by himself, and when he finally finished, the old stingy bastard gave him just ten bob. Max put a sign on the back of his ute that said 'Yes, it's my ute, and I'm not helping you move in case anyone else has got any ideas'.

*

There was an apprentice one year younger than Max. His name was Bob but they all called him Nitro, because his farts were extremely loud and the smell was unbearable. He was a bloody good bloke and he and Max became very good friends. Nitro was getting married, and he asked Max to be his best man. They had been drunk many times together and stood back-to-back during fights outside pubs on many occasions. He hadn't missed any of Max's football matches, so of course Max said he would be honoured.

Nitro was getting married today at two-thirty. Max was racking his brain to make sure he hadn't forgotten anything that was the best man's responsibility – wedding cars booked, wedding ring ... Shit, if he lost that, there'd be hell to pay, so he tucked carefully it into his jock strap, hoping he wouldn't have to use the toilet before the wedding. On second thoughts, maybe it wasn't a good spot to keep it after all.

His mum said, 'Now have you got clean undies on, Max, in case you have an accident and have to go to hospital?'

'Jesus, Mum, if I have an accident, I will shit my pants anyway, so does it really matter?'

Max had had a haircut and was looking great. His wedding suit was hanging in the FJ along with his polished shoes and socks. The idea was that he would get dressed at Nitro's place and then they would head off to the church together.

'I'm going now, Mum,' he said.

'Tell Nitro we hope he has a lovely wedding and a wonderful rest of his life with his chosen partner.'

Max was singing to himself, thinking what a fantastic day was ahead of him. He had done everything on his part, double-checked and triple-checked. Nothing could go wrong. Shit, what's that banging and scraping? Then he heard it, the loud roaring of the engine somewhere under the ute. The bloody muffler and pong box were dragging on the ground, one of the few things that hadn't been fixed yet. *Shit*, thought Max, *I'll have to stop. How can this be happening now!* He stripped off to his singlet and underpants. The muffler was still too hot to handle, and he had nothing to hold it back in place.

'The wire coathanger! You're a genius,' Max said out loud, bending and twisting the wire hanger till it broke.

He was about to climb back under when a car went past with some kid baring his arse out the window.

'Dickhead!' Max shouted.

He thought about making a phone call, but Christ knows where the nearest phone box was. He was sure he could fix it good enough to get where he was going. Back under the ute, the muffler was cool enough to touch. He shoved it all back in place, wired it up and headed off in his undies.

'Jesus,' Nitro's mother said, 'Max, we were getting worried. Look at you! Where's the wedding suit?'

'In the ute,' Max said, 'and the wedding ring is in the glove box.'

'Boys!' she said, 'Who would have them! I will get all that while you get in the shower – and tell Robert I want to see him.'

'Now, Robert, you two are to go straight to the church.'

'Where else would we be going?' replied Nitro.

'Knowing you two, who would know?'

The two of them sat in the vestibule opposite the minister, Mr Chambers, who was seated behind his desk. He had a short crewcut that looked ridiculous with a moustache. He wore his black cassock and sat quietly with his legs apart. Max couldn't believe what he wasn't seeing – he had no pants on under the cassock! He started nudging Nitro, they both started sniggering which turned into muffled laughing, and when you're not supposed to be laughing, it's hard to stop. What they didn't know was he had been swimming and still had on his bathers. The church bells rang out which was the sign that the bridal motorcade had arrived.

Max looked at Nitro and said, 'Last chance, mate.'

As time went on, Max continued his friendship with Joey. Now they both had cars, they often went ice skating at the St Moritz ice skating rink. They were a pair of buggers who would pick out the girls who were struggling on the ice and whiz past, clicking their skate under the foot of the girl who would fall on her arse. They would then stop to apologise, help them up, show them how to skate and then take them to Luna Park for a ride in the Tunnel of Love.

Max would often say, 'Mine's all right, Joey. Yours isn't too good. I think yours fell out of the ugly tree and hit all the branches on the way down', even if it wasn't true. 'Mind you,'

Max said, 'I have seen some ugly and shitty looking blokes as well, so what's good for the goose is good for the gander, I reckon.'

When they weren't going skating, they continued their Saturday night ritual at the town hall dance. It was at one of these dances that he met a girl who took his fancy, and after the dance he asked her if he could take her home. She lived with her parents in the eastern suburbs and her name was Valda. Bugger, he remembered the ute was off the road getting a paint job and a canopy fitted, which meant he would have to take her home on the bloody train. Shit, he would have to buy her ticket and his own, too. He bummed some extra money from Joey and took her home. By the time they had done the expected 'kiss and tell' stuff up against the neighbour's fence, the last train had long gone. He was now faced with a twenty-something-mile walk home, but at least he had enough money left for four steamed dim sims from a place called Fong's Chinese Restaurant.

Max's ute was now back on the road, and he was thinking, *Do I keep seeing Valda?* Then he thought, a smile from a pretty girl doesn't mean she wants to go to bed with you, but a bloke would be a fool not to take it as far as it might go, so he pushed on with their relationship.

Chapter 5

Max the fireman

Max couldn't see himself working in a factory the rest of his life, so he took two days off work and went into the Eastern Hill Fire Station for an interview with the Melbourne Metropolitan Fire Brigade that proved to have a successful outcome. The Chief Officer told him he would start his training in four weeks' time. Good news – fantastic news! – as Max knew he wouldn't be spending the rest of his life clocking a card in a factory, making money for a bully owner who didn't appreciate what the workers did for him. Besides that, he had higher expectations of himself, places to go, things to do and to grab some of the excitement that life had to offer. Adrenaline pumping was the key to it all, he said to himself.

The next day at the factory, he climbed the concrete steps to the office. The lowlife owner was there talking to the office lady. The way he looked at Max and said, 'What are you doing up here?' Max thought he really was a prick.

He said, 'I'm here to give a week's notice.'

'No, you're not,' the owner said, 'you're sacked.'

Max knew he was never going to get the week's pay that, in those circumstances, he was entitled to. The lady in the office looked stunned, and you could see her thoughts were the same as Max's.

'You're a mean, miserable bastard!'

Well, with all that had just happened, Max knew it was time to get out of Dodge. Back in the factory, he briefly told Nitro what had happened.

He said, 'At the end of this year, my apprenticeship finishes, and I'll be out of here in a flash as well.'

Max said, 'Please stay in touch, mate. I'm off on another journey and the road to my success will always be under construction. I've got dirt to scratch and eggs to hatch, and I'm determined to follow through on my dreams.'

Max's cousin, Keith, was starting a three-week holiday and asked Max if he wanted to go.

Max said, 'Why not? I don't start training for another four weeks.'

Keith had a small Ford Anglia, so they decided to go in Max's FJ ute which now had a canopy on so they could pack their stuff in the back and sleep in there if it was raining; otherwise, they would sleep in two small tents. They decided to go to Mildura; that's where Fred's mate and his wife lived. If they needed to, they could scam a couple of nights there.

Max said that when they got to Aunty Silvy (that's what the kids used to call her) and Uncle George's house, just really to say hello, it was 4 pm, and the pair of them were already half cut. George was an alcoholic and Silvy wasn't far from one either. George would go to bed with a half-drunk long-necked bottle of beer beside the bed with a teaspoon shoved in it to stop it from going flat. *What a load of bullshit,* thought Max, *couldn't see a bloody teaspoon doing any such thing. Bloody urban myth.* They were both a couple of rough diamonds, but good caring people.

Silvy said, 'Listen to me, you two boys, there's a big dance on tonight at the Municipal Hall. You play your cards right, you might get a couple of sheilas and you can bring them back here. We're having a party tonight.'

The boys got to the dance. It was a typical country-style set-up with the girls all lined up down one side of the hall waiting for the blokes to ask them for a dance. Max went down the line, asking girls if they would like to dance. The first half dozen said, 'No, thanks'. Max wondered why they were standing there if they didn't want a bloody dance, particularly with a good-looking bloke like himself. Something must be wrong. He checked his fly in case it was open and his little dolly was hanging out.

Keith was busy dancing with some tall skinny sheila, so Max had another go down the line. This time he cracked it. Irene was rather plumpish with some nice features, but not quite good enough for his little dolly to stand up and clap, but she wanted to dance, and she was very light on her feet. She and the tall skinny girl who Keith was with were friends and had come down from Berri for the weekend, so the boys decided to take them back to George and Silvy's party.

By the time they all arrived at the party, it was in full swing, with all there fairly well under the weather. Silvy kept making suggestive remarks about what the boys would be doing later that night. Max had made no promises to Valda, and she had gone to Queensland with her girlfriends, so he reckoned it was all fair play, and besides that, it looked like his girl had a nice comfortable body.

The next night, Keith had gone somewhere with the skinny one, so Max told Irene he would take her out to dinner. He explained to her that he was on holidays and didn't have an abundance of money so he asked her if it would be all right to go to a Chinese restaurant. Irene was happy with that, and they were given a nice table for two with a candle flickering away, kind of like a romantic mood setting. They started an idle chat. Irene was a schoolteacher, teaching the bubs grade and Year One at primary school. All of a sudden during a break in chatting, the silence was broken when Irene let out a gigantic fart.

She said, 'Oh, Max, that was lucky. For a minute I thought I might have shit my panties.'

It was not often that Max was stuck for words, but this was one of those times. You can meet someone for the first time and straightaway, you know that this is the person you want to spend your whole life without. He knew he had wasted his money on dinner, money that he didn't have a lot of, and he'd be saying goodbye after the meal. His little dolly would just have to wait.

*

Max fronted up on the scheduled day at the big main fire station in Melbourne along with six other recruits. It was all very confronting – fire trucks parked on polished concrete floors, brass helmets, jackets and axe belts hanging all around the walls on hooks. Up high was apparently what was called the watch room behind glass walls, and Max could see dials, small red and green lights blinking on and off, an array of small clocks that looked like they weren't there to tell the time and a big board in front of a padded seat. The board was full of holes with cords hanging out of some of them and a dude sitting there with headphones on. The Chief Officer's name was Jackie Paterson, and he was the one who welcomed them and gave an introduction to the training they would receive and what was expected of them. The training would be 9 am to 5 pm. Max thought, *Let's get the adrenaline pumping! Let's get this show on the road!* A few weeks later, he was absolutely knackered, and yet he was fit, not long from playing football.

'So now, Max,' his dad said, 'sit here and tell us all about the training.'

Max began. 'There's these ladders called pompier ladders. They have one single strand running up the middle with a horizontal tread attached and a big steel hook on the top. You have to run the ladder very quickly to stop it swinging left to right. The training tower is four storeys high with a pair of open windows. You hook the ladder on the window ledge and run up, climb in the window, lean out, haul up the ladder and hook in into the second-floor window. This goes on until you reach the top floor, and then back down the same way until the instructors think we are proficient at it. We would have races, two teams racing to the top and down.'

'What if someone missed their footing and fell? Sounds dangerous!' his mum said.

'They have a big rope net at the bottom with about ten blokes spread out around it hanging on to it.'

His father said, 'Well, if it's so safe, explain to your mother about the ten stitches in your head.'

'Trust you to bring that up!' Max said. 'I was just about at the top window when I looked across to see where the other team was, a bit like I did in the billycart race with Joey. I lost my footing and fell backwards off the ladder. I thought I was a goner for sure, but the net was there; it was obviously there for dickheads like me. I fell on the outer rim of the net, bounced out, cracked my head on the concrete and woke up across the road in St Vincent's Hospital. I wondered if I would be the only one to ever fall off the training tower in future, but thank you for bringing this up again, Dad. You just can't help yourself, can you? Well, I guess a failure is like fertiliser: it stinks but it makes things grow faster in the future.'

Max went on outlining the training. 'They put these breathing things on us called Protos. They are designed for use in a contaminated environment. It's a self-contained system which consists of a cylinder of oxygen and an air reservoir or breathing bag containing an absorbent, which removes the carbon dioxide. It is then mixed with a fresh supply of oxygen and reused. It's a cumbersome thing in confined spaces like drainpipes because we have to push the bag along in front of us to get through small openings. The instructors blacked out our face masks and shoved us into some sort of drain system. The object was to get through to the other end around bends and obstacles. The idea was to see who might be claustrophobic and panic and so end your career as a fireman. I shit myself in the first five minutes inside the drain, but I said to myself, "I wanted the adrenaline ride, boy, so get on with it". I could hear blokes moving behind me, so I knew if anything went wrong, I wasn't going to die alone. When I emerged outside, I saw the so-called drain system was made of plastic tubes laid out above ground for the exercise. Sometimes in life all it not as it seems to be. I was angry at myself for being such a pissant – lesson learnt.'

Once a week, schoolkids visited the station, and the recruits were used for demonstrations. The ladder they used for firefighting was called the Magirus ladder and was the biggest in the Southern Hemisphere. However, they couldn't have anything bigger than that due to the Victorian registration rules for width on roads. How bloody ridiculous, the rules of the nanny state! This was not your run-of-the-mill delivery truck; it was a lifesaving vehicle. That's why the ladders with the hooks were there because some buildings were taller than the Magirus ladder. As Max was to learn later in life, it was not the only poorly thought-out decision by the government. Anyway, this ladder would set itself up under the four-storey training tower to perform a rescue for the schoolkid. All the recruits took their turn each week to be rescued.

'This week, Mum, it was my turn. The ladder came up to the top floor and a senior fireman on the ladder attached me to a harness. The ladder moved away from the tower, and I was told keep my hands close to my body and jump, looking down. I thought, "Shit, what if this doesn't work or has a malfunction?" Oh, well, you only live once, but if you do it right, once is enough. I just needed the chance to do it once. The pulley on the cable is designed to evaluate my weight, compensate for it and lower me slowly but it took a few seconds to work this out, so for a small amount of time, I was free falling. To me, it felt like there was enough time to hit the ground, and having already fallen off this bloody tower once, I said, "You're an idiot, Max!"'

The theory and practice training went on for three months. Max was now accredited as a driver. The test to get your licence, if you already had Victorian heavy-duty license, was to drive this open-air fire appliance with a ladder on top around the city. It had a gear stick three feet long and a crash gearbox that required doubling the clutch and listening to the engine revs between changes. There were only four of them left who'd completed the training and all of them had passed the driving test.

Nearing the end of training, a big grass fire happened somewhere out the back of Coburg. The almost-trained recruits were hustled to one of the two grass fire trucks as someone yelled, 'Thornton, you're driving.'

Talk about an adrenaline pump, Maxy boy, he thought, *This is what it's all about*, as he drove up Sydney Road the wrong side of the trams, lights flashing and bells ringing through the red lights, adrenaline coming out of every pore in his body. *This is fantastic, but will my training hold up when we get to the fire? Well, it's only a grass fire anyway.*

They were the second unit to arrive at the fire. The grass was two feet high, but the flames were four or five feet higher and the wind was gusting big time.

The officer said, 'Get around the back behind the fire we'll cut it off from there.'

Max took the truck and the crew to the other side of the fire, and they had got the hoses out and the pump running when suddenly a newspaper reporter appeared, filming too close to the fire for his own good.

Max called out to him, 'Get out of there, you idiot!'

He took no notice and kept filming.

Max said, 'Hose the bastard.'

They hosed him and arse overhead he went. The wind suddenly changed direction, and the only way out now was through the burning grass. They had a bit of a group discussion and decided it was going to be up the guts with tons of smoke, so back through the fire they went, melting anything that was plastic, like taillights and indicators.

Max was allocated a station and his career as a firefighter began. Day shift was 7 am to 3 pm, afternoon shift 3 pm to 11 pm and night shift 11 pm to 7 am, then two days rostered off; the duration of each shift was two days. A Z day, as it was known, was an extra day off, allocated to bring them back to five days to compensate for their six-day week. They had to provide their own bedding; most of the blokes like Max had fold-up wire beds with a mattress and blankets or a sleeping bag that they folded up and put way after their shift.

'We cooked our own meals in the kitchen area and ate at a table in the dining area,' Max said, 'and I don't know how many times I was halfway through cooking a meal when the alarm bells would go off and we'd have to leave it all and go. Needless to say, it was bloody ruined when you got back.

'There was a woman called Margaret who was always on the late-night radio talk program from midnight to 4 am, and if it was my turn in the watch room during those times, it was a laugh to listen in. She was always half or fully pissed, and she would keep laughing; the radio announcer would get a lot of mileage out of her. When he'd had enough of her, he'd say, "You have to go now, Margaret. There's someone else on the line", and she would say, "I'm going to ring the fire station now to talk to Jimmy". I don't think Jimmy existed, but she didn't know that because she was always pissed, or half-pissed. Once she was in the fire station phone system, they would keep passing her around all the stations, and I think everyone told her he was Jimmy. Well, if nothing else, it broke the boredom in the watch room during those hours, and it was actually quite funny.'

The watch room at Max's station had rows of clocks, one for each street fire alarm in the area of the station's responsibility, small red and green lights on panel boards indicating pump pressure in the sprinkler system at that location and a small switchboard that linked up eight other fire stations which included No. 1 Station Eastern Hill. There was a ten-minute time-out button you had to keep pressing in case you fell asleep. If you missed the ten minutes in time-out, an internal alarm rang in the watch room and you had one minute before all the main alarms and external bells rang. This meant everyone out had to get out of bed thinking it was a call-out, and you would not be very popular.

The red fire alarms on the corner of some streets had to be checked and tested every so often and was usually done by the junior fireman on a bicycle. On one of his day shifts when Max was the junior fireman, he peddled the bicycle to the first street fire alarm. The alarms had a small round glass window within easy reach to break the glass. Once broken, it gave access to a button which, when pressed, activated a clock in the watch room. The particular clock that sprung into life and the number the clock hand moved to indicate the street fire alarm location.

Max used his key to open the alarm. Inside were spare glass squares and a phone. When he picked up the phone, a voice said, 'Hello, Max. Press the button.' A metal disc with pegs was activated and a gyroscopic wheel hit all the pegs as it went round; the number of pegs on the disc corresponding with the number the clock stopped at in the watch room. The bloke in the watch room said, 'Smith and Grant Street.' Max said, 'Roger that.' He then rewound the disc, closed and locked the door, and thought only another twenty-five of these things to go!

The station officer's name was Gordon. He played on the half forward flank for Essendon and had kicked seven goals the year Essendon had won the premiership. On Max's return to the station, Gordon said, 'Just in time to finish the shift, Max. You haven't been waiting in a pub somewhere, have you?'

'Not bloody likely!' said Max.

Usually on the day and afternoon shifts, hoses that had been used on a previous night shift were scrubbed, washed and hung up to dry, vehicles checked and cleaned, the station concrete floor polished and, of course, your brass helmet, unless you were lucky enough to have a shift in the watch room where you could sit on your arse and watch the activity.

It happened on a Saturday night, somewhere near midnight. Everyone except the watch room shift was in bed, when the bells went off, the PA system blaring 'Fire alarm, Smith and Grant Street, hose carriage only'. Sometimes the call would be 'All gear, all gear', but not this time. The hose carriage, as it was called, went to every call-out with five firemen on board. Max was not driving this time; he was in the back seat. On arrival, there was nothing to be seen; no one was there. Max was instructed to radio back to the station. He grabbed the mike in the vehicle and said, 'Glass broken, machine run down, nothing showing.' The alarm was reset, and the glass replaced.

Max recalls: 'It was pissing rain so back at the station the vehicle was chamois dried, and we went back to bed. Half an hour later, bells on again, "Alarm at Smith and Grant, hose carriage only". Back we went. The alarm was on the corner of a block of shops. The call-back was the same as before – glass broken, machine run down, nothing showing. Back to station, chamois the vehicle and back to bed. But this time, the police had been asked to sit down the street and watch to see who was doing it, so we should get this prick whoever they were. Well, bugger me, sure enough, when we got there, the alarm was again activated and the police were standing next to it. "No one has come near it," they said. "We have been sitting just down the road and have seen no one." Still pissing rain, so back to the station and – you guessed it – chamois the bloody vehicle.'

This time when the fire crew arrived, the police were standing there with a small boy and his parents who lived on the premises of the shop. The boy's bedroom had louvre windows just a small distance away from the front of the alarm. The boy had been poking a stick out the window, breaking the glass and activating the alarm. The police explained to the boy and his parents that prank calls like this could seriously affect response time to a real fire and could even mean the loss of a life. While the police were lecturing the boy's parents, Max could see the crew trying to conceal a smile, thinking about the boy's ingenuity, but the kid needed to understand what he did was wrong.

Max thought he should have been made to come and wash the fire appliances as a punishment, but that was not the call of a junior fireman.

Chapter 6

Engaged and married

Max struck up enough courage to ask Valda's parents' permission to get engaged, although he knew he was not her mother's favourite person.

He had once sat on their new cream-coloured vinyl couch and a blue biro in his pocket had leaked into the couch; the stain was never able to be removed. She had once told him he never put the cap back on the toothpaste properly when he was staying there, so he cut a hole in the side and squeezed it out from there, much to her disgust. Another time when he turned up after playing football half pissed and suffering with what he now knows was concussion, he was sick in the toilet. Thinking he had done a thorough job at cleaning it up, he decided not to mention it to anyone. Unfortunately for Max, Valda's mother used the toilet next, and Max was in the shit.

'Jesus, Max, you've been sick in there. It's all over the wall and down the back of the toilet.'

Bloody hell, Max thought, *I will never get this woman to like me.*

He was there once on a Sunday. When it came time for

lunch, Valda's mother called her into the kitchen and left him sitting by himself while they had lunch. Max thought, *How bloody rude is that!* So, he went away and bought fish and chips and sat in the lounge eating them while they were in the kitchen. When Valda's mother saw this, she went crying to her room. Max thought, *Serves you right, you rude person.*

Sometime earlier, when the twins Max and Dorris had their twenty-first birthdays on the farm, all those in attendance were going to stay the night due to the distance to travel – but not Valda. Her mother said, no way known, it just wasn't going to happen. Mrs Thornton rang her and explained the girls would be sleeping in the house and the boys in the shearer's quarters, but no dice. Valda's girlfriend and another friend, Scrooge, were of course allowed to stay overnight, but now they had to drive all the way back to take 'you know who' home, so their night was fucked as well. As you can well imagine, Max wasn't a great fan of Valda's mother. On the other hand, her stepfather was a really nice bloke.

However, they did say yes to the engagement. They lent Max Valda's mother's car one night and when the car came back, its front end wasn't right. Max told them about it, and they said he must have been driving it up the gutter. *That's what my father said about my bike*, Max thought, *not true then and not true now.* Some smart arse 'know it all' at the Holden plant where her stepfather worked told him that's the only way it could have happened – 'liar, liar pants on fire'. However, when the car was checked, the steering arm and wishbone were loose, and the front end was out of balance. Mind you, no one ever apologised to Max for being accused of the damage.

Whenever her mother was present, Max had to be very careful. He always felt like he was being tested by her for something he hadn't studied or prepared for, and on a couple of occasions, he was ready to give it all the arse. The problem was, Max was still a larrikin, but he was trying to live at the same time in both worlds: carefree and settling down.

*

On his way to an afternoon shift before he was married, he was hit on the driver's side by a car coming through the intersection on a red light. He somehow found himself in the gutter across the road from his pride and joy ute, which was now fucked. He was loaded into the ambulance and taken to the Alfred Hospital. Someone must have rung the fire station because the Station Officer was at the hospital not long after Max arrived.

'You just can't stay out of the limelight, can you, Max,' he said. 'The X-rays show a cracked kneecap and broken arm. We will get you back as soon as you're able. You can sit on your arse and operate the watch room until the Medical Officer deems you fit to return to full duties.'

Max asked if they would go to the shop and tell Valda what had happened. Valda told his parents and that's when the shit fight started. Fred went off his brain.

'Why weren't we told first? We're his next of kin, not you. You're not his wife yet. We deserve to be told by the authorities, not second hand by you.'

This didn't help the relationship between Valda and Max's family.

The driver of the other car was charged by the police and the court found in favour of Max. On the advice of his Station Officer, Max engaged a solicitor to negotiate with the other party's insurance company, and consequently Max's new car was born – a powder blue Valiant AP6 S series. Chrome spoke wheels, front and back bench seats, Borg and Warner push-buttons transmission … it was almost worth going through the pain to get this baby, Max reckoned. The FJ ute that he'd loved and cherished had gone to God, but the Valiant had certainly softened the blow. Healing time and physiology exercises, particularly for his knee, were long and arduous, but eventually he was back on full duties.

*

Max and Valda, although not married yet, purchased a small milk bar which she could run while he remained in the fire service. But once the grocery stores, which were much bigger, were permitted to sell milk, the writing was on the wall for the small 'mum and dad' stores. Their milk bar was one of the casualties.

However, there was always someone ringing the watch room on night shift offering outside work. Two night shifts were followed by two days off, and if those days fell through the week, you could get four days of extra work as well as the fire brigade. Max was no stranger to this scenario. He had driven buses in the suburbs where passengers paid at the door, picnic buses up to the snow at Mt Buller and Pioneer buses when the Clipper was a good-looking bus. He had driven delivery trucks, taxi trucks furniture vans and a hearse for a funeral company. He had unloaded oranges off the train at Spencer Street railyards, dug house foundations, worked on the loading line at Cottee's drink factory and at WD and HO Wills tobacco factory shovelling tobacco on to a conveyor belt.

So, he knew all about the extra work you could get.

When Max worked with the furniture removal van, he was very quick at packing crockery. He could pack a set of twenty china dishes in ten minutes or if you wanted forty of them, he could do it in five minutes.

On one of Max's night shifts, some bloke rang the station looking for someone to drive his delivery van for about six weeks. He had broken his leg and it was in plaster. He thought a relay of firemen on or coming off night shift could keep his van on the road. He would pay cash at the end of each day.

'Anyone want this job?' the bloke in the watch room announced on the PA.

'I'll take it,' Max said.

After his shift finished at 7 am, he headed for the address in Beach Road. It was a private address with a very big side yard. In the long grass was this very ordinary looking, white, pug-nosed Morris van with a flat tyre. *That can't be it*, Max thought. He went into the house, where the bloke was sitting in his bed, and sure enough, he had his leg in plaster. He introduced himself and gave Max the paperwork for all of the day's pickups and deliveries. He said the van was out in the yard.

Max said, 'What? The one with the flat tyre in the long grass?'

'Yes,' he said, 'Sorry about that. You'll have to take it off and get to the garage to be fixed.'

Max thought he should just clear out then and there. He had a feeling this was not going to be a good day, but he was there now, and he didn't want to waste a day's pay. The sliding door was jammed half open and couldn't be moved and the seat looked like it was fixed to some sort of fruit box bolted to the floor. *You've got to be kidding me!* he thought. But, to his amazement, the bloody thing actually started. So, he took the wheel off and got it fixed.

He did about twenty deliveries around Melbourne with the seat swaying all over the place.

'I nearly fell out through the open door twice,' he said to one of the ladies named Genny at a delivery, and she was very sympathetic.

On his way back at the corner of Collins and Swanson streets, there was a cop in the middle of the intersection directing traffic. He waved Max into the centre ready for the right-hand turn. Max and the van stopped right next to the cop. He was looking in through the open door at what Max was sitting on with a look of astonishment on his face.

Max said, 'Whatever you're thinking, you're right, but it's not my shit heap, and life's a bitch sometimes, sir.'

The cop made some signals with his white gloves and said, 'Away you go, son.'

Max put the van in gear, let the clutch out and the tail shaft fell off from the differential. He couldn't explain what the look on the copper's face said, but it wasn't good. With his and some bystanders' help, they pushed the vehicle to the side of the road. In the only lucky break for the day, Max found somewhere to buy a shifting spanner and some bolts the right size and length. They were only mild steel and he knew they wouldn't last the trip back, so he bought a second set. Sure enough, he got as far as Luna Park and it fell off again: the mild steel bolts had sheared through. He got under the shit heap and reconnected the tail shaft with the second set of bolts.

When he arrived back, he told the owner what had happened. Max thought he didn't seem fazed about it at all

– 'Good. It should be okay for tomorrow.' This bloke obviously knew nothing about engineering.

Max said, 'I won't be back tomorrow. I have another job to go to, but I'll try and find another idiot.'

Max was paid and he left. Back at the station for the second night shift that night, he asked if anyone wanted work the next day. The bloke who said, 'Yes, that would be me' was two years senior to Max and was full of smartarse remarks to those who were junior to him. *What an opportunity!* thought Max. *It's party time.*

So, he said, 'Small van, no heavy lifting, no problems. The owner is a nice bloke, has his leg in plaster. You'll have to go into the house when you get there.'

With two days off after night shift, he didn't see the smartarse till the day shift. When he saw him, the bloke said, 'Shit, Max, you wouldn't believe what happened. I got as far as Luna Park and the bloody tail shaft fell off.'

Unfortunately, Max couldn't hide his smile, and the smartarse said, 'You're a bastard, Max! You knew that was going to happen, didn't you?'

Max said to him, 'Well, mate, if you sit by the bank of the river long enough, you're bound to see the body of your enemy floating by.'

'What does that mean?'

'If you don't know, mate, I haven't got the time to start explaining it by drawing you pictures.'

*

Valda worked in the Health building in the city with one of her girlfriends, Janette, whose boyfriend's nickname was

Macca. He and Max became good friends, so much so that Macca joined the fire service as well. His nickname became Black Mac, not because he was black but he just had dark olive skin. Max was best man at his wedding and Mac would be best man at Max's wedding. Max and Mac were always in the shit with the girls. They were either late getting back from the pub or had some harebrained plans that were destined to failure, and to make it worse, they'd look at each other and start laughing. Unfortunately, these two sheilas had no sense of humour whatsoever. *Someone's going to have to change*, Max thought. Problem was, he couldn't see it being any of them.

The Eastern Hill Fire Station (No. 1 Station) was invited to play a picnic football match against the Nar Nar Goon Club and the local pub. Max and Macca were among those selected. They took the girls with them in a picnic van, which was normally a furniture van but with fold-down seats along the sides for picnics.

They were all picked up outside the fire station on the Sunday. On arrival, they saw there were eighteen-gallon kegs set up supplied by the pub and barbecues cooking the meat. The Club President welcomed everyone and said the football match would start after everyone had eaten. Max thought, *Shit, this'll be a fun match. We've all been on the booze.* Those who were playing changed and ran onto the ground amongst a mixture of clapping and booing, depending whose side they were on. Max's opponent looked like he might be an Olympic weightlifter, but he also looked like he had drunk his share of booze and somebody else's, so Max reckoned he could handle him.

Max said to him, 'Bloody hell, who's that over there?'

He said, 'That's one of the barmaids from the pub. There's another one playing as well.'

She had blonde hair tied back in a bun, which did nothing for her well-lived-in face. She probably hadn't looked too bad ten years ago, but her body had also been well lived in and had since gone bad on her. Max made some smartarse remark about her which he thought she heard, because she took out her teeth and pulled a face at him.

The game was now on. Max said, 'We were running down the wing, me and Macca, passing the ball back to each other. I ran in and kicked a goal. I was standing in the goals sucking up the applause when the barmaid came running up and punched me fair in the nuts and said, "That's for the smartarse remarks." Macca came running in, and I said, "Christ, did you see that?" He's laughing and I'm holding on to the family jewels in pain.'

After the match, which they lost, Max was sitting on a seat and the blonde barmaid came over. She had a bucket of ice and a pot of beer.

She said, 'The beer's for you and the bucket of ice is for your nuts.'

'What? Do you think they're on a bloody string and I can just lower them in?'

'It's Max, isn't it?'

'Yes.'

'Good game today, Max. Thanks for coming. Enjoy the beer and the ice. Call into the pub one day and I'll shout you a beer.'

'Thanks, I will,' Max said, but he knew he probably wouldn't.

*

Mac's wedding and Max's went off without a hitch, although Max could see his new mother-in-law smiling to convince everyone she was happy and proud of her new son-in-law. Max knew she was probably sticking pins in a small Max doll under the table at the reception.

Sometimes he saw her flying over the fire station on her broom, but she never waved.

Chapter 7

Fire stories

Sometimes Max and Valda were invited to Sunday roast at Max's parents' place. After the Sunday lunch, Max was asked about some of the fires he had attended.

'Where do I start?' he said.

'Well,' they said, 'pick out the most memorable ones.'

'There are two that will stay in my mind forever,' he said. 'I was one of the crew on the hose carriage on the afternoon shift when we were called out to a house fire. We arrived about the same time as a nearby station's appliance. The middle and right side of the house were well alight, and it looked like the fire was working its way down the left side of the house in the rafters. We forced open the front door. Budget and I went left, the others to the right. (Budget was his nickname, don't know why. He wasn't from my station.) The fire on the right seemed the main issue. Outside, more hoses were being connected to help control the flames, although we knew the house was gone.

'I could hear someone crying. We crawled down the passage close to the floor where any oxygen would be. Imagine, if you can, being blindfolded and led into someone's house to walk around with no idea of the layout or where furniture and obstacles are. What if there were some stairs going down? You will be arse over tit, and all of this with smoke you to have to breathe in. (We only use Proto breathing apparatus in known contaminated areas.) Budget and I struggled down what we hoped was a hallway towards the crying. We found a door which was a child's bedroom. The fire was just starting to come through the ceiling. Standing on a small bed was a little girl – best guess, four years old. Hot embers were falling onto her hair and her pyjama sleeves had caught fire. We brushed the embers off her hair and did what we could with her pyjama sleeves.

'I said, "What's your name, darling?"

'She said, "Annabella".

'She was having trouble breathing, and so were we. I took off my brass helmet and said to Annie, "Put your face in there and breathe." There was no time to go back the way we'd come, as the fire was now in the hallway, so we carefully opened the window, mindful of a fresh oxygen supply to the fire.

'I said, "You're going out, Annie," and with that, I threw her out.

'A crew were now coming up the hall with hoses. We wouldn't have known that when Annie went out the window, but it meant we could now go out the way we had come in. The crews that were hosing from the outside must have seen Annie unceremoniously come out the window because by the time we got outside, she was already in the ambulance that had arrived, having her burns treated and on oxygen. We were coughing and dry retching.

'I said to one of the ambo blokes, "You haven't got a smoke, have you?"

'"Shit, you've got to be joking, mate! You've had enough smoke in there to have had fifty packets of smokes. Here, put this on," and passed me and Budget an oxygen mask.

'"How's Annie?" I asked.

'"Some small burns to her arms and one hand. We will be taking her to the hospital, but she will be fine," he said.

'Her parents didn't make it; they were in the other part of the house. After Annie's time in hospital, her grandparents, who had flown down from somewhere up north to be with her and take her back with them, brought her to the station. We sat her in the hose carriage and on one of the ladders.

'Her grandmother said to me, "She wants us to call her Annie because that's what the fireman called her."

'Annie looked at me and said, "You're the one who threw me out the window, aren't you?"

'"Yes, I am, darling."

'"Thank you," she said.

'I held her hand and we walked out to their car. I often wonder where that little girl is now.'

'What a lovely story,' Max's mum said, 'but so sad about her parents.'

Then Max said, 'Then there was the William Booth Memorial disaster. It was a Salvation Army Hostel for homeless men. There has been much written about this disaster. If you were to read some of the earlier reports from the media, some reporters were putting their own interpretations of what happened and what the living conditions were like. I can only tell you what I remember and what I was faced with on arrival.

'Our fire station was not called out to the disaster in Little Lonsdale Street in the city, but the Station Officer was told to attend. I was his driver, and we took the station's car. By the time we got there, Little Lonsdale Street was crammed with appliances and ambulances. It was a beehive of activity. I joined the crews carrying or helping to bring the men – some dead from asphyxiation, others dazed and incoherent – as far down the stairs as the second landing. The smoke was still quite thick, and it wasn't long before I was dry retching on the floor of the foyer. In what looked like a lunchroom, firemen and others were attempting to revive some of the men and others were being taken out on to the street.

'The fire had started on the third floor in someone's cubicle; early reports were that someone had fallen asleep smoking. I think the reports are now confirmed that an illegal heater was to blame. The fire had spread to the fourth floor as well. The place was like a bloody rabbit warren. The cubicles looked like they had been erected in a large floor space. The original ceiling was much higher, so the cubicle tops were covered with wire mesh. I think the walls of the cubicles were three-ply sheeting. There were dozens of these cubicles which meant there was a maze of narrow passageways leading from what I could see to the one that led to the toilet and shower block. This is where the asphyxiated men were found.

'When I walked down the passageway that led to the shower block and the stairs, I could see where their handprints had been marked on the scorched walls while trying to find their way out. This is my opinion only, but I think they were coming out of passageways to join the one going to the stairs, forming a daisy chain, but the first man who was leading the push kept going into the shower block instead of going to the right and down the stairs. Of course, everyone else followed. Remember that the place was full of thick smoke, and they were moving by feel only.

'It will take a long time for people to forget that 1966 disaster where some thirty forgotten men lost their lives. The first responding firemen will have more firsthand experiences to share.'

'What a damned shame,' Max's father said, 'even though they were homeless men with probably no one to mourn them.'

One of the weirdest fires he went to, although he was there after the fire, was at the Jam Factory in Chapel Street. The fire had occurred on the afternoon shift, and as Max was on the night shift, he had been allocated the first fire watch at the premises. Fire watch was when you were sent to make sure the fire didn't reignite during the night. You were sent there with a container of coffee or tea if you were lucky. A hose was left there sometimes, depending on the circumstances. The shift was usually for two hours when you would be relieved, although sometimes it may have been all night, depending on where you were.

Max said, 'When I got there, I did the usual walk through the place. Everything looked okay, so I sat down, took off my brass helmet and made a cup of tea. It was then that I heard this hideous laughing coming from somewhere in the building. *Shit, what's that?* I grabbed my torch and did a search. *Christ*, I thought, I'm here by myself. *Maybe I should use the fire alarm outside and get some bloody help. Bugger it!* I kept looking in the dark with the torch. The laughing seemed to keep moving. *Fuck this, I'm going to make a call.* When I got back to the tea urn, my brass helmet had been damaged. *That's it, I'm getting help.* I used my key in the alarm and the fire appliance came from the station with the police. They found this fellow, who it turned out was the one who started the fire destroying the Jam Factory. He had recently been sacked. Bloody scary at the time, I tell you.'

The family were mesmerised by all this and couldn't wait to hear more if Max was willing to tell them.

'There was a kitchen fire in a house with simply a pot on the stove. At first it looked like no one was home. However, after gaining entry and extinguishing the small fire, a woman appeared from the bathroom in a bath robe.

'She said, "My God, look at all these firemen in my house, and here I am with nothing on."

'She opened her robe and, bugger me, she did have nothing on. As I have said many a time, a wink and a smile from a pretty woman doesn't mean she wants to go to bed with you but a man-would be a fool not to take it as far as it might go. Well, someone did go back once, she reported it and his employment was terminated. Turns out maybe he was a fool. Make your own mind up about that.'

Max continued. 'One night, we got in the vehicle to go on a call and there was this bad smell, but when we returned to the station and searched the vehicle, there was no smell to be found. This went on for some time with the smell getting worse. One afternoon shift, I was polishing the floor along where the jackets and brass helmets hung on hooks on the wall, and there was that smell. Someone on another shift had unscrewed the top crest of the helmet, which is hollow, put a dead rat in there and screwed the crest back in place. Every time the bloke who owned the helmet got in the vehicle, it stank.

'Do you want me to continue?' Max said?

'We are fascinated!' they said. His sister Dorris said, 'You could write a book about this stuff.'

'Well, one day I just might.'

Max related another story. 'It was a Friday, maybe 3 am, when we were called out to MacNamara's pub. A man was asleep sitting outside his second-storey window in his pyjamas. The call was for both a hose carriage and ladder vehicle. We used no sirens or flashing lights in case we woke him and he fell. I was working the controls of the ladder. Someone went up, and as the top of the ladder hit the windowsill, the man woke up. We grabbed him and brought him down. The publican took us into the pub, we laid our brass helmets on the bar, and he opened some long-necked beer bottles and filled the pot glasses for us. I wished I had a camera to capture the scene of helmets on the bar between pots of beer at 3 am.

Those photo opportunities only come once in a lifetime, and it was missed.'

While they were in the pub, Macca said to Max, 'Was that you that fell off the roof into the hedge at Toorak the other night?'

'Yeah, well, don't go on about it, mate. I've still got all the little holes in me from the branches where they pulled me out. There are things that happen that when you talk about it later on, they are funny, but they're not bloody funny at the time.'

There was a fire in two shopfronts in the main street in Prahran. The fire crew split into two groups. Max went with the group down the side of the shops. The people who were living upstairs were now out on the street, so each crew member picked a window on the second floor and went up the ladders. There appeared to be no fire upstairs, so Max opened the window and lowered himself in. The upstairs was full of smoke, as black as the inside of a dog's bum. He kept lowering himself in, but there was no bloody floor! He was hanging there by his arms, ready to drop into Christ knows where, and he was sure the brass helmet on his head wasn't going to help the fall.

'Well, here we go,' Max said as he let go. Down he went.

'Shit! Trust me to pick the only window over the stairs!'

He was sitting on his arse in the stairwell in the smoke, licking his wounds and pride, when the others came through from the front of the shop.

'Don't sit there on your arse, Max,' someone said, 'Get up and help.'

'Yeah, thanks for that,' replied Max.

The family kept asking Max for more stories.

Max said, 'All right, just one more – and that's it.'

The fire crew was on the afternoon shift when they were

called out to a fire at the Glaciarium ice skating rink in City Road, South Melbourne at about 5 pm on Good Friday, a stinking hot day. When the crew got there, the fire had really taken hold. The hoses were quickly rolled out and connected to the street fire hydrant.

Max and another fireman raced into the foyer with the branch pipe. Unbeknownst to them, the big Magirus ladder with the Dennis pumps had arrived and they connected Max's hose to the pump. The pressure was ramped up to get a suitable pressure at the top of the ladder but that meant Max and his mate were going to cop the extra pressure at ground level. The branch pipes they were using had no on/off valves, and although they had backed part of the hose into a corner to take the first surge of water, it still came through at a great rate. Max and his mate were flung from one wall to the other in the small front entrance. The branch pipe was large and heavy and if they let it go, it would snake through the air and could kill somebody, 'particularly me,' said Max.

The only communication they had was a small, black, cannister-type claxon horn with sounds produced by pushing the plunger. One horn meant water on; two horns meant water off – that's if anyone was close enough to hear the bloody thing. It was a really dangerous fire. The roof was collapsing, and they just managed to get out. It eventually took about ten fire appliances to save the surrounding buildings.

*

A fireman mate of Max's was always talking about going to the Melbourne Cup, so this year they decided to go. John was to meet Max there as he lived on that side of town. Because there were a few Johns, they called him JW. When Max arrived at the prearranged spot at the racecourse, JW was nowhere to be see. Having no way to contact him, he thought, *this is going to be a shit day, here all by myself.* However, Max managed to find a telephone box inside the races and rang JW's place. He was told JW's dad had been taken to hospital and JW had gone with him. *Well, that's it, then*, Max thought, *just me against the bookies.* He didn't like his chances.

Race one was a hurdle. When the horses jumped from the gates, Max's horse didn't have a jockey. Apparently, the girth had not been secured properly and when the horses leapt out of the gates, the bloody jockey fell off.

Max was really pissed off, screaming out, 'You're gotta be kidding me! What mental moron is responsible for that shit?'

Just to add insult to it all, the jockey walked back down the track right past Max carrying the bloody saddle.

Max said to the idiot, 'Someone needs a foot right up the arse, mate.'

The bloke standing next to Max said, 'If I was you, mate, I'd go home now.'

He should have! Having run out of money by the second-last race, Max decided to go and, on the way out with what little money he had left, he bought a pie. It was one of those sloppy, soft ones and as he went to take a bite, someone knocked his arm and the pie hit the deck and squashed flat.

'Give me a break!' Max said to himself, as he walked under the track to the car park. Now he really panicked – he could not find his car. Sure enough, his new, powder blue Valiant was gone. Not only that but he had no bloody money. He went to where the police on track were operating from and reported it missing.

I'll have to get a taxi home and pay when I get there. Christ knows how much that will cost, he thought.

The next day, he rang the number the police had given him. They said they had his car, but the news was not good. It has been involved in a fatal accident and the driver was killed. There were no other cars involved and the prick who had stolen it was dead.

Max and Valda's milk bar was right next door to Dorris's sandwich and lunch shop. They lived above the milk bar, but it had only a small area at the back, and as a baby was on the horizon, it would now be far too small, so they decided to sell and rent somewhere else.

'At last,' Max said to Joey a couple of months later, 'our baby boy was born at the Bethlehem Hospital today. We called him Martin.'

His hunt for another car resulted in a blue two-toned FE Holden station wagon, hardly new but quite a nice car with plenty of room for young Martin's pram and the many other odds and ends needed for travelling with the little tacker.

'Maybe things are on the up and up,' said his mate, Joey.

Chapter 8

Friends

Max's diversionary paths of employment meant that past friendships were, over time, eventually lost, or at best, only renewed annually, but this was also rare. As Max pointed out to Joey, 'You can make new friends easily, if that's what you want, and you should endeavour to do just that. You will need someone to lean on when the going gets tough. Just make sure you choose them carefully. Everyone will need some sort of support from a friend over their life's journey. Damned right, there's no need to go it alone in tough times.'

Max had made a lot of new friends while courting his wife Valda in the early days, and they would remain his support for his entire journey.

Joey said, 'I'll get a couple of beers and you can tell me all about them.'

'Well, first there's Brewster – my age and height, about five foot ten, a thick-set moon face, large work-like, rough hands from plumbing and digging drains, a no-nonsense bloke, but a bloody prankster and non-stop talker. I once saw him talk to an old bloke for that long, the old bloke took out his hearing aids when Brewster wasn't looking ... although they say, beware of the man who doesn't talk and the dog that doesn't bark. He is a military history buff and has to know the technical data of anything that's mechanical and moves. He is a maniac for asking questions about comic strip characters, like who Ginger Meggs' best friend was, who were the ugly sisters or who was Snoopy's best friend. He knew them all, of course; drove us mad. He had an early model VW Beetle. Bought it new; he always had more money than the rest of us. He was more advanced in his apprenticeship than we were, so he was better off. He later bought a Jaguar while we were still driving older cars – and I might add, Joey, still paying them off.

'I remember, after a footy match at the MCG, six of us went to a Chinese restaurant in China Town. No one had any money, but we knew Brewster was always rich. However, Brewster told us he that he didn't have much money this time. Well, we didn't have any, or not much anyway, and I said to him, "Yeah, tell us another one, mate."

'Anyway, we went in and we all ordered up big, smiling at Brewster. He was laughing and telling us he couldn't pay. Well, he was right. I went out the toilet window into the laneway; the others went out the front door with the Chinese man after them. I must say, though, Joey, we took up a collection amongst ourselves a few weeks later and went back and paid the Chinese man and had a rather smaller meal. Brewster, as I said, is a bloody prankster, but you couldn't watch him all the time.

'Fourteen of us went to another Chinese restaurant sometime later. He went to the toilet down a passageway. Ten minutes when I went through the door into the passageway, Brewster saw me and held the toilet door open for me. I said,

"Thanks, mate" and went in. It was one of those toilets that didn't have a urinal, just a toilet cubicle. While I was having a wee, I heard a woman's voice.

'"What are you doing in the ladies' toilets?"

'I said, "That can't be right! You must be in the men's toilet."

'Sure enough, Joey, it was the ladies' toilets. That bastard must have been passing the ladies' toilets, saw me and held the door open.'

'I remembered what I had been told many times – things aren't always as they seem. My father had told me to believe nothing of what I read and only half of what I see. Of course, when I got back to the restaurant, he had told everybody. The whole restaurant laughed and clapped. He is like you, Joey, a good friend, and will be so for life. You'd better get us another beer, Joey, if you want to hear more.'

Joey came back with another beer so Max continued.

'Now this bloke is another kettle of fish. I'm calling him Scrooge and at the risk of hitting him too hard, which is difficult, he's another good friend for life. Scrooge, I'm guessing, would be five foot seven, a round, very friendly face with a roly-poly body. Now you've seen how quick a magician can make things disappear; well, this bloke is lightning fast. We never saw his money at all, and he also had a burglar alarm on his wallet. He could fumble for his wallet better than anyone when it was time to pay, and when the beer was paid for, he would magically find it. His wife said it was our fault because we all just laughed at him.'

Joey said, 'How could you all put up with that sort of shit all the time?'

'Well, we all got a lot of mileage and laughs out of it, I guess. There are so many stories how this bloke can miss out on paying, whether intentional or not. He is a trade teacher at RMIT, teaching apprentices in the foundry industry, so he has access to various projects they make, things like differently shaped lead sinkers. Of course, he gets them to make the ones he wants. He drives a grey Standard Vanguard sedan, which unlike most of us, he owns.'

'Okay,' said Max, 'get another beer and I'll tell you about Gus.'

'Jesus,' Joey said, 'we're gonna be pissed before the end of this.'

'Gus lived with his parents next door to Valda. He worked in the bank and later became a bank manager. He drove an old Wolseley, when it was going. He had the mechanical aptitude of a doughnut. I doubt he could hang a picture on the wall. Whenever I was at Valda's place, I would be next door fixing the lawn mower or Gus's car. He must have been good at figures, but he wasn't much good at anything else. He was to take a girl out to dinner, but she lived way over on the other side of town. We told him it would take about forty-five minutes to get there, and we marked all the pages in the street directory for him. You know, Joey, you can sometimes tell by watching someone if they're confident. He had to follow the pages at night in his car, yet he was having trouble finding the pages we marked for him in the street directory, and that was in daylight. I thought this girl, whoever she was, had no hope of going out to dinner, not with Gus anyway. Gus eventually arrived back home at about 11.30 pm. He told us the next day he didn't find the girl's house and he got lost on the way home.

'At the drive-in, all cars are parked on a slight incline for better viewing of the screen. The car behind Gus's kept blowing its horn, eventually the bloke banged on Gus's window and said, "Turn your bloody lights off!" His lights weren't on, but he was sitting there with his foot on the brake so the car wouldn't roll backwards. What do you think of that, Joey?'

'Which bank's this bloke at, Max? Some poor bugger has to sit in front of this bloke at the bank and ask him for a loan.'

'Now Harry is different from all of us. He's the smallest one in the group. He has the gift of the gab – he could sell ice to the Eskimos. He drives an FX Holden that I think was an ex-army vehicle and he walks with a limp, the result of a skiing accident at the Melton Weir. His brother was driving the boat and had to swing away to miss another boat and Harry skied into the rock wall. He is different in the sense that while we were gallivanting around on weekends, he was cleaning shop windows. He is more into making money than the rest of us are. Amongst his customers are several banks, office blocks, chemical companies and factories. Over time, Harry has, to his credit, built up a good business, although I suspect along the way some of his business deals and manoeuvres have been questionable. I'm not suggesting he's broken the law but he plays very close to the line. One day when we were all having a beer together, we said as a joke, "Harry, giving you the keys to a bank would be like giving Dracula the keys to the blood bank". All jokes aside, good luck to him. He has worked hard to get where he is, considering some of the setbacks he had. His factory once burnt down, and his boat caught fire while he was towing it along Beach Road. He originally owned an old Austin 7. When Coles caught fire, there were police and fire brigade vehicles everywhere and fire hoses across the road. Harry went straight through the lot, running over the hoses. A cop jumped on the running board to get him to stop, but the cop was so busy with the fire and other traffic he didn't ask Harry for his licence. Lucky for Harry, as he didn't have a licence – he was only seventeen. Sometime later, Gus and Harry went to Sydney in the Austin 7, and on the way back the car shit itself, so they pushed it into the bush and hitchhiked home.'

Joey said, 'Well, he's certainly had a lot of luck.'

'I couldn't agree more,' Max said, 'but in your life's journey, you start with a bag full of luck and an empty bag of experience. The trick is to fill the bag of experience before you empty the bag of luck, and to his credit, I think that's exactly what he has done. Let's have another can of VB and I'll give you the lowdown on the last one in the group. There are more blokes coming and going in the group but I'm only introducing you to those I am closest to.

'His nickname is Johno, his early car was a VW Beetle and his girlfriend's name is Margo, whom he promptly put up the duff. None of us knew about this until they announced they had secretly snuck off and got married, so we never got a chance to go to the wedding. He wasn't always chubby and round like a bowling ball, but he is now, and because of the size of his beard covering most of his round face, his eyes give me the impression of two piss holes in the sand. He lives with Margo now in his mother's house with his daughter. He is now driving a LandCruiser wagon, albeit an older one, and, I might add, he's a maniac behind the wheel. He also suffers from sleep apnoea. Sometimes when he asks you a question, you look around to give him an answer and he's asleep. When I'm in the car and he is driving, I've got to keep watching him in case he falls asleep, so I only go with him if I have to.'

'Shit,' Joey said 'that's bloody dangerous! He could have an accident.'

'Yes,' said Max, 'he has had many accidents, mainly due to his maniac driving rather than falling asleep. He wasn't all that good on the tools. It was always "rough enough is good enough", and he always had these harebrained ideas that were doomed to failure. But I'll say this for him, he always gave it a go. Lucky Margo had a good job.

'Originally, he did his apprenticeship as a butcher and worked some time in a butcher shop. He was the perfect person for that role, bullshitting to the ladies buying their meat, telling them how young they looked, spreading the gossip he would get from other women and telling them they were the only ones he gave this special cut of meat to. Only my opinion, but he would have been better off with his own butcher shop. Having said all that, he is a nice bloke and would do anything for a mate which he has done for me on occasions.

'Sometimes in our early days, before we were all married, we would ring the nurses' quarters and ask if anyone wanted to go out. Most times, the four of us would be lucky because the girls knew they would all be going out together. We took some girls to the drive-in on one occasion and at interval, Johno said to me, "I've just realised I have been massaging her elbow, thinking it was her breast".

'"Christ', I said, "did she say anything?"'

'"No, but she kept giving me this funny look."

'"You must have realised her elbow was hard, not soft like a breast is."'

'"Well, I thought she was getting sexually excited, and her breast had gone hard."'

'"Jesus', I said, "you're as dumb as dogshit, Johno!"'

Chapter 9

Ambo and other jobs

Sometime later, Max's voice began to deteriorate. When you think about the fires he attended, breathing in smoke from bedroom fires in rundown apartment blocks, breathing in the fire-ridden remains of piss-stained mattresses and vomit-stained blankets and anything else that might have been in the room, smoke from rubber tyres at a tyre factory, paint and thinners at factories – never mind the houses and buildings that were built using asbestos! And of course, they went in to all these places with no breathing apparatus – no wonder he was losing his voice.

Things were just getting worse for Max. After a visit to the brigade Medical Officer about his voice concerns, he had now been strongly advised to seek different employment.

'I'm not giving in,' Max said to himself. 'Ambition is the way to success and persistence is the vehicle you arrive in. I don't remember who said that but it's true. If you don't go when you've got to go, when you do go, you'll find you've gone.'

With the help of the brigade, he began employment with the Victorian Civil Ambulance Service.

His first posting with the ambulance was to the Russell Street Station in Melbourne's CBD. The Station Officer on his shift was a bloke called Peter. He was a fit-looking sort of a dude with a medium build of five feet ten, a well-trimmed beard and dark short hair. He was also very patient with Max as the new kid in town.

There were two ladies in a glass enclosure called the call centre, not unlike the watch room at the fire station. These ladies took the calls for ambulance call-outs. Max learnt later their names were Gabby and Dee, and the lady called Gabby was married to Peter, the Station Officer on his shift.

He was introduced to Stuart who would be his partner. He was a senior ambo, and he would be guiding him through his early days and instruction on advanced lifesaving medical procedures, using their specialised equipment. Max was also required to attend night training classes once a week for the next eight weeks.

'Hello, Max,' he said, 'Never be afraid to ask a question. There are no dumb questions in this work. You see that 1960 Chrysler Royal Ambulance over there? That will be ours on all of our shifts. We will share the vehicle with two other crews to cover the twenty-four-hour period.'

He showed Max where the name of the crews and their vehicle number were and the shifts in the week ahead were listed. The uniform consisted of a shirt, collar and tie, pants, shoes and socks and a pullover, jacket and a peak cap.

Max said, 'Spoofy looking uniform!'

Stuart said, 'Looks good for patient transfers, and company image of course, but bloody useless for working a crash scene. You wait till your hat comes off and stood on by others at the scene, and the tie is a pain in the arse in confined spaces.'

Max said, 'Sometimes, you think you would like to see who is actually on these committees that make these decisions, in this case what an ambo would wear. I wouldn't mind betting the poor bloody camels were designed by a committee. And then there's the one where we need to have a meeting to decide who's going to be at the next meeting.'

Stuart then explained how the crew system worked. He and Max would rotate as driver or attendant. The attendant's role was to operate the two-way vehicle radio and on arrival at a house, for example, the attendant's role was to enter the house and gain information on the situation. But as Max was to learn, most times they would both go in, and it proved more than once a better system when urgent care required two sets of hands.

Max's first lot of shifts were at night and was mostly uneventful until about 1 am, they were sent to a dwelling in the suburbs at the back of a shop for a probable early childbirth. Entry to the dwelling was via a back laneway, then through a back yard at the rear of the shop. The back yard was a of drink crates, old shop fittings and boxes. This time, Max went in by himself, as Stuart had pointed out it would be good for him to get some experience in getting patient information and stretcher access if required. Stuart called the station and Max worked his way in through the minefield to the back door.

He called out, 'Hello, ambulance here.'

A voice said, 'Thank God! Come in.'

There was a large lady sprawled out on a recliner chair, five small kids of various ages and, he supposed, the husband, all in a small lounge room.

Max said, 'Hello, darling, what's your name?'

'Rose.'

'Okay, Rose,' said Max, 'how far apart are your pains?'

'About two minutes ... here's another one coming now.'

Shit! Max thought. 'Okay, Rose, what hospital are you booked into?'

'Oh, I'm not booked in anywhere. I haven't even seen a doctor yet.'

Max went back to the vehicle to grab Stuart and fill him in on the patient information and then they went in through the minefield with the stretcher carrying Rose.

They were now in the ambulance with Max in the back with her, because it was his turn as the attendant. *Just your night, Rose!* thought Max. Stuart had radioed the station and they had received approval for her to go to the Royal Women's Hospital. They only got as far as Princes Bridge when the baby decided it was time to see the world. She was a large lady, and this was her sixth child, so the baby simply popped out. The necessary bits and pieces were saved in a kidney dish and handed to nursing staff on arrival at the hospital. The grin on Max's face looked like it might stay there forever.

Sometimes if Max and Stuart had a low-key job like a patient transfer and had to go down Swanston Street where the tram stops in the middle of the road at the lights, they would turn the driver side window washer to the right so they could squirt the people waiting for the tram, who, of course, wouldn't think for a minute it would be coming from an ambulance. Just a bit of harmless fun in their world of gloom, but it wouldn't be tolerated by the head honchos.

More marital activities meant a little girl had just been born; Max and Valda called her Anne. Four in the family now, so they moved to a nice little cottage on half an acre on the edge of town, and that's where they celebrated Max's birthday. Valda and Max's friends and family were there, Max, Joey and Nitro burning the meat on the barbecue as usual. It was a foregone conclusion that Max would have to make a speech to thank everyone for coming. Max was a storyteller and so here was the opportunity for another one of Max's tales. His theory was to never let the truth get in the way of a good story as long as you kept to the facts, but there was nothing wrong with adding a bit of colour.

'Last week,' said Max, 'we were called out to a house in Collingwood for a body that was found. The house was one of those old two-storey terrace houses. Inside, the owner and several builders were renovating and replacing the old stairs with a spiral staircase, and part of the old earthen plaster wall had come away, revealing what looked like where an old doorway had once been. The builders had looked in through a small hole and seen what they thought was a body. Now that the ambulance had arrived, they knocked a large hole through so we could get in. The room was the size of a small bedroom, with no furniture except for an old-fashioned wooden kitchen chair. We all froze at what we saw next. The skull was turned grotesquely to one side like it was trying to look at something, what was left of the skin had leathery yellow look, the pelvic girdle had almost come away from the lower spine and the left arm, now just mostly bone, was on the floor next to the chair. The smell wasn't all that good either. Everyone's opinion was that the door had been purposely hidden. The coroner arrived, and we left.'

'So, who was this person?' they said.

Max said, 'A few days later, after forensic analysis, it was verified that this person was indeed the 1932 Irish hide and seek champion.'

'That's the last bloody time you're going to do that! We've been caught by you before, bastard,' said everyone.

Catching public transport for shift work was becoming a pain in the arse. Valda needed the car for the kids, which was fair enough. Stuart and Max's shifts were fairly mundane, mostly patient transport and the occasional suicide, either attempted or successful. They knew when they got there which was which: if the police were sitting in their car outside the house, the person inside was dead; if they were inside, it was likely the person was still alive.

Trips to the mortuary at Spencer Street were not at all pleasant, particularly after a long weekend. There was a large room called the holding room, full of bodies after a long weekend. They were in rows around the walls on gurneys, like hospital beds would be in a ward. Some of the bodies' postmortems had been done with stomachs stitched up rough as chaff bags. The place would be a beehive of activity – swinging doors opening and closing, the sound of buzz saws heard from another room.

Max said, 'You know, you get to see things that no one should have to see, but I guess there will always have to be first responders. If you can't do that sort of thing, there is no shame. Some things that you see will take time to erase in the mind and others will remain for a lifetime, like a small boy crying on the side of the road with police, and his parents dead inside their crushed and mangled car. You need to be able to sweep the sadness away and get on with your work. Having to pick up someone's head from the railway line when assisting the coroner and putting the head in a separate body bag to go to the morgue will probably be with me forever. The past becomes like a dream, even if the details are blurred, and there are memories that will shape us and mould us into who we will become, and there's no changing that.'

The straw that broke the camel's back was during a patient transport. It was a stinking hot day so when they entered the air-conditioned hospital, they took off their hats and placed them on the end of the stretcher while they were in the hospital. Someone reported them for not wearing their bloody hats and back at the station, they were paraded before the CEO for a reprimand. Max was really pissed off but kept his cool. *Never miss the opportunity to keep your mouth shut*, Max thought. Max wondered what he would have said if he knew he and Stuart had been squirting people at the tram stop.

This incident, plus travelling via public transport to meet difficult shift times, took their toll and were beginning to affect the harmony of family life with Valda and the kids, so Max handed in his notice to leave. As disappointing and regretful as it was, it was deemed necessary at the time. A farewell was arranged for Max, and he gave them this short poem that he had written for them to keep, to remember his short but memorable service.

> The sirens echoed through the night, carried along
> on the breeze,
> The red and blue flashing lights, throwing their image
> at the shadow of the trees.
> An ambulance racing through the night, warning the
> public of its plight,
> Yes, they're coming; it's a promise on the wings of the
> night.

The names are not important, only the nature of their
pain.
Their priorities are focused on how their bodies are
lain.
So when you hear our sirens, please move over and
give us a go.
We are on our way to help someone, and it might be
someone you know.

Max was now at a loss as what to do. Valda had found part-
time work at a fish and chip shop on Friday and Saturday
nights when Max would be home and able to look after
Martin and Anne. The child endowment was five shillings
a week for each child under sixteen, so they knew he'd have
to get off his arse quickly to bring money in to support the
family. Because of the urgency, he did what he said he would
never do again and went back to work in a factory as a sheet
metal worker, but not at the factory where he'd done his
apprenticeship.

The factory was divided into two sections: one side did air-
conditioning duct work and general fabrication; the other side,
would you believe, made electric hot water units. Because of
his previous experience in this field, he was put in charge of
this area, so here he was clocking a card in a bloody factory
again. The first couple of months weren't too bad because
he could make changes and procedures to streamline the
production. All of this became a challenge for him as he was
known at the factory as a perfectionist, particularly with
the younger workers, because where Max was concerned,
nothing they ever did was good enough. However, they soon
learnt that if you did the job properly, you got the accolades.

When that happened, Max didn't seem like a bad bloke after all.

The weekends and social activities were mostly spent with the families of Brewster, Scrooge and Johno, and because Brewster was a plumber who sometimes installed electric hot water units, he was interested in the manufacturing process. If a new unit leaked into the drip tray in the roof and water continually ran out the drainpipe outside the house, the unit in the roof, which was gravity fed, would have to come out through the roof at great expense.

Brewster said to Max, 'Christ, Max, don't they test these things before they go out?'

'Well,' Max said, 'let me tell you what sometimes happens, although very rarely. After the copper internal cylinders are welded, they go onto a test bench where all the welding is checked for leaks. A sticker is placed on the cylinder and signed by the person who tested them. They then go into the outer casing and are filled with insulation, usually wool or granulated cork. From there, they are electrically wired and the unit spray painted. Now here's what can happen. When drilling holes to rivet the labels on the outer case, a small sleeve goes over the drill to ensure there's not enough of the drill bit exposed to piece the internal copper cylinder. If the drill sleeve can't be found from where the last person left it, the lazy buggers try to do it without the sleeve. Most times they are successful; however, there are the times when they are not, and that's usually when it's eventually got to come out of the roof. Mind you, when this happens, the person who tested for leaks and the person who put the labels on are very nervous, but more often than not, it's usually a hole in the cylinder opposite where the label is on the outer case. It's a very expensive exercise, as you would know, Brewster, which the manufacturer must pay for, so I don't have tell you what happens to the dude responsible.'

With Max's money now coming in and that from Valda's fish and chip shop job, they were managing financially. The rent was being paid on time but there was no money for a snazzy lifestyle. However, Max was not happy helping someone else filling their pockets with what he was doing, and he hated factory work. You went home knowing exactly what you would be doing the next day, and he hated that.

Max knew he could get work with any of the companies or places he had worked for when he was in the fire brigade, so he went to work for Lindsay Fox (whose slogan was 'You are now passing another Fox'). You could take the truck home ready for the next day's early start, which meant Valda could have the car every day. Unlike his previous work with Fox, which entailed deliveries for Cottee's drinks in between his shifts with the fire brigade, this time the truck was allocated to Victa Plaster Board. Plaster boards were loaded at the factory by forklifts but unloaded at housings sites by hand. You needed to get to these sites while the workers were there to help unload. It was really hard work unloading big heavy plaster sheets by yourself.

Max and Joey made a point of seeing each other once a month at the pub for a catch-up. They didn't see each other as much these days; the old days had gone now they each had a family.

Joey was now working at General Motors Holden in Fisherman's Bend.

Max asked, 'What's going on at GMH these days, mate? Anything exciting?'

Joey replied, 'We are building a new red motor that's superseding the grey one. It has a seven-bearing crank shaft, full flow oil filter and hydraulic valve lifters.'

Because Max had rebuilt his Holden motor with Joey, he knew what all that meant.

'What about you, mate?' asked Joey. 'You're still restless, aren't you? I can tell.'

'Buggered if I know what's wrong with me, Joey? I can't seem to settle down in one job. I've had two jobs already since I left the ambos and now my shoulder's playing up from carrying plaster boards at building sites. So, I'm going back on the buses.'

'Does Valda know?'

'No, not yet.'

'Are you pleased with that?'

'I am,' Max said, 'but I'd be happier if I could find my place in life, work-wise that is. You know, mate, somewhere with security and the chance of advancement. I can't see that happening with anything I'm doing lately. Look at you, Joey,' Max said. 'Big company, GMH, you've got security and huge advancement opportunities. I'm very happy for you, mate. Now, buy a bloody beer!'

'You are going to have to make a substantial decision soon, mate. The road to success is filled with dead kangaroos that couldn't make their mind up which way to go.'

And Max knew that, most times, if you waited too long to make a decision, the opportunity would be gone.

Back on the buses, it didn't take Max long to learn again that dealing with the public was no mean feat. However, his good breeding under the Australian flag was his best security against other people's ill manners.

On an early morning run to meet the train to Melbourne, the bus was running a little late due to an accident ahead of the bus. Most of the people on the bus had to catch this train. There was one stop two hundred metres from the station where some women got off who worked at the cotton factory, so he didn't stop and went on to the station so that about thirty people would not miss the train as the next train would be another thirty-minute wait. Max reckoned the ladies wouldn't mind walking back that small distance so the others wouldn't miss their train and he had told the passengers this over the bus PA system. The ladies, however, when they got to work, rang the bus company, complaining the driver didn't stop at a registered legal bus stop. Max was hauled over the coals and told, regardless of the circumstances, the bus must stop if required for passengers to get off. The trouble with common sense is that it's not very common. Max thought, *Well, there you go, a bunch of women with no morals who couldn't care less if thirty or so people would've been late for work.* The uncaring attitude and lack of moral support for the others on the bus just continued to promote a selfish world, and he wondered whose flag they were taught under. They were all from another country whereas 'our' people would have said, 'Yeah, go for it, mate' – well, he bloody well hoped they would have.

On another occasion there was an old lady who walked with the aid of a cane and whose house was between bus stops. She was often seen by Max to struggle back to her house. So, when there were no other passengers, he helped her by stopping at her house and not the bus stop. Well, that didn't last long either. He was once again reported by some busybody wanker and again was hauled over the coals.

'You can't do that, Max,' the transport manager said. 'If she falls while getting off the bus at a non-recognised stop, we will be sued.'

Max was going to put his sixpence worth in but decided to never miss the opportunity to keep his mouth shut, so again he said, 'Yes, sir'. But he thought, *You're not allowed to help anyone are you, Max? I just bet that would be right up the alley of the ambulance-chasing solicitors.* Mind you, the transport manager was right, but it still stank as far as Max was concerned.

Valda's parents had bought another house, and as they weren't selling the one Valda grew up in, they asked Max and Valda if they would like to rent it at a reasonable rate. The house was in the same area as Valda and Max's friends. Valda's girlfriend, Joan, whom she went to school with, also lived close by; she was married to Scrooge.

What a coincidence! thought Max. *This is the house of many memories, most of them bad for me. But that's in the past, and to tell you the truth, I often got a laugh out of it all.*

So, Max and Valda moved in. The house was a neat, pale buttercup yellow, or creamy yellow if you like, and weatherboard like most of the houses in the street. Gus was no longer living next door. He had married like the rest of their friends, and they had all been married in the same church as Max and Valda.

Chapter 10

Army training

Max was still wrestling with his job, so he sat down with Valda one night to discuss the best outcome for their future.

Max said, 'With my fire and medical experience, I could probably go into one of the services as a medic. Not the Navy – I'd never be home. The Army is probably the best one where that's concerned, and I might be able to get a direct entry. They provide uniforms, free medical, security and housing and, most of all, huge opportunities for promotion. What do you think, Valda?'

Valda said she would reserve her judgement until they got more information. Max spent the day at the recruiting building in Melbourne, getting the lowdown on entering the service. Once again, he sat down with Valda to discuss the issue.

'Right, this is how it happens. I would be guaranteed to go into the medical corps, but the bad news is I would still have to do the regimental training, which is six weeks in New South Wales. I would be away from home during that period. The Army sends a portion of soldier's pay home to their wives, so you would always be guaranteed an income while I'm away; in fact, that procedure continues whether I'm away or not. At the end of the six weeks, I would be sent to the School of Army Health to verify my knowledge, after which I would be posted to a unit and the family moved at department expense to wherever that was. I know the six weeks away would be hard for you, but at least your family and friends are close by.'

'Bloody hell, Max,' replied Valda, 'it's a huge change in direction for all of us, and we would be moving away from all our friends and family.'

'Well, hopefully I would get a posting here in Melbourne, but that's not guaranteed.'

Valda said, 'Can you just leave if you don't like it?'

'No,' Max said, 'but you only have to sign on for three years and then you can leave if you wish.'

The next few days saw lots of serious talks about pros and cons.

Eventually Valda said, 'Look, Max, I know you're still restless and don't like the mundane same day in, same day out work, so I guess if this works, it will give you the satisfaction of an interesting and good long career.'

'You know, Valda, sometimes a true journey doesn't begin until the wrong one ends.'

'It's 1968, Max, and you're twenty-six years old. You haven't got many more chances for a career with a pension. The kids and I will manage the six weeks because I know you're ambitious, and I'm sure you will make a go of it. The kids and I will tough it out. Don't dare get shot, you hear me?'

'Yes, ma'am!'

Jesus, Max thought, *I hope she doesn't think that twenty-six is so old the only thing you can get hard is your arteries.*

Max fronted up for his medical in Melbourne. There were no problems as at twenty-six, he was very fit. However, he failed the hearing test. They told him he had a high tone hearing loss and might not be suitable for enlistment. They would send him to a Collins Street specialist for an assessment.

Shit, you gotta be kidding me! thought Max, *Bloody sheet metal work in a factory all those years with loud banging almost nonstop every day.* There had been no health and safety regulations, no hearing protection in any of the places he had worked, and he had never seen anyone wearing them. It was all just excepted as the norm, and now look what was happening. Max was really pissed off that it had come to this.

After his review with the specialist, he was given a report to take back to recruiting. He sneaked a look at the report and almost kissed the old lady who was walking past. The report he read said, 'Mr Thornton has a slight high tone hearing loss but is within the bounds and would not hinder him in the Service.' So Max Thornton was enlisted in the Royal Australian Army, and so began his and his family's next journey in life.

He now had two weeks before his training started, and a party was organised. Everyone was there – Brewster and wife Suzy, Scrooge and wife Joan, Gus who by now didn't have a wife (but that's a story for another day), Johno and wife Margo. Harry and his wife couldn't be there but sent their best wishes and good luck.

All his friends were very sceptical about Max's decision for his future, and he hoped it would not be an end to close friendships. But they all wished the family good luck and that whatever their dreams and ambitions were, they sincerely hoped they would all come true. Max had found that the harder you worked and the more you persevered and had a go, the luckier you got. Luck very rarely comes free of charge.

Leaving home was a sad occasion, with long embraces with Valda, hugs and kisses and lots of tears and cuddles with little baby Anne and cuddles with Marty who was now two years old.

On the bus to the Regimental Training Battalion at Kapooka near Wagga Wagga, Max met Frank. He was also twenty-six, and they were definitely the oldest ones on the bus. National Service had started, so most of the recruits on the bus were Nashos (National Servicemen). The whole thing didn't seem right to Max, and he said to Frank, 'Look, it's supposed to be conscription at a certain age unless you've got medical issues like flat feet, is that right?'

Frank said, 'Yep, that's right.'

'So how come they do a raffle? Names in a barrel and if your name comes out, you're in; if not, you're exempt? That's just not right. Look at it this way. Mrs Brown's son has gone off to Vietnam because his name came out of the barrel, but Mrs Smith's son's name didn't get drawn and she can see him next door with his mates at the barbecue, boozing and laughing. Shit, Frank, I might be wrong, but conscription is not a bloody raffle. How do you think Mrs Brown would feel if her son came home from Vietnam with no legs, or doesn't come home at all, and the kid next door is still partying with loud music? It's not the kid next door's fault, mind you. Anyway, Frank, we've got bigger fish to fry waiting for us than to be concerned with shit political decisions. Look at us, we could be half these kids' fathers ... well, not quite, but you know what I mean. You know, when there's thirty or so people together, there's always four types in amongst them: a bully, a comedian, a smartarse know-all and a crybaby, and I guarantee you Frank, they'll all be on this bus.'

The bus arrived at Kapooka early afternoon and was met by four little upstart Corporals.

Max said, 'Did one of them say, "Do you mind getting out of the bus?"'

'Actually,' Frank said, 'he told us to move our no-good arses out of the bus. We are not civilians anymore, neither are we soldiers; we are a piece of shit nothing.'

Max said, 'I don't think I like this bloke. I know who the piece of shit is. I know at these training camps, a fair amount of play-acting goes on, but at the same time, you can pick the ones who, in among the mandatory play-acting, are naturally mean pricks. The others, aside from the bullshit, are probably good blokes doing what they're told to do. That's my early summary for what it's worth.'

They were marched off, actually as more of a gaggle, to the quartermasters store to be issued their gear.

Max said, 'That little man that taps on the window at LP Alexander's tailor shop must've come to life and he's working in here. What a joke! The soldiers behind the clothing counter were throwing the clothing to us and the soldiers on our side of the counter were measuring us. This is how they did it. One bloke walked down the line of recruits, putting his hands around our heads and calling out "$3^5/_8$", "$4^7/_8$", "$6^1/_2$", and slouch hats would be flung over the counter for us to catch. The greens were measured the same way. The bloke that wasn't doing the hats called out, "Looks like a 32", "Looks like a 38" and so on.'

They later found out that none of these items fitted. They all looked like a bag of shit. Even after swapping clothes and hats with everyone, they still didn't look all that good. One of the Nashos said, 'If God wanted me to be in the Army, he would have given me green baggy skin.'

Next, it was off to the armoury to be issued with a 7.62 self-loading rifle (SLR). During the next six weeks, there would be map reading, field craft, weapons training with the SLR and the sub-machine gun (SMG), marching and weapons drills, three-mile runs and obstacle courses.

It didn't take long for the four types to rear their heads, and because Frank and Max were the oldest, they became the 'go, fix it' men.

The bully was persecuting and pushing around the crybaby.

Frank said, 'What do you think?'

Max said, 'We need to fix this real quick.'

He found him and thumped him – end of problem. Although Max had learnt early in life, when a mosquito had landed on his testicles, that sometimes violence wasn't always the answer.

The rifle bolts were kept in a box by the staff. Prior to going to the rifle range to be handed out, they would take a bolt from the box and call out the last three numbers of the serial number.

'Here's an example of six bolts being handed out,' Max said, '423, 768, 469, 768, 257, 884.'

During the call of the numbers one day, someone yelled out, 'Bingo.' *Ah, there he is*, thought Max, *the comedian, I knew he was here somewhere.*

'I'll give you bloody bingo,' the Corporal said. 'Now we will all run to the range instead of marching.'

'Is this the part where we're having fun?' Frank commented.

'I think there's a lot more of this sort of fun to come,' Max said.

Frank and Max were in 19 Platoon and were billeted in a two-storey dormitory with rooms down each side of the passage, two to a room, with the showers and toilets at the end of the passage. The bugle played reveille at 5 am every morning.

'It's still bloody dark!' said Max.

They had to hit the parade ground for roll call with the bottom sheet off the bed. Breakfast was 6 am and room and locker inspection at 7 am.

'On one occasion,' said Max, 'it was pissing rain the morning we were on parade. When we got back to our rooms, the remaining sheets off the beds had been thrown out into the mud.'

'Jesus,' said Frank, 'when they picked the staff for this place, someone obviously left the idiot bag open.'

'Bastardisation at its best,' said Max.

In the platoon was a recruit called Fran. He could only square gate; that is, when you swing the left arm, left leg goes instead of left arm, right leg. When someone marches like that, it looks ridiculous. They could not get him to march properly no matter what they did. Whenever they marched anywhere, he had to be at the back of the squad. He was not allowed to go on the parade ground for any of the drills. He just could not keep in step with everyone else.

Frank said, 'Funny how some things stick in your mind, Max.'

'What's that?' said Max.

'You know the map reading classes where we change bearings from grid to magnetic and vice versa, and we learnt these mnemonics to help remember them? Well, here's how

I remember them: magnetic to grid is MGA as in 'car', and grid to magnetic is Grand Mother Sucks, and if I never get anything else out of this bullshit, I won't get lost,' Frank said.

Max and Frank thought the March Out parade was a lot of bullshit pomp and glory about nothing. They would have been quite content to just get on the bus and go home. Anyway, the parade went off without a hitch, but Fran wasn't allowed to be part of it.

When the bus arrived in Melbourne, there was a car and driver waiting to take Max to the School of Army Health at Healesville. He was told he would be staying on the fairway. Sounded good, but when he saw the tents, Max thought, *Jesus, it's bloody winter, I'll freeze!* The tents were called eleven by elevens and slept four people on stretchers, with two red fire buckets hung outside each tent. *When I was a nobody, I stayed in a building. Now I'm a Private, I get a tent. How does that work?* he thought. There were ten of these tents in two rows of five, which meant when full, there would be forty soldiers here for medical training of some sort. Healesville is also where medical and nursing promotion courses were run. The next medical course was not due to start for three weeks and although Max wasn't going to attend it, he had to wait for it to start to be assessed. In the meantime, those waiting did general duties.

The good news was you could leave the school on weekends; the bad news was Max had no transportation to get home, where he now hadn't been for seven weeks, although he had stayed in regular touch. On the first weekend, he managed to bum a ride with someone going back to Melbourne. Once in the suburbs, he could use public transport the rest of the way. It was fantastic to be home with the family. Marty kept asking where his gun was. Max didn't have one, but he told Marty he wasn't allowed to bring it home.

Given the car had to stay with the family, Valda said, 'How are you going to get back, Max?'

He said, 'Yes, big problem. I suppose I'll have to walk and hitchhike.'

'Jesus, Max, it's eighty kilometres!'

'There's no other way. I have to be back there for the Monday morning parade or I'm AWOL.'

Max had worn his uniform home because he reckoned he had a better chance of a lift; someone was more likely to pick up a soldier than just any bloke. He knew his chances of a ride in the suburbs was next to nil, and he was right. He guessed he had walked about ten kilometres to get to the Maroondah Highway, when about two kilometres up the highway, a car stopped.

'Yes, you beauty!' Max yelled.

Even better, the bloke was going further than Healesville. He was a young bloke, Max guessed about twenty, with a slim build. He looked a bit like Joey except he had long hair and a stud in his ear. He was driving a rattly old 1945 Dodge. It had a large hole in the floor where it had rusted out, and you could see the white centre lines going by under the car. Max didn't care. It had four wheels and was going in the right direction, and he had thanked the bloke more than once for stopping.

'You might have to do this several more times,' the bloke said.

'Looks like it,' Max said, dreading the thought.

He arrived back at the school about 11 pm that night, and by the time he got his gear ready for Monday's parade, he was knackered. Turned out he had to do this three more times, and he wasn't as lucky as the first time. On one occasion, he didn't get back till 4 am and it rained the whole way.

The medical course started. Max was tested and passed all the requirements. The subjects were anatomy and physiology, treatment for sucking chest wounds and traumatic amputations of limbs, CPR procedures, broken limbs and general first aid. Well, if Max thought this was the end of being away from home, he was sadly wrong. He was now told that, because of his experience and likelihood of quick promotion and advancement, he was to now go to Western Australia to the Special Air Services unit at Swanbourne Barracks for further training. It had nothing to do with the SAS itself; it just happened to be where the course was being held. It could have very well been held in Melbourne, but oh no, the furthest point away from Melbourne as possible.

Shit! Max thought, *what am I going to tell Valda? I'll have to go if I want to move up the promotion ladder, considering my age.*

Valda had already had her share of hardship, managing day to day with the kids without support from a husband, particularly when the kids were sick with all the things that little kids get from time to time. Max could see himself at the end of this new career. Really hard decisions had to be made now. His time was up in three years when he could opt out, but then he would be nearly thirty years old with still no security for the family. It was a no-brainer for Max; however, Valda was part of the family decision making.

'I'm not happy, Max, but the family will support you, and I'm speaking for Martin and Anne as well as myself. I know you won't let us down. The Army sends us money each week, so financially we will be okay from that point of view at least.'

More goodbyes and a barbecue with everyone and the usual comments from Brewster: 'I hope you know what you're doing, mate, but then again, I know you and your tenacity so I'm reserving my judgement. Go, get 'em, Maxi boy, and we will make sure Valda and the kids are okay. Just do what you have to do.'

'You see,' Max said, 'this is what I mean when I say you must have good friends through your journey of life. It's so important to have someone to rely on in times of need. Just be careful you don't overdo it as it can quickly wear thin, and remember, it's a two-way street.'

He knew that only too well, having been on the other end of it when supporting his friends. He knew that if they were good friends, they would return the favour when needed.

Just before Max left for Perth, Anne rode her little bike into the front gate, somersaulted over the top and broke her arm – not a good time to happen!

Max and one other soldier called Bruce boarded the *Overlander* train for Adelaide, with an overnight stop there and then on to Kalgoorlie. The train arrived at Kalgoorlie at about midnight. On the opposite platform was the *Westlander* and a change of trains was necessary due to different size rail gauges.

Max said, 'Lousy bastards, couldn't pay for a sleeper for us, could they, Bruce? We've had to sit up all the way. I'm going to sleep up there.'

Max climbed up and slept in the overhead wire luggage rack.

The next morning, they had something to eat from the small kiosk on the train before it arrived in Perth. An Army Kombi van took Max and Bruce to the barracks where they were billeted with eight other blokes in a long dormitory with five beds down each side; the showers and toilets were outside the building.

On day one of the course, they met the Sergeant who would be their instructor for the duration. He was of medium build and had a chiselled jaw, with a middle-aged spread and a bald patch on the top of his head that, Max guessed, meant he wasn't far away from retirement. His name was Ernie, although they called him Sergeant Harrigan. He was an easy-going bloke and absolutely suited to run a course like this one. Max immediately liked him.

'Okay,' he said, 'welcome. Have you all settled in?'

They gave him their travel documents for the return trip home. They were introduced to the subjects to be taken in the following four weeks: typing of medical documents such as admission and discharge sheets, doctors' patients notes, referrals to specialist and other hospital or clinical documentation, along with an introduction to the *Army Law Manual* and how to use it along with other Army administrative manuals.

Max said to Bruce, 'Typing? You have to be joking, mate. I can't see me mastering that in four weeks.'

To pass the typing test, you needed to type forty words in five minutes without a mistake. Max thought, *No way!* and after two weeks of practice, you could have cut off nine of his fingers and he wouldn't have been any slower. Unusual as it was, they were all good blokes and everyone got on famously. During their nights and days off, most of them would go out together.

It was during time off on a Saturday when the US *Long Beach* was docked in Perth, taking on supplies and doing minor repairs. They were in the pub with a bunch of Marines. Max introduced them all to a game called Dead Ant.

'If you hear someone call out, "Dead ant", you lie flat on the floor. Last one down buys the drinks.'

The Yanks had never heard of this, but being half cut with booze, agreed to play. There were about thirty of them in the pub lounge. Max and Bruce waited until they saw a Marine coming through the crowd with a tray full of mixed drinks.

'Now's the time,' said Max, so Bruce yelled out 'Dead Ant'.

The Marine threw the whole tray of drinks into the air and threw himself on the ground.

'Jesus, I can't believe he did that,' said Max.

'Bugger me,' said Bruce, 'I wonder how much that tray of drinks cost.'

Everybody pissed themselves laughing, except for the publican, who admitted later it was the funniest thing he had ever seen in the pub, and of course the Yanks were spending a lot of money. There were a lot of locals in the pub and after the laughter died down, the locals began to mix with Max's group and the Marines. Later that day, they were all invited back to someone's house. The owners were a middle-aged married couple, and by this time everyone was well under the weather.

'We were all swapping bits of uniforms,' said Max, 'We couldn't swap ribbons because we didn't have any, but they all wanted our slouch hats, which we couldn't give them but promised to try and buy one for them at the barracks.'

'The Marines' uniform was very close to our summer uniforms,' said Max, 'and if you swapped the slouch hat for their cap, it was hard to tell the difference of who was who until you spoke, as the accents were very different.'

The end of week two came and Max was still fumbling on the bloody typewriter. He had managed twenty words with only one mistake. That wasn't bad you know, particularly with only one finger.

The US *Long Beach* was now leaving and all the friends the Marines had made were there to see them off, along with a crowd of locals. Max, as promised, had bought a slouch hat for a marine, which he was now wearing with his summer uniform. The tender boats were loading the Marines on, and the Marine whom Max had given the slouch hat to shook hands with Max and said goodbye as he jumped on the tender boat.

Max was now mistaken for a Marine by a shore Military Policeman (MP) and shoved on to a tender. It didn't take long for the Yank MP to find out who Max was when he yelled out, 'Hey, you mental moron, get me back up there.'

The MP said, 'Goddamn, man, you looked like a Marine!'

'Bullshit!' Max said.

During the third week, the SAS asked Sergeant Ernie if anyone wanted to do a first static line parachute jump. They were conducting a jump for first timers on the weekend and Sergeant Ernie's fellows would be welcome.

Static line jumping is where you hook up the static line cord to a cable in the plane. The other end is connected to the top of the parachute deployment bag, and as you exit the plane, the static cord is pulled tight so the deployment bag is released from the container, which means you don't have to do anything – except pray.

'It's purely voluntary,' Sergeant Harrigan said, and explained it was a great opportunity to jump with the SAS, something not likely to happen again once they left the course.

Only three from the course of volunteered: Max, Bruce and a bloke called Trevor.

The training was most of Saturday, which included familiarisation and fitting of equipment, aircraft drills, how to exit the plane with a stable body position, landing and controlling the canopy and how to operate the reserve parachute. After training, they all went to the other ranks' club at the SAS centre for drinks. Max wanted to know where he could get a set of worry beads from.

The jump was the next morning. Bruce didn't seem to be worried about it, but Max was going to check his pants after the jump to see if he'd pissed himself.

'We jumped from around three thousand feet,' Max said. 'The jump master called out, "Stand and hook up", and one by one in safe intervals out we went. Someone yelled out "Geronimo". The next bloke said he had forgotten the Indian's name, so he said "Hiawatha". When it was my turn, the jump master said, "What are you going to say, Thornton?" I said, "Foo was here" and jumped out. We had instructors jump with us and help with advice on guiding the canopy. What an experience! When the chute opened, I was pulled up and when my pulse returned to normal, I was gently gliding down. What a fantastic view! The landing jolt was harder than I imagined, or maybe I didn't get it right – you're supposed to do a para role when you hit the deck. Bruce didn't piss his pants, and neither did I.'

During the last week of the course, a man in a pub gave Max and the rest of the course participants the address of a reliable tattooing place in Bassendean, a suburb of Perth. Some of the blokes were thinking of getting a tattoo. Max said he'd think about it. They were invited back for a barbecue at the people's house where the party was with the Marines. Their son was away in the Air Force and his Austin A40 was not being used. They were sure he wouldn't mind it being used by the boys for the last week they were there. It would keep the battery charged and the wheels turning. It would be good for it. After the barbecue, it was driven back to the barracks. Now they had some wheels, it was decided that some of them would check out the tattoo man.

Max said, 'We went after the course finished that day. It was a private house and pretty late when we got there. Because it was late, he wasn't all that interested, but he said if the four of us got tattoos, he would do it. Trouble was, Max hadn't decided if he was going to have one, but he was sort of pressured into it, as the others wanted one and they had driven a long way. Max studied the pictures in the tattoo book and said, 'Okay, I'll get one.'

The next day on the course, the four of them had a bandage on their arms.

Sergeant Harrigan asked, 'What's with you four?'

They told him they had tattoos.

'Bloody idiots! I hope you didn't get a name on there you might be sorry about one day.'

The course finished, and they took the car back, said thank you and did the goodbye stuff.

They said, 'We're sorry to see you go. You're a good bunch of blokes and we wish you all well.'

Back at the barracks, they received their first posting via a signal (same as a telegram in civilian terms). Trevor read his.

'Fantastic! I'm going to the Middle East.'

Max said, 'What? Give me a look. No, you're not going to

Cairo, you're going to CARO – Central Army Records Office in Melbourne.'

'Bugger,' said Trevor.

Max read his and he was going to the same place. Not what Max wanted, but as a Private soldier, he guessed it was like the new apprentice – you get the shit jobs in the beginning. He knew Valda and the family would be over the moon to finally have him home for a couple of years and for any further postings, they would all be going together. He rang home that night to give her the good news and that he would be home in two days. He would ring when he got off the train and could she come and get him. Max had five days before he had to report to Albert Park Barracks, so quality time was spent with family and friends. Even in the small time away, the kids had changed in size and character. He was concerned that with constant time away, he would miss a certain amount of time watching them grow. Sometimes, when you start a new venture in life, you don't realise the hardships that could follow, he had said to Valda, but they were both very aware of it now.

Chapter 11

Climbing the Ladder

Max arrived at the front gates at Albert Park Barracks but had to wait for someone to come for him as he didn't have a security pass. A Warrant Officer took him to Block B where the medical records office was located. The barracks consisted of eight blocks, A through to H. The headquarters building for medical was a separate building. Max was introduced to the staff at medical records, which comprised one Captain, one Warrant Officer, one Sergeant, two Corporals and four Private soldiers, all National Servicemen. Additionally, there were five public service personnel and two part-time doctors.

These doctors were there to read and approve, or not approve, soldiers' repatriation claims. When soldiers' files left the office, a lady called Ali marked the index cards as to where they went. Outlying medical units such as hospitals and unit regimental aid posts would send the original forms, after a soldier had seen by a doctor or medical staff at his unit, to Central Medical Records Office (CMRO) where they were filed manually on the soldier's medical file. These documents were held and used to substantiate any claims that were made by the soldier for repatriation after he was discharged, so it was important the documents found their way to the correct soldier's file. Max knew it would be the most boring shit posting you could possibly get, a daily bundle of fifty documents to manually find and file on a soldier's file; however, Max approached it with professionalism, and it wasn't long before it was recognised that his professionalism and leadership skills were wasted in this job. He was subsequently recommended to attend a promotion course for the rank of Corporal.

The promotion course would be held at Meares House at Watsonia Barracks, also known as Meares House Yallambie in earlier days. It was purchased by the Army from a Doctor Meares and family and used for quadripartite exercises and some training activities, and that's where Max would be going. 'Bugger me,' he said, when he found out he would have to go away three times for this promotion. He needed to do three subject courses: A (weapons and drill), B (his corps subject, medical, at Healesville) and C (military law). Each time you were promoted to another rank, you did the same courses again, albeit at a higher level. The course didn't start for another three weeks but, Jesus, he'd not long been home. Valda would cut his nuts out when he told her.

The duration of the first course was three weeks but was live-in, which meant you couldn't go home on weekends, as it was seven days a week. Max's age and life experiences were far superior to the younger soldiers, but he wondered if they were good enough for fast promotion in the service. Life and military discipline were a far cry from the civilian world he came from. Well, he'd find out, wouldn't he.

The first hurdle now was to win the approval and the congratulations he hoped he'd get from Valda. He knew she was keen to see him do well after all they had been through, particularly her times alone with kids as a young mother, and all those long drudging walks he had done to Healesville at night, sometimes in the rain. But Valda was the one who would have the bad end of the stick, alone again with the kids, although she did have family and a good circle of friends. Max wondered if he was trying to convince himself that everything was going to be roses.

'Well,' Valda said, 'what can I say, Max? You are getting what someone thinks you're worthy of. And you know what? The money will be better, and we can certainly use that. Just keep doing what you do best, play nice with the other kids – and don't get bloody shot!'

Valda and the kids drove Max to Watsonia Barracks and dropped him off at Meares House.

'What a lovely old two-storey house, Max! Fancy living here in the old days. The owners must have had a lot of money.'

'Yes, dear, they certainly did.'

There were twenty participants on the course and, like Max, all were nervously unpacking their gear in their upstairs allocated rooms. Nervous because they had just met the two Warrant Officers Class 1 who would be running the course. It was a bit like 'good cop, bad cop': one was all military, up the guts, no bullshit and bombastic; the other was a more understanding officer who, Max thought, knew how everyone was silently dealing with the three weeks to come. Max made a mental note of the man's demeanour and how he engaged with the soldiers, given his much higher rank. He spoke to them not as equals but as humans. Max took this on board for when, if ever, he would be the same rank as that man, a Warrant Officer Class 1, a long way off, if ever. He never forgot how that Warrant Officer dealt with those junior to him. *That's what leadership is all about*, thought Max, *firm, fair and friendly.*

Max would learn a lot of leadership skills from this man during the course. His name was Warrant Officer Stuart Dodds. He had a really short crew cut, as you would imagine, and when you saw his physique, he was big but not intimidating. His face was one of knowledge and trust, someone you'd like next to you in the trenches at war when the shit hit the fan.

The first two days were classroom lectures on leadership skills. Guess who gave that lesson? Max was not surprised at all. The other bloke's name was Warrant Officer Nelly. He gave the lessons on weapons drill and formations, and told the course, in no uncertain manner, that their parade ground drill with weapons would be well scrutinised, so they needed to put the practice in with long hours at night on the parade ground, and they would need everyone working together if they were all to pass this course.

Everyone had been allocated morning jobs like mopping and polishing floors, polishing staircase banisters, cleaning the toilet block, and of course, there was their own gear.

'We wore greens for the entire course,' Max said, 'and they had to be washed, pressed and starched, along with boots spit-polished to a mirror shine. Our rooms and allocated jobs were inspected every morning at 6.30 am, breakfast at 7 am, first lesson 8 am with some of us in the classroom and others on the parade ground, depending on what you were being instructed or tested on.'

Mostly, the weekends were left free for students to study or use the parade ground to practise their drill or weapons lesson. There was a row of fruit trees at the back of Meares House and Max used these at night to practise his drill lessons. He could imagine the trees were his squad on the parade ground and gave his orders to the trees, hoping the psychologist wasn't watching.

Everyone got one practice drill lesson assessed and marked to see how they were progressing and how much more work or practice they would need to do before the final drill assessment.

'There were four Warrant Officers, one on each corner of the parade ground,' said Max. 'The idea was that the squad were all raw recruits, and you had to teach them the particular activity you had been allocated.'

One of the students performed badly, and the Warrant Officer asked the course if they thought his brain might have been 'too tense'. They all agreed that the student was probably very tense. The Warrant Officer said, 'No, I mean his brain was two-tenths the size of a normal one.'

The lesson Max had been given to teach was fix and unfix bayonets; for ease of instruction, these lessons were taught by numbers. The student instructor would march the squad onto the parade ground, size and number them, open order march, explain the lesson they were going to have and give a complete demonstration of the activity they were going to learn. This was then followed by a demonstration of the same activity by numbers: for example, on command one, you will do this; on the command two, do this and so on till the activity was completed. The instructor then did the action, one by one and the squad copied him. Within the forty-minute lesson, hopefully the students were able to, in some way, shape or form, complete the activity, like in Max's case, when it was his turn to fix and unfix bayonets.

The students on the course were from all Army corps – infantry, signals, engineers, ordinance, medical, psychology and one musician from the band corps – a mixed bunch of blokes who all got on pretty well to achieve a common goal. The time came when they were given the lessons they would be tested on. Max's lessons this time were to strip and assemble the 9 mm pistol and saluting on the march. He had to present a classroom lesson of his own choice, but it had to be a subject from his corps. He chose sucking chest wounds and cardiopulmonary resuscitation (CPR), both of which he was proficient in and knew the instructors would know bugger all about, so he only had to watch his presentation skills. He could bullshit as much as he wanted to where the topic was concerned, but if he did, it would be minimal. This was the last week of the course, and they had all had enough. They were looking forward to the final test and getting out of Dodge. One person failed the weapons test and two failed the parade ground drill lessons – they would be coming back at another time for retesting – but Max was clear and on his way home with Valda and the kids.

Valda had arranged to go to Phillip Island on the Sunday to take the kids to see the Penguin Parade. They were joined by Scrooge and Joan in his pastie-shaped grey Vanguard, and Brewster and Suzy in their walnut-shaped VW Bug (who didn't want to put the engine in the front like everybody else). Max said the only thing that looked like a car was his FE Holden station wagon.

Martin thought the penguins were little people and wanted

to know if penguins had knees. Anne was too small to know what was going on.

Next in Max's promotion courses was subject C. It was only a two-day course with no live-in requirement, so he was able to go home overnight. The first day was simply how to use the *Army Law Manual* and the different sections that applied to various laws within the military. Max was amazed that the Australian Army was still using the *British Law Manual* that had sections about cruelty to your horse combined with other sections not relevant to the Australian Army. Max thought they were like a mob of mice following a British military Pied Piper around. Max asked the instructor why, in 1969, the Australian military didn't have their own law manual.

'You know what,' the instructor said, 'we're working on it!'

Max had no worries about the exam the next day because the promotion course he had just finished also dealt with the law manual. There were thirty questions to find answers to in the book and give the reference to legally substantiate that charge at a hearing or court-martial. Max could not find the answer to one question (and he didn't think anyone else found it either): 'What does the conductor do in the Australian Army?' What does this conductor actually do? Is he in the Army Band or does he stand on a hill and conduct the lightning? After further investigation, he discovered the Australian Army doesn't have a conductor! At least, he is not called that; he does the same job but is called an Ordinance Liaison Warrant Officer. He is the 'go-between' for the military and civilian suppliers for items purchased and costing. Max reckoned that whoever wrote that question came out of the same idiot bag as those individuals who threw their sheets in the mud, and someone needed to tie that bag up.

The last promotion course to do now was subject B. The course was due to start in four weeks. For this, he had to go back to Healesville for another two weeks away from home, but he was getting there. The course was fourteen days straight with no coming home on the weekend, and there was no way Max was going to bloody walk there and back again. By this time, Valda had pretty much come to terms with Max's absence and had her routine at home down pat. Max had a considerable amount of gear he would have to take with him this time. He drove the car to Healesville with Valda and the kids, and she would come back for him in two weeks.

The course was run by two Warrant Officers and a Sergeant, along with a Major who gave only one or two lectures. The Major's favourite, annoying saying, was 'Defluff your navel.' *Jesus, what's wrong with these people?* thought Max.

There were several outbuildings, each set up for two people. Max and a bloke called Ted were placed together. Just up the path from their hut was where the trainee nurses were billeted so they had to walk right past Max and Ted's hut to get to their quarters.

Max said, 'We were sitting on the steps of our hut, cleaning our gear ready for the course to start the next day, when four girls walked past and stopped to talk to us. We slowly walked up the path with them as far as their enclosed veranda, but did not go beyond that bound, and stood there finishing our chat with the girls. They went in and we walked back to our hut which was only fifty yards away.'

The next morning, Regimental Sergeant Major Chandler came into the class and said, 'Day one and we have a discipline problem already. Two soldiers on this course were seen in and out of the bounds area at the nurses' quarters, contrary to unit standing orders. Please identify yourselves. You will both be charged today with disobeying unit standing orders and could be taken off the course.'

Max said, 'Come on, Sir, let's be fair about this. We didn't go in, and you've got us staying fifty yards away. Where is the bound line?'

The Regimental Sergeant Major said, 'If I were you, Private Thornton, I would keep my mouth shut, particularly in front of the Commanding Officer when he hears the charge today. That's if you want any chance of staying on this course.'

'Well,' Max said, 'day one and I'd managed to stand on my dick already, but I wasn't going to miss the opportunity to keep my mouth shut. We were found guilty, of course, fined ten shillings and two days confined to barracks.'

Max was told he would be staying on the course, but if he ever came back to that unit again, which was seriously doubted, he would know better.

'March them out,' said the Commanding Officer.

After the course lectures finished, for the next two nights, Max and Ted had to do kitchen duty for the two days confined to barracks.

The course included three days out in the bush at Healesville in the wet. *Next time I have to do this, I'm wearing pantyhose against the bloody leeches!* thought Max. The ground was wet and soft underfoot, and on a night exercise, Max slipped over and buried the end of the barrel of the rifle into the soft dirt. As there was only a pull-through cleaner on a cord, Max couldn't get the dirt out, so he poked a stick up the barrel which promptly broke off and stayed there. *Should be really interesting in the morning when Major Defluff Your Navel does the weapons inspection,* Max thought. No matter what Ted and Max did to the rifle, it just made it worse. Max didn't see the funny side, but Ted did. His rifle was clean.

Next morning on the bush parade, Major Defluff Your Navel went down the line looking up the rifle barrels. *Here he comes, my turn. This will not be good*, Max thought. The Major held the barrel up to the light and looked inside.

'He really didn't need to,' said Max, 'I could have told him it was going to be as black as the inside of a dog's bum. The look on his face was priceless, and I was trying my hardest to stop grinning.'

He said, 'What's all that?'

'Dirt and a stick, Sir.'

'Get it out and report to me when you have.'

'Well, Sir, that will have to be back at the unit because we don't have a solid pull-through cleaning kit out here. The Warrant Officer said it will have to wait till we return to the unit.'

'Can't seem to stay out of trouble on this course,' Max said to Ted.

The last night out in the field was a night navigation. It was absolutely pouring with rain. Three Warrant Officers and Major Defluff Your Navel had been placed at compass magnetic bearings as checkpoints; Defluff was at the last checkpoint. Everyone missed the last checkpoint in the dark by about fifty yards. Dickhead Defluff was sitting somewhere close by but didn't see or hear them go through. Back at the camp, the exercise was now declared non-tactical, and although it was still raining, a big fire in a drum was very welcome. Someone said, 'Where's Defluff?' He was still sitting somewhere out there in the pissing rain waiting for people who weren't coming. One of the instructors had to go and find him.

Max and a bloke called Bob had worn their wet clothes the entire time, but now the exercise had finished, they put on the dry stuff they'd saved for the last night. They clipped their hootchies (tents) together and crawled into their sleeping bags. They had each made a pannikin of hot tea, when someone spoke. As they both turned, they spilled the tea and soaked their sleeping bags.

'This fucking course has been nothing but trouble for me,' Max said to Bob.

The classroom content was more about leadership qualities, a small amount of medical treatment, the field ambulance role, and layout and patient evacuation from land and air, in particular the system being currently used in Vietnam. Considering the altercations and mishaps that had occurred, Max was more than pleased it was over. He did however start a friendship with a Sergeant called Harry, and they became close friends throughout their whole careers.

Valda arrived safely and the family were together again. Two weeks later, back at the barracks, Max's promotion order came through and CMRO had a new Corporal – Max Thornton.

He sent his shirts to the army tailor at the barracks to have the stripes sewn on, not because Valda couldn't sew but the tailor knew exactly where they were to go. Max couldn't help glancing at his reflection in shop windows as he walked past with his new stripes. He went to the pub where Fred drank to show off in front of his old man's mates, and to silently say, *'See, when I make my own decisions, I will always be successful'*, a sort of 'I told you so'.

A promotion barbecue was held at Max and Valda's house,

and he thought he actually saw the mother-in-law smiling. She might have even been happy for him. In all fairness, she did give him a kiss and congratulate him. Perhaps she thought more of him than he gave her credit for, but it was early days.

Back at the unit, they congratulated Max on his new promotion and the daily mundane tasks continued. Max was back in the saddle again on a new horse, but he still had some saddle sores from the previous course – he now had a charge on his record, albeit a minor one. Trouble and mishaps seemed to follow Max wherever he went.

Some months later, Max was required to report to the headquarters building; a postings Major wanted to see him. On the way there, Max was trying to think what he might have done wrong. *I bet I'm going to get a kick in the arse for the charge on the course*, Max thought. The postings Major was sitting down so it was hard to tell his height, but he was a podgy sort of bloke, bald as a badger's arse, in his late fifties, Max guessed.

'Come in, Corporal Thornton,' said the Major. 'How did you enjoy the course?'

Max thought, *Here it comes*, but no.

The Major said, 'There is a Sergeant's position available, working with a Colonel who is one of our specialists. You would be working over here in the HQ building. You will be promoted temporarily straightaway, but you will need to complete your courses by the end of this year (1969) to become substantive. How do you feel about that, Corporal Thornton?'

Bugger! Max thought, *I'm just starting to have a stressless and happy time where I am. However, when one door of happiness closes, another opens, so don't look too long at the closed door, Max, or you will miss the one that's been opened for you now.*

'Yes, Sir, I would be pleased to take the position, and thank you for offering it to me.'

'You were offered the position because you were recommended by those you have had contact with. Today is Wednesday. Be here in the shape of a Sergeant on Monday. That's all, Corporal Thornton.'

Max knew the Corporal who worked in the quartermaster store, so when Max asked him for the necessary patches for the rank of Sergeant, he said, 'Christ, Max, who do you know? The ink hasn't dried from your promotion to Corporal yet.'

Apart from going home with great news, the best was yet to come. He would now be a member of the Sergeants Mess, which is considered by all ranks, officers included, to be the best mess in the Army. He could hardly contain himself. He couldn't wait to give Valda the news. Who knew what sort of reward she might give him? (Whether she did or didn't isn't going in this book!)

The new posting was another one of those clerical medical positions, which really didn't suit Max, but he didn't want to look a gift horse in the mouth. Once again, he hoped he had enough experience to carry the rise in rank. Final medical board results were sent to his new posting for confirmation, scrutinised by the Colonel and sent on for further actions deemed necessary. There was one particular medical unit that sent correspondence which needed correction a lot of the time, which Max had to redo, and as time went on, the Colonel realised Max was fixing these errors. Max didn't mind, and he wasn't going to dirk some poor bugger at the other end.

Unfortunately, the Colonel said, 'Sergeant Thornton, get on the phone and tell the Sergeant at that unit we are not fixing them. In future, they will be sent back.'

Shit, thought Max, *why have I got to do this?* but then realised the boss wanted it done at the Sergeant level. So Max made the call.

A Captain, who Max called Malice for reasons that will become apparent, answered the phone. Max said who he was and wanted to speak to the Sergeant. The Captain said he wasn't there at the time but that he would pass on the message. What Max should have said was, 'It's okay, Sir, ask him to ring me back.' However, he didn't and told Captain Malice exactly what the Colonel had said. *Big mistake, Max!* What Max didn't know was that this Captain was the department head and was really pissed off that a bloody Sergeant had told him they weren't measuring up (albeit the Colonel's words, not Max's), and he had also managed to piss off the unit Sergeant as well. He was now going to get a foot up the arse from the pissed-off Captain.

On the plus side of things, Max had completed his courses for Sergeant, so he was now at a substantive rank. It was nearing the end of the year 1969, and it was a tradition to invite the officers to the Sergeants Mess for Christmas drinks, so Max invited the Colonel. Max noticed a Major looking at him.

He said to the Colonel, 'Do you know who that is? He keeps looking at me.'

'I'll introduce you to him. Major Malice, this is my Sergeant, Max Thornton.'

Shit! Max thought, *that's who I spoke to on the phone. He's been promoted.*

He didn't look happy to see Max. He didn't shake hands and just nodded. Looks can tell you everything.

The group started talking football and the Major was making outlandish statements about how good Collingwood was.

Max said, 'Sometimes you can be one-eyed about a team.' *Big mistake – again – Max!*

The Major had some sort of eye affliction. Max meant no disrespect; it was simply a footy term often used, but he knew how it had been taken. Max spoke to the Colonel later about it.

'Don't be ridiculous, Max. He wouldn't have taken offence.'

Max thought, *Yeah, well, we'll see, won't we?*

The usual Christmas celebrations were underway. Max and Valda always had to go to her mother's on Christmas Day for lunch. There was no alternating between Max's parents on Christmas Day, so Max's parents always had to be satisfied with the Boxing Day visit, which was always a sore point. Valda's mother insisted on it at her place every year. 'Bloody selfish and inconsiderate,' Max said, but then again, there was never any love lost between Valda and Max's family.

The kids were growing up fast, Martin was now three years old and Anne was now one. On Christmas Day, Max would have to drive the kids to Dorris's house where his parents were for the Christmas lunch. They only had time to spend about an hour there, having been told not to be late back for the Valda family lunch. Valda never ever went with Max on that Christmas Day visit to Dorris's. You couldn't make it any harder to celebrate a family Christmas even if you tried.

Max was always walking on eggshells at Valda's parents place in case he said or did the wrong thing. After the lunch, everyone was quietly relaxing, so Max sat in a comfortable chair, making sure he didn't have a biro in his pocket, and fell asleep for a short while. When he woke, everyone was on the back lawn and the kids were playing with the dog. *Ah, there they all are*, he thought as he walked straight into a closed glass door. He staggered out, nose bleeding and bruised face. He just seemed to create his own storm when he was at this place. It was always an uphill battle for him.

Chapter 12

Off to Vietnam

National Archives of Australia Fact sheet 164:

In 1964, a fourth period of National Service was introduced. In May 1965, new powers were introduced by the Coalition Government which enabled the sending of national servicemen overseas.
At this time, Australian soldiers were involved in conflicts in both the Vietnam War and the Indonesian Confrontation.

In order to meet these overseas conflicts, the Menzies government deemed it necessary to raise the Army's numbers to 40,000.

All 20-year-old males were required to register with the Department of Labour and National Service, and a 'birthday ballot' was introduced. This ballot randomly selected the names of those registered by their date of birth and it was these men who would now be required for National Service, the commitment being two years of full-time service in the Regular Army along with three years part-time service in the Citizens Military Forces (Army Reserves).

Aboriginal and Torres Strait Islander men were exempt, along with theology students and those who were medically unfit. Men who held a conscientious objection to war would be given exemption provided they could prove their objection was based on religion grounds.

University students, apprentices, married men and those who could prove that National Service would financially disadvantage them were granted a temporary deferment.

Over 15,300 national servicemen served in the Vietnam War from 1965 to 1972, there were 200 killed and 1,279 wounded. The issue of conscription, once again, provoked a debate within the Australian community, large anti-conscription and anti-Vietnam war demonstrations were prevalent. These comprised of mainly university students and other members of the community who held the belief that both conscription and involvement in the Vietnam War should be banned.

The National Service scheme was abolished on 5 December 1972 by the newly elected Labor Government. However, it would take time to discharge all of the National Service Soldiers, so the Government offered a war service loan to those National Service men who elected to finish their time; thus, allowing a slow flow through that the system could handle.

What upset Max about that was that there were National Servicemen who were conscientious objectors who stayed home in Australia who would now get a war service loan, the same loan earned by those who were sent to Vietnam and risked their lives and those that came back missing limbs, and that included wives of deceased National Service veterans who were rightly entitled to a war service loan. Didn't seem right to Max, as it was all done to alleviate administrative issues.

In 1970, the Vietnam War was still going on and Max was told he would be sent there this year. He was to be posted to the 1st Australian Field Hospital in the Province of Vung Tau for a period of one year.

'Shit!' Max said, 'I didn't expect this, not so soon anyway.'

He was only a new Sergeant on the block and to be sent into a war zone ... Valda would be really worried about this.

'Jesus,' Valda said, 'I'll kill you if you get bloody shot, Max.'

Prior to leaving for Vietnam, Max, like everyone else in the same position, had to attend the Jungle Training Centre at Canungra in Queensland. Along with all his field gear and civilian clothes was the bolt for his rifle, which had to be removed before the weapon was loaded into the civilian plane's armoury. The large, soft, green bag that everything was packed into was lovingly called a struggle bag, so named as its very composition made it a struggle to carry. Three Army trucks were used to carry the struggle bags, with pickets to ensure nothing fell out the back of the truck. Max happened to be standing next to a Military Police Sergeant who threw Max's bag on, and Max threw the MP's bag on. They were all herded into Kombi vans for the trip to Canungra.

On arrival, there were two huge piles of struggle bags that you needed to sift through to find your own. Max couldn't find his bag, and when there were no bags left, he came to the realisation that his bag was truly missing. Max reported this to a skinny little Sub-Lieutenant (one pip), who Max thought was about one step up from the Boy Scouts.

He said, 'Not to worry, Sergeant Thornton, we will get you reissued with your DP1 gear.'

This was the gear you needed for overseas deployment. He obviously didn't give a shit about Max's personal gear.

Then Max gave him the bombshell – 'What about the bolt for my rifle that's in there?'

'Jesus Christ,' he said, 'what's it doing in there?'

'You're obviously not aware, Sir, that you can't fly with the bolt in a weapon. There was more risk of losing it from my person on the plane than the Army losing a large struggle bag. Just shows you how wrong you can be, doesn't it, *Sir*.'

The pipsqueak came back later and said, 'I have spoken to the baggage pickets and they assure me nothing fell out of the trucks. It obviously didn't go on the truck, so you must have lost it before you arrived in Queensland.'

Now that Max was a Sergeant who wasn't going to take this shit from a prick who had come out of that hole in the idiot bag.

He said, 'Later in life, when you get some time up and experience, *Sir*, you will come to realise that when a Sergeant tells you something happened, you can take it as gospel, if you get my drift.'

He secretly hoped this bloke didn't check how long his service as a Sergeant had been.

A day later, the Lieutenant told Max he was going to be charged for losing military equipment, specifically the bolt from his weapon. Max could have told him he had a star witness, the Military Police Sergeant who threw his bag on the truck.

Fuck him, thought Max, *he needs a lesson in life, cocky little bastard.*

On the day the charge was being heard, the Lieutenant asked Max who the Sergeant in attendance was.

Max said, 'Say hello to Sergeant Shepherd from the Military Police. He is here to burn your arse, Sir.'

The charge, of course, was dismissed. The Commanding Officer who had heard the charge asked the Lieutenant to stay behind. Max reckoned he knew what that was going to be all about and he decided for the remainder of the course, he would fade into the background and keep his mouth shut as he didn't know where this Lieutenant would fit in during the training. He had to be issued with another rifle from Canungra which turned out to be a bonus. When the tower water jump happened, you jumped with your rifle, but because Max had one of their weapons, they told him not to take it on the jump, which meant Max didn't have to dry and clean a weapon like everyone else did. More time for him dedicate to other course tasks.

They were put into platoons and course participants were allocated certain roles. A signals corps Major was to be the platoon commander, and Max was to be the platoon Sergeant. Each platoon was being tested on harbouring up techniques. Harbouring up is where you stop for the night, and the sections go in clockwise one by one and take up defensive positions while the perimeter is checked, cleared and declared safe. If you got the training wrong, you did it again until the platoon got it right.

'When our turn came,' Max said, 'the platoon commander

said, "Is there anyone here who has never done this before?" There was one Private soldier who put his hand up. He was from the service corps and was going to Vietnam to work in the ASCO canteen that sold watches, radios and other general items. *Thank Christ for that*, I thought. We called him ASCO for the rest of the course.'

The platoon commander said to ASCO, 'Listen carefully, son, we don't want to have to do this twice. Take a good look at Sergeant Thornton. When we go in, wherever he goes, you go hang on to him if you must, but don't lose him. Do exactly what he tells you. Are we clear?'

'Yes, sir,' said ASCO.

They crept into the Queensland jungle. It was pitch black. Max was silently placing his section into their positions by hand signalling. When he looked behind him, shit! ASCO was gone. Where to, who knew? *Well, we'll find him when we stand down*, thought Max, *that's if he's not bloody lost out here. As long as he stays still, we might get away with it.* The platoon commander was having a nervous breakdown until they found ASCO sitting out in the jungle.

Max said to ASCO, 'You will be sleeping in the hootchies with me tonight.'

Max clipped two hootchies together and set up their sleeping gear. All ASCO had to do was make a brew. Max explained how to do it.

'You unfold the little metal stove, ASCO, and use one of these hexamine tablets. You don't eat the tablet. You light it just like you would a firelighter, then put the pannikin of water on the stove to make the brew.'

How hard could that be? Max thought as he was kept busy with his other section Sergeant responsibilities.

'Jesus!' Max said, 'You're supposed to unfold the bloody handle from under the pannikin. ASCO, you're as dumb as dog shit. How do you think you can get it off and drink the brew without the bloody handle? Thank Christ you're only going to work in the canteen over there.'

They were all taken through the jungle and shown examples of Vietnamese booby traps and how to pick the early signs of their existence. The course finished with a five-mile hike up Heartbreak Hill with full packs and rifles. On the way up, they shared carrying the general purpose machine gun (GPMG), which was heavy and cumbersome. There was one soldier worth mentioning, for all the wrong reasons, being called Private Sook in this story for legal reasons. He wouldn't carry the GPMG, was against any discipline and was disrespectful of anyone with rank, particularly Sergeants. Max made a point of talking to the Major about him and wondered how he could have been missed by the trick cyclists (Army slang for psychiatrists). He was going to be a big problem wherever he went, particularly for Sergeants, and someone needed to do something about it. Whether they did or not was not Max's problem. He had reported his concerns to the next chain of command and that's all he could do.

A large going-away party was organised with all in sundry. Even Slim, Nitro, Brewster and Macca were there. Max was sure some of them thought he might not be coming home. At times, it seemed like a bloody wake. Max reckoned he could hide behind a sandbag as good as the next person, so he quoted a later movie of Arnie Schwarzenegger and said, 'I'll be back'. Max convinced Valda it was better to say the goodbyes at home to alleviate the sadness and tears at the airport. He knew he probably wouldn't handle it all that well either. She said once again, 'Don't get shot, Max, and play nice with other kids.'

When Max arrived at Essendon Airport, Sergeant Shepherd was there. They shook hands and had a laugh about the skinny little Lieutenant at Canungra. Sergeant Shepherd's name was Brian and they would stay together on the journey to Vietnam.

Max and Brian flew out to Sydney on an Ansett Boeing 727. The embarking and staging were at Chowder Bay in Sydney. As usual, the Army applied its usual 'hurry up and wait' policy, so they were there two days before leaving. They were free during the day but still had roll calls each morning regardless of rank. Brian was going to stay out overnight. Max didn't ask him where he was going but said, yes, he would cover for him on the roll call. When they called out Shepherd, Max simply called back, 'Here, Sir' and said the same for his name. *Christ,* Max thought, *something like this shouldn't be that easy!*

Although Max had been A1 dental checked just two weeks previously, they were all required to be checked again, a waste of time. But he couldn't believe it when the dentist told him he needed two fillings. Then again, this was a contract dentist obviously making the most of a good thing.

'Now, Max, do you usually have an injection for a filling?'

'Mate, I have to have a bloody injection to go to the dentist.'

They flew out to Vietnam with Qantas via Darwin and were to keep a civilian shirt ready to put on in the plane before going into the terminal at Darwin while the aircraft was being refuelled. This was due to the anti-Vietnam rallies in Australia.

'They must be joking,' Max said to Brian. 'We will be standing there with a civilian shirt on over our bloody uniforms.'

Brian said, 'Who thinks up this shit?'

'Well, they still haven't tied up the idiot bag yet, have they? Normal people wouldn't believe this stuff.'

Back on the aircraft, it was a dry flight, no booze for obvious reasons. Next stop, Vietnam. The landing at Saigon was crucial due to the huge amount of military aircraft activity using the runways and because of the danger of enemy activity. The Qantas aircraft needed to go straight down and land first go. This was the first moment Max's brain realised where he was, and from now on, it was all fair dinkum stuff. His training was over.

On the ground at Saigon, they were in the American system and were billeted in prefabricated buildings overnight, waiting for on forward movement the next day. Max was amazed how different things were with the Americans. The urinals in the men's toilets looked like a funny-looking wash basin.

Max was now good mates with Brian, so he said, 'Never seen anything like this! Don't eat those pink lollies in the basin, mate. They'll give you indigestion.'

'Thanks for that, dickhead,' Brian said.

Max and Brian flew to Vung Tau in a Caribou Army aircraft. There were two of these that provided a shuttle service, called Wallaby 1 and Wallaby 2. They flew over large bomb craters, reminding them again that they had arrived in the country. Once again, due to enemy ground fire, the Caribou flew high and came down fast to land. Max reckoned the Caribous looked like they were made of fabric stretched over a frame and glued. They made a lot of noise and shook like buggery but were one of the military's most reliable aircraft.

The Australian Field Hospital was situated within the

Logistic Support Group, along with Military Police, ordinance, engineers, vehicle workshops, bomb disposal pits and the ASCO canteen. All the buildings except the hospital were of timber construction and sandbagged. The Sergeants Mess and Officers Mess were on top of a sandhill; the hospital, Other Ranks Mess and main kitchen were down on the flat ground.

Max and Brian headed off to their respective units. *Expect the unexpected, that's what they say*, Max thought. When he entered the Sergeants Mess, who should be sitting there but Major Malice and the Commanding Officer. Max knew his rank didn't warrant a Major and a Colonel waiting to say hello.

Malice said to Max, 'Sergeant Thornton, you are in my unit now and I will be watching you closely.'

Jesus, Max thought, *what's wrong with this bastard?* And what was wrong with the Commanding Officer, listening to those petty vindictive nasty comments directed at a new arrival in the unit, whom neither of them had ever served with previously. Malice would have fitted nicely into the sadistic Adolf Hitler family of misfits. Birds of a feather, Max guessed. So, if Max wanted confirmation of what Malice's opinion of him was, he just had been given it. *I know one thing for sure*, Max thought. *I will sit by the banks of the river for as long as it's necessary till your body floats by.*

The two birds left the Mess, the hawk and his pigeon, the Malice bird. This man would be what Max referred to as a promotions blocker. And where Max was concerned, it would prove to be right; he had no substance or morals at all. All Max had to do now was stay out of trouble. This was going to be a David and Goliath struggle, but it was not yet time for the slingshot.

Max was introduced to the members who were there at

the time; some were on duty as the hospital ran 24/7. At 10 pm, the Regimental Sergeant Major whose name was Blacky said good night; Max and some others stayed on. What Max didn't know was the Mess had to close at 10 pm. Max didn't know that as he'd just got there, but the others would have known the rules. So, with the help of others, Max had stood on his dick again. There, however, was no let-off for Max and he was fronted to the Commanding Officer along with the others. *Nice work,* Max he said to himself, *I suspect you've made Malice very happy.* Although one may not realise it at the time, sometimes a foot up the arse is actually good for you, although this one seemed bloody unfair. If you make a mistake, you learn from it, you acknowledge the mistake and you move on; that's what people of substance do. However, Max's opinion of the RSM wasn't very high. He obviously had no balls sneaking around outside. He should have come into the mess, chastised everyone and dished out his own punishment. Instead, he went wimping to the Commanding Officer the next day and had us all paraded. He never spoke personally to anyone of us about it, not what you would expect from a man of his standing, and Max uses the term 'man' very loosely. He had no morals or substance of any kind, either.

Well, Max, you're going to have a peachy time here, aren't you? A tough year coming, but I'm also bloody tough, so they can all get stuffed, and we'll just see who's standing at the end of all this shit fight. Christ, how do people with no morals, social and management skills get these bloody positions? I suppose it's all got to do with what you've got to pick from at the time.

Max's work was on the medical side and Malice's was administrative, so hopefully, Max thought, he would be able to keep out of his way. But that did not stop Malice leaning on Max whenever he could. Max put in for a change of shift for night shift for one night. It came back not approved by Major Malice. He was certainly proving he was a small child in a grown-up's body but to get Max by the short and curlies was just not going to happen, so *xin loy* (tough shit) to all those others there that might be masquerading as bloody humans.

Chapter 13

Angels, Vampires and Jolly Green Giants

Max had various roles: supervising the staff of the admission and discharge section, monitoring the dust-off radio and working in triage when casualties arrived by choppers. The term 'dust-off' originated due to the amount of dust that is made when the helicopter hovers and lands to pick up casualties.

Max referred to the choppers as 'angels in the sky'. In Max's original notes, Valda found a drawing of a helicopter that Max had done and a poem he had written during his time in Vietnam, apparently written for his grandchildren to read in years to come.

Off the coast of Vietnam in the Sand Hills not far
A Medical Unit stands ready for casualties, from afar.
Their Call Sign is Vampire.
A blood sucking host
But they're saving the Blood for those who need it the
most.
The call to Vampire breaks the warm silent Air
And Marks the beginning of their Dedicated Care
They look like Dragon Flies from a long way out
But as they get closer you'll see they're Angels no Doubt
They're carrying our Wounded and those that are sick
And once they get here, they'll be cared for real quick
Although they were welcome and gave the wounded
a new breath

Sometimes they also brought with them death
The nurses were the earthly angels to comfort and care
Someone for the sick to lean on, an answer to their pray
When all seems lost, dark and bleak
The sick found an angel at their feet
The love for humanity lets them care for all,
the suffering and sorrow becomes their call
So if Grandpa or Grandma have a tear in their Eye
Give them a Hug and a warm friendly smile
their minds on the angels and the wounded that came
from the Sky

312586 KJW, 4 February 1971

The field hospital was a facility of one hundred and six beds: fifty surgical, fifty medical and six for the ICU unit. The hospital call sign was Vampire. Max and his staff were responsible for the early notification of casualties by dust-off (angels) to ensure the right medical staff and doctors were in attendance when the casualties arrived. When the inbound chopper called 'Vampire' on the radio, they would advise Max of their estimated time of arrival. According to how much time there was, the hospital departments would be notified by field phone or by siren. If by siren, everyone in the unit had to attend the helicopter pad and the triage section until the requirement of relevant personnel was known.

Max often flew with the American dust-off angel 451 and its crew. The pilot's name was Bruce, who became a lifelong friend. During one of Max's flights, he heard a gun ship chopper talking to its base.

'Gun ship Grey Nurse, this is Wide Minnow. Over.'

The gun ship answered, 'Fat Fish, this is Grey Nurse. Over.'

Wide Minnow replied, 'I repeat, this is Wide Minnow. Over.'

The gun ship replied, 'Roger, Pregnant Tuna.'

They called their base call sign anything but the correct one, just for a bit of fun.

'Wouldn't be tolerated in our system,' said Max. 'Our mob's got no bloody sense of humour. Even in a bloody war zone, everything must be crossed and dotted. The bloody fun police never give up.'

Bruce and the dust-off angel crew gave Max his own flying helmet with a picture of a cartoon kangaroo with the words 'Bloody Kangaroo' on the front. Max said to the crew, 'What I can't understand is, why kamikaze pilots bothered to wear a bloody helmet.' Nobody else knew either.

On one of Max's stays at the American base at Long Binh, he used their cartographer's office to design, paint and cut out a cartoon image of a vampire bat. The finished bat was three feet high with a drip bottle attached to its foot. Max took it back to the field hospital and it was hung in the Sergeants Mess at the front entrance by himself and a bloke called Alan in 1970.

Not long after Max had arrived, the sirens went off and Max hot-footed it in the dark through the sand hills as a short cut. Bad choice – Max was now missing. When they found him, he was stuck right inside the big coils of barbed wire set up on the boundary. It took an hour to get him out, bleeding like a stuck pig.

The field hospital was full of interesting characters and made the twelve months a little more bearable. The mortician's name was Chuck, an American attached to the unit. He could be found lying on the post-mortem stainless steel slab with his head on the rubber block reading a book in air-conditioned comfort. They didn't see much of him socially. Max thought he lived in Vung Tau with a Vietnamese girl. Then there was a dental staff Sergeant who appeared to be, well, let's just say under the weather most of the time. It was discovered he had been injecting the bowl of oranges in the dental clinic with vodka. He had promised one of the bar girls in town he would get her false teeth fixed, but he was going home on rest and recreation (R&R) for a week, which everyone did after six months. He asked Max to pick up the teeth for him and hang onto them till he returned. The bar girl gave Max her false teeth. He put them in his pocket, went back to the unit, stripped off and left his clothes on the floor. Next morning the clothes were gone. The washerwomen had taken them while he slept. *Shit*, Max thought, *the bloody teeth! Two people aren't going to be happy, particularly the bar girl.*

Several of the Australian units in Vietnam had a football team. The hospital team often had to play substitutes, depending on who was available from the emergency staff, and when a dust-off angel came in, everyone became emergency staff. It was not uncommon for a game with the hospital to be suspended and played again on another day. The hospital needed a set of decent football jumpers. As Max's family had been Essendon supporters since 1920, Max wrote to the Essendon Club, asking for a set of hand-me-down jumpers for the boys serving in Vietnam. They declined, saying all their jumpers were handed down to the lower grade players in the club. The Essendon Football Club were a wealthy club. Max considered they could have, and should have, done better for the boys serving their country in a war zone. He was bitterly disappointed, and he told them so.

*

When Max's turn came for R&R, he flew home with Pan Am Airlines, along with American soldiers going on R&R to Sydney. One week home was nowhere near enough, but that's what it was. Martin knew who he was, but Anne was very standoffish, being too small to remember who Max was. Max took Valda to the German Hofbrauhaus restaurant in Melbourne. The kids were being looked after by Valda's parents, so on the way home Max suggested they not go home but stay at a motel, but he couldn't get Valda to agree. Max didn't understand why. Valda and the children were staying at her mother's, and so was Max. There was no privacy there, which only made Valda's decision not to go where they would have some privacy only worse. 'Just ring your mother,' Max said, 'and tell her we are staying out. I'm sure she will understand.' But it didn't happen. There were obviously other reasons she didn't want to go to the motel, but Max didn't want to go there. He'd have to go back to Vietnam wondering why she wouldn't stay at a motel, which Max considered important and so she should have as well. Max tried not to think about that too hard; after all there was no guarantee he was coming back.

There was not enough time to see everyone, just immediate family and to shop for requests from those few who had asked Max to get for them. Max had promised to deliver presents to John Gillespie's wife who was expecting their first child. He delivered the presents and had a cup of tea with her and told her, 'John sends his love'. John was a dust-off medic on board a chopper. When Max returned to Vietnam, Corporal John Gillespie's dust-off chopper had been shot down and his body had not been found. *Jesus,' Max said to himself, 'just as I was telling his wife he sends his love, he had been shot down. A bloody waste of a young life and a child coming into the world without its father. Sad, so sad.'* Max viewed the crews' bodies; their faces were so badly burnt that their teeth were protruding ungainly from their faces. The helicopter was completely burnt out and John's body could not be found. He was listed as Missing in Action.

John's remains were found some forty years later. He was found by a group of Vietnam veterans who took it upon themselves, at their own expense, to go back and try to find his remains. You have to wonder how much time the Army spent searching, and who was in charge of the search

– although it was in a war zone, and to be fair, it was also enemy territory. Why, then, when the war had ended, didn't the government organise their own search now that the area was safe? You can't help being disappointed in our leaders when they keep telling us the Army is our family. Max said his heart goes out to those Vietnam veterans who went back and found their mate.

*

Flying in and around Vietnam was a large helicopter, an H-47 Chinook, lovingly called the Jolly Green Giant. Sometimes when Bruce and his chopper crew were staying overnight in the Sergeants Mess, they would mix up a drink they called the Jolly Green Giant. They mixed it in a big bowl with vodka, gin, rum and scotch, and cream de menthe liqueur to give it the nice green colour. It was so smooth and moreish, which tempted them to drink more than they should have. They had to help them put one foot in front of the other to get them to their beds. They only fell for it once.

The Officers Mess tried in vain to get the crew into their mess, but Bruce and his crew soon learnt the Sergeants Mess was the place to be. Max, of course, was delighted, and so was Bruce once Max had passed on some pertinent information regarding Malice's comments to him when he had first arrived.

The Australians certainly lived differently to the Americans in Vietnam at Long Bihn, who had clubs with five-piece bands and female singers. Max said when their Sergeants Mess had a function, they would invite the nurses. The music was provided by a soldier from the signal's unit. He was a one-man band with cymbals strapped to his knees, a mouth organ on a wire frame round his neck and a guitar. Good old Aussie improvisation at its best.

*

Casualties came and went. Max and a visiting Sergeant who was from the service corps were in the mess at about 9 pm when the field phone rang. Max's staff advised him of a pending dust-off carrying an acute appendicitis that required an appendectomy. The relevant personnel had been advised. The Sergeant said, 'I don't I suppose I could watch the operation?' Max said he would ask and spoke to the surgeon, who incidentally just happened to be a Collins Street specialist on a three-month detachment. He said he had no issues with that. Max helped the bloke put on the boots and gown and took him into the theatre. They stood him up on small steps so he could get a good look. The idiot fainted.

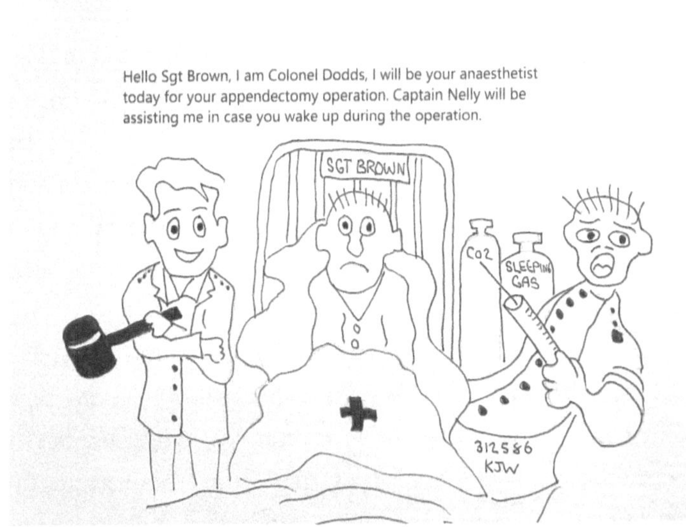

At one stage, apparently a young soldier was told by his mother when he went home on his week-long R&R that he didn't look well. He told her he felt sick all the time and was losing weight. She made him promise he would go to the hospital when he got back, which he did. While he was in hospital, all sorts of tests were conducted by pathology but no abnormalities were found. However, the patient's condition worsened, and he was placed in the intensive care unit. Max was the duty Sergeant on this particular night and stopped in at ICU for a brew. While he was there, the patient's monitor alarm went off: his heart had stopped. Max and the Nursing Officer on duty pulled him out of the cot, that had sides on, to the floor where they could perform CPR. Max said he did the compressions and the nurse used the air bag for ventilation. At one stage, they saw his pupils start to dilate in reaction to the light – and then nothing. The doctors arrived and took over from Max. Sadly he didn't survive.

On one particular dust-off chopper with casualties, there was a dead-on-arrival with a gunshot wound to the chest; one small hole, that's all. The pathologist Major was to do a postmortem and Max was to assist. The chest was cut open and the sternum pulled up out of the way, revealing the soldier had drowned in his own blood. The blood was removed and measured; a 7.62 rifle round had lodged in his spine, and as was explained to Max, had he survived he would have been a paraplegic.

On Christmas Eve 1970, up in the battalion area at Nui Dat (call sign 'Red Earth'), a handful of Sergeants were having a Christmas drink in their Mess, all standing with their backs to the door. Private Sook (yes, that's him from Canungra) walked in and opened fire, killing two and wounding another.

They came into the hospital by chopper. Amongst the possessions of one Sergeant was a letter from his wife, which Max read as part of the identification process. It said that the presents for the kids were under the tree and on Christmas morning, they would all be thinking of him and praying for his safety and his return. It was now Christmas morning and Max was staring at their father's dead body, shot by a misfit that shouldn't have been in the system in the first place. Max had seen and been part of many sad things in his life, but standing over this soldier's body and reading this letter really made him extremely upset. He said he would be sad about this for a long, long time.

'I don't care how strong you are, it brings a tear to your eye and a stab in the heart. What are they doing here? What are any of us doing here, paddling around in a winless war where there can be no end, a shameful waste of young Australian lives?'

Max said these sad and raw circumstances, seen there almost on a daily basis, intensified the significance of life and made him realise with keen awareness how precious life is and the loved ones with whom we share it. It was only now that he was beginning to understand how important this is and what it all means. Life is so precious and can be so short, cut down without warning. We should endeavour to love and share what we have, while we still have it.

During a section advance supported by armoured personnel carriers (APC), a Vietnamese interpreter jumped off the APC on to a mine. When Max looked at what was left, his head and face were untouched, his eyes hadn't had time to glaze over, but the rest of him was only two feet long, just a mixture of bone, fingers, feet, leaves and sticks. What a devastating mess.

'I also remember,' said Max, 'a female Viet Cong (the enemy) with gunshot wounds to the hip was brought into ICU. The X-ray showed what looked like a hand grenade inside her vagina. The ICU was cleared and the two Warrant Officer bomb disposal blokes put on surgical gloves and shoved their hand up to grab it. What a surprise to find out she had a big role of American dollars wrapped up in a banana leaf up there!'

Across the track from Max's hootchie was the bomb disposal dugout operated by two Warrant Officers. Max had been down in there on several occasions but not while they were disarming bombs or booby traps. The dugout bunker was about the size of a normal bathroom with a work bench, a vice, large magnifying equipment, flexible manoeuvrable lights and various tools on a shadow board. Misery had struck again; both operators were killed when a mine went off while they were working on it. They were the blokes who had retrieved the money from the Vietnam woman's vagina. A service was held and the bodies flown home. More grief for loved ones at home.

Max could never get over the fact that they could save soldiers with traumatic limb injuries, limbs blown off their body and half their skull missing, and then someone with one small bullet hole would be dead. Medically, he knew why, but it was hard to get his head around this sometimes.

Max often spent time with Brian, the MP Sergeant, mainly just to chew the fat and trade information. Max said, 'You know, Brian, it's got that way now that whenever I hear a chopper coming, I know it's going to be some poor bugger's death or misery, meaning usually lifelong changes for those waiting at home, and somewhere there will be someone crying for that loss or misery.

'A small child, maybe one year old, came by chopper yesterday from a village that had been bombed with napalm. All of the child's body was exposed, and clearly visible were the fumes of napalm rising from the child's little red and blistered body, with a faint white glimmer of the child's small white teeth in a sea of red blistered skin. Such a sad thing to look at. I wasn't used to having wet eyes, but I think tears are the words the heart can't express, and these sorts of things tend to haunt you for a long time.'

Max was going to have to learn not to let his feelings come from the heart.

'There's no way you can help by sharing the sorrow with an unknown grieving family, and on the other side of the coin, there's no bloody happiness to share in a place like this. Nothing could be done for the child except wash and bathe the skin, which was done in the operating theatre. The child was then placed in a cot and left to lie in pain under some sedation for the last two hours of its life. Now you tell me, Brian, we are in a war zone in a country that's full of death and destruction. Why didn't they quietly give the baby an injection in theatre to end the suffering? They knew the baby had only a matter of hours to live.'

Brian said, 'But what about the Hippocratic oath to maintain life that doctors have to swear to?'

'Don't give me that bullshit. Under the circumstance faced with here, that's just a scapegoat term for no common sense and a lack of humanity. And don't stress yourself out about the Geneva Convention, either; they are shooting down our dust-off helicopters with wounded soldiers on board with our medics. There will come a time in everyone's life that you will do something you wouldn't normally do, but you do it because it was the right thing to do at the time. Putting that baby to sleep was the right thing to do, there and then.

'Whether people realise it or not, at the end of life's journey, there will be things you did that you shouldn't have, and things you didn't do you should have, and that, my friend Brian, is life. As far as this war is concerned, killing a few mosquitoes won't fix anything. You need to drain the swamp, and that's not going to happen. Let me put it another way. We are only treating the symptoms of this war; the actual disease will just roll on. We're just the puppets in their bloody Punch and Judy show, and when this is all over, this country will go back to what it considers its own normality without our bloody interference. This will just have been a sheer waste of young lives. I want to go home and forget any of this happened. I wonder, though, if anyone ever forgets the things they had to do or what they've seen, in a continued environment of some poor bugger's misery. I think, when all of this is over, the secret will be to learn how to live with it, and to keep the good memories up front.'

*

A bunch of letters from some schoolkids in Melbourne had been sent to the hospital and were handed out to the hospital staff to read and answer. Max took one.

> Dear medical person,
> My name is Sandra Benson and I am in Grade 5 at
> the Moreland State School. My mum said there are
> no gum trees where you are, so I'm sending you some
> gum leaves. I hope you like them. The leaves are

falling in Melbourne. The green leaves are now red, orange and yellow and everything looks lovely. I don't know if the leaves are changing colour where you are. I am sorry you are in a bad place and I hope you come home soon.

This letter touched Max's heart and would become one of his nicest memories. Max answered the letter.

Dear Sandra,

Thank you for your nice letter and the gift of the gum leaves of which I will treasure. Yes, autumn in Melbourne is a lovely time and the gift of the leaves you sent me is testimony to the beauty that exists in all things, big and small, Mother Nature's magic. It won't be autumn here until September, but it won't be as beautiful as Melbourne. And your childhood will also be the most beautiful and colourful season in your life; don't waste it. Yes, we are in a bad place, Sandra, but we are doing good things for good people, so we must all keep thinking of happier times, and you should look for the good things in life, wherever you can find them. Thank you again for your nice letter. It made me smile and will make my time here a little more bearable. I hope you have a million lovely dreams that all come true on your journey through life. I will keep your letter with me until I come home. *Sergeant Max Thornton, 1ˢᵗ Australian Field Hospital, Vung Tau Vietnam, 17 March 1971.*

*

On one of Max's stints as duty Sergeant, he was sitting in the duty room when a voice behind him said, 'Get up.' Max turned to see a soldier pointing his rifle at him.

The soldier said, 'I want the regimental Sergeant Major.'

Max said, 'Well, I'm only the bloody Sergeant, but I will find him for you.'

Max rang the Sergeants Mess on the field phone and said to the RSM, 'Someone wants to see you right now, and I mean right now. You got that?'

You wouldn't normally speak to the RSM like that, so Max hoped he got the message that something was wrong. Max added, 'Be careful, it's dark down here.'

Five minutes later, two MPs arrived and took the dude into custody. The RSM had been smart enough to get the message.

The HMAS *Jeparit* was due to dock with the next day with supplies. In June 1966, the Australian National Line cargo vessel MV *Jeparit* sailed on her first voyage to Vietnam. The vessel had been chartered by the Department of Shipping and Transport to carry supplies to the Australian forces engaged in the Vietnam war. However, after five voyages, some merchant seamen refused to man the vessel. To overcome this difficulty, crew members who were prepared to continue to serve in the *Jeparit* were supplemented by a Royal Australian Navy detachment. The ship was eventually commissioned, and this would be its fourteenth trip in RAN service.

The bosun of the *Jeparit* turned up at the hospital for an injection for his International Health Certificate. Max convinced him to stay the night at the Sergeants Mess, as the bosun would not be involved in the unloading of the ship and the Military Police would be doing the security. The bosun is like the regimental Sergeant Major of the ship, so Max asked him how much steak he could get.

He replied, 'Bring on board three cartons of beer and I'll find three cartons of steak to swap.'

Max had finally learnt how to cover his arse, so he told the Commanding Officer where he and two others were going and why. Up the gangway they went, carrying the booze only to be met by a Lieutenant from the Military Police who ordered them off the ship. He was obnoxious and had that small man syndrome. He wouldn't listen to their explanation, so off they went. They were waiting on the dock when the bosun, dressed in civilian clothes, arrived from town. Max explained what had happened. He said, 'Wait here'. He boarded the ship and came back out in full navy uniform, stood on the deck and called out, 'Come aboard.' They grabbed the booze and headed up.

Max was a little bit behind the rest of them, and when he got on the deck, they had disappeared. Then the MP Lieutenant appeared.

'I told you to get off the ship,' he said.

'Bugger me,' said Max as he went back down.

He had no sooner got on the dock when the bosun reappeared on deck and called out, 'What are you doing down there? For Christ's sake, get up here.'

Max called back, 'Well, you stay there or I'll get the arse again.'

A week or so later Max and his two cohorts were fronted to the area commander over the incident. The MP Lieutenant had obviously had the shits, because on board the ship the bosun outranked him, so he had written a formal report. Max's Commanding Officer was aware of their visit to the ship and the details of the incident, so they had his support. *'You're learning,'* Max said to himself.

Some months later, the Lieutenant turned up at the hospital. He was going home and needed his medical documentation which included his International Health Certificate that listed his current inoculations for overseas travel. *Well, well,* thought Max, *payback time!*

'We don't have your IHC,' said Max.

'What does that mean?' the Lieutenant asked.

'It means, Sir, that you'll be getting all of your inoculations again and be issued a new IHC. You do remember me, don't you, Sir?'

He knew very well why he was getting the injections, and there wasn't a bloody thing he could do about it.

Max told Brian the story. 'We did it with the bluntest needle we could find.'

Brian said, 'You know, Max, he wasn't liked much at the MP base either.'

'He hasn't learnt yet,' said Max, 'that it's not over till the fat lady sings.'

*

Max's unit received a signal (the same as telegram) to say that a farmer had found Max's struggle bag in a ditch – the one Max said hadn't fallen out of the truck as he was leaving Australia. The Army sent an officer to Max's house with his personal belongings.

He said, 'Hello, Mrs Thornton. I have brought your husband's belongings.'

In shock, trembling and on the verge of collapse, Valda managed to whisper, 'No one told me he had died.'

'Oh, no,' he said and told her about the bag.

What a mental moron! Sometimes Max had to remind himself it was the Queen's commission he was saluting, not the idiot wearing it.

*

Max had heard the old saying many times: 'The trouble with common sense is that it's not all that common'. This was the case with the dust-off radio equipment. It was an AN/PRC-77 set, not designed for long-distance communication. On one of Max's stays with the Americans, he scammed a powerful radio system from their signal's personnel in exchange for a quantity of Australian beer. They flew down with the equipment and installed it no problems, and they could now talk to the field ambulance at Nui Dat, which hadn't been possible with the toy radio they'd had. They could also talk to a dust-off chopper further out, giving them more time to prepare for the wounded they had on board.

The quartermaster said, 'Shit, Max, how do I take this on charge with our equipment?'

Max thought, *Jesus, these people have been brainwashed about paperwork. We're still in this war zone, it wasn't brought here by us, it's not on the books and the Americans would have left it behind like they have done in the past with equipment they don't want, and they obviously didn't want this radio because it was gifted to the hospital.*

What the quartermaster should have been doing, if he wanted to play with paperwork, was put in a request for a radio that was fit for bloody purpose. Max said this radio would have arrived years ago, and they must have realised it was not up to speed and that the scope of the communication required here deserved better. They should have done something back then instead of worrying about this bullshit now.

Along with procuring the radio, Max also managed to obtain a four-door fridge for the Sergeants Mess and enough timber to enclose the back deck, which he and a Warrant Officer called Alan built. All of this material was given to Max by the Americans, war zone style – no paperwork required, all done on the Sergeants' old boy network. Max bet the hospital wrote off equipment and deemed it expendable so they could leave it behind when they went. There's a saying in the Army – CDF, common dog fuck – and in some cases, it was absent. Some of these people would never learn, as long as their arse pointed to the ground, how to operate and get things done in a war zone and as such, sometimes the fastest and best way was not the paperwork way. Put it another way, you don't always have to dot the i's and cross the t's when in a war zone, and this sort of trading had been going on since World War I.

*

One evening, Max's mate, Brian, the MP Sergeant, came for him.

'Put your greens uniform on, Max. I'm taking you with me on my rounds of the bars in town.'

Unless you were an MP, you were not permitted to wear uniforms in town, unlike the Americans who did. Max thought that the fact that the MPs had invited him on their patrols, and in uniform, meant he'd be safe from any disciplinary action, although he suspected it was unofficial. Brian's idea was to take Max to several bars where they would be under the impression he was also an MP, and given the fact that the MPs could close the bars for not complying with certain rules, any future visits to these bars in civilian clothes would see him offered certain privileges and drinks at no cost. Anyone who visited these bars with Max from then on could never work out why Max was getting all the special treatment.

'What's going on, Max?' they would say.

Max would simply say, 'I'm just one of life's hidden treasures, and maybe they know what side their bread's buttered on.'

His invisible MP image remained intact.

There were certain bars that were monitored by the military health system where the bar girls were required to be checked for venereal disease. They were issued with a card that had to be punched once a month with the date they were checked. Soldiers who wished to partake in the ladies' pleasures could check the card to see how current their last check was. If the bar girls test was positive, her card was taken from her until her test was negative. The pathology Major, who was a female, would go to the Vin Loy Vietnamese Clinic to conduct the tests, but she had to have an escort. On some occasions, Max would drive her there.

On the way, the Major said to Max, 'I hope you don't use these girls, Sergeant Thornton.'

'No, Ma'am,' said Max.

When they got there, there was a long line of bar girls down the passageway, so they had to walk down the line passing them. The Vietnamese word for love or sexual attraction is *mình anh*. As they walked past these girls, some of them recognised him from the bars. They were calling out, '*Mình anh, mình anh*', and touching Max. The Major just looked at him and raised her eyebrows.

Shit, Max thought, *how bloody embarrassing!*

Chapter 14

In PNG

Max's 'favourite' Major had finished his time in Vietnam and was leaving. On his return to Australia, he would play a significant role within the posting and promotion section. Max knew what that meant for him, and he reckoned it would be all bad. However, he would watch, wait and see what transpired.

In an interview with Major Malice, Max was asked where he would like to be posted. Max thought, *Well, it doesn't really matter what I say; I won't be going there.* So, Max asked for a Queensland posting and, sure enough, he was posted back to Albert Park Barracks in Melbourne. Another case of Malice making sure he had a shit posting. At least he'd be back in Melbourne, with friends and family.

The flight home from Vietnam was enjoyable on Qantas. With free booze all the way, it was called the Champagne Flight and arrived in Sydney at 1 am. Flights to various other states were not till the next day, and the soldiers were not permitted to stay overnight in the airport. Some of them with Max got a taxi and the driver took them to a friend's motel.

The owner opened the door in his pyjamas, and when he saw who they were, said, 'Come in, boys. You're more than welcome'. He opened the bar and gave them rooms if they wanted them, all at no charge.

That was more than Max could say about the public during the welcome home march when abuse eggs and rotten tomatoes were thrown at them. *Bloody university students and long-haired louts, all of them oxygen thieves with the brains of a beanbag. Tomorrow's leaders!* Max thought. It was lucky the soldiers were disciplined and didn't break ranks; otherwise, they would have beaten the shit out of them, but somewhere in the objectors' journey of life, they would learn their mouths would be responsible for their broken noses.

The RSL was no better. The older veterans had not come to terms with the fact that Vietnam veterans were in fact returned soldiers and they were treated with contempt. They were the new kids on the block, invading their private little den, and they didn't like it. They were told, 'You can't come in', or they let them in under sufferance. My, my, how things have changed – they now need them there and the general public to keep their bloody clubs afloat.

'It was too late for me,' said Max, 'I'll just pay my respects on Anzac Day. The RSL to me is just another club among the many where you go out to eat.'

Unfortunately for Max, bad things that had happened to him were carved in his memory. Anything leaving a bad taste seemed to stay forever, and he could add the Malice prick to that list, along with the RSL.

On return to Australia, they landed at Melbourne's new airport at Tullamarine. Soldiers were getting off the plane and kissing the ground, family and friends were waving and smiling, some were in tears. Valda had obviously told the kids to run to their father. Marty came running towards him with Anne sheepishly following.

She looked up at him and said, 'Mummy said you're my daddy. Are you my daddy?'

Max said, 'Yes, I am, sweetheart', and picked her up.

She soon smiled, and he gave them both a kiss, along with Valda. Of course, he had never forgotten the fact that she wouldn't stay at a motel when he was on R&R, and that had stayed in his mind the entire time he was away.

When they got home, everyone was there, with much shaking of hands, hugs and kisses and the usual mothers' tears. There were presents to open for Valda and the kids that Max had brought back, along with a reel-to-reel tape of Fred's favourite music, none other than Bing Crosby. Nitro hadn't lost the ability to fart, Joey was just as slim as he was before and Scrooge had a burglar alarm in his wallet. Brewster was as talkative as ever, Gus needed directions to get home and Harry was still limping.

Max said, 'I see nothing has changed.'

The next two weeks were spent entirely with Valda and the kids, with a lot of personal and social catching up to do. Max made sure the two weeks off were not wasted. The FE Holden wagon was getting past its prime, so he bought an FB station wagon almost the same colour as a sort of coming home present. It even felt good to mow the bloody lawn and do the edges. Max was looking forward to some normal life with his family.

Max was going back to where he started as a Private at Albert Park Barracks. He was now the section Sergeant, and a new Warrant Officer and Captain had been posted there, but most of the civilian staff were the same. Max knew them all and they knew what to expect from him, so the transition was easy.

As time went on, Max found that all was not what it appeared to be where some of the public servants were concerned. On one occasion, a male member of his staff was caught by gate security staff with his bag full of soldiers' medical documents that he couldn't be bothered filing into the soldiers' medical files. These documents would be pertinent to any claim the soldiers might make regarding an injury or incident during their service. You would think his employment would be terminated, but he was simply transferred to another department within the barracks.

The department buildings within the barracks were labelled A to H, so when he rang another department to speak to someone on a military matter, it seemed reasonable when told the person he wanted was currently in G Block, only to find out some time later that the G Block being referred to was in fact the bloody George Hotel in St Kilda, where they only came back from lunch to sign off at the end of the day. These people were processing soldiers' pay increases, promotion authority, transfer applications and posting details, and those soldiers in outlying units were waiting for notification of approval for these issues. Max knew now why sometimes these things took a long time to reach the soldier's unit.

'Mind you,' Max said, 'they weren't all like that, so we shouldn't shoot all the dogs because some have fleas.'

Another one of Max's male staff, it was discovered, kept a flask of whisky in the toilet flush tank. Disciplinary action was controlled by the public service, which left a lot to be desired, Max thought. He did, however, enjoy his time in the

Sergeants Mess where the president of the Mess was a medical corps Warrant Officer Class 1, Alan, whom Max had served with in Vietnam. He and Max had hung up the vampire bat that Max had made in Vietnam.

Max rang the barracks barber one day for a haircut. The barber said, 'No worries. The Chinaman at the dentist', and promptly hung up.

He rang the bloke back and said, 'What's that mean?'

'See you at 2.30 – tooth hurty', and hung up again.

Max thought, *Shit, I've got to get out of here. All work and no play makes Jack a dull boy.*

In this case, it was Max, and as a result, Valda got pregnant, the baby being due in the last week of November.

Max played cricket with the medical corps cricket team. Their caps were green and gold with the insignia MCC. Every Wednesday afternoon, they played against other unit teams from the RAAF and the Navy. Wednesday afternoon was sports afternoon, the official time out for the entire Australian Army. Max was no Donald Bradman but could hold his place in the team.

The baby and Christmas weren't far away. Martin was six years old and Anne was four. Managing financially was getting harder, and at one stage to be able to meet a financial deadline, they had to pawn Valda's engagement ring and retrieve it the next payday. In an attempt to alleviate this situation, Max took on extra work. He would leave the barracks at 4 pm, strap a vacuum cleaner on his back and clean six classrooms at a Catholic girls school every night, go home for tea and then go to a factory that dyed big rolls of material in different colours in a big pressure cylinder. He worked there from 7 pm till 11 pm, arriving home around midnight. The whole process started again the next day. The extra money certainly helped to give the children what other kids had, like school excursions, swimming lessons and other activities that all cost money.

Then out of the blue, Max was offered a posting to Papua New Guinea (PNG). It was a family posting so they would all be going. *Don't tell me I'm getting a decent posting!* Max thought. He said he would accept the posting if a promotion was involved. When you're posted overseas, you are automatically out of the promotion chain for that duration, as they're not going to bring you all the way back, family included, to fill a promotion posting. Max was told the position was for a staff Sergeant, so Max accepted it.

He spent a period of time learning pidgin English at the RAAF Language School at Laverton. Sergeant Harry, whom he had met at Healesville while on course, was also there, being posted to PNG as a Warrant Officer. Harry and Max would become lifelong friends and spend many postings together. His posting order from New Guinea was in English and pidgin English and read like this: 'bilong dispela yia i girap long 29/12/72. i go inap long 27/1/76.' Translated into English, this means 'Max is going to PNG on 29 December 1972 until 27 January 1976.'

His little girl was born on 28 November and was called Arlene. There would now be five of them going to PNG. However, it wasn't that easy.

'How come I'm not surprised?' Max said to Valda, 'I have to go unaccompanied for a few months until the house is available and then I fly back for our removal, which includes the car. Then we all go to PNG together.'

The night before Max left for New Guinea, Arlene, still

a little baby, cried all night so Max had to put her in the car in the bassinet and drive her around the streets until she fell asleep, so not much rest for him either prior to departure.

Max arrived in PNG and was met by the staff Sergeant he was replacing. He was transferring to the education corps and Max wondered why. Two weeks passed, and Max enquired about his promotion. PNG Headquarters Administration rang Canberra and were told the position had been downgraded to Sergeant. Suddenly, Max knew why the staff Sergeant he was replacing transferred out of the position. Max spoke to the Captain Medical Officer.

'Those bastards knew this position was being downgraded, they would have been notified to adjust their establishment documents, and they knew when I got here that I wouldn't be promoted. Worse still, I will be out of the promotion chain for the next three bloody years! I bet that bastard Malice is involved somewhere in this.'

Max couldn't believe someone could blatantly do this to one of their own senior non-commissioned officers. Someone in Canberra (colloquially referred as Bullshit Castle) would have known about this and he knew who that would've been. Max decided he wasn't going to let this get him down and was even more determined to see his career through, whatever that meant.

*

The regimental aid post for soldiers (the same as a civilian medical clinic) and family aid post (FAP) for soldiers' families were operated by the Captain Medical Officer and a Sergeant medic; the FAP had a civilian nursing sister. Both these departments used the same doctor and were in the same building, the left hand-side for soldiers and right-hand side for their families. The doctor would go to one or the other as required according to the medic or nurse's initial assessment.

On one particular occasion, neither the nurse nor the doctor was at the clinic by lunchtime. It was discovered that the doctor had gone AWOL (absent without leave) and the civilian nursing sister had gone with him on the midnight plane to Australia. Well, you reckon that didn't put the cat among the pigeons! The nurse was married to the Australian police commissioner who was in PNG overseeing the Australian and PNG police force. What a bloody drama this unfolded! The system would no doubt go after the young doctor because he would owe the Army time for his medical training, and no doubt they would have notified the Medical Practitioners Board as well. Who knew what the police commissioner would do.

The doctor must have had his trail motorbike in for repairs when he shot through, because after Max returned to Australia, he received a letter from his replacement asking for approval to pay the repair expenses and get the bike. He must have been told the bike was Max's. Max replied and explained the circumstances and that the doctor owner would never be coming back, and maybe if he took Max's letter with a statutory declaration to the military and civilian police, that might suffice to allow him to get the bike. Otherwise, it would probably be sold by the repair shop after a suitable time elapsed. It wasn't Max's bike so he couldn't give him the authority; anyway, that's all Max could think of.

Quite a lot of the staff in Max's section had trail motorbikes. On weekends, they would go trail riding in the hills amongst the old war bunkers and pits, then have a picnic on the beach with their families. The Colonel in charge of the section didn't favour the activity, as he didn't want half his staff off work with broken limbs. However, curiosity eventually got the better of him and he and his wife came on the picnic. During lunch, the trailbikes were lined up on the beach. The Colonel couldn't help himself and asked if he could take one for a ride, against his wife's better judgement, so off he went. Half an hour went by and there was no sign of him. Everyone was worried. They knew where he had gone was quite challenging, particularly for someone who hadn't ridden a trailbike, so they decided to go and look for him. Max was riding through the war rubble and rocks, looking left and right, when he saw an arm waving from down in a culvert. Max went to check. The Colonel was lying against a rock with a lacerated leg and a swollen ankle. Max said he was sorry he was laughing, but he couldn't help it as he remembered the Colonel's concern about injuries to his staff.

Back at the unit during the next week everyone had to try and keep a straight face when they went into his office and saw him sitting there with his foot up on a cushion and a walking stick against his chair.

*

Max happened to be in the quartermaster's store one day when they bought the new Pacific Island recruits in for clothing. They were issued only sandals until the rank of Sergeant, then they would get shoes and socks. One of the recruits' feet were so big they stood his feet on a large piece of paper and drew round his feet to get his sandals specifically made. Think about how big a pelican's feet are – well, now you get the idea.

Warrant Officer Harry had been allocated his house, but his family wouldn't be arriving until the school term was over for the children. Max moved out of the Sergeants Mess and moved in with Harry until his family arrived. Harry's houseboy's name was Jonnas. He had little experience as a houseboy, so he needed to be introduced to household items that he had never seen before.

Harry had one of those sausage-shaped old vacuum cleaners. He said to Jonnas, 'You put the hose on this end, and it sucks. If you put the hose on the other end, it blows. So, when you're cleaning the floor, you put the hose on the end that sucks.'

'We left the house and went to work,' said Max. 'When we came home, the houseboy was cleaning the floor with the hose on the blowing end of the vacuum cleaner.'

Harry said, 'No, no, Jonnas, you have to put it on the suck end.'

The houseboy told Harry he had washed the floor. Now he was drying it.

Max said to Harry, 'He's got you there, mate.'

Harry's house was at Taurama Barracks and Max had been allocated a house at Murray Barracks about twenty kilometres away, both in Port Moresby. Max went back for the family. He had given the heads-up to a Sergeant who was looking for a house to rent in Melbourne. Valda's parents agreed to renting the house to him and his family when Max and Valda moved out. Their furniture and car were uplifted and on the way to PNG. Max and family stayed the night with Max's cousin, Keith, and his wife and they drove them to the airport the next morning. Max told Valda that they would be staying in a hotel for a couple of days until their furniture arrived.

Their house was high up on concrete stumps, high enough for a carport underneath. It had polished wooden floors, sliding aluminium windows all round and large ceiling fans in each room. The houseboy's hut was in the back yard away from the house; it was the size of a garden shed with a bed and small stove, very primitive but more than he would have, otherwise. Valda would often buy him food to cook from the marketplace and they paid him the amount that was required, which Max thought was a mere pittance, but once again, more than he was used to.

'We had a barbecue not long after we moved in,' said Max. 'Fair dinkum, some of the houseboys were as useless as the pope's testicles!'

Max spoke to him in pidgin, 'Yu mekum wanem.' (What are you doing?)

The houseboy said, 'Mi wasim plet.' (I'm washing the plates.)

Max told him, 'No ken wasim ol plet pepa.' (You can't wash paper plates.)

A lot of families in the barracks had a dog for extra security. You couldn't take the dog back to Australia, so the dogs usually changed hands with the replacement family, or a family with no dog would take them.

'When we arrived,' Max said, 'we had no dog, but one of the doctors was leaving and we agreed to have their dog, a German Shepherd.'

The family went and picked up the dog and put him in the car. He was a nice-looking dog. When they got home, they opened the car, the dog jumped out and that was the last they saw of him. Max told the kids he would have gone back to his old house. They looked everywhere for a couple of days but couldn't find him. A week later, the opportunity to have a black labrador came up, so they took this dog and called him Buka, as the Buka tribe have the darkest skin of the Papuans. They all became very attached to the dog in the three years that followed, and when it was time to leave the dog behind, the kids were heartbroken.

'We love this dog, Dad.'

'You probably won't understand this, but you will when you're older: it's better to have loved and lost than never loved at all. Buka will be well cared for with the doctor and his family who had just arrived. When we get back to Australia, we can get another black lab puppy.'

'Can we call the new dog Buka?'

Max knew that you don't usually call a new dog the same name as the last one because it could have a different temperament and personality, but most lab's temperaments were pretty much the same and the kids were attached to the name.

He said, 'Yes, okay, we will.'

Max was very careful not to make a promise he might not be able to keep down the line, due to circumstances beyond his control. Small children don't understand the part circumstances play when a promise isn't filled.

In PNG, wives were advised to be careful how they dressed, and not to walk around the house scantily clothed. *Some wives needed to find out how the air was getting into their heads*, Max thought. Their only purpose in life would be as an organ donor, as they took no notice of what was being told to them, walking around with hardly anything on, giving the uneducated houseboy the wrong idea, which led to all sorts of problems, as you could imagine. Because it was so hot, some of the wives would walk around the local marketplace with tiny shorts and a halter top with their boobs hanging out. Those who were sensible wore a moo moo, a long, loose-fitting dress.

In the time that they were there, it was reasonably safe. PNG was still under the Australian government as it hadn't yet received its independence. The police commissioner was from Australia and Australian police oversaw the Pacific Island police, but there were still rules to follow. It wasn't one hundred per cent safe, and Port Moresby was full of bad locals, with orange stains everywhere from spitting betelnut saliva on walls and footpaths. When in town, the idea was you left your car unlocked and windows down so they could climb in, find nothing and leave, instead of them smashing the window to find nothing. Women were advised when driving alone to keep car doors locked, but some people just didn't listen.

'You have to realise, some of the Papuan people had not been long away from their remote villages,' Max said. 'I'll give you an example. When I ordered band aids from the supply store, why did I get razor blades?'

The supply Sergeant took Max to the shed and showed him the bins. 'You see, Max,' he said, 'bin number six (for band aids) is empty, but bin number 7 isn't, so their assumption would be, what's in bin number seven must be nearly the same as what was in bin number six, so that's why they gave you, in this case, razor blades.'

Max and his mate were given a stolen burnt motorbike from the police. Max said, 'We had parts sent from Melbourne and rebuilt the bike, a 250cc Suzuki which we raced motorcross at the Granville Speedway on Saturday nights.' Young Martin had a PeeWee motorcycle he raced with other kids during the interval. They never won anything, and Max had his foot run over twice.

They made a trailer for the motorcycle and took it to get registered. It was pouring rain, and the PNG inspectors were sheltering under the building. Max and his mate pulled up on the inspection pad and one of the inspectors came over and checked the trailer lights.

He said, 'Ol lait bilong trela, bilong you i no wok.' ('The lights on your trailer don't work.')

Max said, 'Bullshit. You get in here and I'll look.'

They weren't working, but Max said, 'Ol i wok nau.' (They work now.)

The bloke said, 'Okay, im i good pela tru (That's really good),' and they registered the trailer.

Even with a fair understanding of the language, sometimes it was difficult. Max was trying to contact Warrant Officer Harry on the phone.

A voice answered, 'Hulo.'

Max said, 'Hoosat he stop.' (Who are you?)

'Mi tea boy tasol.' (I'm the tea boy, that's all.)

Max said, 'Yu laik toktok wantaim Warrant Officer Harry.' (I want to talk to Warrant Officer Harry now.)

The tea boy said, 'Emi no stap, emi no save, emi stap long hup.' ('He's here somewhere but I don't know where.')

Once a year, the medical unit would be taken by a military landing barge, called a LHD or LLC, and dropped in by helicopter into remote areas for glaucoma testing, to put in water wells and explain the benefits of washing and excreting downstream from where they took their water. The Commanding Officer was a British exchange officer. On one occasion, they had set up camp some five hundred metres from the local village. They also had some Pacific Island soldiers with them to help with the local language when communicating with the villagers. Max enjoyed these trips. At night, he would gather the children around a fire and tell them the stories in pidgin of Red Riding Hood (Lik Lik Red Pela Hat) and the Three Little Pigs (Tripela Lik Lik Pik). Max said he loved to watch the looks on their faces and their expressions as the stories progressed. He could see their brown eyes staring at him in the flickering of the fire as he began the story.

'Bipo tru, tripela lik lik pik i stop long bus. Ol i no got haws, na i gat wanpela waildok tu. Em i stap long dispela bus.' ('Once upon a time, three little pigs lived in the bush. They had no house and a wild dog lived in the same bush as them'), and to the delight of the children, Max finished the story.

On one particular morning, the British exchange officer told Max he could hear pigs making noises in the bush behind his tent at night. Max made some discreet enquires and discovered that one of the Pacific Island soldiers, who was from this village, was humping one of the girls from the village and was doing it in the vicinity of the officer's tent; hence, the grunting noise that was heard. He was Morris, the PNG transport Sergeant.

Max said to him, 'Mi bin stap Olsen you long baksait bilong haus sel.' (Were you here last night with a meri?)

He said, 'Yes'.

'Yu mekim wanem?' (What were you doing?)

'Mi slip wantaim wanpela meri.' (I was humping my girlfriend.)

'Well, Morris, I suggest you find somewhere else to hump her.'

These island and bush trips among the coconut trees were always an eye-opener for Max to see what little they required to survive on. On one occasion, he watched four small native boys walking along the water's edge. The smallest one was carrying half a coconut shell full of hot embers; the others had a piece of sharpened fencing wire and a piece of bicycle rubber tubing. The boy with the coconut shell started a fire on the beach while the others were in the water. They came out with a handful of small fish, cooked them and were on their way, all in the space of thirty minutes. *See now, there is a good example of parenting*, Max thought. *It's not what you do for your child, it is what you teach them to do for themselves.*

At the end of the field trip, Max gave some surplus supplies like band aids, bandages and throwaway items such as plastic tweezers to the Catholic mission. The nuns were most appreciative and wrote a letter of thanks to the area commander, telling him what a good boy Max was. The commander said as good an act as it was, it was not permitted for legal reasons. So Max was once again in the shit. Max's dick was getting sore from standing on it.

Max was asked if he wanted to deliver some drugs to Manus Island where the Australian Naval Base was, but he was told not to go on a Friday if he wanted to come back that day. The fishing was so good that the Navy took you out on their work boat, the *Caribou*, which always 'broke down' on Friday on the island but magically fixed itself on Monday, so he should plan for a weekend stay, which Max said was not hard to take. It was seafood heaven, with an abundance of lobsters, bugs, mussels and oysters to pig out on. Unfortunately, he only got to go once, and he couldn't come up with a good enough reason for a second trip.

The following year, as part of a team, Max went on a field survey which was being done on Manam Island, locally known as Manam Motu, where a live volcano was bubbling away. The villagers had their outrigger canoes on standby in case the volcano erupted. Mother Nature would give them their early warning when all the birds began to fly back to the mainland in large flocks. There was a vulcanologist on the island and the team had his okay to head up to the crater. From the moment they started to climb, the drums started to beat, and they went nonstop until they left the island. They would be blamed for making the gods angry if the volcano became active. They did what they needed to do to help the local villagers and then left.

After completing twelve months in PNG, Max and his family were eligible for free travel back to Australia, with two weeks' leave. Max and Valda decided to take the kids to the Gold Coast where there was an Army holiday centre called Mallaraba. By the time they got through Customs in Brisbane with three kids, they had missed the bus to the Gold Coast, and it was already 6 pm. A nice taxi driver took them there at a very reasonable price. They were all buggered when they got there and decided they would rent a car the next day.

They rented a yellow VW Beetle from a place called Rent A Bomb, and that's exactly what it was, but it turned out to give them a lot of laughs. They took the kids to all the fun parks, the bird sanctuary and to feed the dolphins, and the kids thought the platypuses were fantastic. Max said he thought they were probably a duck designed by the same committee that was responsible for the poor bloody camel. The VW really was a bomb; they had to push it twice. In the end, they were given one that was slightly better.

The weather was good enough to spend lots of time with the kids at the beach. Two weeks went by too quickly and soon they were on their way back to PNG. Valda was expecting another baby, due sometime in April. 'That's what happens when there's no television,' Max said. After lengthy discussions, he had a vasectomy at the military hospital at Taurama Barracks. He regretted riding his motorcycle home the same day as the surgery, particularly when he rode it up the gutter.

Martin and Anne went to the Murray Barracks Primary School where there were about thirty other children of military parents. At one of the parent-teacher nights, Valda asked why Martin never got any homework.

'He gets homework all the time, Mrs Thornton, but he never brings it back.'

Martin had definitely told them he never got any.

His sister Anne said, 'He hides it under the outside stairs,' and sure enough, it was all there. Little bugger.

Valda went into hospital for the birth of their fourth child, born on 4 April 1974, a dual citizen child whom they called John.

If you wanted to buy a car in PNG, you had to have brought your own car with you. You then had to have owned the new car you bought for at least twelve months to be entitled to have it shipped home. Max had been keeping his eye on the market for some time. An XW Ford Falcon station wagon almost new, another blue and white car, was for private sale. The owners were going overseas and couldn't take it with them. Max was running out of time for ownership, so he bought the car.

If you had to be an idiot before you could mature, then these two were the perfect example. Harry and a bloke called Bugs, who worked in pathology, often visited the Sergeants Mess at Murray Barracks on their motorcycles. The road from

Taurama Barracks was a narrow gravel and dirt road with deep monsoon drains either side. These two idiots would get a skin full of beer, then race each other back to their mess at Taurama Barracks. Harry was about twenty metres behind Bugs when he watched him skid off into the drain. He decided to keep going and get the Army ambulance from the hospital where they both worked. Worrying about Bugs, he increased his speed and on the last bend before the barracks, Harry misjudged the corner and went over the handlebars into the monsoon drain. The driver of the car that stopped to help Bugs was now on the way to get the ambulance when he saw an arm waving from the drain. 'Jesus, that's two them now,' he said, and continued on for the ambulance.

The ambulance would be coming from the Taurama medical centre where these two idiots worked. It had six beds and a staff of ten (now eight), one doctor and two Nursing Officers. The ambulance picked up Harry and then Bugs.

'Shit! What happened to you? I can't even rely on you to go and get help,' Bugs said.

The hospital staff had no idea who would be in the ambulance when they opened the doors and found these two idiots. Bugs had a fractured fibula (the thinner bone in the lower leg) and Harry had a fractured radius (the bone in the forearm on the thumb side) and they both had minor cuts and bruises. The doctor discharged them after two days, providing they stayed at home. Harry had his arm in plaster and Bugs had a sort of boot cast.

Max couldn't believe it when the two of them came hobbling into his mess at Murray Barracks. There were bets of up to five to one that they wouldn't make it back, and they didn't. The doctor and the Nursing Officer opened the ambulance doors, and there they were, two Warrant Officers, bleeding again.

The doctor said, 'Right, you two, that's it. Lieutenant Roper, get these two into the ward. Strict bed rest and no privileges.'

Being around Warrant Officer Harry always seemed like a suicide mission. He had already been demoted twice on his way up to his current rank. Max and he were on their way past the PNG guards at the main gate one night. They had been to a function and were in uniform and had had more than their share to drink. The guards gave them a salute with their weapons. Harry wasn't happy to just go home; he had to stop and lecture the guards on the way they'd saluted.

Max called out, 'Jesus, Harry, come away.'

A car pulled up and a man in civilian clothes approached and asked what was wrong.

Harry said, 'Nothing to do with you. Now piss off.'

The mystery man in the civilian clothes said, 'Excuse me, Sergeant Major, I am Wing Commander Mackenzie.'

Max thought, *Don't do it, Harry!* but he did.

'Bullshit,' said Harry. 'You could be Father Christmas for all I know.'

The next morning, sure enough, they were called to the HQ Building. Go into that office, they were told. Harry and Max walked in, and sitting there in all his regalia was Wing Commander Mackenzie.

He said to Harry, 'Now, Sergeant Major, do I look anything like Father Christmas?'

'No, Sir,' said Harry.

Mackenzie said, 'You will be the Duty Officer for the next week, and take the little fat Sergeant with you as the duty Sergeant. You are dismissed.'

Max said, 'Bugger you, Harry, I've now got to live in for five nights as the duty Sergeant. Guilty by association, that's what this is. You're a pain in the arse sometimes. But I suppose, like I keep saying, to be old and wise, you first have to be young and stupid.'

The time had come to start arranging the trip home, but Max wouldn't make the same mistake the Colonel and his family did. They had gone to the airport at midnight on the wrong night and then had nowhere to go because their house was now empty. Mind you, the Colonel tried to blame everyone bar himself, but being able to blame someone else they say shows good management potential, apart from getting the movements staff offside.

Max had trouble trying to get the Colonel's air-conditioner back to Australia. Once the movement staff found out whose it was, the air-conditioner was going nowhere. Eventually, Max managed to get it shipped using the old boy network in the RAAF. To add insult to injury, when Max got back to Australia, this bloody Colonel took him to task because it took so long for him to get his air-conditioner home. Max remembered the old saying: a complaining tongue reveals an ungrateful heart. How true that was in this case. Bloody prima donna, he was lucky to get it at all! He had no idea how much trouble Max had gone to just to get it on a plane. It just happened that Max knew the flight Sergeant in the RAAF, so he was able to ship it outside of the Army system.

'You see,' Max said, 'just another example of when serving outside Australia, the senior non-commissioned officer system works when the military one doesn't. Otherwise, everyone would have told the Colonel and his air-conditioner to get stuffed. Another officer who hadn't learnt yet that if you piss these people off and start throwing your weight around, it doesn't matter what rank you are, it's not over till the fat lady sings.' The staff at movements were mostly Warrant Officers and Sergeants; they were the ones that did the movement details and ticketing. The officers might have their superior rank clout, but it paled into insignificance compared to the well-oiled and maintained senior non-commissioned officers system. That's why they got everything. 'Imagine,' Max said, 'with all the problems I had to get his air-conditioner onto a plane, all done as a favour for me from a friend, yet when I returned to Australia and saw him, there was no thanks, just bloody whinging about how long I took to send the air-conditioner, even after I explained the problems. Bloody ungrateful, and he did it in front of other officers which made me look bad.' Max was getting sick and tired of being blamed for things he had no control over, particularly when he went out of his way to fix someone else's bloody problem. All this surprised Max, because Max's previous opinion of this person was that he was a decent officer.

Chapter 15

Moving around

Having spent another year in PNG, when Max went to arrange his family's trip home, they were entitled to one more trip back to Australia at no cost to them. After that, the Army would still have to fly them home. Max asked the movement Sergeant to put those costs towards his family going to Manila, and then onto Singapore where Valda's parents were staying, and from there to then home to Brisbane where his car would be shipped by boat.

As far as organising the trip was concerned, the movement Sergeant had said, 'No problems, mate. Give me a couple of days to put it all together for you.'

The flights were booked along with three days' accommodation in Manila and then on to Singapore.

The kids had a wonderful time both in Manila and Singapore, with the exception of Anne getting locked out on the balcony seven floors up. Martin, with his gung-ho hero attitude, climbed from another balcony onto the one Anne was stuck on to save her. They were now both locked out on the same bloody balcony, but he probably gave her some comfort of not being there by herself. They were all down at the pool and saw what was happening. They rushed up and let them in.

They took the kids to the Singapore Zoo and at the entrance, there was a monkey on a chain. John was still in a pusher and the bloody monkey jumped in on top of him. As quick as a flash, Max grabbed the monkey and threw him off. They also went to the Tiger Balm Gardens with the Buddha displays. Martin couldn't do as he was told, climbing on statues and carvings with some Indian kid, where signs specifically said, 'No climbing'.

Max had been assured by the Royal Automobile Club of PNG (RACPNG) that they would liaise with the RACQ in Brisbane to pick up the car and hold it until they arrived. It was another four weeks before the family arrived in Brisbane, where Max rang the RACQ from the motel. The bloke at the RACQ said they had been trying to reach Max for weeks to let him know they hadn't been able to pick up the car as they didn't have Max's authority. Max asked where the car was and was told it was in the government bond shed on the dock and that he would have to pay the bond and storage fees to get it, and that it was going to be quite expensive.

'Shit!' Max said, 'four kids, a mountain of luggage and no bloody car.'

The cost to get their car used up almost the rest of their holiday money, just leaving enough for fuel and two motel stops to Melbourne.

Valda's parents were back in Melbourne and in their new house. Max, Valda and the kids were absolutely buggered when they arrived, only to have Valda's mother tell them that they couldn't possibly stay there; she wasn't having four kids in a brand-new house.

Max said, 'Jesus Christ, Valda! What's wrong with this woman? They're her bloody grandchildren. She said we have to go and stay at your grandma's house.'

Max was speechless. On top of that, he would need to get a part-time job somewhere for four weeks because they had now run out of money. So much for a holiday! No one was offering to help with money, and at the end of all this, they would be driving to New South Wales where Max's next posting was. What a bloody nightmare.

Max managed to get a job with a taxi truck company delivering parcels for the four weeks which saw them through financially.

*

Max was now posted to a small unit that did bugger all except look at mosquitoes and insects under a microscope. To help with the monotony, Max and some soldiers put in a large fishpond and filled it with fish. They also built a horse float for Simpson the donkey, the medical corps' mascot. There was absolutely nothing to do except while away the two years. What a bloody waste of a Major, Lieutenant Warrant Officer and a Sergeant. They could have tacked this unit onto the field hospital, it was so small and insignificant by itself.

The Army had its own housing estate, all government housing contained within six of seven streets adjacent to the military camp at Ingleburn, NSW. These houses had been built during the war and had been renovated to some degree for current use. The kids caught the bus to school. Anne was becoming the bossy one, and where they were concerned, she was like a mother hen. Arlene and John were smaller and younger, so they were happy to go along with Anne's bossiness. Martin was in another category. When he wasn't bouncing off the trampoline over the neighbour's fence to break his arm, he was climbing out the bedroom window with Max's air gun, or off somewhere on his horse, Pepper. He was a bigger mother hen. It was generally considered that if any of the family were to have a short life, it would be Max, due to his type of employment, or Martin, due to his dumb acts.

John was still looked on as the baby. He came in one day and said he had a new friend.

Valda said, 'That's nice, John. What's his name?'

'Daydadatee.'

'What?'

'Daydadatee,' he said again.

'Where does he live?' said Max.

'He lives just up there,' pointing out the window.

It took a little while, but Max and Valda eventually worked it out. Daydadatee was John's imaginary friend.

By now, all had well and truly settled in, and the family routine had been established. One night at 10.30, there was a loud thumping noise in the kids' room where the double bunks were. Max and Valda went in to find John on the floor with a dislocated shoulder. The other kids said he had fallen off the top bunk, but Max could tell that was not what really happened. However, it was more important to get John to the hospital. By the time they got back home, it was 1 am. As far as the fall off the top bunk was concerned, the kids had obviously made some serious promises about secrecy. Max suspected that Arlene had something to do with it and he'd probably be told what really happened at the appropriate time when they were all older.

'Good morning, let the stress begin,' said Max. 'Look what John's managed to do now, Valda. He's got his head stuck through the ladder holes of the double bunk.'

It took ages to get him free, and he had red ears for two days.

Arlene's girlfriend had her own horse which she knew did not like two riders on its back, but she put Arlene on the horse with her anyway. The horse promptly bolted and threw them both off. Arlene badly damaged her temporomandibular joint in her jaw and was taken by Army ambulance to the Children's Hospital, with the rest of the family plus the dog following by car. Not to be outdone, Anne went on her bike the next week to get the sausages from the local shop; she fell off and dislocated her shoulder.

This posting was becoming a bloody nightmare. Not only was it a something-nothing career for Max, it was one disaster after another.

Max said to the family, 'This must be the part where everyone is having fun! And if I were you, Anne, I wouldn't smell any flowers today – a wasp might fly up your nose.'

The local Presbyterian church was surrounded by five acres of land, and Max rebuilt the fences for the church in return for the use of the land for their horses. Max's horse was an Arabian stallion called Jed; his breeding and show name was Jedarie. The kids' horses were also kept there. Martin was earning some money at the riding school by escorting riders who had hired horses; he did this on his own horse, Pepper. All their horses had their own individual personality, just like the kids had: Martin's, boisterous, loud and bloody devious; Anne's, bossy and 'goody two shoes'; John's, too little just yet, but whatever it was at the moment was nice; and Arlene's, forward thinking, always had some shifty move planned to stick it up Martin and never worried, particularly when she jabbed Max accidentally in the groin with a hot sparkler on Guy Fawkes night.

Max thought, *You soon realise when you have kids growing up that you can't change someone's personality. You can change their mind using logical reasoning or bribes, but you get what you get with their personality.*

*

The Army had just acquired 566,000 hectares on Yampi Sound, one hundred and thirty-five kilometres north-west of Derby, WA, which included both the Kimbolton and Oobagooma stations. A survey of the proposed training area was being conducted by the military, and Max volunteered to be part of the advance party which would only be for one week. The advance party included a road convoy of stores and supplies, non-perishables and beer, all loaded into steel containers on a Diamond Reo semitrailer in Perth, with steel containers for those supplies. On arrival in Derby, the advance party group hootchied up in a paddock of salt plains, only to find out later it was the caravan park. Four of the group would be in Derby for the week to liaise with local contractors for the supply of perishable items and fuel and to ascertain air strip availability. When, the main body arrived, they would head out to the survey area, Kimbolton and Oobagooma stations.

There were more people in Derby than usual, all there for the Boab Festival Ball and the Boab Cup. The Army had rented a brown Ford Falcon sedan for the advance party until the military vehicles arrived with the main body, and sharing it around sometimes proved testy.

There were two pubs in Derby, the Boab and the Spinifex. The Spinifex pub was holding the Calcutta for the Cup. (A Calcutta is the selling and drawing of raffle tickets, and an auction of each horse in the selected race.) Three of them went that night, leaving one behind, 'who was as full as a boot', Max said. The Calcutta was in full swing when they arrived, and the outside barbecue area was packed. The bidding eventually got to the race favourite, a grey horse called Kimberley Gunsynd. The bidding was up around $800. Just as the auctioneer was calling, 'Going once, going twice, any more bids?', their drunk friend came in, and seeing his mates, he called out, 'Hey there', and waved. The auctioneer said, 'We have another bid – it's now $820.'

'Shit,' Max said to the others with him, 'he's got no idea what he has done. He wouldn't have $8 in his wallet!'

Well, luck was on his side. Someone else made a late bid and he was off the hook. Not that he knew anything about it. To get rid of him, they threw him the car keys and told him to go sleep in the car. They had already met the police Sergeant as part of their liaison with the community. He was smiling when he said, 'Hello, Max. You need to come and collect one of your blokes. We locked him up last night for his own good, and he won't be charged.'

'What's he done?'

'He went to sleep in the wrong car last night with his false teeth on the dash. The owners didn't know who he was, so they rang us. We knew who he was, so we gave him a bed for the night. There's no further action, and we will keep it to ourselves.'

The day before they left for Yampi Sound, an old timer asked the Lieutenant where they were all off to. When the Lieutenant replied that they were going out to Yampi Sound, the old bloke said, 'I wouldn't be going out there now, sonny. It's going to rain like buggery, and you'll be stuck there for weeks.'

The Lieutenant said, 'What rubbish! The Army survey revealed it hasn't rained here this time of year for decades.'

'Well, be warned,' the old bloke said.

Out they went, the heavens opened, and down she came in buckets. The dry crust on the ground surface broke and down went the vehicles, some of them to the tops of their wheels. The Diamond Reo was hopelessly bogged, and they couldn't get to the supplies because another idiot who had escaped from the idiot bag had loaded all the steel containers with their doors inwards. They were going to be unloaded by forklift, but that was now out of the question. Max asked why that was done, to be told it was in case someone stole things from the truck when they were stopped on the road overnight. *Well*, Max thought, *they were all padlocked so why didn't they just have a roving picket at night?* They were all stranded there with the donkeys and emus for weeks on end, with helicopters having to bring in supplies. Max guessed the old bloke must have been pissing his pants laughing; it would have been very 'emu-sing' for him!

Max was better off than most of them. He had an education course to go on, so he was airlifted out and flown back on a C-130 Hercules returning to Sydney after a supply drop. Max's education had only gone to Form 3 (Year 9), the requirement for an apprenticeship, but now things had changed. Further promotions required Year 10. He would now have three months full-time schooling at the Army education centre and then sit the Year 10 exams. Max hadn't been to school for a long time, and he was never an A student. It was tough on everyone at home, with the four kids and long hours at night studying. He was lucky the education centre was close by so he could come home each night. When the exam results came in, Max thought he must have been given someone else's results. He would have been happy with seven ordinary passes, but he obtained three distinctions and four credits.

*

With many years of not being considered for promotion or a decent posting, particularly with top annual reports, many officers were starting to enquire why Max was being held back. So much so that on the next visit from the posting team from Canberra, which included Major Malice, Max was advised to make sure he had an interview.

Even though Max was not on the Major's list to be interviewed, there was an opportunity for him to request to see Major Malice. Max was finally going to have it out with him.

At the interview, Max said, 'Sir, the reason I have asked to see you ––', and that's as far as he got.

Malice jumped up in his usual abrupt manner and said, 'You haven't asked to see me, Sergeant Thornton. I've asked to see you,' which, of course, was bullshit.

Max said, 'Settle down, Sir, no need to throw the toys out of the cot.'

Well, that really pissed him off.

He said, 'Don't start quoting those smartarse one-liners to me. I don't care what a lot of senior officers in Canberra believe. I am not your stumbling block.'

It didn't take long for Max to realise Malice was definitely the elephant in the room. Like the old riddle – What can an elephant do at a children's Christmas party? Anything it likes – that's what he was doing here.

Don't do it, Max, don't miss the opportunity to keep your mouth shut. Your time will come. Although it was probably too late for that now, as Max's makeup didn't allow him to listen to bullshit, particularly from someone with no substance or scruples, and have to listen to statements he knew weren't true. Why was this man making it so hard for Max to be just who he was and what he was good at?

During Max's medical training, he had read the old treatment for drowning was to give the victim a smoke enema, blowing smoke up the rectum. It was eventually discovered it didn't work, that it was all bullshit; hence, the term 'blowing smoke up your arse', and that's what Major Malice was doing with Max right now.

Max thought, *What's the point?* A heated discussion with this bloke wasn't going to do his military career any good, and besides that, this obnoxious officer wasn't going to be in the service forever. Max would wait. When it comes right down to it, all a man's got left is his values, and if he sells them out, there's nothing left. Malice obviously knew nothing about that. He was a self-opinionated bully, and where Max was concerned, was rude and bloody obnoxious. There will be people you meet in life whom you have a dislike for, and that's quite normal. The word 'hate', however, is a whole new level, with significant undertones you would imagine used in extreme circumstances only. Max said he has never hated anyone in his entire life. However, this officer was in danger of being the first.

'As you wind your way through life,' Max said, 'you will meet people in a position of power who should have never been put in a position dealing directly with other human beings. This officer is the prime example.'

He just didn't have the balls to talk to Max about it and continued to deny any knowledge of it when challenged by other officers. Max had also seen at times where Warrant Officers had taken a dislike to a soldier for no apparent reason, and could make it difficult for their advancement, although once the soldier was posted to a different unit, that could rectify itself. Sadly, his blocker was in a much higher position in Canberra, which meant Max was trapped. So, Max would just wait.

It wasn't long after that when Malice took his retirement, and on the next posting team visit, Max was shown a document written by a very senior Army officer from Canberra. It said, 'This Sergeant is now to be appropriately considered along with his peers for promotion and postings.'

The posting team said, 'Don't ask to see this document again because it won't exist. Pack your bags, Sergeant Thornton. You're being posted to the military hospital in Brisbane on promotion to staff Sergeant.'

It felt like something that had been incredibly wrong had now been fixed.

Max said to his Commanding Officer, 'Correct me if I'm wrong, Sir, but right is right and wrong is wrong, and this has been wrong for a bloody long time.'

Max was glad he had kept his mouth shut during the interview with Malice. It was quite obvious he had been held back by this prick, and the so-called stumbling block had now been removed, albeit after nearly ten years. It's hard to understand that there must have been officers in Canberra who knew or suspected this was happening but chose to stick their heads in the sand rather than do something about it, like use their balls and show some bloody substance, square their shoulders, stiffen their jaw and get it investigated. This one man had almost destroyed any respect that Max had for commissioned officers whose promotions were mainly based on time served in rank or their medical qualifications, unlike Other Ranks promotions that were performance based and judged alongside their peers.

Max said, 'I've met some bloody idiots you wouldn't let look after your dog, which is why it's important to remind yourself you are saluting the Queen's commission and not necessarily the person wearing it. Mind you, there are idiots in all rank structures of life and there have been some dodgy senior NCOs I've meet at times. However, my respect was held intact by the many very fine officers that I've served with, real men and women with bloody substance and character. With some extra training, they might have even made good Warrant Officers, not some pissant dude that belonged behind a desk in Canberra, concerned only about his or her own promotion and career. It's how you carry yourself and have the right principles of life that matters.'

The school term had another six weeks to run before the kids finished school. Changing schools was hard enough for them, so Max and Valda ensured the change was always at the end of the year. This meant that Max would go to Brisbane unaccompanied. Before Max left for his new posting, he was asked to be one of the four Sergeants to give the royal salute to the Queen Mother for her eightieth birthday at the Opera House during a Royal Gala concert. The Queen Mother was the medical corps' Colonel-in-Chief. The Sergeants were required to go to Sydney two days early to practise the movements with rifles, chrome bayonets, white web belt and white gloves. Gordon Boyd was the compere on the night, and when they heard him say, 'On 4 August (the Queen Mother's birthday) ... ', they marched onto the stage of the Opera House in full dress uniform with medals. As the Southern Command Military Band started playing, the four Sergeants gave the royal rifle salute to the Queen Mother. She wasn't present but it was being beamed to her in England on the night. What an honour! Max quietly said to himself, *Where are you, Major Malice, you prick? I hope you're watching this performance of your favourite Sergeant.*

*

Max had by now his new rank sewn on all his uniforms and arrived at the hospital in Brisbane.

'Well, hello, Staff Sergeant Thornton,' a voice said.

Max turned to see none other than Warrant Officer Harry, who was now the regimental Sergeant Major of the unit.

'Jesus, there's no getting away from you, is there?' said Max.

Harry told Max there was only one other person living in the Sergeants Mess, a female. He said she had long flowing hair and was quite a looker.

'You know, Max,' he said, 'Mary and I are personal friends of you and your family, so behave yourself.'

A happy hour was arranged in the Mess with all members to welcome Max. That's when he was introduced to the only other person who was living in the Mess. With the RSM smiling with that smug look, Max looked her over. She looked a bit like an egg on legs, and she definitely was hiding balloons. She did, however, have nice long hair, and apart from drinking altar wine, she was a nice, caring person, but there would definitely be no need for Valda to be concerned. Max was posted to the hospital as the chief clerk. He and his staff were responsible for the unit's pay entitlements, annual leave and compassionate leave, movement of personnel by air and road, discharge procedures and documentation. In other words, he was going to be their military mum and dad.

It was getting close to Christmas, so the officers were as usual invited to the Sergeants Mess for Christmas drinks. Knowing the officers liked their canapés and little party treats, the Sergeant cook made some plates of small bite-size lamingtons. Every second one was actually sponge rubber coated over which looked identical to the real ones. Max watched as two officers standing next to each other began to each eat a lamington. The one who had the dummy lamington couldn't understand how his mate had managed to eat his before he realised his was sponge rubber. This happened a number of times around the Mess, and then they started testing them before eating. They never seemed to learn to be more on their guard when in the senior non-commissioned officers' domain.

The family had now arrived and had settled in to a nice two-storey house in Moorooka, a suburb of Brisbane, where Max was now coaching the local junior football team called the Roosters. Max's boys joined the team when they arrived. As Max had said they would, they brought a black labrador and called him Buka. They took the dog to the kennels while they were away, but when they went to get him, they were told the dog had died and the vet didn't know why. They didn't seem to have much luck keeping a dog, and once again, the kids were devastated.

Major Robin was the Pathology Officer; he was also the unit prankster, and sometimes bloody annoying. He was under the impression no one knew it was him. There were five ladies in the typing pool. On arrival one morning, they found the typewriter letters had all been tied together with cotton, and their swivel stools wound up to the maximum. His favourite trick was attaching a prawn under your desk drawer, which you found some time later by the smell. Another trick he had, that Max fell foul to, was when he used an invisible dye that went black when in contact with skin, often used by the Military Police to catch a thief. In this case, Robin convinced his Sergeant to smear it over Max's pool cue in the Mess. When Max played pool at lunchtime, sometime later his hands were black. Max threatened the Sergeant, who had been sucked in to be the Major's pigeon, with extra duties if he didn't help Max retaliate.

'This is what I want you to do,' said Max, 'Put this solution on the earpiece of the Major's phone and I will ring him several times.'

The Major had been shopping with his wife that day. She asked him what that black stuff was all over his ear. The thing about this dye was that you couldn't wash it off. It had to wear off. One up for Max.

As it turned out, RSM Harry and Staff Sergeant Thornton were a perfect pair for a unit like the hospital. They both had the right amount of temperament and management skills for a unit like this. Then it all happened without warning. A severe rash attacked Max's hands and feet, red raw and skin falling off. Max was admitted to Greenslopes Hospital where he remained for eight weeks with drips in both hands and feet. The final diagnosis was 'skin disease of unknown origin'. After four weeks with the rash not being as intense, the Army ambulance took him home for the weekend, and he rode around in a wheelchair until they took him back on the Monday.

No one in the skin ward was in danger of dying and they weren't really sick, so apart from the ailments, the ward was a jovial place, and the nursing staff were kept on their toes. Max said they were a good bunch of young, fun and caring nurses. The matron, however, was not as sympathetic to their pranks, but given her role, she wasn't a bad old stick; there were times where even she had to crack a smile. The patients were able to smoke in hospital, so some of Max's engineer mates made a wire frame attached to the roller bedside table with a hole to put a cigarette, and a tray underneath to catch the ash. Max's hands were bandaged like boxing gloves with drips in, so he couldn't hold a fag. The bloke in the bed next to Max would put the fag in the wire frame and light it for him, and all Max had to do was smoke it.

When Max eventually returned to his office, there had been a female Lieutenant posted to the unit for administrative duties. In Max's absence, she had taken it upon herself to change the complete layout and the routine. Max was ropable and he and his staff changed it all back. Who the bloody hell did she think she was? That was not the way to do things, Max told her in no uncertain terms. This office was his domain, not hers, and it was also more the way she had done it. She complained to the Commanding Officer and was told, not in so many words, to keep her busybody fingers out of Staff Sergeant Thornton's area. His department ran very smoothly, thank you. Not long after this, the Lieutenant was posted elsewhere.

When you go to hospital, they place an identification band on your wrist, and every time they come near you to give you a procedure, the staff ask you who you are and when you were born. You'd think they'd know after the first couple of times who you were, wouldn't you? Well, when Max was posted to the hospital in those days, this procedure didn't exist.

A young soldier was due to arrive at the hospital in the afternoon for a vasectomy. He rang the hospital to tell them his wife had just given birth, so could he come in the morning instead. He was told that was okay and not to have anything to eat or drink after 8 pm. What happened next was bloody amazing. There was a roofed-in walkway running between the hospital wards: surgical on the left, medical and rehabilitation on the right, with the internal layout of all the wards being identical. Most of the patients in the rehab ward were mobile and they could get around. Now this next part is sketchy – was this patient sleepwalking or was he dopey from medication? Who knows, but he went for a stroll and wandered into the surgical ward and got back into the wrong bed. Obviously, no one saw him and the nursing staff that changed at 11 pm had not been told the vasectomy dude wasn't arriving till the morning, so when they did a bed check, everything seemed normal. Every bed was occupied and the chart with the vasectomy bloke's name was hanging on the end of his bed. Everything seemed shipshape. There were no procedures for the vasectomy soldier till the morning, so they let him sleep.

Next morning was a classic. The nurse wandered down to his bed with a razor shaving mug and brush to shave him for his procedure.

She woke him up and said, 'Good morning, time to shave you for your vasectomy.'

'What? Not bloody likely!' he said and shot out of bed.

It didn't take long to sort out what happened. Whenever Max went to hospital after that, he knew what could happen without those wrist bands.

Amongst the patients in this hundred-bed hospital was an SAS paratrooper who had injuries from a parachute accident. The hospital staff brought him down to the Sergeants Mess for morning tea in a wheelchair. Looking through the mess window, the pool, tennis court and the Mess clothesline were visible. Hanging on the line were a pair of bras.

'You've gotta be kidding me,' he said, 'Who owns those? You'd get more updraft in them than my parachute.'

'Well,' Max said, 'there's only two of us living here, and they ain't mine.'

The local police would often visit the Sergeants Mess to spend time drinking with the members because the drinks were cheap, which was considered to be good for everyone's benefit. However, it was later discovered that on some visits, some of the police had placed stickers on the rear bumpers of cars to indicate the driver had recently been drinking. After this, the police were subsequently banned from entering the unit, albeit having to unfairly shoot all the dogs because some had fleas.

*

During Max's posting to the hospital, Exercise Brahman Drive commenced with some six thousand solders involved from the 1st Division of six task force units based at Enoggera

Barracks in Brisbane. The headquarters of the division were based just outside Charleville, with task force units spread as far away as Quilpie. Various command posts had been set up along the road between these two areas. The watchdog post manned by the Military Police was the first crossroads outside Charleville; all other command posts were set about a kilometre back from the road. The task force was practising quick ground recovery from an enemy over hundreds of kilometres in western Queensland, with the medical units practising casualty evacuation by road and air.

Max had been seconded to be part of the medical operations command post. This was the first time the Army had practised these manoeuvres on such a large scale since World War II. Max was on the radio listening watch in the command post and related the saga that followed.

'About sixty kilometres away towards Quilpie, a woman with four children in the car had driven under the tray of a turning semitrailer at about 9 pm. Due to the infrastructure and facilities the Army had on hand so close to this incident, they were requested to provide assistance. A helicopter was to be dispatched to the field ambulance location to pick up a doctor and a medic and fly to the accident site. However, this couldn't happen because the exercise helipad at the field ambulance wasn't cleared for night landing. The staff offered to surround the helipad with vehicle headlights because the pad was in a huge, cleared area but were told regulations would not allow that, so it was not approved. Thirty minutes had now elapsed since the call for assistance and all were still buggerising around with regulations versus common sense. Eventually someone made the decision that the chopper could land at the crossroads where the MPs were; whoever that was must have waved a magic wand as the crossroads suddenly became a cleared night landing site.

'The plan now was to drive the doctor and the medic to the crossroads and get the chopper. When they arrived, there was no chopper waiting for them, and at that moment, the civilian ambulance went rushing past. The doctor decided not to be a part of this shit storm any longer and they took off in the Army ambulance behind the civilian one. A short time later, the chopper arrived at the crossroads, advising that there was no sign of the doctor and that he was advised by the MPs that they had gone. What a bloody balls-up, and bloody embarrassing to be part of it!'

Regulations, rules and procedures are put in place for individuals' safety. However, Max had been around long enough to see how many times, after careful consideration in an emergency, common sense was sometimes the best action during an over-regulated procedure. As Max was listening to it all unfold into shit, the civilian ambulance successfully picked up the casualties and transported them to hospital with no assistance from the bureaucratic balls-up, or what the Americans would call a cluster fuck. You would think that one helipad at least would be cleared for night landing, wouldn't you?

It's the same old stuff the politicians and senior Army officials hand out: we've got this, and now we've got that, and we can do all these things ... And that's probably right, but actions speak louder than words, and you need team leaders with a brain who can organise and run the show. That's how simple it is, but do we have such a thing? Yes, we do, but not in the political world or the services in Max's eighty years of watching. It's there out in the private sector earning a fortune, so you're never going to get the best of them into government positions or the services. Oh, don't worry, those that Max is talking about now who are in charge have the brain power, but the little box in the corner of their brain called common sense is non-existent.

*

Max's father, Fred, came all the way by bus to Queensland from Melbourne to visit. Max took him to the RSL for a drink and a game of pool on the Saturday afternoon and was told by Valda dinner would be at 6 pm. Max said they rang for a taxi at 5.30, but being Saturday night, it didn't arrive till 6.30, getting them home by 7 pm. Max tried to explain to Valda what had happened, but she refused to believe him. She was so bloody obnoxious and rude, reminding him of exactly what her mother was like. Max's father was so upset he went back to Melbourne on the next bus after only a two-day visit.

On the subject of mothers, Max said his was no bloody angel either. Fred and his mate, who was called Uncle George, were good at playing the ukulele, and at parties they went to, they would always sing along around a keg of beer. Every time just before they left for a party, Fred could never find his ukulele because Alice had hidden it, which she always denied. There would be a huge argument, with Fred eventually finding it. Alice was so bloody devious, and after Fred died, the ukulele was never found. She probably burnt it.

After Alice and Fred had been to an annual ball at the factory where Alice worked, she would cut herself out of the photo of the two of them that was taken there. *Christ*, Max thought, *what was that all about?* She was such a jealous person at times and caused considerable problems over the years. Having said all that, she was overall a good mother to Max and Dorris, as probably Valda's mother was to her. Max had forgiven his mother for making him drink barley water when he was sick, and for the mustard plaster between brown paper on his bare chest when he went to bed to break up a tight chest cold. He thought his parents and Valda's mother just lacked the necessary social skills of life, and when you have to keep dealing with people that are hard work, it wears thin in time.

*

The posting cycle had again been implemented for Max. He felt he'd been up to the task and the opportunity of the role he'd been given at the hospital and welcomed the thanks from all members of the unit for the caring support that he had given them. It made the at times previous shit postings over the last ten years more bearable. His posting to the military hospital would always be a memorable one.

Chapter 16

Back to the future

Max was now posted, again on promotion, as the Warrant Officer Class 2 Company Sergeant Major to a camp hospital in NSW. It was the end of the school year, so the family travelled with him this time. Max was the sort of bloke who wanted to get from one location to the other without too many delays, so when they stopped for fuel, the family were told not to muck around too long while he was filling the car.

At the second stop, everyone jumped out and went into the shop while Valda paid for the fuel and Max was in the car waiting to go. The back seats of the XW Falcon station wagon were folded down to make a bed with a mattress, blankets and pillows. The kids often hid under the blankets, so when they told Max that young John wasn't in the car, he just said, 'Yeah, very funny', and kept driving. Again, they said, 'Dad, he really isn't here.' Max stopped the car and looked. They were not kidding – John wasn't bloody there. They had travelled about ten kilometres by this time and had to turn around and go back. There was John, waiting outside holding hands with the owner and bawling his eyes out.

'Jesus, I hate this shit,' Max said.

Then there was Anne in the back seat telling Max, 'Martin's touching me. He's doing it again; he's touching me!'

'If I have to stop the car, Martin, you'll know all about it. Leave your sister alone.'

Max looked in the mirror and he could see Martin secretly elbowing Anne where he thought no one could see.

'I can see you doing that, Martin. You really are going to get it this time.'

Whenever they had to travel, Max would wake up and say, 'Good morning, let the stress begin.'

The house they moved into was very comfortable. Next door was a Warrant Officer and his family. He was the Company Sergeant Major from the district support unit close to the hospital where Max was and held the same position.

The street had its own pet magpie called Maggie, which would visit different houses in the street. It would fly onto the window ledge of the kitchen and keep tapping with its beak until you opened the window. After being fed, you might not see it again for a week, as it would be visiting other houses. One time, Max was lying under the car and couldn't find the small spanner he had put on the ground next to him. He crawled out for a better look and saw the magpie waddling up the driveway with the spanner in its beak.

Soon after they settled in, Martin and Anne started their first jobs. Anne started as a junior at the local bank and Martin was working at the mines for a tyre and wheel bearing company, repairing and maintaining the mine trucks' large wheels.

The hospital where Max worked was a ten-bed facility, with an outpatients department, which held a daily sick parade for soldiers from surrounding units. The staff consisted of the Commanding Officer, a doctor (Major), a Nursing Officer (Captain), a Warrant Officer (Max), two Sergeants, three Corporals and ten soldiers. The unit transport was one ambulance, two Land Rovers and a Holden ute, with any ongoing specialist treatment coming from the district hospital. The barracks also contained the military infantry centre. The barracks, or camp if you like, was quite large.

Once again, Max got roped into coaching the junior footy team. Martin was now playing with the big kids, and young John was playing in the team Max coached which was what normally happened. Max was no super coach but it gave him the opportunity to instil into the kids' heads the lessons from footy that would also be needed for their own successful life's journey, like setting goals, teamwork, determination, selflessness, discipline and perseverance.

Eventually, Max was asked to play with one of the camp area cricket teams.

Jesus,' he said to himself, *'they can't be any good if they're asking me to play. They've gotta be bloody hard up.'*

As it turned out they weren't all that bad. They didn't win any finals, but they did all right.

*

Doctors aren't usually all that military minded, but that's not necessarily bad. Their role is primarily to be the doctor there, which applies also to the Commanding Officer. Of course. Max's role as the company Sergeant Major was to make sure that any military matters occurring in the unit were seen to correctly and efficiently. He was also responsible for the soldiers' welfare and discipline.

Max had gained a vast amount of administrative and military experience, but it hadn't prepared him for what happened next. The soldiers lived in huts with six beds in each hut. They told Max they were too scared to sleep there for another night. They said they saw one of the empty bed mattresses sag down as if someone had sat or lain on it, but there was no one there. They had seen this happen twice before, and they were all scared witless.

'Maybe we could sleep with you tonight, Sir.'

Max said, 'Bullshit. You won't be sleeping with me, even if you were tattooed on my arse.'

Max arranged for them to sleep somewhere else that night and gave the problem to the Army padre. What he was going to do about it, Max had no idea. Max had offered to go into the room with a can of smoke and a dead chook, wave it around and throw some feathers in the air around the room, but that didn't go over too well with the soldiers. The padre's idea, which worked, involved taking the bed away and replacing it with another bed from a different hut.

*

Max was having a drink with the bloke next door during a happy hour in the mess.

'So, how's it all going' the bloke said.

'No problems workwise, everything smooth and shipshape,' Max said, 'but things are very fragile at home. I think all the moving around and being away all the time has taken its toll, with the family circle of parents and relatives not being around for the past ten years. Bickering, arguing and yelling, we can't seem to agree on anything. It's not doing the kids any good either. Makes you not want to go home. It's not something that's just happened. It's been like this for quite a while, and we've just kept hanging in, probably more for the kids. I don't know ... Anyway, it's bloody fragile.'

Max sent some flowers home for Valda and when he got home, she had said not to buy her flowers. They were just a waste of money, and they just die anyway.

'Jesus Christ', Max said, 'she just doesn't get it. It's not the material part of the flowers that counts; it's what they're trying to say. I'll never send or buy her flowers ever again if that's what she thinks of them. Mind you, I'm not the goody two shoes that Dorris tells me I think I am. (Shit knows where she gets that from.) I'm the last person to be called good. I guess she's still got that little sister trait – poke a stick at Max and see what happens. I love my sister, but she's not getting off that easy. The one thing little girls still have when they become women is the incredible ability to keep poking us blokes with a stick. Don't get me wrong, I'm a great lover of women, particularly the balloon smugglers. I'm simply making an observation.'

Someone in the camp had a motorbike for sale. Max thought if he had that to ride to work on, then Valda could have the car. He was $200 short of the price and any money in the bank was for family emergencies. Anne said that as she was now working, she could lend Max the money, which he thought was a very nice gesture, and he would think about it. It wasn't a good practice, Max thought, to borrow money from your kids, but he did it anyway. Little did Max know that in years to come, the shoe would be on the other foot with the kids on many occasions.

On weekends, a few of the blokes would go to a place called Hole in the Wall at Mungo Brush near Tea Gardens in New South Wales and camp there on weekends. It was only about an hour's drive away and the tailor fishing there was excellent. On one of their trips, Max took Martin with them. Early on the second morning, the tailor fish came on the bite with gusto. Everyone was pulling them in one after the other, everyone that is except Martin, who was fishing next to Max with exactly the same set-up as everyone else. Martin kept coming over to Max to see if he was doing anything differently, and he was getting really pissed off. Max tried not to let him see that he was laughing. Eventually, he did start to catch some tailor and you couldn't get the smile off his face. For Max, it was a damned nice weekend with his son. Unfortunately, young John was too young to be taken, but Max knew his time would come.

Max and three of his mates brought an old small wooden caravan and took it to Mungo Brush. They dragged it in to through the sand dunes to a clearing the ranger said they could use, and it was well and truly used it on weekends for the next two years. By the time all were being posted away from New South Wales, the old van was hopelessly stuck in the sand. They contacted the ranger who came and looked at it. It was decided to set fire to it, and the frame or what was left was taken away. What they did was a good example of first getting approval and then taking care not to damage the environment, and you would usually find everyone was happy. That wouldn't happen these days, though.

*

The posting team had arrived from Canberra, minus that prick Malice who had retired, and were busy interviewing soldiers, asking where they would like to be posted. Max knew it would be more like 'this is where you're going next'. Because of Max's rank, his interview was conducted casually over drinks in the Sergeants Mess.

'How do you feel about going to the School of Army Health, Max?' said Warrant Officer Kenny.

'Bullshit,' said Max. 'I don't want to go anywhere near bloody Healesville, and besides that, it's not a suitable posting for a family with members who need to find work. Go and buy the drinks and come back with a better offer, one that doesn't include bloody Healesville.'

Kenny came back with the drinks and said, 'What if we told you the school was moving to Portsea a month after you get there? If you take the posting, we would send you to Chowder Bay in Sydney to do the Training Development Officers (TDO) course. You will be promoted to Warrant Officer Class 1 and become the senior instructor for all courses for Sergeant, Warrant Officer, Lieutenant and Captain. You will also be the school's subject master for military law.'

'That's a better offer than the first one.'

Kenny smiled.

'You're a bastard!' said Max. 'You knew the school was moving from Healesville and you knew I'd initially say no. It's a good posting and a good way to get my twenty years up, so thank you – and yes, I will go.'

Max knew the entire family would be over the moon. The family circle would be intact again with Valda, Max and the kids back with lifelong friends. Max was allocated a house in Sorrento. They had always been lucky with houses, and this was no exception. The kids all had their own rooms, they were close to the beach and five minutes from the Portsea Army Camp. The family volunteered to take a police training dog for two years, a lovely German Shepherd called Kaiser. The police would collect him for training as a guard dog for the jail. The boys joined the Sorrento Football Club and, you guessed it, Max was coaching football again. Martin was playing with the seniors and John was playing with the juniors, the team Max was coaching. The girls were doing girl stuff like netball, gymnastics and basketball. Max bought a boat for waterskiing with the kids and fishing with a couple of his mates. The fishing in Port Phillip Bay was excellent and so was crabbing. *You couldn't help but love this place*, Max thought. *Make the most of it as they probably won't leave us here too long, I bet, particularly if they find out I like it.'*

Max attended the TDO course which went without incident. On one occasion when Max rang home, Valda said Martin wanted to speak to him, and not to yell at him.

'Hi, Dad. Sorry, but I burnt the Mini Cooper.'

'What do you mean, burnt?'

'You know,' said Martin, 'burnt to the ground.'

He said he was taking the mower to Anne's girlfriend's place to mow the lawn. The mower was in the boot and the handle must have touched the battery and the car caught fire.

Valda had said not to yell at him. Max thought, *Christ, he couldn't have done more damage if he'd taught a woodpecker to play our piano with its beak.*

The School of Army Health Training Cell was split into two sections in the same building: a basic training wing and an advanced training wing, which was where Max's office was. The advanced training wing consisted of a Major, who had replaced Geoff (a Major whose career with Max went back as far as Vietnam when they were both Sergeants), a Captain, a Warrant Officer Class 2, two Sergeants and Max, the Warrant Officer Class 1.

The Major and the Captain did very little in instruction and the two Sergeants were mainly developing and writing training packages. One of those Sergeants was a female whom Max called Marion when at social functions. She occasionally did some instruction and was a good hand. She was a mad Hawthorn supporter and had fallen in love with Dermott Brereton, not that Dermy knew anything about it. Max and his WO2 would do most, if not all, the instruction for Sergeant, Warrant Officer, basic officers course and some for the advanced officers course. The school had two Warrants Officer Class 1: the RSM and Max. The RSM was the President of the Mess Committee and Max was his deputy. It was the most satisfying and constructive postings of Max's military service.

Structured into all courses was a field exercise for three days. On the second day of a Warrant Officer's course, the RSM came into the field to tell Max that the Major General from training command would be at the school the next day. The whole unit was to be on parade, and that included this course.

Max said, 'No way! Does this bloke know these people have been in the bush for two days? They will have to come back in and have only one night to get their uniforms ready for a parade. We're not doing it. They can all go on the bloody parade without us.'

The RSM, whose name was Ollie and was a good friend of Max, said, 'Listen, mate, it's a direct order from higher command. Sorry, I know how you feel, but that's it.'

Back into the school they all went. Max went home to get

his uniform ready for the parade to find that Valda had been told by the RSM about the parade and she had Max's uniform ready to go.

The morning of the parade, Max was apologising to the course for the inconvenience and explained it had nothing to do with him. There were three courses being conducted at the school at this time; their numbers plus the staff meant about a hundred were on parade. The command came from the RSM: 'Band by the centre, parade by the right, quick march.' The band started playing the tune of 'Colonel Bogey March', known in the services as 'Hitler had only one brass ball'. Max marched his course onto the parade ground to see that there were guests sitting on chairs next to the dais where the visiting officer would be taking the salute.

Max said, 'What's Valda doing there?'

The parade was brought to attention and the black staff car, with the flags indicating who was inside, came onto the parade ground. The Major General took his place on the dais and spoke over the microphone.

'It gives me great pleasure on behalf of the Australian Army and the medical corps to present this commendation to Warrant Officer First Class Max Thornton, for his exemplary service and leadership, as the senior Warrant Officer instructor here at the School of Army Health.'

'Shit,' Max said to himself, 'these poor bastards are all here because of me! How bloody embarrassing.'

After the parade and the march past and then the usual bullshit of scones, cups of tea and the mandatory photos, Max couldn't wait to get his white gloves, the Sam Brown belt and his medals off and get back to the field exercise to complete the course.

Max couldn't help but smile to himself when he remembered being at this school when it was at Healesville, when he was on his first course and the Commanding Officer had told him, when he'd been charged, if he ever came back to that unit again, which was seriously doubted, he would know better. *Bloody shame he's not here now*, thought Max.

Later in life, Max would be disappointed that his mother and sister weren't given the opportunity to be present when he received his commendation, but Valda and Max's parents never really got on, so he suspected that was why. Also, he thought about his sister never being notified when he came home from Vietnam, either. *Well*, he thought, *you can't choose your bloody family, can you?* Although, in all fairness, his sister and Max weren't all that close back then, due to all his time away interstate or overseas. *Let's leave it at that*, Max thought. *If I try to delve into this too much, I'll be the only one in the rubber room.* It's not unusual for the wives not to get on with their husband's parents and vice versa. Max was also man enough to admit there are two sides to every story, and he was probably part of one of them.

Warrant Officer Timothy, Max's second-in-command, was a dedicated soldier. What he lacked in finesse was more than made up by determination and loyalty. He was an 'up the guts' type of bloke without the ability to realise when the situation required a quiet 'this is how it's done' approach. He needed to develop his own style of instruction and not follow Max's sometimes unconventional methods.

To illustrate this, Max told Tim he had designed a four-hour exercise called 'A day in the life of an administrative officer'. Every unit has one problem child, and the star of the exercise was an imaginary Lance Corporal Murphy. The exercise consisted of a number of field phones in the model room, linked to a separate small room for each officer, the phones in the model room being manned by school staff. All sorts of military problems and issues were delivered by hand to each officer's room in-tray to be dealt with a written reply and reference used from the military manual and placed in their out-tray to be collected and marked for the correct remedial response to the issue. The officers were also annoyed throughout the exercise with phone calls from Lance Corporal Murphy with his family problems.

That night after the exercise, Max learnt the officers were going to a local restaurant in town. Max got dressed up as Lance Corporal Murphy, with a name tag on his jumper. He marched into the restaurant where they were all sitting amongst civilian diners and said in a loud voice, 'Look at these Army officers, all wining and dining. I'm only a little Lance Corporal who wants to go home to his sick mother, and they won't let me go home.' Then he marched out. Max said, 'I'll bet they spent the next ten minutes explaining to the people in the restaurant about the bloody Murphy exercise.'

Max said to Tim, 'See? You need to put your own stamp on training to make it interesting for the students. They will pick up on the different antics of each instructor and look forward to a change in pace and the different, light-hearted style offered during instruction, and some light-hearted activity sometimes doesn't go astray. I know for a fact students will sometimes lay bets for money among them themselves prior to a lecture on how many times a particular instructor might say "for example" or "you will soon learn". So, good instructors should be aware of these things. It makes the more boring lessons more interesting for students. And that's why, my friend, you need to develop your own style. You will find it will be very rewarding, and the student results will reflect that.'

Military instructional periods were structured for forty-minute periods, so a certain number of lessons could be fit into one day. If you went overtime, the instructor coming after you had less time. Timothy could never seem to keep to these times, mainly due to students throwing him red herrings. Most of the time, it was Max who had to follow Timothy's lesson. It was an annoying itch that Max would have to scratch. Sometimes the courses were split into small classrooms like out-buildings for particular topics, but mostly lessons were conducted in what was called the Model Room. The Model Room was like a large theatre with a stage, tiered seating and a lectern on the floor in the middle of the room. The seating was long benches with seats fixed along the rows and room underneath for your feet, which meant, from down on the floor where the instructor stood, you could see underneath. On day one of a new course, they would all be seated there waiting for the Commanding Officer's opening address. Max was always accused of sitting the female students at eye level. Most of them would be wearing dresses – well to start with. Max always smiled when he saw the look on the Commanding Officer's face as he looked up. Max never admitted he did it on purpose, nor did he deny it.

The Model Room could be very daunting for some and, like Timothy, they used the lectern in the middle of the room as a security blanket, much the same way a child uses their teddy bear. When it was time for Max to 'scratch his itch', he used one of several ways he'd devised to give Timothy the message that his forty minutes were up. At one stage, he came through the stage door behind the curtain. Timothy was glued to the lectern with his back to the curtain. Max quietly began to sweep the floor behind him. The students started laughing, Timothy turned around, and Max said, 'Your time is up, now get out.'

Not wanting to do the same thing twice, Max borrowed a large wax blowfly from the Health Section. It was about a foot long and six inches across, and very realistic with artificial hairs on its legs. The Model Room had very high rafter ceilings. Max threw a fishing line up over the rafters, attached the other end behind the curtain on stage, tied the fly to the line and pulled it up out of the way. Timothy, as usual, was starting to go over time again. Max slowly lowered the fly and the students began laughing. Behind Timothy, about head high, was the fly swinging on the almost invisible fishing line. Unbeknownst to Max, Timothy eventually made a huge fly swat and kept it in the lectern. The next time Max lowered the fly, it was swatted with enough force to almost destroy it; pieces came off it everywhere. Max said, 'You are in deep shit now, mate.'

Major Robin, the so-called phantom prankster who was at the military hospital when Max was there, had been posted to the training wing. *He's another one who hasn't learnt. It's not over till the fat lady sings*, thought Max. *He is really going to cop it now. Hello, party time!* Major Robin also happened to be the supervising officer of the Sergeants Mess, although in all the time Max was in the Mess, he failed to see any significant role this officer performed, apart from being invited along with the Commanding Officer to official functions like formal dining-in nights, making it easy for Max to target him.

Formal dinners were full of pomp and glory: Mess blues, white dinner jackets, bowties, medals and cummerbunds. The junior Sergeant became Mr Vice, whose role was to ensure all the members were moving into dinner when the agony bags (bagpipes) started playing. The doors would then be closed, and he announced to the President of the Mess Committee that the Mess had assembled. No one knew who would be saying grace until the President called their name. 'So you needed to have something ready in case it was you,' said Max. The mandatory speeches were done, dinner was served by the stewards in white jackets and gloves, and after a dinner of four courses, the port and cigars and or cigarettes were passed around. The port decanters were passed to the right and were not allowed to touch the table.

Christ, Max thought when he first saw this years ago, *who thinks up this shit? Not only that, but once you're in the closed dining room, there's no going out for a piddle, or anything else for that matter.* So, it was a case of being careful how much you had to drink before going in the dining room. On rare occasions, there would be a mixed formal dining-in night where you took your wife. The rules for being able to leave the room were somewhat relaxed on these occasions for obvious reasons.

Once, Max took a port glass over to the dental clinic and had a very tiny hole put in the bottom of it. This glass was then placed where Major Robin would be seated. The members' port glasses were filled, and the Royal Toast was conducted. Slowly, a reddish damp stain began appearing on the tablecloth under the Major's port glass. The hole was so small next to the stem it was impossible to see. Each time he filled his port glass, the stain on the tablecloth got bigger. He eventually realised he was on the blunt end of a joke. *Round one to me*, said Max to himself with a smile.

The next regimental dinner was only a week away – round

two for the Major prankster. Max took one of the Mess's old cutlery knives to the workshop and carefully cut the blade from the handle. Now he wanted to carefully glue them together, but not too strongly. The bloke in the workshop told him he had just the stuff he would need. Max went into the Mess while they were setting it up for the dinner and made sure that this knife replaced the one set at the table where the Major's place name was. With the usual pomp and glory, and everyone dressed like the pox doctor's clerk, in they all went. The main course was steak and pepper sauce. Max recalls, 'Our hero prankster started to cut his steak. As he was pushing down on the knife, well, bugger me, it broke, sending the handle and his fingers into the sauce.' Max could hardly contain himself and pretended he didn't see it happen. 'I could tell he was really pissed off, but what could he do with everyone watching? He just had to grin and bear it. Look don't get me wrong. Major Robin was quite a nice bloke, but I owed him from days gone by.'

Max knew when he retired there would be a dining-out regimental dinner to farewell him, so he would save the best for last.

*

One of Max's extra regimental appointments was to audit the financial books of the soldiers club and the property in the Officers Mess each year; the same for the Sergeants Mess by a nominated officer. Max knew the carpet bowls in the Sergeants Mess were missing, so while he was auditing the Officers Mess, he pinched theirs and marked them as missing.

When the officer did the audit of the Sergeants Mess, he said to Max, 'These carpet bowls look like ours.'

Max said, 'Don't give me that bullshit, Sir, just because yours are missing. These are ours, so don't get any idea. You'll just have to fill out a lost property report. The Officers Mess should take more care of their things. And if the Officers Mess had a Warrant Officer Supervising Officer, they might still have their carpet bowls. You need to take more care of your equipment.'

There was an annual shoot-out at the rifle range between the Officers Mess and the Sergeants Mess, and Max was asked by the Officers Mess to organise the event and lay out the rules. A bad move by the officers, letting Max organise the shoot! That was like putting a fox in with the hens; now they had no hope of winning. The weapons used would be the 7.62 self-loading rifle and the 9 mm Browning pistol. The self-loading rifle would be one hundred metres lying supported, fifty metres kneeling and twenty-five metres standing, each of these with a twenty-five-round magazine.

During Max's service and mandatory qualifying shoots at various rifle ranges, he had earned the right to wear the crossed rifle badge; however, he never wore it. Max didn't know what the overall expertise of the officers would be, so he said to Ollie that they needed some sort of an edge on them. Max said, 'Leave it with me, mate. I'll come up with a plan.'

The target butts are a long trench that the operators stand in to raise the target frame up and down. Attached to the frame is a paper target with a bull's eye marked with points. Max's idea was to have the Privates operate the target butts and use what Max was calling a 7.62 pencil, which was just a simple pencil the same thickness as the bullet. The idea was that after each of the Sergeants Mess members fired, the soldiers were to poke holes with the 7.62 pencil in the target where the most points were marked. When everyone came up to the butts to check the scores, the holes would already be there, and given that only the butt operators were permitted in the butt during the firing, all should go well. Max needed to offer an incentive, by way of a bribe, for the butt operators, so he made a visit to the Soldiers Club and spoke to a Corporal.

'Here's the plan, mate. The Sergeants Mess will give your club five cases of beer and you pick the butt operators you can trust to keep their mouth shut.'

As the bet with the officers was for ten cases, Max reckoned they were looking good. The twenty-five-metre pistol range shoot would have to be fair dinkum, as the black figure targets were out in the open and there was no way to fudge anything. Max wasn't too worried; they should be way in front on points after the rifle range, he said. During the shoot, the officers couldn't believe how badly they were doing and how good the Warrant Officers and Sergeants were doing, and the soldiers were doing a remarkable job with the 7.62 pencil.

Max said to the officer in charge of their mob, 'You blokes will never get the job of sniper. I've seen how good some of you are with a compass, so there goes the forward scouts job, but that's where we come in, Sir – the dynamic Warrant Officers and Sergeants to your rescue. They're good at everything. We gave you every chance to win, we even offered you soft pillows to lie on, and glasses of wine with canapés.'

The officer told Max that was bullshit, but very good bullshit.

Max was also asked to organise a triathlon for military and civilian competitors. The triathlon was to finish at the Army barracks. Max wanted to erect one of those large overhead finish banners at the finish line. He rang the local high school and asked the school principal if they had a finish flag or knew where he could get one. The principal said that they didn't have one but one of their students had just come back from Finland and he would ask her.

Max said to Ollie, 'Is it just me that's out of step with the rest of the world? There should be some sort of an invisible protective suit you can wear to shield you from idiots. Correct me if I'm wrong, mate, but at the end of a triathlon, the banner doesn't say Finish – it says Finnish!'

*

The kids were beginning to find their own way in life, albeit they were still living at home. Martin was about to turn twenty-one, Anne would soon be nineteen, Arlene was thirteen and John, the baby, was thirteen. Max was approaching the twenty-year mark in the service and was thinking about retiring. He was now forty-five which wasn't old for what he did, but to stay another ten years wouldn't alter the amount of military pension by a great deal, and it certainly wouldn't be enough by itself to sustain a good income. He also considered that the older you were, the less attractive you would be for any future civilian employment. So, a decision had to be made very soon.

Once Max retired, they'd need somewhere to live so they decided to buy land and build. The War Service Loan was a lousy $25,000 and couldn't be used for just land; it had to be for a house and land package. Valda's grandparents had given her some money to help with buying the land, so along with what they had, there was enough to buy a block nearby. Max told Valda that if he was going to retire at the end of the year, the house needed to be built by then. She agreed but said that they should do this whether Max retired or not. They would need to make a move sooner or later, so they should just do it anyway.

The Christmas holidays had started, the family hadn't moved into their new house yet and the atmosphere at home wasn't the greatest. They had good friends coming to stay for Christmas, which Max hoped would ease some tension.

Scrooge arrived ahead of his family. Max asked him if he had brought his wallet.

He felt in his pocket and said, 'Shit, it's not there!'

'Come on,' Max said, 'fair go, mate.'

'I'm not joking, mate,' he said.

Valda came out and said to Scrooge that Joan was on the phone. He left his wallet at the chemist, and that she would bring it with her. She gave him the wallet when she arrived, and he said there was $50 missing.

'No, there's not,' said Joan, 'You told me you had no money, so I gave you $50 and that's in there.'

Scrooge had just been found out and said that he had $50 in his cunning kick for emergencies.

'What bullshit is that?' she said, 'You never go anywhere you'd have to spend money, Scrooge. Look at the wallet – it's covered in cobwebs.'

Max said, 'Nice try, mate, but no cigar.'

The next day Max and Scrooge were going to the pub for a drink and to bring back some wine for the girls. While Scrooge was trying to get his shoes on, he commented to Joan that he didn't have any money.

Watching the shoe saga, Joan said in frustration, 'Don't do it like that. Undo the laces properly.'

Scrooge ignored her, still struggling with his shoes.

'You're not listening to me,' she said. 'Christ, nobody told me when you get a husband the ears are sold separately.'

She started trying to get his shoe off but couldn't as he had his toes curled up. Suddenly the shoe came off and money went everywhere.

Max couldn't stop laughing. 'Jesus, I almost wet my pants.'

'It's your fault, Max,' said Joan, 'You and Brewster both keep laughing at him. He thinks it's funny, so he keeps doing this skimpy stuff with money, and he gets away with it.'

Max had four crab pots anchored fifty metres offshore at the Portsea barracks. He had a very small dinghy to row out to check them and had filled the electric copper ready to cook the crabs when he and Scrooge came back with the catch. The dinghy was really only a one-person boat so it was fairly cramped. The current was getting stronger with the outgoing tide, so Max had tied the dinghy to the crab pot anchor weight. Fumble fingers Scrooge somehow managed to knock the rowlocks into the water, so now they could only paddle. They let go of the anchored crab pot and tried to get to shore. 'Far out,' Max said, 'now we're two hundred metres offshore.' They threw out the little piddling dinghy anchor and waited for a boat to come past.

'Here comes one now,' said Scrooge, standing up and waving his arms.

'No, not that one,' Max yelled out, 'that's the bloody police boat.'

The police boat was a giant next to the dinghy. The police looked down, shaking their heads – two idiots in a plastic tub, no life jackets, no safety gear. Max told the police that it was Scrooge's dinghy, and Scrooge had made him get in. Their answer to that was 'bullshit'. They were kind enough to give them a warning and towed them in as far as they could. Max had to jump out waist deep and pull the boat in. Scrooge stepped out onto the sand bone dry, then told Max he couldn't swim. They were gone for hours, of course, and Max was accused of being in the pub and having no thought for anyone waiting at home. It didn't matter what Max said, and once again, things became unpleasant.

Mind you, there were times when Max probably overstayed his time at the Mess or the pub, but this wasn't one of them. To be very fair, though, Valda had to put up with quite a lot from Max. There were times when he wouldn't get home till the early hours of the morning, or not at all. His rank allowed him to have his own room in the Sergeants Mess, with clean uniforms and civilian clothes along with personal items. So sometimes he would stay there, particularly if a new course had just started.

When Scrooge and Joan were leaving, Max reminded Scrooge his fishing gear was still in the big boat. Scrooge was a teacher at RMIT and had had his students make his sinkers. On a particular fishing day in Max's boat, he asked Scrooge if he could try one of the sinkers. Scrooge and Max thought no more of it. When Max climbed into the boat to get it ready for Brewster's arrival, he sat there in disbelief – the bugger had cut the sinker off Max's bloody line.

'Jesus Christ,' Max said out loud, 'I provide the boat, the fuel, the bait and a stay here at the house for the family, and he cuts the bloody sinker off my line!' He was that pissed off he sent him some sinkers in the mail with a note saying, 'If you're that bloody hard up, keep these.'

*

Max had notified Canberra he would be taking his discharge in April. Ollie was doing the same as Max, so there would be two Warrant Officer Class 1s being dined out at the same regimental dinner, and Major Robin would be there as well. The final round for Robin would now come into play.

The stewards were setting up the dining room for the night, folding the starched white napkins into little waistcoat shapes with a black paper bow tie and little black paper buttons stuck on. Max asked the lady to unfold one and he filled it with baby powder. This one, of course, was placed for Major Robin. On the night, Max watched the Major carefully take the bow tie and buttons off. Because the napkin was starched and stiff, you needed to hold it up and shake it. And that's when it happened – baby powder went everywhere. The Major now had white hair. Even the dignitaries from Canberra were laughing.

Max moved next to the Major, bent down and said, 'Now we are even, Sir.'

He said, 'You! I might have bloody known. They were all good pranks, though, Max. I might use them myself someday. By the way, Sergeant Major, thank you for your service and your support to me here at the school. I wish you well in your future endeavours.'

At the farewell dinner during the speeches, Max was asked how you know when it's time to retire, what he had learned about life in general and what were his best service memories.

Max simply said, 'You should count your life by the smiles you've had on your journey, not the tears, and try and live your life in such a way that you wouldn't be ashamed to sell the family parrot to the town gossip, and good luck with that. You will wake up one morning and realise that the system has changed so much that you're now in a place that you shouldn't be, but it's given me the chance to see life with new eyes, and I will have unblemished memories accumulated over twenty years of service that will last me a lifetime. I have accumulated many lifelong friendships along the way; some of them are here tonight. I loved what I did here with training, and I intend to keep doing what I love after my discharge from the service. To all I have worked and been associated with over the twenty years, let me say it's been an honour, and I wish you well with the remainder of your careers. Thank you.'

*

About 9 pm a week later, Martin was doubling up with pain.

Come and let me look at you,' Max said, and told Valda, 'He's got appendicitis.'

Max and Martin headed for the small hospital. The doctor on call happened to an Army doctor who knew Max. He said, to save bringing in two theatre nurses, Max could assist in theatre, but they must ask the patient if that was okay.

Martin said, 'Of course it's no problem.'

So, out came Martin's appendix.

Sometime later, Max was talking to Timothy outside the Sergeants Mess by his vehicle, when he realised he should have got fuel earlier. Timothy asked if he would get home okay and Max told him he had twenty litres of fuel on the back of the four-wheel-drive Nissan, and he would use that. When Max started pouring the fuel in his vehicle in the dark, he realised something was not right – no fuel smell. He had been pouring bloody water into the vehicle. What Max didn't know was that Martin's car had a leaking radiator, so he had emptied the fuel out of Max's container into his car and filled it up with water to take with him to work. When he had come home, he put the Jerry can full of water back on Max's vehicle and hadn't told him what he had done.

'Jesus Christ,' Max said, 'I'm going to kill this kid before he gets too much bloody older.'

Chapter 17

Civilian life

On his discharge from the Army, Max took up the position of Defence Reserve Ranger at Portsea. He used this position while he put together his resume for a more prospective employment opportunity.

His role was to monitor the safety at the live firing range and the grenade range, general tractor mowing and training area allocation. The money was bloody pathetic, but he knew he wouldn't be there long. At the target end of the firing range was a high mound and behind that was the ocean. During live firing, red flags were flown on the cliff top, and a couple of picquets were posted to watch for small boats that might fish in the danger zone. Once, when a small fishing boat was spotted in the zone, Max was advised by radio, and he drove to the Portsea police station where the police helicopter was. The Police Sergeant was also the pilot.

'I couldn't believe it,' Max said. 'We flew out over the fishing boat, but the police chopper had no loudspeaker system. We had to put a message in a plastic bottle and drop it into the bloke's bloody boat. Talk about the Keystone Cops!'

The field ambulance wanted to use the training facilities, so Captain Jane Roper was doing the liaison with Max. He had known Jane for many years, back when they were both Sergeants and Warrant Officers. She had been awarded the Alice Appleford Award for her outstanding performance as a nurse within the nursing corps, which was similar to Max's commendation. They had never served in the same unit but had attended courses and meetings together, and along with others, had had long conversations over drinks at the mess after the meetings. Max knew her marriage over the years was not healthy and they had talked about their marriages on occasions. They were not what you would call close, and they had never had an affair. Jane had transferred from nursing to medical and was offered a promotion to Captain. So here she was.

Max took her on a tour around the training area in his Land Rover. Max was interested in the tax-free money at the Army Reserve. Jane said if he was interested, he would be welcomed as the training Warrant Officer at the field ambulance, the same rank he had prior to retiring. The Army Reserve could be done alongside full-time employment, so it sounded okay. Max said he had given it a go for a short time. It all seemed a bit of a waste to him; however, the money was good.

There was a position available for Captain, so they sent Max to the 'trick cyclists' for assessment. When Max left the assessment, he was still Warrant Officer Thornton – *you're obviously not allowed to hammer the round pegs into the square holes if they don't fit*, thought Max. His opinion was that they'd discovered he was far too intelligent to be a Captain, and his heart wasn't really in it anyway.

Colonel Davis was Commanding Officer who restored

Max's faith in who they gave the Queen's commission to –
sometimes they actually get it right! Max was asked if he
would organise and run a four-day navigation and map
reading field exercise. Max and Captain Roper packed the
trailer and Land Rover and headed off as the advance party
to map out an exercise area for the navigation. They were now
up in wet, cold leech country, and it was snowing heavily. The
ground and timber lying around were wet and mildewed. The
fire would have to wait till the main party arrived the next
day. It was going to be a freezing cold night.

'Where are the sleeping bags, Warrant Officer Thornton?'

'I don't know. I thought you put them in the trailer.'

'Well, that's just bloody wonderful! We are going to freeze
our arses off.'

The trick now was to get their sleeping bags to arrive with
the main party, without the unit knowing they didn't have
them. Max said, 'Leave that to me, Ma'am.' He drove down
to the local town and rang the quartermaster and told him to
pack extra sleeping bags in case some of the soldiers' bags got
wet during the exercise. When the unit arrived, Max helped
himself to two sleeping bags.

While Max was in the small town ringing the quartermaster,
a nice-looking Dalmatian dog came past with only three legs.
Five minutes later, the dog was followed by a man with only
one leg. Max thought about asking the man if it was his dog,
or if he could get a photo of him with the dog. He decided it
was probably a sick joke and probably wasn't a good idea to
ask him. Look, fair dinkum, you couldn't make this stuff up!

*

After the exercise, Max saw an advert in the newspaper from the Shell Oil Company of Australia, seeking a suitable person to write the leaders' notes for their driver awareness training program, and then to present the courses to their drivers Australia-wide. The position would only be for that program. Max thought, *Well, once I get a shoe in the door, who knows what might come of it?* and the money was fantastic, more than double what his military wage was. Max thought, *How long has this sort of money been available while I've been ginning around in the service?* Max sent his resumé to Shell in Melbourne. It took an incredible amount of time before Max had a reply. What he didn't know was that they had advertised Australia-wide and the number of applications took a lot of time to go through. The letter asked Max to come for an interview as they had placed him on the short list for the position.

The day of the interview, he was at the Army Reserve unit, dressed up like the pox doctor's clerk in suit and tie. He borrowed Captain Roper's briefcase, something he had never carried before; he thought he looked like a bloody nerd. The Captain was going into the city on military business in the staff car, and she would drop him off at Shell House in William Street, and if the timing was right, she might be able to pick him up after his interview.

He stepped into the main foyer of Shell House, much bigger than what he had expected, with three security staff seated at the reception counter. Max told them who his appointment was with, and they gave him a pass and directed him to the lifts. He needed a nervous wee, so he asked where the toilets were, and off he went. He came back past the security staff and nodded and smiled, but when he got to the lift, he realised, as he was not used to carrying briefcases, that he had left it in the washroom. 'Shit,' Max said. So, back past the security staff to the washroom, grab the briefcase and back past the security staff for the third time. Max thought he heard them saying to each other, 'This bloke has got no hope of getting a job'.

The personnel officer was waiting for him when he got out of the lift, she introduced herself and they went to her office.

'Make yourself comfortable, Max. Did you bring the documents we asked for?'

Max said, 'Yes', and promptly opened the briefcase upside down. All the documents fell out on the floor under her desk. So now Max was groping around on his hands and knees. 'Christ, Max, fair dinkum, you've got no hope of getting this job,' he said to himself. 'She's probably thinking, is this the person we're getting to get to talk to twelve truck drivers in a room together?' She was very nice about it, 'Not to worry,' she said, and the rest of the interview went without a hitch. She thanked Max for coming and said she would be back in touch.

The good Captain must have finished her business because she was waiting in the staff car outside.

'How did it all go?'

'Well, apart from leaving the briefcase in the toilet and opening it upside down at the interview, the answers I gave to her questions were to the best of my ability. If I had to do it again, my answers wouldn't change, so I guess if I'm good enough I'll be selected. Time will tell.'

Max was now doing some (tax-free) time with the Army Reserve and killing time as the defence ranger. Less time was being spent at home, which wasn't helping the relationship, and if he was successful at Shell, it was only going to get worse. As time went by and Max had heard nothing from the interview, he had convinced himself he hadn't been successful. Then, out of the blue, the letter arrived notifying he had been selected from all the national applicants and was to come back in for further instructions. Max would spend the next four weeks working at Shell House writing the leaders' notes for the course. The training would be conducted at The Entrance on the New South Wales central coast, Monday to Friday, and he would fly home each weekend. Every driver in Australia would be attending the course, twelve at a time, which meant probably a year to complete. There was another person selected to assist with the training, but he turned out to be a dud. There was also a requirement for Max to form a company, as he would be considered a private contractor for this training role. Max and Jane subsequently formed their own company, called Sempcom Petroleum Transport Trainers, which covered these requirements.

Max suggested to Shell that he knew the ideal person who could come on board to assist him with the training. This was approved by Shell and Max contacted his old friend, Ollie, from the school at Portsea who came on board as the second instructor.

Valda said, 'What's wrong with you, Max? You can't keep still. Why must you keep going away? Why can't you stay home?'

Max's marriage was all but buggered. He knew the more time he spent away, the less arguing and stress took place which helped keep the peace in the house – not an ideal situation and one that couldn't be sustained. Someone once said, 'Life is like riding a bicycle: if you don't keep moving, you lose your balance', and besides, it's harder to hit a moving target. That was Max's slant on it, anyway.

The plan for the Shell training was that Max and Ollie would fly to Sydney and meet up at the airport with the drivers, where a coach would be waiting to take them to the venue at The Entrance. Not as easy as it sounds as they soon found out. First, there was finding the drivers who were spread all over the airport, usually found in one of the airport bars. Then there were those who didn't want to be there and needed to be pacified. Their thinking was, 'What can these two blokes teach me? I've been doing this job for ten years.' It would take a few courses to get the word back to those yet to come that they would actually enjoy the week away and might just learn something.

'As you can imagine,' Max said, 'we had them all – whingers, scammers, red raging unionists putting the company down whenever they could and those who were there to cost Shell as much as they could at the bar during Happy Hour each night. One driver found out you could get your clothes dry cleaned while on the course, so he brought his bloody suit. Another bloke had a second suitcase for all his Mylanta for his boozing stomach ulcer. Yes, we had them all – and in among them, were some hellish nice blokes.'

On Thursday nights, the course would go to the local RSL for the evening meal where they always had a band playing. The drivers soon named this 'Grab a Granny' night due to the age of the patrons. There were many slogans like that introduced as the course progressed. The barman at Happy Hour wore a white shirt and a bow tie, so the drivers called him Propeller Neck. Wednesdays was allocated as a half-day outing, and they all went to Old Sydney Town by coach for the afternoon, all paid for by Shell, of course.

These drivers were really being looked after, but sadly,

some just didn't get it. The thinking by some was that Shell obviously had an ulterior motive. Ollie and Max agreed that somewhere down the line, the bean counters would work out who was costing them the money, and fuel deliveries would be turned over to contractors. What these drivers didn't fathom was they'd be out of a job with Shell, and it wouldn't be as good as they had it now.

*

The separation from home during these courses and coming home on weekends was no longer tolerable. Max left the family nest. As hard as it was, everyone needed happy circumstances for whatever was left of their lives, and it had not been a happy house for a long time. Max hoped that someday down the line, the children and Valda would understand that, as bad as it seemed now, it was the right thing to do for everyone's happiness. He loved his family, he adored his children, and to some degree, he blamed himself for choosing careers that destroyed the family unity, and while he still had some issues from his tour in Vietnam, they weren't entirely to blame. Max hoped that like himself, they would be thankful of the wonderful times that they'd had as a normal family, with lots of laughter and some tears. Nobody can predict the future, and as he had often told young John, nothing is forever.

Unfortunately, what happened now was that family, relations and friends chose sides, who they would support and who they would disband, causing more damage and misery to already irreparable circumstances.

Jane must have decided that what Max had done, she should have done a long time ago, for exactly the same reason

– happiness. Now she would have her own demons to deal with.

Valda's brother was a solicitor so Max knew the vultures would be coming. Max decided not to give them the satisfaction arguing who gets what. He simply said he didn't want anything. 'Well, that stopped them farting in church,' Max said. He wondered what they would do for the rest of the day now they had nothing to haggle over. Well, they found a thread; they later tried to suck money from Max when there was plainly no entitlement. Max said, 'Bloody ambulance-chasing lawyers – they're not far removed from car salesmen and bloody estate agents.' He told them to piss off. Max had given all he had worked for and was leaving it all for the children and Valda, and he couldn't be fairer than that.

Max and Jane now stood on the street with nothing but the clothes on their back and very little in the bank. Max hadn't thought about it much, but now that he did, he realised he had nothing to show for all those years of struggle and perseverance. Jane was no different, and even if they pooled their resources, they still had nothing substantial. However, Max had managed to keep his boat! 'Well, I guess we start again,' they said to each other. 'There's no point waiting for someone to give us a cuddle; there's no one coming anyway.' Max and Jane decided to move in together, and whatever happened now was entirely up to them.

The drivers' courses were in full swing. Jane was still in the regular Army, working not far from their rented town house on Beach Road, so there were no pressing financial problems at this time.

Max had to go to Sydney for a meeting and while he was there, Jane rang and asked if he would go and see her brother Duncan.

'Sure,' said Max, 'where is he?'

'He's in the Parramatta Jail.'

'What!'

'I'd better tell you about my brother, Duncan, so you know what to expect. Some years ago, Duncan had a motorcycle accident and lost his leg. He also had some frontal lobe damage and as such, sometimes leaves a lot to be desired. He had several speeding and parking fines he hadn't paid, and he'd been given time to pay by the court on several occasions. In the end, the judge got sick of his bullshit excuses and sent him to prison to cut out the fines, so there you have it,' Jane said.

Max had never been in a prison before, so it was quite an experience. Max had never met Jane's brother, Duncan, and that was quite an experience as well. He looked like Jesus Christ with long hair and a beard. You could have been excused for thinking he had been in there for years. A haircut and a shave would change his appearance considerably and wouldn't bring unwanted attention to himself. Max said he spent the thirty-minute visiting time with him as promised and left it at that. Duncan's dramas and issues is a separate story for another day.

Max and Jane decided to get away for a few weeks, so they went with Max's sister Dorris and her partner Graham on a road trip. Halfway across the Nullarbor, they camped for the night and sat around a nice big fire. It was a perfectly still, crisp and cold Nullarbor night. Every star in the sky must have been out on a black velvet landscape, a perfect example of Mother Nature's majesty. She was giving them her million-dollar view. Looking up at it could easily send you into a different world all of your own, turning you into an instant dreamer, lost in the beauty of the outback. It reminded Max of the song about when you wish upon a star. The sad part about this is, there are people who live and work their entire lives in the city who will never experience what they were seeing now. 'Look at us,' Max said, 'out here in the middle of nowhere – wide open spaces, room to move and breathe, the envy of the world.'

What they didn't know was the train line from Adelaide to Perth was just behind the tree line and, right on queue, the Indian Pacific came out of the dark. The driver must have seen their fire, and he blew his horn.

Jesus,' Max said, 'it gave me goosebumps.' Then he said, 'If we were in the planet's sixth-largest country in the world, Pakistan, with its population of 245 million, we certainly wouldn't be sitting here by ourselves, and the train that just went past would've had ten thousand people all over the roof like bloody ants. This is Australia, my friends, and don't you ever forget what a wonderful country we live in.'

Max thought that Dorothea Mackellar summed it up perfectly when she wrote:

> I love a sunburnt country,
> A land of sweeping plains,
> Of ragged mountain ranges,
> Of droughts and flooding rains.
> I love her far horizons,
> I love her jewel-sea,
> Her beauty and her terror –
> The wide brown land for me!

'We've explored almost all of our planet but there is I'm sure much more to discover things we haven't yet seen or even imagined. The silent view we get from the sky of the universe is just the beginning, and I'm quite sure of that,' Max said to the others round the campfire.

*

Back in the mad, tear-arse bustle of the city, there was no room for the boat at Max and Jane's town house so they got membership at the local motor yacht squadron. The clubhouse was on a small island just off the Mordialloc Creek with a footbridge for members to get to the club.

On their first time there, Jane had gone across and Max was going to put the boat in their allocated berth then meet her at the club. The berth was in the creek on the island side but the tide was out, so Max couldn't get the bow of the boat all the way to the island bank to tie off. Max jumped off, and to his dismay went down to his waist in black mud. On the balcony of the pub on the opposite side of the creek were people having lunch. They all stood, cheering and laughing, Max gave them all the finger and dragged himself onto the island.

He was dressed in his white slacks and white pullover ready to meet the commodore for the introduction to club members. Jane was talking with the commodore when Max arrived. She said, 'Here he is now.' Then she saw him. Max was covered in black shit from head to toe, and the smell was bloody putrid.

'Hello,' Max said, 'I thought I'd make a grand entrance for my first visit.'

Jane went to get some clean clothes from the car while Max hit the shower. The commodore suggested to Max that they get a photo for the club scrap book. Max ensured that there were no photos taken, and the rest of the afternoon was pleasant. But Max couldn't see the boat staying where it was for long; it wasn't a suitable mooring.

*

Max would get Jane to take him to the airport on Sundays for the training at The Entrance and pick him up on the following Friday to enable them to have the weekend together. After a few months, they decided to alternate; every second week, Jane would come up to The Entrance. There was no difference in cost than if Max went back and forward, it broke the monotony, and gave Jane a break away from home and a chance to see how it was all going at the sharp end.

On one of the weekends when they were staying at The Entrance, the prawns were coming in. The hotel chef said if they were able to catch some prawns, he would cook them for them. The river was just across the road from the hotel with a hire boat shed.

Max said to Ollie, 'Let's hire a boat for a couple of hours and get a couple of nets.'

Off they went. It was now dark, but they had a torch.

As they sat in the middle of the river looking for the prawns, Max said, 'Look at all those lights coming down the river. I can hear voices.'

About six blokes walked past the boat, waist-deep catching the prawns.

They said, 'How you going, boys? Catching any?'

'Christ,' Max said, 'look at the number of prawns they've got. How many have you got?'

Ollie said he had four, and Max had five – bloody hell!

They had hired a boat when they didn't have to, and all they had to show were nine bloody prawns.

They went back to the hotel and the chef said, 'How did you go, boys? Give me the prawns and I'll cook them for you.'

Max said, 'We gave him the nine prawns, and he couldn't stop laughing.'

'Jesus, you blokes are bloody hopeless.'

'See,' said Ollie, 'you need local knowledge.'

*

When Max and Jane got home, they decided to go and look at Lake Nagambie for the weekend. They paid for an onsite van near a jetty on the river with an outside fireplace near the van. After they got a fire going that night, Max walked out on the jetty with his fishing rod. He couldn't see the jetty that well in the dark and ended up walking right off the end into the river.

'It was deep and bloody freezing cold, and I was fully clothed,' said Max. 'It frightened the Christ out of me. I came up so fast and cracked my kneecap on the jetty getting out.'

By this time, Jane was standing on the end of the jetty, wetting her pants laughing. Max wasn't impressed. Luckily, the fire was going well. Max changed into dry clothes and stood by the fire, shivering his arse off with a painful knee for the next hour.

The next morning in the shower block, some bloke said to Max, 'Hey there, mate, did you hear some idiot walked off the end of the jetty last night?'

Max said, 'Bugger! No, I didn't hear anything about that.' *Jesus, it doesn't take long for the word to get around, Max* thought. *Funny how when you want any good news to get around, it doesn't go anywhere.*

They bought a large, old caravan and paid for a vacant site on the water's edge with its own jetty. Jane would pick him up at the airport on Friday and they'd go to Nagambie for the weekend, unless she was coming up to The Entrance.

Max and Jane saw a little old mud brick cottage for sale out in the boondocks on six acres. Jane thought it was very rustic and charming, Max thought it was very something, but whatever it was, it was more bloody rustic than charming. However, at least it was a start, they thought. They approached the bank in Nagambie for a loan. Although they were earning good money and the property wasn't a lot of money, about $150,000, they had nothing and no collateral.

Max said to Jane, 'I wouldn't get too excited. We probably won't get the loan.'

They waited with bated breath over the next day or so for the reply. The young lady who was the bank manager must have liked their style, or more likely felt sorry for them. Anyway, whatever it was, she gave them the loan.

Now that the cottage was empty and they actually owned it (well, more the bank than them), they headed out to the place with Dorris and Graham with smiles on their faces for a detailed look.

Max said, 'Christ, Jane, it's worse than I thought it was. I don't think the bloke that built this place owned a spirit level or could read a tape measure.'

It was more of what you'd call a fixer-upper, and it needed a lot of that.

Jane had taken her long service leave to move into the house and get it to some sort of liveability while Max was away through the week on the drivers' courses. The house had 240 volt power to the power outlets. The lights were 12 volt solar, but they soon discovered the panels on the roof were buggered and the lights were hooked up to two old 12 volt car batteries on the back veranda. They weren't any good either, so after five minutes of light, the house would be in darkness. Jane was in the house through the week by herself, with no neighbours for miles around, and at night the place was quite pitch black. Max had a coil of festive-style cable, the one you can screw a globe into wherever you like. He plugged one end into the 240 volt wall socket and ran the cable round inside the house, in and out of all the rooms, then screwed the globes in. When you switched on the power, every light in the house came on. Jane was sure the house would be visible from outer space. It didn't look all that professional, but it did the job and gave Jane some sense of security while Max was away.

The mud brick walls were six inches shorter than the roof line, meaning there was a gap, allowing things that flew, crawled and wriggled or walked to enter the house at night. Max had to make a frame over the double bed with netting to ensure there weren't any unwanted 'friends' sharing the bed with while they were sleeping.

The slate floor had been laid directly on top of the dirt, so that was going to be a big job to fix. The slate would have to be torn up and a concrete slab would have to be laid from within the house. There was also no town water, and out the back was a large concrete water tank with moss growing on the sides in places where the water had been seeping through the cracks. A smaller corrugated tank was mounted high on a platform with an electric pump to pump the water from the bottom tank to the top tank, which gravity-fed the house taps.

The water pressure was that bad you had to run around under the shower just to get wet. All the black polyester water pipes were lying above the ground, another example of that lazy attitude, 'who cares what it looks like as long as it works'. It certainly didn't look great, and it didn't bloody work. There was also a small dam on slightly higher ground with a pipe that gravity-fed the toilet with brown muddy water – well, sometimes it did. What it did have, however, was a creek running through the property; whether it had water in it all year round, time would tell.

Further down the property was a small bungalow-type building in fair repair with a large hornet's mud nest across the doorway. *I could think of some people I'd like to be the first ones in through that door*, Max thought.

The whole place reminded Max of Footrot Flats. All it needed was a border collie, so they bought one to make the place complete and called him Skipper. When he was little, only a couple of months old, Max put him in a box on the back of the motorcycle and rode into the paddock. The grass was very long, and before he knew it, Skipper had fallen out. It took Max some time to find him in the long grass.

The toilet had a wooden door with no handle, just a hole where the handle should have been. There was a slide bolt on the outside of the door to lock it, stopping it from blowing in the wind. Max was on his way to the top paddock one day when he noticed the bolt wasn't in place, so he slid it across and left. He had to come back some time later to get something and he heard Jane screaming out, 'Max, you fucking idiot! Let me out!' She was obviously in the toilet when he'd locked it. She was lucky he came back when he did, and so was Max.

Max was good with his hands – at least that's what the girls used to tell him at the drive-in movies anyway, he said. He could fix most things, and if it could be built with a chainsaw, he could. He was probably what you called a bush carpenter, but he was no builder, so all of the structural work would have to be done professionally. On one of his many trips to the hardware and builders supplies, he saw a sign that said, 'Husbands choosing paint colours must have a signed note from their wife'. *How true that was*, Max thought.

Two ladies from Melbourne owned the block of land next door. Max and Jane wanted to extend their property and kept asking the girls if they thought about selling it. They told Max that there was no way they were going to sell, so stop asking. Each weekend, the ladies would come for the weekend and spent many hours planting native shrubs, hundreds of them. Jane had been given a couple of goats from a work colleague, much to Max's amazement.

'What on earth do you want goats for, Jane?'

Jane thought about this and said, 'Well, they are quite cute', and she made an enclosure for them.

One week when Jane was at work and Max was away, the goats escaped. Jane found them on next door's block, contentedly eating their way through all the native plants the ladies has spent arduous hours planting. The next weekend when the ladies arrived and saw all their shrubs eaten to the ground, they were so distressed and asked Max if he knew how this could have happened.

'Hmm,' Max said, 'could be rabbits or kangaroos,' which there was no shortage of in the area.

They threw their hands in the air and said, 'Okay, Max – we are selling if you are still interested!'

They now had fifteen acres and put some sheep on the place

to keep the grass in the paddocks down along with a ram that Jane called Rambo. Skipper was bringing the sheep down one day with Rambo coming along fifty metres behind the rest.

Jane said, 'Look at him, Max. He's not going to be any good; he's buggered. Look at his balls – they are dragging on the ground.'

Max said, 'If I'd just humped thirty females, my balls would be dragging on the ground, and I would be buggered as well.'

It wasn't long when lambing time came and nearly all the ewes had twins.

Max said, 'What do you think of Rambo now, Jane?'

'Yeah, okay,' she said.

Because Max was often away for long periods, he bought Jane a mobile phone as he wanted her to be able to call for help if needed. The road to town was called Kangaroo Alley.

He showed her the phone and she said, 'Ring me, Max.'

He rang her and she said, 'Oh, look. All the numbers light up. It's about time someone thought of the deaf people.'

'What!' said Max.

'Well, they won't hear it ringing, will they, Max, but at least they'll see it.'

Jesus, Max thought, *maybe it's true what they say about blondes*, and said, 'What about when they say hello? They are deaf, remember!'

Jane just smiled and kissed him.

A bloke who was a retired Sergeant whom Max had known when in the service now moved into the area. He told Max that he had run into Major Malice in Melbourne the other day, who had retired as Lieutenant Colonel. He was telling Malice that he had bought a property near Max and Malice responded with, 'Good luck with that.'

'Jesus,' Max said, 'this bloke is bloody sick. We've all been out of the Army for years and this prick is still at it. But if I'm still pissing him off, I'm happy about that. I'd like to pay him a non-social visit. I'm not surprised about the rise in rank; people like him can almost promote themselves.'

*

The Shell driver programs had come to an end and Jane had retired from the Army. The money that was coming in was drying up.

'If something doesn't happen soon, I might have to sell pies at the football,' Max said.

They broke open the piggy bank and had enough money to have a cheap Chinese lunch and go to the movies in the local town.

Once, Max was working in the top paddock and had to come back to the house for a hat. He heard what sounded like someone moaning or talking, and called out, 'Hello. What's happening?' Then he heard Jane call out for help.

She had both her hands caught under the spring-loaded sewing machine platform. The sewing machine was constructed with the machine on top of a platform which, when released, drops the machine down level, making a flat bench top. Jane had tried to release the platform to lower it, but it got stuck. She put her hands under the platform and it dropped down, spring-loaded with the weight of the machine on top, jamming both her hands under by the wrists. She was stuck, unable to move or use a phone, and calling out from inside the house wasn't heard by anyone outside. The dogs had kept running backwards and forwards, licking her face with love, but making no attempt to go and get help.

'I got her arms out,' said Max. 'They were very bruised and the skin was broken, and of course she was very upset and in tears. That's when I realised how important it was to have some way of her not being stuck for days on end if something happened while I was away.'

Max went to visit Les on the hill at the next property. He told him what had happened and gave him their phone number, and then said to Jane, 'This will be the plan. When I'm away, I will ring you twice a day, at midday and 8 pm. If you do not answer after my second try, I will ring Les, and he will drive here to check if you are okay. We need to put some safety plan in place because you are virtually in isolation and vulnerable. Look what's just happened!'

A nod is as good as a wink to a blind man.

Chapter 18

Max the trainer

One door closes and another one opens, or so they say, and that's exactly what happened. The aviation section of Shell rang Max and wanted to see him in connection to training. Shell House was now on the corner of Spring Street, a very impressive building. Max met Kevan Gosper who was the CEO of Shell Australia at that time. The who's who of Shell Aviation were all at the meeting. Max was more relaxed this time and didn't make a gig of himself.

They explained that, though refuelling aircraft was not new to the Shell refuellers, they had never had formal training, and as such, no training program had ever been written and there was no format. This was right up Max's alley. He was well versed in job and task analysis and the specialist panels that were required to write such a program. Max explained they didn't need to have a refuelling expert; they could use the specialist panel for that. The job of the task analysis team was to view the tasks list in priority of procedure, safety and risk, and identify shortcuts or bad practices that may have fallen through the cracks over time.

Max said he would need to spend time refuelling aircraft at

Tullamarine with the workers and also spend time at the airport fuel farms, where the fuel came from. He would need to do this before the task analysis was done at airports around Australia. They were more than happy with Max's experience and agreed a contract be drawn up and arrangements made for Max to attend the faculties prior to the task analysis around Australia. Once this was done, Max and Jane's company, together with a specialist panel that Max would convene, would write the training program for Shell refuellers Australia-wide, and then the company would conduct all the training.

Max said to Jane, 'This will be a two-year commitment, and what's more, I won't have to sell pies at the football.'

However, he knew from old it wouldn't be without some drama. Four weeks travelling around Australia with airfares, hire cars, hotel accommodation and meals wasn't going to be cheap. They were contractors, so they would be paying up front and submitting receipts to Shell on a thirty-day reimbursement system.

'We need to use someone else's money,' Jane said, so Max paid a visit to a travel agent, who agreed to do all the bookings once they gave them their movement details. No one got paid until Shell paid the invoices in the thirty-day period, then everyone was paid via the travel agency. It was a good deal for all concerned: the company didn't have to outlay a large amount of money, and the travel agency had to put on another girl just for this project – a win for everyone.

Max arrived at Tullamarine for his first day to do his mini refuelling apprenticeship, so to speak, and this is where the fun started. Unbeknown to Max, Shell was moving quietly from the current system that used two men to one-man refuelling, and the refuellers knew Shell was trying to bring this in. When Max arrived, they saw him as the forward scout to survey for the change and report back to Shell. The union delegate banned him from the tarmac and would not allow him to talk to the refuellers. The refuellers station (lunchroom and amenities) was airside, the main Shell aviation administration building was outside the airport. *Christ,* Max thought, *the Shell aviation manager at Tullamarine can't just arrive airside without notifying the refuellers of his arrival. A regular refuellers' man cave!* Max wasn't going to get mixed up in who was controlling what or whom.

Eventually, after several meetings with the Tullamarine manager and the union delegation, Max was accepted on to the airport apron for the reasons he was meant to there, albeit under suspicion. Once again, Max met some damned nice blokes who'd had no choice but to fall into line with the militant minority if they wanted to keep the workplace peace, sad as it was. Max ignored all of this. It wasn't his issue, and what he'd seen and heard wasn't going back to Shell, not from him anyway. But he suspected they were well aware that he was just in the wrong place at the wrong time. Fortunately, most of them came to understand what Max was about, and for the most part he was well accepted, both airside and at the fuel distribution farm on the other side of the airport.

What Max knew about refuelling before this you could write on the back of a stamp, but he was a quick learner, had a photographic memory, and he wasn't going to be working as a refueller. Although twenty years ago, it might have been different, considering the difference in money compared to the military – more than double.

*

Back at the property, Jane had taken the 'Old MacDonald had a farm' song literally. The place was alive with things that walked, flew and ran, things that snorted and quacked, and she still had the goats out the back that had eaten everything they could reach, regardless of what it was made of.

Max said, 'We fenced off the dam for the ducks and a built a mud brick hootch to keep the foxes out at night. On the first night after it was built, we were trying to get the ducks out of the dam and into the hootch. Jane was swimming around the dam in her pants and bra, but when she got near them, they'd duck under and pop up somewhere else. "Come out of there," I said. "You'll bloody drown, and the ducks will still be there!"'

The geese were another issue. To get in to check the eggs, Max needed a rubbish bin lid and a broom handle to protect himself from the ganders. It wasn't long after Max got bitten on the arse that the geese went. Jane was keen for Skipper to have a girlfriend, so they bought a female puppy and called her Maggie. They got on famously, and after a period of time, too famously. When Maggie was on heat, they put her in the old geese enclosure which was concreted twelve inches under to keep the foxes from digging in. They reckoned that would keep Skipper out. No such luck. Where there's a will, there's a way. Skipper came up to the house, his face bleeding.

'What's done that?' Jane said.

'No idea,' said Max.

When they went down to check on Maggie, they found out that Skipper had chewed a hole in the bird wire wall and, of course, helped himself. And after nature had run its course, five border collie puppies arrived.

The only animal they didn't have was a horse. One of the Shell tanker drivers owned a riding school, and he had a horse that needed to retire. He told Max he could have the horse as he knew it would be going to a good home. Max borrowed their horse float and picked up the new addition to the farm. The horse was called Stocky; in its younger days, he had been a stock horse. He was a lovely gentle horse and the kids, no matter how small, could sit on his back with no saddle or bridle. Stocky would just wander around for as long as the kids wanted him to.

By now, Max had completed his familiarisation and mini apprenticeship at Tullamarine Airport. The travel agency had their schedule with flights and accommodation all booked, the schedules and visits times had been sent to the refuelling depots, so all was good to go. Max's sister Dorris and her partner would look after the property while they were gone.

It was one of the most interesting and satisfying experiences of all the task analysis programs Max had been involved in. He did the field work and Jane deciphered handwritten notes onto her laptop at the end of each day. After about a week, the training program started to take shape.

The smaller country depots took more time. They were contracted out by Shell but still needed to conform to the Shell standards, and their checks and balances were audited by Shell. These depots took receipt of the aviation fuel from the road tankers, Aviation Gasoline or Jet A1, sometimes both. Water checks, density range and temperature were performed before any fuel was unloaded. Water drains on coalescer filters was also done daily, along with filter monitors being checked. All these procedures had to be written into the course package, as these checks were the last line of defence before the fuel went into the aircraft. These tests were routinely conducted at the major airports, but the further into the country the depots were, the more responsible the refueller had to be. He was absolutely the last line of defence for those about to fly.

The job and task analysis went without a hitch, the travel agency did a fantastic job and all went like clockwork. Dorris and Graham managed not to kill themselves on the motorbikes, and the chooks were still laying eggs.

*

When Max and Jane returned home, Dorris said to Jane, 'By the way, I've been meaning to ask you: how does your family feel about you and Max?'

Jane related that in the beginning, her mother Aileen thought Max was having a midlife crisis, despite Jane telling her at great length, and trying to reassure her, that the relationship with Max was something special – in fact, incredible. Jane said for the first time in her adult life, she knew that she had found her soulmate, someone that she knew she was meant to be with, to spend the rest of her life with.

The time came when she had to introduce Max to her mother and her siblings.

'It started with a trip to Victor Harbor, where they all lived,' said Jane, who had flown over a few days previously, as Max was working in Adelaide. She had given him directions to her sister's place at Back Valley, several kilometres out of Victor Harbor, on a country road with no street lights, which didn't instil a great deal of confidence in Max, as he would be arriving after dark.

Jane said to him, 'Don't worry Max, I'll put a light on the gate.'

Well, after much driving backwards and forwards, Max eventually saw the minuscule green light from a glow stick!

'So, the introductions began,' Jane said, and as she had silently predicted to herself, within half an hour Max was on a roll. Within a couple of days, he had won the whole family over. By the time they were due to leave, Aileen in particular thought the sun shone out of his bum.

'Well,' Dorris said, 'I'm very pleased for both of you.'

Not long after, Jane's mother came to stay for a week while Max was away. One of the polyester pipe elbows above the ground had split so they decided to fix it. Max had a large box of fittings they could use to replace the one elbow. When Max got home, they showed him quite proudly their handy work. They had used five different elbows and four joiners to get the pipe round the corner. With tongue in cheek, Max said, 'Good job, ladies.' He wishes now he had taken a photo of their work.

They had also been feeding the bloody cockatoos and there were fifty of them in the afternoon on the front lawn. (Mind you, they weren't going to get much from what Max was calling the 'lawn'.)

'Christ,' Max said, 'don't do that. When we're not home, they will eat the wooden windowsills and the glass window will fall out.'

Aileen said, 'Oh, bugger.'

Jane said, 'Oh, shit.'

While Max was away at Shell in a meeting, the phone rang in the meeting room. 'It's for you, Max,' they said. Max picked up the phone to hear Jane crying her heart out. She told him that last night, the foxes had dug a hole in the back of the mud brick duck hootch and killed all the ducks. Max was very sympathetic about it, but as he was in the middle of the meeting, he said, 'I'm so sorry, love, I'll have to ring you back later.' They decided not to replace the ducks.

Everything seemed to happen when Max was away, leaving Jane to deal with it by herself. Sadly, Stocky developed a stomach tumour and had to be put down. Of course, Max was away again. She hugged Stocky's head, kissed his forehead and said a sad goodbye. Jane had become very attached to the horse, so having to have him put down by herself was a very stressful and a sad occasion.

Again, in Max's absence, Jane had to suck it up and take charge of organising the shearing of the sheep. With much bravado, she told Max not to worry; this would be right up her alley. Jane had become a very proficient farm girl. She could drive all the farm appliances, hook up and mow with the slasher, drive the forklift, jump-start flat batteries and change plugs and fuel filters, and had a heavy truck licence to boot. The only thing she wasn't really keen on was the way the shotgun would recoil into her shoulder.

When Max arrived home, the sheep had all been shorn and fly sprayed.

'Looks like you've done a good job, my farmer girl.'

She told Max it was all going according to plan until she tried to back the trailer full of sheep up to the sheepyard loading ramp. She lost count of how many goes she had; it had probably taken an hour. She was so bloody stressed, and so were the sheep. Max silently wished he'd been there with a videotape.

Jane worked as the administrator at the part of the local hospital that was a nursing home. The elderly residents had a pet lamb that one of the nurses would take home for the weekends. The nurse was going away for the week and asked

Jane if she would look after the lamb. They loaded the lamb into Jane's Nissan Patrol and off she went. Max was working in the paddock when Jane arrived in tears.

'What's wrong?'

'The lamb must have jumped out of the car window,' said Jane.

'What lamb?'

Jane explained why she had a lamb in the back of the Nissan. She had opened the sliding window in the back to give it some air. When she didn't see it jumping up and down, she thought it was lying down. When she got to the mailboxes and got out of the vehicle, she realised the lamb was gone. Jane was crying again.

'How am I going to tell the residents at the nursing home that I've killed their lamb?'

Max said he would go back in his ute and look along the road, although he didn't think there was much hope with the lamb jumping out at a hundred kilometres per hour. The road to town wasn't a major highway, just a single carriageway, with bush close to the road on both sides. Max drove slowly, carefully looking on both sides of the road for a dead lamb – more the case, he thought, than something running around going '*baa, baa, baa*'. By the time he reached the town he had found nothing, but on the way back he couldn't believe what he saw – the bloody lamb standing at the edge of the bush. Max stopped, opened the ute door and the lamb jumped in on top of him. *Now how could a small lamb like this survive a fall at a hundred kilometres with hardly a scratch? Jane will be a happy girl*, Max thought.

Suffice to say, Jane wasn't asked to babysit the lamb again.

'You don't have much luck with sheep, do you, dear?' Max said.

*

The specialist panel to draw up the final training package went for two days. Jane looked stunning in her red outfit and kept them all in check, particularly when the union delegate threw in the red herrings.

Max was starting to feel like he was born old. There had been a lot of water under the bridge that had washed up a mixture of sad and lovely memories, some that would make him sad for his entire life, but where Jane was concerned, she was the wind beneath his wings, and he loved her for just being who she was. Max knew they wouldn't be where they were now without her influence and expertise. He knew he was going to marry her one day, although he considered her to be way above his pay grade.

Three weeks later, a pilot course was scheduled at a hotel at Tullamarine that would run for four days. The panel consisted of a senior refueller from each of the major airports and two from selected country depots, one from each of the larger tank farms, the occupational health and safety manager from Shell House, the Shell Australia aviation manager, and since Max had included a segment of the course for first aid and CPR, the Shell Head Nursing Officer. She was also on the specialist panel. All the attendees were given their own copy of the proposed manual to follow as the modules were presented over the four days. At the end of each module, time was allocated for discussion. The proposed course modules to be presented by Max were:

- environmental issues
- occupational health and safety overview
- manual handling

- communication and working shift
- emergency procedures
- protective personal equipment
- spill procedures, apron and depot
- first aid (life support awareness)
- work clearance and permit to work system
- aviation static electricity
- quality control
- product receipt and release
- filtration equipment
- tank farm (distributor maintenance: daily, weekly and monthly testing)
- operational checks
- refuelling procedures – overwing and underwing
- defuelling aircraft.

The pilot course was well accepted, with some vigorous discussions along with the occasional addition and deletion of content that may have suited some locations but not others. Max explained the content might not be relevant for everyone but there will be those on the course for whom it would be, so he turned the decision over to the Shell Australia aviation manager, who decided the content was to be for all locations and should not be changed, a decision that was out of Max's pay grade. If the dog can bark at the gate better than you, you should use the dog. And if he's barking when he shouldn't be, it won't be you who gets yelled at.

Shell had decided that the courses would be held at a motel in Brisbane as most of the participants would be from New South Wales or further north, and since they were paying for travel and accommodation, it was their choice. Max's travel and accommodation would be reimbursed as per the contract. Each of the state aviation managers had been given a roster to attend an end-of-course dinner to present the refuellers their certificates of attainment. One by one, the courses rolled by with the usual attendance of wags and dags, and for the most part, it was considered worthwhile with successful outcomes.

During one of the courses, Max said his room phone rang at 11 pm. It was Jack, one of the course participants, who told Max he had just sat on the needle of a used bloody syringe that was stuck between the cushions on the couch.

'Bugger!' Max said, 'Go down to reception and I'll meet you there.'

Max asked the motel receptionist to ring the police, and when they arrived, a bit of a battle started. He explained what had happened to the two female cops. It was like talking to the Keystone Cops, female version.

The large one with the crew haircut and nose hair hanging out said, 'Well, what do you expect us to do?'

'Well, let me explain it this way,' said Max, 'I must make out my own report for the Shell Company head office and explain what actions I took. In my report, I will be saying I rang the police so they could get the particulars of the person last in that room, track them down and find out who they are. Are they just an old person using insulin or a junky on drugs? The hotel won't give me that information. So, the decision of what you do is entirely yours. Let me put it another way: if your arse had just sat on a used syringe, what would you want someone to do for you?'

'The one with the nose hairs glared at me,' Max said, 'and I knew if she could have got away with it, she would have rammed her black baton up my arse and twisted the end because she knew I was right. Before she did me any anal damage, I said, "Thanks for coming" and took Jack to the hospital for blood checks.'

Fortunately, it turned out that it was an insulin user who had accidentally lost the syringe in the couch, so Jack's HIV worries were over.

However, the worries from the course were not over for Max.

'Fair dinkum,' Max said to Jane, 'I've just had a call from Avis Rentals. They want to know where their bus is.'

'Well, where is it?'

'Last time I was in Brisbane, I gave the bus we use for the course to a refueller to take back to Avis because I had to refuel a 767 going to London, so we need to ask him what he did with it.'

After making a couple of phone calls, it was discovered the idiot refueller had parked it in front of the arrivals terminal and it had been towed away. The dickhead was too lazy to take the bus all the way back to Avis.

Max said, 'Why didn't the tow bloke just tell Avis to move their bloody bus?'

To further complicate matters, now that they had their bus, they wanted to know where the back seat was. Because some of the refuellers couldn't drive the bus with more than twelve seats, Max had said to take the back seat out, so it obviously hadn't been put back in. Max told Avis to take the bus to the Shell airport workshop and they would put it back in for them. A classic case of 'if you don't do it yourself, it doesn't get done'. Max usually saw to all these things himself, but because he had had to do the refuelling and only had enough time afterwards to catch his flight home, he had handed it over to one of the refuellers – fail!

Shell decided to put the distributor refuellers through separately on their own course, and that would take at least a year after the training for the Shell employee refuellers was finished. The distributor courses would be run at Bankstown Airport and that's where Max learnt to fly a Robinson R22 helicopter, lovingly called a Robbie. The Robbie is a two-seater helicopter used worldwide because of its reliability, mainly for training, mustering and personal use. It only has a range of about four hundred kilometres. Max calls them Puddle Jumpers.

He obtained a recreational pilots licence, sort of like the bubs grade of licences. Max knew he wouldn't be able to keep it current because reviews were required every ninety days if you weren't flying all the time. In a dream world, Max would have loved to have completed the next two steps for a private and commercial licence.

Chapter 19

Cootes, cockie and wine

The property that Max and Jane had purchased sat between a host of vineyards.

Max said to Jane, 'What do you think about putting in a vineyard?'

Jane's response was, 'Do we know anything about grapes?'

'Not a bloody thing,' said Max, 'but I can enrol at Melbourne University in the Dookie Agricultural section and learn what's required.'

And so began the journey into the nectar of the gods. The first person Max met on enrolment day was the bloody union representative – unbelievable! She wanted to ensure Max joined and paid his fees. Max wondered if there was a union representative at the primary schools yet. It didn't take Max long, mixing with the students at the university, to realise you can have a degree and still be an idiot. You shouldn't confuse education with intelligence. The family on the neighbouring property had become friends, and after discussing what Max and Jane were doing, they decided to follow suit and pool their resources, and of course they were going to get the benefit of what Max would learn. A name had been chosen and registered as 'Ainslie Crossing'; the neighbours would eventually choose a name for their own vineyard.

The bulldozers and diggers came in and dug two dams. Max and Jane decided while the machinery was there, they would get the ground prepared for a swimming pool as well. The paddocks were measured and marked for deep ripping and post holes were drilled along the rows. The inside of the house was a mess as well while they put a new concrete floor in and had the walls extended to meet the roof. Max wondered if they were doing too much all at once, but they both realised the need to get it all done while they had the money.

Jane was now working at the local hospital, which at least kept her away from the mud and upheaval around the property through the day. The property was too far out of town for workers to go back and forward so they would all bring their morning tea and lunch with them. Unfortunately for two of them who left their ute door open, the dog ate their lunches. Max said he shouldn't have laughed, but he couldn't help it.

Jane arrived home from the hospital after work and said that the electrician was here; he had followed her down the drive. Max asked if he had eyebrows.

'What?'

Max said, 'Never trust an electrician with no eyebrows.'

One of Johno's hare-brained ideas was to go into business with ground spas, so a purchase was made, and he arrived with it to install. Max, Johno and Brewster dug the hole for the spa, with that idiot Brewster in the hole with the arse out of his pants. About a week later, the spa was operational, and just as well because Johno had come off his dirt bike in the bush and was now lying in the spa with the skin off his legs.

Apart from the heavy machinery that cleared and pushed the trees down or dug the dams, all the hard labour of the vineyard set-up was done with the help of family members. Max and Jane had their own tractor, truck and forklift so that helped, but hundreds of holes for planting had to be drilled using a handheld motorised auger. One of the most difficult tasks was crawling along the bottom wire, clipping the dripper pipe and outlets on. Max could never explain sufficiently just how backbreaking all of this was.

The bench cuttings had been purchased from a credited phylloxera-free area. There are three grapevine zones – exclusion, risk and infested – and they had to be strictly adhered to. Phylloxera is an insect pest of grapevines. These almost microscopic, pale yellow, sap-sucking insects feed on the roots and leaves of the vines. The resulting deformation on roots and secondary fungal infections can girdle roots, gradually cutting off the flow of nutrients and water to the vines. Although there is no cure for phylloxera, you can plant grafted phylloxera-resistant American rootstock.

'While waiting to plant, we buried the cuttings upside down them in brickie's sand,' Max explained. 'Then, if all the preparation hadn't been hard enough, it rained like buggery for the next four days. There's an old saying: if you want the rainbow, you gotta put up with the rain. Well, we had to do just that.' The cuttings were starting to bud and needed to be planted, and the pre-drilled planting holes were now full of water. The crew took specialty soil to all the holes in wheelbarrows, two of them on hands and knees bailing water out of the planting holes before the cutting and then the soil going back in. However, after bailing, the bloody hole kept filling up again with water. By day three and still raining nonstop, everyone's clothes were covered in mud and soaking wet. They just took them off at the back door each night and put them on again the next day. Unpleasant for the first five minutes, but then you were soaked again so, it didn't really matter. Some of the crew managed to keep a sense of humour but some spat the dummy. Brewster kept poking fun at Les's wife, telling her that her fingers weren't going up the hole far enough, but she didn't see the funny side of it, packed up her bongos and went home. It was day six before the last cutting was planted. Jane said it was the worst time of her entire life.

Because of the weather, it was not ideal conditions for the plants. The worry now was how many cuttings would take. It was hard to tell because they were all budding in the sand, and they needed to go on through into the soil which had more water in the planting hole than in normal circumstances.

Max said to Jane and the family after the planting, 'The sun doesn't just hang around over one family, you know, so let's hope it's hanging around our family today. Remember, the same sun that melts the ice can also harden clay. Jane and I can't thank you enough for the tremendous effort you have given us this past week.'

The next week was taken up with the folding of plastic grow guards, placing them over the plant and clipping to the bottom wire.

A ten-bay shed had been built with a workshop at one end and a temperature-controlled shed at the other end for wine storage. Three 60,000-litre water storage tanks had been installed at the end of the shedding, ready to be filled from the guttering. The pool was about to be filled by the water tanker from town, and the electrician had finished in the roof and was leaving with his eyebrows intact, which has to tell you something. The pumps to the drip lines and feeder suctions from the dams were operational just in time for the hot weather.

'Mother Nature amazes me at times,' Max said. 'When the drippers came on, the small, frilled neck lizards hung upside down on the drip line, taking moisture from the drip head. Anything else that walked, crawled, wriggled or flew took advantage of the cool water.'

Max didn't mind sharing, as long as the vines kept growing.

*

Max's earlier prediction about the Shell tanker drivers was about to happen. Shell had realised that what they did best was refine fuel and sell it; they weren't meant to be a transport company. They sold off the trucks and paid off the drivers, and they had also had enough of some of their refuellers, so most of them were shown the gate. The Cootes tanker group had now taken over the refuelling, which meant Sempcom would be training their refuellers.

Max had been slowly guiding number one son, Martin, in the fuel industry direction, and as such, he had secured a job as a Shell refueller at Tullamarine Airport. So now that the refuelling had been moved across from Shell to Cootes Transport, he would be one of their refuellers along with others who were taken across from Shell. All the Shell refuellers had to be interviewed and those who weren't considered troublemakers would now be employed by Cootes.

Sempcom had also been awarded the contract at the two major gas tanker loading facilities to run the driver induction courses; once again, a training program had to be written.

Jesus, it's like a bloody octopus! Max thought. *The tentacles are strangling me, and I can't be in two places at once.*

Sempcom would now have to be in full swing to accommodate the new workload. It had now been contracted to write the training package and conduct the induction training at Elgas, Origin Energy, BHP and Esso. Max said they were called to a meeting with Cootes, who were taking on a large portion of the Shell deliveries system, a large step in size for the company. Shell had insisted that all contractor drivers have the same training their drivers had previously been given by Sempcom. Management at Cootes had said to Max that Cootes had to either grow or get out and that Max was going to have to do the same.

Back at Ainslie Crossing, which was fast becoming a good-looking vineyard, some heavy decisions needed to be made. Max and Jane realised they just couldn't handle all this by themselves. So, seeing they were sitting in a vineyard, they did what anyone else would do – they opened a bottle of wine, maybe two. They both agreed to ask Martin and John to join the company, and as they had been asked by Shell to run an instructor development course, they would need to put them both on the course; that is, if they were interested.

The course participants were from a variety of mainly fuel-orientated companies. The training was quite stressful for the two boys, a big change for them with many strange and new topics and a lot of after-hours work on the five-day live-in course. They needed this qualification to be part of the team. The modules the boys were faced with along with other participants were:

- leadership
- communication

- training and instructional skills
- job and task analysis
- training management plans
- developing training objectives
- lesson plans
- assessment tools
- external and internal training validation

Max became the outrider assessor and trainer under contract for Cootes. As it required a lot of travel to meet drivers at loading and unloading sites, Cootes gave Max a new company car. After a few weeks of Max catching the drivers not complying with safety regulations, they secretly arranged to have his numberplate changed to CTG 007 (Cootes Transport Group, James Bond). Max didn't mind; he let them have their fun. Max's nephew Simon came on board to help with the workload and his help while they were busy was appreciated.

At different intervals, Max would stay in Melbourne, usually in Frankston for the week. Max had some time ago spent a week at Frankston, but now he was at Esso/BHP at Long Island Point at Hastings on the Mornington Peninsula. When he checked his phone at the end of the day, he had a message from the Homicide Division. *Christ*, Max thought, *what do they want?* Max rang back and spoke to a Detective Ringbone (should've been bonehead!) He told Max that two police officers, Gary Silk and Rodney Miller, had been shot dead in Cochrane Road, Moorabbin at 2 am on 16 August 1998. A witness had seen a car, the same colour as Max's apparently, with the same numberplates at the scene that night. He wanted Max to verify where he was when the murders had happened. Max told him he moved around in different states each week and he would check with his office timesheet to see where he was at that date and time.

Max rang Jane and told her what had happened and asked her to check where he was. She looked at the timesheets and told him he was in Frankston. How could he verify his movements on that night? He had been staying in a motel by himself and they wouldn't be able to account for his movements at 2 am when the shooting occurred. Shit! Now he was really worried; even though it wasn't him, he would still be a bloody suspect. He decided to let Cootes know because it was their company car he was driving.

When he arrived at Cootes, the receptionist told him the police had been there asking who that car was allocated to, and of course it was to Max. After a day or so, Max remembered that the original numberplates that had supposedly been seen had been changed long before the shootings, so someone else would be using those plates, not him. Max decided to do some of his own investigation. He rang the VicRoads registration branch in Dandenong, and guess what? Those original plates were still on the shelf; they had never been re-issued.

Why couldn't this bonehead detective have checked that himself to save the worry for Max and Cootes, even though everyone knew it would hardly have been Max who had done the dirty deed? Max had great pleasure in ringing the bonehead back but had to leave a message. He gave him the numberplate information from the registration branch and asked him if he wanted himself to come in and help him with his job, because he didn't seem to be doing too well on his own. Max never received a response.

Sometime later, Max was telling the story to a police officer who drove tankers for Cootes part-time. He told Max if someone sees part of a numberplate and a car colour, they do a digital check on cars of roughly that colour and start ringing owners for their whereabouts on that night to try to match the missing numbers that hadn't been seen by the witness. Just another bloody Max Thornton saga.

*

Back at Ainslie Crossing, Max and Jane had a phone call from friends in Nagambie, Eddy and Betty, asking them if they wanted to join them on a houseboat for a week on the Murray River. As it turned out, the dates were free, but Max was a bit sceptical about it because he knew they were heavy drinkers, and once they were on the boat, they would be stuck with them for the week. However, these friends could be a lot of fun, so they took the chance and said yes. Bad move!

They met them at the houseboat departure point, paid the fee, including a large deposit in case of any damage, and unloaded their clothes and supplies for the week. Max and Jane took a case of scotch and Coke cans, a case of beer and half a dozen bottles of wine, which they knew would be more than ample. However, their friends took on board eight cases of beer, three cases of white and two cases of red wine. Just as well there was a large icebox on the boat to store the booze. They were going to share the driving of the boat, one day on one day off, so every second day you could relax on the top deck, have a drink and sunbake. The deal was that the day you were in charge of the boat, you didn't drink alcohol until the boat was moored for the night.

Max didn't go anywhere camping or on trips like this without his chainsaw, so when they tied up the boat for the night, they could cut wood for the fire. The first night they tied up to the bank and ran out the boarding ramp, they soon had a nice fire going and all was well.

Eddy had a bad habit of leaving the flywire door open when he went in and out, letting in the bloody mosquitoes, and Max had to keep going up the plank to shut the door. At one stage when following Eddy up the plank to get a drink, and as usual Eddy leaving the door open, Max closed it after he went in. When Eddy came back out, he walked straight through the closed door, flywire and all.

'Jesus,' Max said, 'look what you've done.'

It took Max an hour to put it all back together again. Eddy was no bloody help; he was already half-whacked. Max thought, *Yeah, well, I knew this shit was bound to happen.*

'You just can't relax when they're driving the boat,' Jane said. 'They just keep drinking.'

If Max saw the boat starting to head for the bank, he would run downstairs and there would be no one at the wheel. They'd be out at the icebox getting another drink. What a bloody nightmare!

One morning, Max got up early and went into the lounge area. Betty was standing there with no clothes on, stark naked, having a beer. To make it even worse, she wasn't good-looking; her body had since gone bad on her. Now if she had been a young chick, Max might have stayed and had a beer with her.

On the second-last night, it was Eddy's turn to dock the boat at the end of the day. The current was fairly strong, and he was trying to get in on a bend in the river between two big gum trees.

Max said to Jane, 'Shit, he's going to try and get in there. No way can this work.'

As the boat went in, the current pushed it across to a huge gum tree and it was evident that a thick branch was going to hit the boat. What made Max think he could hold the houseboat away from the tree he didn't know. Where he was pushing from, there were two windows, the lower window was for the low bunk bed and the top window for the top bunk. As he was trying to hold the boat off the tree, he shoved his arse through the bottom window, and the tree branch went into the bedroom through the top window.

'Shit, shit!' said Max.

There he was with the chainsaw in the bedroom cutting the bloody branches out. Far out! Max rang the houseboat people and told them they would be coming back with two broken windows, so they might like to have a window dude waiting to fix it, as he had been told that there was another party taking the boat out after them. So, the moral to this is: be bloody careful who you trap yourself on a houseboat with.

*

The government introduced a subsidised training program to alleviate the financial burden of training employees for a specific role and introduced a system like an apprenticeship. The minimum requirement was Certificate 3 in training, and much like the apprenticeship, the trainees were required to be given time away from their workplace of employment for specialised training at a registered training organisation (RTO). Sempcom successfully applied to be accredited as an RTO with the government authority. If Jane thought she knew what stress and anxiety were, she soon realised Sempcom was only in its infancy and was about to change once they got involved with the government in training and financial auditing.

No wonder small businesses go broke dealing with governmental bureaucratic narrow-minded thinking – that is, that one hat fits all. Here they were with an office, three ladies working with laptops and computers, photocopying equipment, telephone answering machines, emailing and internet, along with company uniforms for the now seven employees, five company cars with fuel cards, and all with mobile phones.

'Jesus,' Max said, 'I want my mum!'

Jane was now full-time in the office as she was the company CEO.

Martin said, 'What are you, Dad?'

Max said, 'I'm like you, mate, one of the workers. I'm not getting involved with the government shit. People like you and me can leave that to the experts in our office, people like Jane and her staff. Think yourself lucky we're out on the tools.'

The government conducted annual audits, which usually took between one and two days, going through policy and procedure manuals, trainee records, financial records, attendance at classes and duration times with a fine-toothed comb. Although the RTO was always operating one hundred per cent correct, and that they were told on many occasions after audits that the Sempcom RTO was the best in Australia in their industry, Jane always got herself in a tizz.

'Mind you,' said Max, 'the ladies in the office constantly found it necessary to check the attainment results and site visit reports the boys submitted back from the field, who were not real good at dotting the i's and crossing the t's at times. The hard work by the ladies was largely the reason for the excellent audit reports.'

The auditors would check to see if the trainees had been released from their place of employment for the required specialist training. And here lay the problem of the government's 'one hat fits all' scenario which Max constantly explained to the auditors. For example, an apprentice plumber goes to trade school where they have the necessary equipment for them to use and be tested. Good system, Max said, no problems. Now let's take our case of the aircraft refueller. If you look at our facility here, you will see we have a large selection of aviation, gas and petroleum fittings. You want to find a Jumbo 747 or a heavy lift helicopter hidden here or the other twenty-seven varieties of aircraft that require practical assessment. We take them away from their place of employment for the theory, but after that, all other training has to take place at the airport; in other words, his place of employment. And if you want to get technical, although he is at his place of employment, he is with his RTO on that training day, not his normal daily duties, albeit he is at the airport where he works. So, you need to be able to tick off that practical side as 'away from employment'.

'Jesus,' Max said after the auditor had left, 'it's like talking to a beanbag, Jane.'

'What did he say?' she said.

'Well, he stood there with a faraway look. I don't know if he was piddling his pants or just didn't understand. Any decision for policy change for refuellers would be miles above the bloke's pay grade, so don't expect any answers anytime soon. Anyway, hopefully, he will take that information back to the wonderland he comes from, and that's the best we can hope for.'

*

'We're getting real close to picking the grapes,' Max said to Jane. 'We need to do some Baume and Brix tests to check the sugar levels, and we need to balance the damage the cockatoos and smaller birds are doing against the ideal sugar levels that are needed.'

Max was well aware of the amount of money that had been spent on this venture, and this was no time for a slack decision, albeit he was only an amateur in this industry, and family and friends had put a lot of time into helping to get it to this stage. Max went slowly down a selection of the vine rows, taking juice samples. He did this on three different occasions from different areas to make sure he got an overall sample. He used his hydrometer to measure the Baume of the juice samples he had taken to check the sugar levels before picking.

He said to Jane, 'We need a reading of twelve per cent Baume, which is enough sugar to make a wine with somewhere between twelve to thirteen per cent alcohol. Mind you, I'm quoting this technical stuff from the written word of experts in the industry; I'm not that smart. Someone once told me I was the smartest person in the room; I told him I was obviously in the wrong room.'

The hydrometer readings were close enough, given the ongoing damage the birds were doing to the grapes, so the 'go' button was pressed to begin picking.

The vines hadn't grown evenly, and Max reckoned they were probably only picking five acres in their first harvesting. The boys alternated picking and driving the tractor and truck. By the end of day one, they had gone through three packets of band aids, as it was difficult reaching into the vines without snipping fingers with the secateurs.

'First time pickers, all of us,' said Max, and he doubted if they could convince the family to pick again next year, although he might be able to soften them up with a few bottles of wine.

The vineyard for its first harvest only yielded two tons and filled one-and-a-half barrels, which would make about four hundred bottles. The wine label designed by a firm in Melbourne was quite stunning: it read 'Ainslie Crossing Red Clay Ridge Shiraz'. More importantly, Jane was impressed with the results. They made a trade-off with one of the larger wineries in the area and gave them their grapes in return for one hundred bottles of their finished wine. At the time, it didn't seem like much return for time, effort and money.

Jane said, 'Don't be too disappointed, Max. The vines are still very young, and so are we in terms of experience, knowledge and expertise. And in our temperature-controlled cellar, we do have a hundred and twenty bottles of Ainslie Crossing Red Clay Ridge Shiraz – three years ago, we only had a paddock. With a bit of luck, it will improve next harvest.'

Max and Jane knew from experience that the harder they worked the luckier they got. That's how it had always been for them – hard work and some luck.

The swimming pool was now looking fantastic. At the shallow end was a table just above the water line, with a seating area where the water was up to your waist. There was a hole in the middle for the big umbrella. The locals had started calling the property the Ponderosa in the Green Valley. It was a far cry from the dust-ridden shanty they had moved into.

On one of Brewster's visits, he stripped off for a swim.

Max said, 'Christ, Brewster, you've got a white plastic-looking body, like a window dummy in Myers not dressed yet.'

Brewster said, 'Well, I'm not an exhibitionist, you know.'

Max had used his chainsaw skills and built an outdoor pine

bar on the rear deck near the pool, with a nice long piece of oak timber for the countertop and timber cut into shingles for the front of the bar. He had also brought home from one of his trips to Sydney two one-arm bandit poker machines that now stood next to the bar. In one corner was an electric organ and on the other side of the bar was a small pool table. Nothing fancy, just for a bit of fun.

It happened on one of those warm summer evenings when Skipper was going off his brain barking at the bottom of the organ. The dog was very good at alerting them when snakes were close by.

Jane said, 'I bet there's a bloody snake behind there, Max.'

He said, 'Go and get your gum boots on and stand on the stool. When I pull the corner of the organ out, if the snake slithers out, you'll be safe.'

Max got the shotgun. He could see the body of a large brown snake. The bloody thing had wrapped itself in and around the electrical cord.

'Jesus,' he said, 'I hate snakes.'

So, Jane stood on the stool and slowly moved the organ, enough for Max to get a shot. He gave it both barrels and blew both the electric cord and the snake into many pieces. It blew the plug on the back of the organ clean off, and the house went into immediate darkness when the safety overload switches in the power box tripped.

'See, said Max, 'I told you the electrician who rewired the place would be good. Always see if they've still got their eyebrows.'

The neighbours who had also planted vines came down for a barbecue and the wife brought her mother along as well. Her mother was over the moon when she saw the poker machines.

Max had bought $100 worth of ten cent coins to play the machines; they were only there for some fun and, of course, you couldn't lose any money. After they had all gone home, Max saw that all the ten cent pieces had gone. It turned out the mother had taken what she imagined was her winnings, even though she hadn't put any money in to start with.

'Jesus, Jane, these people vote!' said Max.

You needed to be careful where you were walking in the summer after snake hibernation. Most of them would just scurry away, but the browns were a little more aggressive. You needed to look very carefully, unlike the neighbour's wife who called out to her husband that there was a red-bellied black behind the hay bales. He rushed into the barn, poked the shotgun over the hay bale and shot the shit out of his red tractor's old windscreen rubber, the black rubber with red over spray paint on it.

'We had never seen snakes so close to the house in previous years,' Max said.

'What's bringing them here now?' Jane said.

'Buggered if I know,' said Max, 'but something's attracting them.'

Suddenly it dawned on them both – the bird aviary on the back veranda was bringing in mice, which in turn brought in the snakes.

'Right. That's coming down ASAP,' said Max.

They gave the birds away to friends, but before Max pulled the aviary down, he found a small Major Mitchell galah with a broken wing on the road. He needed to put his work gloves on to pick it up, as its beak was like a bolt cutter. He brought him home and put him in the aviary. Not knowing what else to do with the cockie, Max shoved it in some shade cloth he had put over the bird wire on top of the aviary for extra shade for the birds. A day later, there was this ear-piercing screeching on the back veranda. He went out to find a huge number of cockatoos on the roof of the aviary tearing holes in the shade cloth.

'Shit!' said Max.

'I can't believe they're doing that!' said Jane.

They called the galah Wally. Those who are old enough will remember a cartoon in the *Herald Sun* called Wally and the Major. Since this was a Major Mitchell, out came the name which was suitably apt. Max pulled down the aviary and made a plastic ladder high up into a gum tree near the house, so the galah would be safe from predators, as it couldn't fly, its wing being beyond repair. Wally hung around the house for some months and then disappeared. They hoped that the predators like foxes and wild cats hadn't got him. It was sometime later when Max was out rabbiting with the dog that he saw a galah sitting up in a gum tree.

He said to Skipper, 'That couldn't be Wally, could it, mate?'

Max called out from under the tree, 'Hey, Wally ... Bugger me, Skipper, did you see that? The galah tipped his head from side to side, I reckon that's Wally!'

Well, he hoped it was.

At the vineyard on the other side of the creek, a cooper was re-doing some wine barrels. He had apparently brought his father with him to give him a day out, as he was recovering from an aneurism and some brain damage. While the cooper was working, his father wandered off and it was some time before he was missed. All the local landowners were notified and asked to join the search. Over the next two days Max helped, along with police helicopters, the dog squad and the

SES. The main issue impeding the search was that, beyond the vineyard fence, was the Army training area, about fifty kilometres square. The search was eventually called off, and it wasn't until several weeks later that his body was found by the military during a training exercise. Sad news for everyone concerned.

*

The final conference with Cootes took place in Ian Cootes' office. In the corner was a fantastic old petrol bowser which had been made into a fridge. Max couldn't help admiring it and told Ian he thought it was fantastic.

It was decided that, apart from internal training, there would need to be site visits with drivers while they were unloading at the petrol and gas service stations. This would cover the government regulations for the Level 3 certificate, and for the refuellers, would need to be registered as a practical assessment away from place of employment due to the specialist equipment required for the assessments. The Sempcom trainers would be like outriders and meet drivers at their delivery sites. Once again, this training with the modules and external visits would be ongoing for some time due to the number of company drivers. On many an occasion, Max would spend fourteen hours straight assessing drivers on the road or work.

It was always a worry for Max and Jane that others depended on them financially. Like Max and Jane, all would have mortgage and other financial responsibilities, and while Sempcom was currently in good shape, if you started losing contracts, you'd have to start losing staff. The main reason the company was successful was because they were good at what they did and were now sometimes called to meetings with the Australian Liquified Petroleum Gas Association (ALPGA). They were well thought of within the overall fuel industry, and it needed to stay that way. Max was always reminding the boys in the field that they were the company's billboard, and their performance would reflect the company's professional standards, and as such, ensuring the security of theirs and others employment within Sempcom.

The builders were now at Ainslie Crossing, adding a mezzanine floor to one end of the house, when a strange vehicle drove in.

Max said, 'I don't know that car. Who's that?'

Jane said, 'Well, I'll be! That's Ian Cootes. I wonder what he's doing here.'

They all said their hellos and Ian said, 'Well, Max, show me around.'

As they toured the property, he asked what was in one of the sheds. Max told him it was only a storeroom, that there was nothing in there that was worth looking at.

Ian said, 'Open it up and let's have a look.'

Max thought, *I hope he doesn't think I've pinched something.*

He opened the door and couldn't believe what he was looking at. It was a restored old Shell petroleum bowser made into a fridge, just like the one he had admired in Ian's office some time ago.

'I don't know what to say,' Max said.

Ian said, 'That is for the excellent and loyal training support you have given our company over the years, Max. This is to show our appreciation.'

An engraved plaque was on the door of the fridge which read:

Presented to Max Thornton from Cootes Holdings
For the excellence in Training and Safety Management
Over the last 10 years
September 2001

Jane was in the background smiling and smirking, because she and Martin had known about this for some time. Somehow, with the help of Paul Cootes, Ian's son, they had managed to sneak it into the shed just recently while Max was away.

Chapter 20

Reaping the Rewards

Max and Jane decided to slaughter a lamb and Jane asked Max if he knew how they were going to do it. Using his short answer technique, Max said, 'No.' Well,' Jane said, 'I suppose we could borrow a video from the library and follow the instructions. It can't be that hard.'

After Max had slaughtered the lamb and it had been hung in the cool room, with Jane making sure Max didn't slaughter her pet lamb Ethel, they set up a large, long table in the kitchen and began to follow the video, called 'Easy steps to cut up your lamb.' It wasn't as easy as it bloody looked.

There was supposed to be eight sections of the lamb to get edible cuts from: the neck, the shoulder, the rib, the loin, the sirloin, the breast, the flank and the leg, from where you would get a shoulder boneless roast, spare ribs, rack of lamb, lamb breast and lamb chops. When they were finished, Max said he couldn't even recognise a bloody chop, never mind anything else. Jane said she thought there were supposed to be four legs. The dogs got far more than they should have. Max said the bloody video was no good, they had no bloody idea what they were doing and would give that feedback to the library when they returned the video.

They decided they would have another go, but this time they would get Max's mate, Johno the butcher, up to show them how it was done. Of course, he was full of bullshit smartarse remarks while he was doing it, which didn't disappoint Max. It was inspiring to watch people who are professionals at what they do. When Johno had finished, he put all the cuts into sealed bags with mint and seasoning and labelled them. What the dogs got you could hold in one hand. Unfortunately, Johno spruced on with more bullshit on how good he was; the worst part about out that was that it was true. But Jane was happy, and Ethel was still roaming in the pasture.

*

The house at Ainslie Crossing was looking magnificent in a now lush green valley of vines that had once been a dust and gravel bowl. This was Ainslie Crossing in her party dress. The vineyard that surrounded the house lawns gave the place a Mediterranean feel and if they didn't get too stressed about how much money they'd pumped into the place, it was a great achievement by Max and Jane, considering they had had nothing in the beginning. Cut into the mezzanine floor were three wine barrels with the front half cut to swing out as doors. Behind them was the house wine cellar with access from the dining room; this was one of Max's 'go to bed and dream up' designs, another project moment.

It would soon be Max's sixtieth Birthday and Jane's fiftieth. They were going to have a wingding event, so they engaged a renowned party hire service, and they planned to have eighty or so family and friends. The party hire men came and set up a very large marquee with a dance floor, tables, chairs and so on. Catering had been contracted out and a four-piece band organised for the night. The band were coming from Melbourne, so their accommodation in the nearest town had to be paid for. Max surrounded the dance floor with hay bales and put the tractor in place under the marquee while it was being erected. All the spare beds and lounges in the house and on the deck would be used for sleeping, some would be staying in town and most of the visitors were bringing their own tents and vans. The theme for the night was 1950s and '60s, and as the guests arrived, it was great to see so many had made such an effort to dress accordingly. Jane had found an old leather jacket in the op shop for Max to wear and she had sewn a motif of dice on the back. For herself, she had made a bright green, full circle skirt with a net petticoat underlay with sequins sewn on in the shape of a poodle.

Max's son, Martin, was MC for the night. Once everyone was seated, he made the first announcement using the band's microphone: 'The helicopter pilot that my dad flew with in Vietnam has sent a tape recording from America for you to hear.'

Martin played the tape, and everyone listened. 'Congratulations on reaching sixty and happy birthday, you little Aussie bugger. Wouldn't it be nice to be there tonight with you? So, turn around Max – here I am.'

Max turned around and there was Bruce, all the way from the US!

'Well, I'm sorry,' Max said to everyone, 'but I'm afraid I'm going to cry.'

What a surprise! Their friend, Denise Bell, had arranged this with Jane. These girls can really keep a secret when they want too, yet there were times when you wouldn't tell some of them anything. Max's inner feelings about Jane had always been that she was above his pay grade, super smarter than him, and he adored her for the things she did. Organising Bruce from America was above and beyond anything Max could have hoped for and a wonderful birthday present. *Damn*, he thought, *she's done it again – beaten me to the punch.* He did secretly love it when she pampered him – but don't tell her that!

Denise Bell and her husband Bob along with a working group spent many tireless hours, weeks and months designing and guiding the book called *Call Sign Vampire*. It is a beautifully presented book of stories and pictures of a proud military medical unit in Vietnam.

Max had wanted to use the occasion, while family and friends were there, to get married but his divorce had not come through, which really pissed him off. No one at the party would have known his plan, although the writing should have been on the wall. Max and Jane had been together for sixteen years, come party time. Max's twin sister Dorris came on board to help with a new plan Max had decided to organise; she arranged for a celebrant to be at the party, introduced as a friend of Dorris, and she was going to perform a ceremony of commitment. Max arranged for the band to play his and Jane's favourite song, 'My Friend', and without further ado, he grabbed the microphone and said, 'Jane, will you marry me?'

Jane was totally stunned but managed to yell out, 'Yes, Max, of course I will marry you.'

Dorris gave Jane a veil and some flowers and the ceremony was performed. This was a huge surprise for everyone and was so warmly received. One of Jane's dearest girlfriends, Frances, immediately stepped up as bridesmaid and Bruce from the US became the best man.

When Max's American pilot and very good friend made his speech, he referred to Max as the Bloody Kangaroo, which is what the Americans called Max when he was in Vietnam. It was what was printed on Max's very own flying helmet that the crew had given him when he flew with them.

He told them that when in Vietnam, Max needed looking after the whole time, 'and often shit his pants during the hairy moments–– '

'––which was bullshit!' Max yelled out.

It was a lovely speech and Max was glad his children were there to hear it.

The night was a huge success, and the band were very good. They knew the best music to play for the different ages that were at the party. The young lady who sang was fabulous and they all rocked on until well after 1 am.

'Mind you,' Max said, 'we had to pay extra for that, but by that time, we were well under the weather and nothing else mattered.'

During the set-up of the marquee, Max had placed a hay bale over the septic pit that was near where everyone would be walking that night. The next day, while packing up, Max removed the hay bale ready to replace the lid. A friend of Dorris who only had one leg was being helped along by her husband and fell down the bloody hole. She was a large woman and had to be lifted out. Max gave them a case of wine to try to pacify them. Jane's friend, Frances, who was a health and safety officer with Workcover, saw what had happened and gave Max a bloody lecture on safety.

*

Two more harvests had now been completed and the tonnage had more than doubled. However, the vineyard was getting hard to manage, even with two part-time workers spraying, pruning, mowing, repairing drippers, clearing small fish out of the strainer baskets in the dam pumps and the many other jobs that go with farming and maintaining a property. Getting pickers to harvest was more difficult each year. This year they paid the local football and netball clubs to do it. The family had lost interest while they still had all their fingers, and to be fair, they had their own lives and work commitments to attend too. Although they were enjoying drinking the shiraz, the volume hardly covered the production costs. With Max and Jane now totally committed to where the bulk of their income came from, it seemed like they were being strangled by the vineyard venture. The seven-day-a-week, ten-hour-a-day schedule coupled with the vineyard's ongoing commitments were just getting too much, and Max and Jane weren't getting any younger. Max said something had to give, and he didn't want it to be either of them. They needed to tame the dragon. It was obvious to both of them the vineyard was the flame blower and would burn their arses if they didn't start thinking about the best way to slay the bloody thing, not tomorrow but real soon. Along with Max and Jane when they were home, and with the hired help they were just coping.

But if truth be said, as hard as it had been to do, they were proud of their achievements. The grapes had been sent as usual to the large vineyard for the wine to be made and graded. Max was of the opinion that the latest pick would yield the best vintage so far. 'We will wait and see,' he said. The latest wine Max thought was so good it should be called a reserve, and so labels were made for 'Ainslie Crossing Red Clay Ridge Reserve 2003'.

The Victorian Wine Show was coming up and they decided to enter their latest wine. This show has the largest gathering of Victorian wines in one place. It's where your wine is benchmarked. Once the judging is done, a dinner is held the night before open day. Only those who won gold medallions were invited to the dinner, and Max and Jane weren't invited, but exhibitors got free entry and a free booklet in which the results were printed. The hall where the exhibition was being held was huge, and there was wine on tables as far as the eye could see. The booklet listed all wines exhibited by number, what table number they were on and if the wine had won a medallion. Jane had the book and looked for the table number their wine was on.

'Well, I'll be. Look at that, Max. We have won a bronze medallion! Only half a point away from silver – not too shabby for a couple of Aussie battlers.'

'You've just gotta keep having a go, mate,' Max said.

They were both so excited. Jane sent Max off to find a chemist shop to buy a disposable camera. They hadn't even given a thought to bringing one as they weren't expecting any accolades. Although Max hadn't said anything, he had been quietly confident that they might get an award; however, he wouldn't have been too upset if they hadn't.

*

While Arlene was visiting, she asked Max if he had ever given the $200 back to Anne he had borrowed all those years ago.

'Shit,' Max said, 'I'd forgotten all about it. Bloody hell, I haven't lost all my marbles yet, but there must be a small hole in the bag somewhere. What brought all this on, Arlene?'

'Anne told me just recently that she never got the $200 back that she lent you. She told me not to say anything, but I knew you would want to know.'

'Jesus Christ, Arlene, she's waited all these years to come out with this, and then tells her sister? I'm the one she needs to talk to. Does anyone else think like me, or is it just me out of step with the rest of the world?'

Max sent Anne the $200 immediately.

*

Shell Aviation were aware of Max's history as a military instructor in PNG and they knew he could speak their language, so he was asked to go there and conduct two separate courses, which meant travelling there twice. Max would be going with a bloke whose surname was Bird; his nickname was Feathers. Max and Feathers had worked together on many occasions. He was very experienced in the aviation industry and was also a good friend of Max. Even though Max knew that most of them would speak enough English, Feathers would be relying on Max if some of the trainees' English wasn't that good, as Max could then talk to them in their own language. Max knew from experience in PNG that just because they smiled and nodded, it didn't always mean they understood. What really surprised Max was that two of the refuellers had been soldiers on one of Max's military courses years ago, and of course they recognised him straight away. When Max came home, he found old course photos of these two blokes, and he took them back with him on the next trip to show them.

Circumstances had changed considerably in PNG, particularly in Port Moresby since self-government, and Max considered it was no longer safe enough for Jane to go with him. Even Max and Feathers needed to be careful where they went, and wherever they went they made sure they were always with a group of the refuellers. They stayed at a large luxury hotel close to the airport. Each morning, a bus would take them to the airport and return them at night. There was a high security wall around the hotel with roaming guards, and on several occasions, gunshots could be heard outside the wall. There was really no need to venture out, as the hotel was huge and had everything you needed, and not just anyone was admitted. Max would have liked to visit Murray Barracks and look at the house the family had lived in when they were there, but sadly that wasn't going to happen. All of the emergency vehicles – police, ambulance and fire brigade – had wire mesh over their windows. Max saw an ambulance go by with a coffin and a herd of people in it; who knows where that was going?

There was now a four-lane highway from the airport to Port Moresby, so a long, high walking bridge had been built for pedestrians to safely cross to the other side. No one used the bridge (they were all still dodging the traffic), because when they got to the middle, there was no escape and they, particularly the women, got bashed and robbed by what they call the rascals.

'Look,' Max said to Jane, 'I'm trying to not to paint PNG as an awful place. I don't know what places like Wewak and Lae are like these days, but Port Moresby is just not a safe place. Lae is the second largest city in PNG, and I wonder how safe that is these days. If I'm offending anyone, I'm sorry, but that's exactly what it was like when I was there this time.'

As far as the course went, it was a satisfying experience. The trainees were respectful, and they had many laughs teaching Feathers the language and listening to him speaking it back to the class.

'Don't worry,' Max said to Jane, 'Not having used the language for several years, I also got some laughs from the students. I know I've said this before, you have to be young and stupid before you can be old and wise, and I'm wondering if I've come the full circle yet. I must be getting close, as I've done my time with the stupid part!'

The company was still going flat out with Level 3 certificate training with petroleum tanker drivers, both gas and petrol. Jane and the office staff had done the financial figures with the expenses of travel and motel accommodation in Sydney for Max and the boys, and it was decided to lease an apartment in Brighton Le Sands. Furnishings were mostly from second-hand stores, and Max put a in a well-stocked bar, though he was the only one who restocked the bloody thing (the boys were very good at emptying it). The apartment could be used by the family if they wanted a stay in Sydney. Jane and Max's sister had stayed there on occasions but were never impressed with having to do some cleaning when they had arrived after the boys had been there. Mind you, the boys never broke anything, unlike the girls who broke the glass coffee table while trying to move it so they could vacuum the carpet underneath.

Max said, 'It's like throwing a stone into a pond – there's always going to be a ripple effect. If you're any good at what you do, the word soon spreads; the same as it does if you're not.'

And that's why the next contract was for Mobil Aviation in Fiji.

As Sempcom owned the training package, there was no need to write a new one, just make some minor changes like deleting the word Shell and inserting Mobile, not time-consuming for Max or the boys but all time-consuming for the office staff. All course materials for twenty participants had to be put together and boxed for air freight to Fiji; this included ten modules of instruction, and handouts, PowerPoint presentations, videos, course daily programs, timesheets and some personal protective equipment. The course participants would be from Fiji, Hawaii and various surrounding islands. Max and Martin would be going as the instructors, and Jane and one of the office workers, Jo, Martin's wife, would go also for day-to-day administrative support. Jane was also accredited to fill in as an instructor on some of the subjects if required.

Max and Jane decided that 2003 was looking like a good year to get married in Fiji. No family or friends, apart from Martin and Jo, were told of this; it was to be a surprise to all when they got home. Arrangements were made for the wedding to take place after the course finished. Jane and Jo did all the planning, and they were all going for a week to Sonaisali Island, where the resort offered a wedding package. Jane said it looked great, so they were 'all systems go'.

The course progressed without too many issues. The modules consisted of theory and practical airside refuelling. The practical work had to be done airside at 6 am, training two refuellers each day. That was the time the 727 needed to be refuelled prior to departure for Sydney, and it also fitted in with course theory time which started at 8 am, so that Max and Martin were back in time for the start of that. One of the course participants was really concerned about the final exam. He was convinced he would fail, and he worried about it for the entire course. After the exam, the students were outside talking to each other about the questions that were on the exam paper.

They said to the bloke who was worried, 'How did you go with the five questions on the back page?'

'Shit,' he said, 'I didn't look there! That's it, then. I've bloody failed the course.'

They had intended not telling him there were no questions on the last page until the results came out, but he was so upset they told him later that day that there were really no other questions. Max had to walk away in case the poor bugger saw him laughing.

Martin had volunteered to do the 6 am practical training and that suited Max just fine. At his age, he'd rather be in bed at 6 am. The smug smile soon came off Max's face when Martin came down with some sort of flu strain. He was really crook, so Max was now the man at 6 am. It wasn't long before they all started to show symptoms of the flu – not the people on the course, just the four of them. This meant no one who was sick or looked like they were sick was allowed into the classroom. Fortunately, it didn't happen to all of them at the same time, so there was always an instructor available each day.

One particular afternoon when the girls had gone for some retail therapy in downtown Nadi, it was Martin's turn in the classroom, so Max decided to get in the car and find a nice quiet beach somewhere. He drove a few kilometres along the coast and found the perfect spot, a peaceful cove. He took off his shoes and socks, grabbed a towel and headed up the beach. The sand was warm and soft and gave his feet a massaged feeling. As he walked along, he found a shady spot beneath the palm trees. There was a light breeze blowing across the tops of the fronds. It was just so peaceful, and right at this moment Max could have been the only person in the world. He made himself comfortable and started thinking how far he and Jane had come in such a short time. It wasn't long before he was fast asleep.

When he woke, the time had slipped away along with the tide, the heat had gone out of the day and the sun was down far enough in the sunset sky to reflect a golden, egg yolk colour across the water's surface. The palm trees were swaying in the gentle breeze and seemed to be dancing in time with the movement of the waves rolling up the soft sandy beach. This was another example of Mother Nature at her best, and she was giving Max a front row seat. In Max's mind, sunsets were the early onset of day's end, slowly turning day into night under the warm glow of the twilight ... *Shit! It's 6 pm*, he thought, *I better get back.*

When the sky turns pink, it's time for a drink. When he arrived, they were panicking.

'Jesus, Max, where have you been? You didn't tell anyone you were going anywhere. We've been bloody worried.'

Max smiled at Jane and said, 'Time and tide wait for no man, and neither does the sunset.'

'What sort of an answer is that?'

'It's the response deserving of the afternoon Mother Nature has given me, and one day I'll sit down with you and try and explain it. Give me a kiss. The bar is open, and the students are drinking all the free booze.'

Jane went to get the drinks and called back, 'You're a naughty little boy, Max. Tell someone where you're going next time, please.'

Jane would learn over time that Max could just disappear and reappear an hour or so later, particularly if he was in town or in the pub with mates.

Jane made some enquiries with a phone call to the island to make sure everything was in place for the wedding, only to find out no one knew anything about it.

'Shit, you're joking!' she said to the dude on the other end of the phone. 'You've got to be kidding.'

Max was hearing all this and said to Jane, 'Jesus, I could escape this yet.'

She looked daggers at him.

He said, 'Only joking, dear.'

Anyway, before they arrived on the island, Jane had it all sorted out. She was, however, flummoxed when they asked her what flavour wedding cake she wanted.

'What do you mean, what flavour?' Jane said.

'Well, you know, orange, raspberry or lemon.'

Max said, 'I heard you tell him he had to be kidding. Do you know where that saying came from, Jane?'

She used Max's short answer technique and said 'No.'

He said, 'Listen carefully and I'll tell you. A Captain and twenty of his men were rowing across the river on a dark and stormy night. It was very windy, and the water was rough and Corporal Dicks was on the bow waving the lantern. He went overboard and couldn't be found. On reaching land, they saw a light coming from a large house. What they didn't know was that this was a house of ill repute. They all crowded round the door and knocked. The Madam opened the door smiling when she saw all the prospective clientele. The Captain said, "We are wet and cold, and we need some care and comfort." She said, "No problem. How many of you are there?" "There are twenty of us, nineteen without Dicks." She said, "You've gotta be kidding me.'"

The wedding brochure showed pictures of a bride in a thatched chair being carried on bamboo poles by large native warriors to a waiting lakatoi-type barge which was rowed out to sea and taken to the beach chapel further down the island. They all thought that would be fantastic for Jane, but here's what actually happened. Jane was carried on a white plastic chair by four skinny local native boys in lap-laps to a boat that looked nothing special which they pulled along the shoreline for a short distance. They carried her up the beach on the plastic chair to an outdoor rotunda where the celebrant, Max, Martin and Jo were waiting with the native ladies' choir from the local village and because it was a holiday resort, they had their own rent a crowd who hung around to watch the wedding.

On the recorded video of the ceremony, you could see Max sucking his finger to slide the ring on; the hot weather had swelled Max's finger. Martin was Max's best man and Jo was Jane's bridesmaid. So, say hello to Mr and Mrs Max and Jane Thornton.

Jane had given Max the perspective on life he needed. They had worked extremely long hard hours together to get where they were in life. The laughs had been shared with the setbacks and disappointments, and now it seemed all worthwhile. Jane would never be the children's mother, but she was a wonderful stepmother to them and they are very lucky, whether they know it or not, to still have both a mother who loves them and stepmother who adores them and shares her love with all of them.

Martin and Jo flew home after the wedding while Max and Jane stayed for another week on the island. The little Hobie

Cat yachts were free of charge, so they decided to take one out for an hour or so. The young Fijian girl who was looking after them pushed them out. They put the sail up, but they had trouble steering the thing. The girl on the beach was yelling out, 'The radar, the radar, use the radar.'

Max said to Jane, 'What bloody radar? This little thing doesn't have radar.'

They worked it out after a while, because of the language barrier, what she was saying was the *rudder*, use the rudder. The rudder was in the centre of the boat. When they pushed it down into the water, off they went into the blue yonder.

*

When Max eventually got back into his office, there was a message to contact a Mr Howie from the South Australian Milk Company regarding some driver training. Max rang the bloke back and told him it was out of Sempcom's expertise: although they were tanker drivers, he doubted milk would catch fire or explode. The Howie dude said he had seen the module headings from the fuel tanker course, and if the product knowledge component could change to the carriage of milk, the course would be perfect. Max told him he knew diddly squat about milk apart from drinking it. Mr Howie said they would give Max all the necessary product knowledge to run the course. Max told him if they ran the milk course for him, they would probably be friends for 'heifer'. He didn't get the joke, so Max let it go.

Because part of the product knowledge was testing the milk in the farm storage tanks, done by the tanker driver prior to loading, in case it contaminated the milk from other farms already in the tanker, Max attended a two-day milk sampling and testing accreditation course. They gave Max a tanker so he could do three farm bulk milk pickups by himself. He did this specifically to stop drivers who might comment, 'What would he know? He's never done a bulk farm pickup.'

The course was one day of theory with ten drivers at a time, and one day for each of the drivers doing practical farm pickups and milk testing, along with defensive driving skills. On one of the bulk pickups, as part of the practical assessment, when they arrived at the farm, the driver being assessed said, 'Wait till you see this woman, Max. She has been wearing the same dress for the whole year.' It was a short floral dress with a pattern of flowers. Not that you could see much of the flower pattern, as the dress was filthy and black and could have stood up on its own. Yet they were obviously very conscience of the strict hygiene requirements of their milk, as their milk had been perfect over many years.

When Max returned to the office, he said, 'Well, that was different, although the only difference really was the milk side of things.'

Max doubted his milk grading certificate would hold much recognition in the big milk picture, and a two-day course wouldn't hold much water, or in this case, milk.

'Well, don't get too relaxed,' Jane told him. 'You have been asked to go to a board meeting at the Bacchus Marsh and Sunbury Bus Company to present our driver training package.'

'Jesus,' Max said, 'how do these people get our company details? We don't advertise. I'm trying to have a bloody rest.'

'You can have a rest when you're old, Max,' Jane said.

Max arrived at the bus depot about an hour early. When he

got out of the car, it was bloody freezing, and he didn't have a jacket. As he had some time before the meeting, he went to a Vinnies op shop and found a bomber jacket. He only wanted it for the day so it would be good enough, he reckoned. When he arrived back at the depot, they called him in to the meeting as soon as he got out of the car, so he headed in, still wearing the jacket. He did his presentation with slides on the overhead screen in the board room and afterwards they took him on a tour through the depot.

Max said, 'Well look at that, a 1965 Bedford bus.'

It was the same model as the bus he had once driven up and down Springvale Road years ago in his other world. He wasn't sure if that impressed them or if they thought, 'Shit, he's old'. He knew, though, his previous bus experience would be of value in terms of securing the contract.

When Max arrived back at the office Jane asked how it all went. Max said he was fairly confident that they might get the contract.

She said, 'Did you do the presentation in that jacket?'

'Yes, I did. Why?'

'Because there is a big tag hanging on the back of the jacket that says St Vincent Op Shop $5.'

'Oh, shit,' said Max, 'That's just real handy.'

Jane said, 'You never know, Max. They might give us the contract because it looks like we need the money, having to buy our clothes from the op shop.'

The company did get the contract, and Max was the bunny for the first two courses before it was turned over to John.

If you ever thought stories about blondes were just urban myths, this might just change your mind. On day one on the first course, Max was talking to the class of eight drivers, but one driver was missing. Then, in she walked, brazen as you like. She was a good-looking blonde, and you could tell she didn't want to be there.

She looked at Max and said, 'Are you gay?'

'What!' Max said, 'Are you kidding? You're bloody late, no apology, and you come out with that?'

She really is dumb, Max thought. *She's poking a stick at the person who will be assessing her driving.*

Max learnt that her husband owned a trucking company, and she considered herself a gun driver; she had that 'better than a male driver' attitude. Max kept her driving assessment till last. She wasn't anywhere near one of the best. She was, in fact, the only driver to run the back wheels of the bus up and over the curb. When Max spoke to her and outlined her written assessment, she was not a happy blonde.

Max said, 'The report is a fair assessment of your skills, which are just adequate for the job you do. It's no good you telling people how good you are; those sorts of accolades need to come from someone else. I'm sorry, but they're not coming from me. Your late arrival on the course and smartarse comments to me did not affect your driving assessment, although they did nothing to portray you as a nice person.'

Now she was really pissed off. Max had envisaged her next move and had spoken to her road manager about her attitude before she had complained about being unfairly judged. Apart from the dumb blonde, the training was a success.

Not long after both the milk tanker and bus training courses, Jane's phone buzzed with a message from the office. A lady from a company call Alexander Transport in New Zealand was in Australia for the next week and wanted to call and talk to them before she returned home.

'Jesus,' he said, 'there's no rest, is there? Do we really want to go to New Zealand?'

Jane said, 'We go where the money is, Max. Don't be such a baby. Let's see what she wants.'

Her name was Hayley Alexander and she introduced herself as the South Island manager for the company which her father owned. A considerable amount of their work was for Shell, which was obviously where she had got Sempcom's credentials from. Max and Jane gave her a tour of the training facility and suggested training modules along with a daily program. She was keen to get the ball rolling as soon as possible, once the groundwork and timetable were set in place to have drivers available to attend the courses. Hayley asked Max if he would be doing the training. He looked at Jane, who used his short answer technique: 'Yes, he will.' *Bugger*, Max thought, *By the time this course is ready to start, it will be bloody freezing over there.*

The plan was for Max to travel to each of the depots to conduct the courses, using an Alexander petroleum company ute for the training equipment. There were depots in Christchurch, Nelson, Richmond, Ashburton, Timaru, Dunedin, Queenstown and Invercargill. The course was only one day, but by the time Max got around all the locations, it would probably take two weeks.

'While I'm there,' Max said to Hayley, 'it would a good opportunity for Jane to visit when the courses are finished.'

Hayley said, 'We would be happy for you to keep the ute for an extra week to tour the South Island with Jane. You will certainly know your way around by then. I will be going back tomorrow, and I will be in touch regarding a suitable date for the training to be conducted.'

For the next two weeks, Max and the boys continued with their interstate training schedules: Max to Sydney, Martin to Brisbane and John to Perth, while the dragon continued breathing fire in the background.

While Martin was in Brisbane, he had been talking with a lady where he was working. She asked him how Max and the vineyard were going these days. Martin told her the vineyard was rocking along, with the shiraz winning a bronze medallion at the Victorian Wine Show.

'Wow,' she said, 'that's fantastic.'

Martin said, 'The company is sucking all our time and energy, making it difficult to keep up. I wouldn't be surprised if they were seriously considering selling the property.'

She said, 'You tell Max not to do anything about that until he speaks to me.'

A few days later, she rang Max and said that she had been talking to Martin and would be very interested if he was thinking of letting the property go, and that she would like to come down with her partner to look over the property. Max told her he would talk to Jane about it, and that he would touch base with her when he returned from New Zealand in three weeks' time.

'Well,' Max said to Jane, 'that would get the monkey, or in this case, the dragon off our back.'

Jane said, 'Sounds too good to be true, but it's a very interesting scenario. We'll wait and see what happens after New Z––' (Max was talking to one of the workers while Jane was speaking to him.) 'Are you listening to what I'm saying, Max?'

'Sort of.'

'Sometimes, Max, you've got the retention rate of a flea!'

When Max got off the plane in New Zealand, he was met with minus temperatures, and it was snowing. He knew he was going to bloody freeze here. The first day was taken up with meetings at the Christchurch head office and preparation of the conference room for the training. Max said he could only do six drivers each day. The smaller depots would only take one day to conduct the training, the larger ones two to three days if all of the drivers were made available. Their rosters had been done in advance for each of the locations Max would be at to ensure maximum attendance, which meant Max would need to stick to the timetable when travelling to the various depots. Max said the heavy vehicle drivers would be much the same the world over: if he removed the few cowboys and dickheads, the rest would be a good bunch of hardworking blokes with families to support, like the rest of us.

The training of eighteen drivers was completed at Christchurch. Max was then off to the depot in Nelson. The Nelson Lakes National Park was home to Jens Hansen, the goldsmith responsible for creating the forty different rings used in the movie, *Lord of the Rings*. One of the original rings was on display and copies could be bought in nine and eighteen carat gold. Max thought that would make a wonderful keepsake, but he didn't think Jane would justify the expense.

He would have loved to have gone to Stewart Island, but there was no time. He now had to travel back over the top of Arthur's Pass. This was a bad mistake, as the snow plough was just closing the road. Max gave the operator a sob story about fuel tankers not being on the road if he couldn't get through. The plough operator told Max to put the snow chains on his vehicle and that he could come through behind the plough.

So here was Max under the ute, freezing his arse off, wet as a shag, not able to feel his fingers anymore and wrestling with the chains, when his phone rang.

He answered it from under the ute to hear a hello, laughing voices saying, 'Hey, how you going, old boy?' and poker machine music in the background. Jane and Dorris had flown to Sydney to see a show and stay in the apartment. They were at the casino having a ball, and had obviously had a few wines.

'Go away,' he said, 'I'm under the ute and can't talk. I'm wet and cold. I'll talk to you later.'

Max thought, *Now if Martin was doing this training, he'd be under the ute, not me. I definitely got the wrong end of the stick.* Max followed the snow plough through the bad part of the road, waved goodbye to the nice bloke and headed back to Christchurch for a nice hot shower and a warm bed.

The next day, Max arrived at the Christchurch head office and handed in the driver assessment sheets. He no longer had drivers to do at Ashburton, as they would all be joining the Timaru drivers, so Max decided to have lunch at the pub at Ashburton. He had his favourite pub lunch, a mixed grill and a pot of beer. There was a small room with about ten poker machines. Max put $20 in on his way out and won the $200 monthly jackpot, much to the disgust of the six locals that were in the pub. Max threw $50 on the bar said, 'Thanks, boys,' and left.

When Max arrived at the Timaru depot, he met the manager and set up the conference room ready for the next day's training. The manager took him to a restaurant for the evening meal, which Max reckoned was a nice gesture.

During the course the next day, a discussion somehow got

started on how long someone should work for. Max was asked what his thoughts were.

'Well,' Max said, 'I guess to a certain extent it's a personal choice. However, as long as you continue working, your life blood is ticking away before your eyes and before you know it, there will be no time left. All work and no play makes Jack a dull boy, as the saying goes. I'm only working till I reach my financial retirement plan; it all takes a bit of balancing. Make the most of today but look after tomorrow. Today is the tomorrow you worried about yesterday.

'I know people in this industry whose attitude was, "I'm here for a good time, not a long time. Live for today; there might not be a tomorrow." So, they spend with gay abandon, living a champagne life on a beer income. Well, there was a tomorrow in each case and now in retirement, all of them are on the bones of their arse and own nothing. It's a bit like going to a party and expecting someone else to cop the hangover.

'If you want my advice, it's this: plan for tomorrow but don't waste today. Keep yourself in good shape, but there's no need to get carried away. The rabbit runs and bounces everywhere and lives for two years; the turtle who just moves quietly around doesn't stress about things and lives for four hundred years. It's most important that you prioritise things in your life like health, finance, family and friends. They're some of the big things that are important, but if we keep sweating about the small things in life, there's no time left to spend on the big important things. And remember, there's always time left for a drink with friends.'

Max slept at Timaru that night and headed for Dunedin the next day which is perched on the rim of an ancient volcano last active ten million years ago. Dunedin is the oldest city in New Zealand; its name comes from Dùn Èideann, the Scottish Gaelic name for Edinburgh, the capital of Scotland. Although Max had never been to Scotland, from pictures he had seen along with travel shows, this place certainly had a Scottish flavour.

'I've been bloody cold ever since I got off the plane,' Max said to the Dunedin manager.

He said, 'If you think this is cold, wait till you get down to Invercargill.'

The course ran smoothly, as they had done at the previous locations, with good results from the theory and practical assessments. Max packed up his gear and said his goodbyes, as he would be heading for Invercargill in the morning.

Invercargill was the home of Bill Richardson Transport World, the largest private automotive museum of its type in the world, with more than three hundred rare vintage vehicles. It was snowing and the roads through the town were iced over. All vehicle movement was restricted to emergency vehicles only, so there would be no practical training that day. They all stayed inside and completed the theory side of the course. The next day, vehicles were back on the road and so the practical training could be completed.

Max's last destination was Queenstown, known as the adventure capital of the world. Max wouldn't be there long enough to bungy jump from the Kawarau Bridge, the world's first and most famous bungy jump. The drivers were egging him on to do the jump. 'Maybe next time when I come back with Jane,' Max said.

Jane was arriving in New Zealand on the next day, so Max made sure he had an early night. She had rung Max the day before, asking if she would need a coat. Max told her to find one with a battery heater inside it. When her plane touched down, there was a bomb scare at the airport. Everyone was ushered out of the airport into the bloody cold snow and the plane sat on the runway for the next half-hour. True to form, when Jane got off the plane, it was blowing a gale and snowing.

'Shit,' she said, 'it's bloody cold.'

They drove to the head office in Christchurch so Jane could say hello to Hayley again and say thanks for giving them the ute for the week.

Max and Jane headed off around the South Island. While Max was doubling up on the trip he had already done, he didn't mind. He took Jane to the hot rock pools in the Southern Alps. They were sitting in the pools early in the evening when snow flurries began to fall, swirling around them like little white moths laying down a white blanket on the tops of the trees and the tops of their head, turning this peaceful place into a purple winter twilight of magic, reaching as far away as the distant mountains and valleys – Mother Nature saying hello again. It felt quite strange walking on the snow in their bare feet, particularly when they knew they were the first to walk on this white blanket of snow. It was quite an experience. The evening meal was also quite an experience. All the restaurant tables had woks set flush in the middle with a gas fire underneath. The chef gave them small cuts of meat and vegetables which they cooked themselves at their table. With a glass or two of wine, it was a lovely way to end a perfect day. The next morning, nature became their alarm clock, and they woke to the sounds of the New Zealand bush.

They moved on from there to Queenstown, where Jane wanted to go skiing. Max didn't think that was a good idea. She had never skied before, and he couldn't see them getting on the plane to go home with her legs in plaster. He convinced her to give it a miss. The training contract and the short holiday with Jane was most enjoyable. They said their goodbyes and thanks at a farewell dinner with Hayley and other company representatives, also enjoyable. Apart from Max freezing his arse off under a ute, both Max and management were happy with the outcome.

*

On their return to Ainslie Crossing, there were messages from the lady who was interested in the property, which meant she was still obviously keen to come and see for herself. Max and Jane made arrangements for her and her partner to visit and stay the night to give plenty of time for discussion, if it went that far.

When they arrived, they were taken on a grand tour of the property in the four-wheel drive Suzuki ute, with no doors for easy access in and out of the vehicle while going up and down the vineyard rows. They looked at all the vineyard equipment, machinery and vehicles that went with the property. They were happy with the place, and the discussions on purchase went well into the night, along with several bottles of Ainslie Crossing Red Clay Ridge Shiraz. They explained they owned two houses in Brisbane that they would have to go back and sell, which meant the sale would be on hold until then. After assurances from their solicitor and some legal agreements were signed, Jane and Max agreed to wait.

The vines were dormant and pruning hadn't started, so Max decided to be the one to go and finish the training of the last four Elgas tanker drivers. Jane would go with him and they would take the caravan to stay a week at Lakes Entrance for a bit of a break. They thought they might start to look around at houses and prices. Not that they were ready just yet, but it wouldn't hurt to see what the market was doing. They stayed at the Lakes Caravan Park and Max drove to work for the two days. Jane stayed in the caravan and spent the time catching up on some office work.

On the weekend, they drove up and down the coast looking at properties and both agreed that Lakes Entrance was as far from Melbourne as they needed to be, and when the time came to move, they were keen on a seaside town. Jane said Max arrived back at the caravan after work and told her he had seen a nice house on two acres – not a paddock, just lawns and evergreen trees.

He said, 'It won't hurt to have a look. What do you think?'

Jane was happy to just look, so Max took her for a drive to the house and they looked at all the aspects they could see from the road. Jane thought it didn't look much from the outside; what they could see was sort of average looking.

Max said, 'Why don't we arrange with the agent to have a look inside and see if the asking price is reasonable for what we would get for our money?'

They arranged to meet the agent at the house, and an inspection revealed a lovely house with magnificent ocean views through large bay windows. It had four bedrooms, a large lounge and kitchen, separate large rumpus room and a very large double garage; in fact, everything about the place was large. What impressed Max even more was the double separate workshop garages. They were very impressed and told the agent they would get back to her a bit later, and they headed off to the golf club for lunch to think about it.

The 'think about it' part was that, even though they had an offer for their other property, in reality it wasn't sold, and they had to consider that this could fall through. Also, they didn't really want another mortgage. They decided to ring their company accountant and gave him all the details. He said, at that price, buy it straight away, as it was an excellent investment. They rang their bank manager and she said to go ahead and make an offer, which they did, which was accepted. So, there you go – they now had two mortgages. Jane was a little stressed, but Max told her not to be such a worry wart. As it turned out, the purchase of the beach house was an incredibly good investment. Max and Jane purchased it in early 2003, and about four months after this, the property market boomed. Overnight, their acquisition was valued at over $500,000 more than they had paid for it.

Moving to the beach house wasn't an option at that stage. It would be a year before settlement would go through on the vineyard, and they hadn't even considered a retirement plan from the business. They furnished the beach house which they named Fairview, having the intention of using it once a month for a break. However, work commitments unfortunately didn't allow for that, and it was more like once in three months that they could get away.

During one of the holiday stays, Max went surf fishing along the Ninety Mile Beach. When he waded out in his fishing waders to get a piece of seaweed off his line, a big wave dumped him under. His waders were full of water, and he was drenched. He drove home and called out to Jane.

When she came to the door, he said, 'Look at me! I'm saturated, and my waders are full of water. Can you get me some dry clothes?'

She disappeared and then came back and said, 'Are your underpants wet?'

'Christ, Jane, what do you reckon?' *Another blonde statement*, Max thought.

*

In a moment of reflection, Max said, 'You know, Jane, life is quickly passing us by. It's a "now you see it, now you don't" proposition, and somewhere inside the old Max will be a young Max wondering where his life has gone.'

Max said he wasn't concerned with dying but he was more concerned with losing his mind as he got older and not being able to do the things he was good at. And he wanted his ghost to feel he had earned his place in the afterlife. But for now, he was just thinking of how much the standards and expectations in Australia have changed.

'It's sort of quietly snuck up on us while we weren't looking, and then when you stop and look around at people and what's going on, it dawns on you. I would be quite happy to be back with my 1956 FJ Holden ute with its bench seat and vacuum wipers, provided it was back in those times. Yesterday, there was a man in the post office in a floral dress and nail polish.'

'Well, that's not normal,' said Jane.

See? That's just it,' Max said, 'there's no normal anymore. Or if you like. everything is now accepted as normal. Progress is healthy and necessary, and I love "outside the box" thinking, but I worry that some of what's going on is moving in the wrong direction. Look, I'm all for change – good change, that is. When I was a small boy, if you wanted to see the tattooed lady, you went to the Royal Melbourne Show or the circus but now they're everywhere. I understand we fought for the right for freedom and to have our say, and you don't have to agree with it. That's what our flag is all about, and thanks to the Veteran in the wheelchair and others who ensured we had that say, I'm having my say now, and I'm happy for you to have yours, Jane. And I bet you, if a young girl has rowboats tattooed on her small breasts, she doesn't realise by the time she is eighty, they will probably be battleships and looking fairly ordinary. Then again, who is interested in someone that's eighty? What could they possibly know. That's why you have to ask a teenager while they still know everything.'

Max said he likes the fact he is married to a lovely feminine woman and she to a robust man that cuddle together like two spoons in a drawer at night. Max said he didn't need to be waking up staring at whatever was tattooed on her boobs, or the picture of whatever was on her bum. They are both quiet, happy looking at each other in their natural form that nature has provided them with – although it's not as good as it used to be and they're looking at it less and less these days. If tattoos turn people on, that's fine and Max is happy that they're happy. But he just doesn't think ladies smothered in tattoos are very lady-like. Maybe getting smothered in tattoos is what they're all about and might be the whole aim of it, that they don't want to be like a lady. However, a small butterfly symbol on the ankle or somewhere privately of their choice is quite sweet and lady-like.

'And now, for Christ's sake, there are some who can't make up their minds what gender they are. A good kick in the nuts would soon remind the boys what they are.'

'Well, people seem more agitated and uptight,' Jane said, 'Have you noticed that, Max?'

'Yes. They all seem to be stressing about someone being better at something than they are, or that someone's got something that they haven't, and they see that as a form of failure for not being able to keep up. It's the "keeping up with the Joneses" syndrome. Some people are trapped in the opinion that they have to compete. They are quite convinced they are seen at a lower level in the community if they're not up to speed with the rest.'

'They're probably worried about being a failure,' Jane said.

'The easy answer to all of this,' Max said, 'is that water finds its own level. I don't understand why these people don't do the same – just find friends with their same level and standing and the same financial rewards. Then I can't see a problem. It only happens when you try to live and play above your means, and that has never been us, Jane. I'll tell you what I've learnt about the definition of the word "failure" during my journey, my little chickadee.

'During our time on planet Earth, we will work, dream and play. We will have our sport and social activities and sometimes we will even have what you might call failures, bad health or bad news. These times will be our most vulnerable and are the times we need friends and family around us. Just be reminded, it's only considered a failure if you haven't given it your very level best. You can't always be the very best, but it's important that it's your very best. Sometimes, even that may not be good enough, so in those circumstances, don't beat yourself up. Aim slightly lower and you will find where your best fit is, and likely success, and where you will be the happiest.'

For example, Max had risen to the top of his rank structure, a Warrant Officer Class 1, and was the highest rank in his Mess and second in charge. But if he had been promoted to Captain, he would have been a bottom rank in that mess with no say in anything. He had decided he was better off where he was.

'Decide on what's best for you and your future, and be sensible when it comes to your capabilities, but don't sell yourself short. And try not to judge the choices people make until you know their reasons. You can be anything you want in Australia, but no one is going to give it to you; you have to earn it. Who and what do you want to be? I had to keep asking myself. Where do I sit now and where do I want to be sitting in the future? If you're already there, you've done well. You know, I remember having this same conversation with Joey years ago where we asked each other that question, what we each wanted out of life, given we were only going to get one go at this.

'Problem is, as I've discovered about life, we tend to measure ourselves against those with whom we work or play sport against, or even family friends, and there lies the problem. It's the natural competitive nature of the beast. There will always be someone better than you, whether it is due to physique, education or simply natural talent. You may not meet them but he or she are out there somewhere. It's the opposite with bad luck and sickness – there's always some poor bugger worse than you somewhere.'

Sometimes Max had to remind himself to stop whingeing and get on with life. He realised along his journey that if he had striven hard and given all he had, then that was the very best he could do. The only person you need to try to be better than is yourself. You're the person you have to be honest with when it comes to how hard you tried and if you gave it your very best shot.

Max said to Jane, 'We are going to see examples of that on

many occasions at the Olympics. They might not win, but they know in their heart they gave it their best. They will go away disappointed but proud, and if you can achieve that same attitude and add the respect of others around you, then you can count yourself as a proud Australian, someone with substance, unlike the grubs who don't or won't stand for our national anthem but will greedily take the financial handouts.

'And where I am concerned, although I realise there is a right way and a wrong way to do things, I have to stop trying to get people to do it my right way. That's the bad way, if that makes any sense. And you know what, in the final analysis, it's your own journey of life. You can take someone with you *on* your journey if you like, but they can't go *for* you. In other words, you must make your own way in life, setting your own personal rules and standards to ensure your journey through life is both worthwhile, wonderful and rewarding.'

*

Although the settlement for the vineyard was one year, for one reason or another, it was almost three years from the time Max and Jane bought Fairview till the vineyard was sold and they made the permanent move. Out went the holiday furniture and in went theirs. The day they moved in, the neighbours were waiting at Fairview for them to arrive.

Max said, 'Look, some people might see that as a good neighbourly gesture. Well, if I go inside and the fridge is full of food and the fires going, I will give in. Otherwise, I see two clinging neighbours who, for some reason, need the friendship of people they don't even know. I could be a mad pervert for all they know.'

Max had learnt a long time ago not to invite people to your house socially until you really know them. If they're the clinging type and not your style, you'll never get rid of them. However, in this case, they turned out to be good neighbours and good friends.

Max and Jane started winding the business down to a manageable size. John, who by this time was married and had two children, took over the business with one of the staff members.

Max recalls John telling him that there might be some evidence the world might not be round, but of course, there's overwhelming evidence that it is in fact round, and none that it's not. Max said, 'Come on, John boy, give your old dad a break, son. Why hasn't anyone ever fallen off the edge of the earth? And if it was flat, we would all be on the same time zone, wouldn't we? How do these idiots in the flat society group explain how it's 8 am in Australia and midnight somewhere else in the world? Day and night is simply dark and light; when it's dark in America, it's light in Australia.'

The person who's putting this stuff in his head must be one of those people who keep escaping from that hole in that idiot bag, Max thought, and he was sort of hoping that's not where he had met him. Max knows John doesn't really believe all of this baloney, though he sometimes likes to weigh up all the pros and cons. It's a con, all right. Next, they'll be asking for money to make square pizzas that fit in a round box. But John's hard work and support at Sempcom had not gone unnoticed. He was a hard worker and a dedicated team member, and he remains a loyal family member as do his brother, Martin, and the girls, Arlene and Anne.

Martin spent some time with Cootes in South Australia. He

is married with two children and was eventually offered the position as Terminal Manager at the ATOM BP's Birkenhead Terminal, Largs Bay. Arlene and Anne, now both beautiful women, were married at Portsea and Sorrento respectively, also having two children each.

Max and Jane are happily retired at Fairview.

Jane said, 'Max will be eighty-two this year but every now and then, you'll still get a glimpse of that cheeky little boy that's still in there somewhere. I've always loved the little boy part of Max with his silly antics, which sadly we don't get to see much of these days. But he can still be that bugger of a kid when he wants to be. I think in Max's early restless life, he was trying to find a custom fit in an "off the rack" world.'

'Getting old is not for the faint-hearted,' Max said,' but I'll never be lonely, Jane, knowing you're my friend, and we will continue to grow old together. Someone once said friendship was like pissing your pants – everyone can see it but only you can feel the warmth. Thank you, Jane, for giving me that warmth and that precious love you can't buy. Right up till the very end, it's going to be just me, and you, my friend.'

Epilogue

The dark shadows of war

When our men and women returned to Australia from a theatre of war because they were ill or wounded or because the war had ended, the disabilities they carried were often permanent ones – lost limbs, disfigured bodies, mental scars, loss of sight and many other injuries that are not visible. Through all the wars that have been waged, these conflicts have been responsible for horrific casualties, not the least being psychological damage. After Vietnam, this was given the new name of post-traumatic stress disorder, PTSD.

The long-term health consequences have been enormous: of the 60,000 troops that went to Vietnam, 74 per cent are classified by Veterans Affairs as having some form of health impact as a result. They may live with physical disabilities, health problems or varying degrees of psychological trauma. Regarding Australian servicemen, 500 were killed, 426 died in battle and 3,129 were severely wounded, resulting in long-term effects. Many more were subject to less severe injuries but still debilitating, such as hearing loss which effects a third of all Vietnam Veterans today. The widespread use of herbicides such as Agent Orange added to the health issues, with data pointing to their families as well. (The statistical data research and writings above are from the Australian War Memorial, Maria Strydon Research Document 2017.)

If Max was honest, he would tell you that, though he escaped virtually unscathed, he has problems feeling warmth within himself or long-term warmth towards others for fear of losing them, like the military friends he has lost, and his long association with death, sickness, destruction, sadness and horror that he saw both in his civilian and military service; some of those memories remaining to this day. These have contributed to a change in his demeanour.

Max has kept these feelings to himself over the years and not spoken about this before, but now seems the right time to explain to his family and friends why sometimes he's not the person he should be, and why his old sunny and infectious personality has been slowly eroded. There are things that break inside you that can never be fixed again He's sorry for any discomfort that he may have caused. To some extent, Valda understood and gave him her support. Jane has always secretly known his struggle and has been a lifeline for him. Max says he started feeling sorry for himself when he was getting on in years and a lot of his old friends had gone.

'We are poorer for their passing, and I miss them. They never leave my mind,' Max says, but he's looking at things a bit different now. He realises he has had a wondrous and joyful life, and that's all that matters. He loves his family and friends who have put up with him all these years, and he takes this opportunity to say thanks for hanging in there with him. Max is very aware of his misgivings, and he works hard at improving. That has proven difficult, but he is still trying hard to be a better person and will keep at it to try and give his family and friends the best of himself.

333

Max's musings

ife is unpredictable. It can be cold, tough and hard and can bruise your ego and hurt your pride. It can disappoint you, make you laugh or make you cry, make you happy or sad. And there are times it will just kiss you and set you down with the softness of a butterfly landing. But like water, it will flow downhill if not checked and channelled to meet your needs, and you shouldn't be afraid to change the flow's direction around life's obstacles. You're in charge of your life's direction, and in most cases, the person responsible for your downfall is only as far away as the mirror. Be mindful of where you are right now. Yesterday is history, tomorrow is a mystery, but today is a gift – that's why it's called the present.

Just be very careful who you let into your heart. Broken hearts mean broken lives. You can't buy real love; it's just not for sale. Although many people will walk through your life, only the true friends will leave footprints on your heart. If you can't make your life at least a small adventure, then it's probably not going to amount to much. A journey through life, from the womb to the tomb, shouldn't be a trip with the motivation to arrive in perfect condition with a well looked-after body, but rather to charge in, up the guts with tons of smoke, body absolutely buggered and knackered, worn to a frazzle, calling out 'Shit, what a ride!'

We are, all of us, so lucky and privileged to belong to and live in this free and easy country, Australia, the place we call home. It belongs to all who love it and abide by its principles regardless of colour and creed, or how long we might have lived here. (By the way, I was born here, and my family and relations collectively have been here for two hundred years). I don't think I should have to be welcomed to my own country like a visitor who comes for a short stay or have to listen to 'A welcome to country' over and over again. This is my country by birth, and in my opinion, 'Welcome to country' is just another example of our politicians appeasing people to ensure their own political survival.

Australia is a country of compassion and courage, somewhere you can feel safe and at ease, a place that is the envy of the world. It is our land down under, and so many have given so much to keep it as it is, in some cases giving their lives to protect the principles of our flag, so our kids can play on the streets without fear of being shot or bombed, with having to change laws to protect us from those that would do us harm.

So, mate, if you don't want to get off your arse and stand when we raise our flag or play our national anthem, perhaps you should help the Aussie veteran in the wheelchair next to you, a real Australian who would be more than happy to stand if he could.

The Aussie group, The Seekers, remind us in their song that we are from all lands, but we are one – we are Australian.

Acknowledgements

To Penny for her loyal support and the painful long arduous hours of typing and correcting my grammatical and spelling errors. Your nagging me to write this book eventually broke through. And I owe you the debt for the birth of this book. You were the wind beneath my wings throughout the journey, and you can be my wingman anytime.

To Fay Gaw for her encouragement to start writing – never underestimate the power of encouragement. To all those friends and others who have given permission to use their names: my twin sister Dorris, and Joe, Lois, John, Dee, Gabi, Genny, Fay, Mick, Peter, Marion, Frances, Graeme and Bruce (Brewster), and Denise Bell for being a caring and good friend in the early days at Ainslie Crossing. Thank you all for your contributions to the book. I hope you all will enjoy the story.

To my children, called in this book Martin, Anne, Arlene and John, for enduring the hardships of growing up in a family that was always on the move. I hope your life was somewhat enriched by your time in Papua New Guinea, Manila and Singapore. To 'Valda' (Leigh) who gave up so much of her life to allow me to achieve my dreams, and who was and is a wonderful mother to the four lovely children she gave me.

I would also like to thank the team at Sid Harta and my

editor, Susan Pierotti, for their expertise, time and advice. This book would not exist without them.

I certainly have had a fortunate life. To all the places that employed me, both casual and permanent, and the people with whom I worked, I simply say, thanks for the ride.

The laughter and memories I had with childhood friends will never end; they were the birth and the foundation of who I am today. It was the innocence and joy in those early days that defined my world. Together, we created our own magic when the only pain in life was a skinned knee. Wherever you go in life, the places you lived and grew up in will seem like long-lost friends, and the memories of your childhood friends will always remain special, and I don't think you ever get those same childhood friendship outlooks again. And while I have some wonderful caring friends to this day, my twelve-year-old and teenage friends will remain fond memories.

About the author

The author's story comes from his handbook of hard times, and to the best of his ability, he has stuck to only the facts. He promised himself during his military career he would one day write a book called *Hardly A Challenge*, a common phrase used then by soldiers in Australia during his service. So here it is.

He is also a talented illustrator, artist and cartoonist. He enjoys playing the piano, but it's doubtful he'd get a guernsey at the Opera House, or for that matter, the Brunswick Town Hall, but he can knock out a tune.

Max and his wife now relax in their quiet seaside property at Fairview which they both look upon as their holy ground, and enjoy fishing, golf and travelling in their motor home with like-minded friends.

This is the author's first creative non-fiction book and he hopes you enjoy *Hardly A Challenge* as much as he did writing it. His military honours and awards are as follows:

- Australian Active Service Medal 1945–75
- Vietnam Medal
- Defence Force Service Medal
- Australian Service Medal 1945–75
- Papua New Guinea Independence Medal

- Republic of Vietnam Cross of Gallantry with Palm Unit Citation
- South Vietnam Campaign Medal (Vietnam Star)
- Chief of the Army Commendation.